Little
Cruelties

ALSO BY LIZ NUGENT

Lying in Wait

Unraveling Oliver

Little Cruelties

LIZ NUGENT

PUBLISHED BY SIMON & SCHUSTER
NEW YORK   LONDON   TORONTO   SYDNEY   NEW DELHI

SIMON &
SCHUSTER
CANADA

Simon & Schuster Canada
A Division of Simon & Schuster, Inc.
166 King Street East, Suite 300
Toronto, Ontario M5A 1J3

This book is a work of fiction. Any references to historical events, real people, or real places are used fictitiously. Other names, characters, places, and events are products of the author's imagination, and any resemblance to actual events or places or persons, living or dead, is entirely coincidental.

Copyright © 2020 by Liz Nugent
Originally published by Penguin Books Ltd.

All rights reserved, including the right to reproduce this book or portions thereof in any form whatsoever. For information, address Simon & Schuster Canada Subsidiary Rights Department, 166 King Street East, Suite 300, Toronto, Ontario, M5A 1J3.

This Simon & Schuster Canada edition November 2020

SIMON & SCHUSTER CANADA and colophon are trademarks of Simon & Schuster, Inc.

For information about special discounts for bulk purchases, please contact Simon & Schuster Special Sales at 1-800-268-3216 or CustomerService@simonandschuster.ca.

Manufactured in the United States of America

10 9 8 7 6 5 4 3 2 1

Library and Archives Canada Cataloguing in Publication
Title: Little cruelties / Liz Nugent.
Names: Nugent, Liz, author.
Description: Simon & Schuster Canada edition.
Identifiers: Canadiana 20200167200 | ISBN 9781501191312 (softcover)
Classification: LCC PR6114.U365 L58 2020 | DDC 823/.92—dc23

ISBN 978-1-5011-9131-2
ISBN 978-1-5011-9132-9 (ebook)

*To my parents, John D and Siobhan, and
my four brothers and four sisters, Peter, Michael, Mary,
Patrick, James, Jennifer, Elaine, and Joanne.
None of whom bear any resemblance
to the family in this book.*

"The awful thing in life is, everyone has their reasons."

—Jean Renoir, *The Rules of the Game*

*A*ll three of the Drumm brothers were at the funeral, although one of us was in a coffin.

Three is an odd number, so there had always been two against one, although we all switched sides regularly. Nobody would ever have described us as close.

As the service began, I became tearful. Without ever realizing it, I had inherited my mother's acting abilities. My living brother and I stood, side by side, at the top of the crematorium while people lied to us about what a brilliant man our brother had been, all the usual meaningless clichés.

His death was sudden. Horrific. The investigation was quick and conclusive. I was not a suspect. I had a sense of freedom and relief I hadn't felt in quite a while. I didn't expect that this air of serenity would last. But I thought I would enjoy it while I could.

My surviving brother was unreadable to me. Maybe he was thinking of our brother's smashed and broken body. Still, even he must have known this outcome was all for the best.

Daisy sat in the pew behind us. She seemed not to be aware of her surroundings, fidgeting and whispering to herself. I caught my brother's eye as her babbling became audible and people began to notice. He reached out and quietly asked her to join us. That reaching out of his hand made me shudder momentarily. She seemed to return to reality and moved to stand between us without any argument. We both attempted to put a proprietorial arm around her, but she shrugged us off. We looked at each other then. The old rivalry resurfaced.

I

BROTHERS

William

Chapter 1

1994

My daughter, Daisy, had just been born, and Susan was feeling the strain of new motherhood. I was twenty-five and trying to get a production company off the ground to make short films with my college buddy Gerald, who wanted to direct, but there were money problems, and I sensed that Filmbase would take some persuasion to fund a new company. Mum had lent me some seed money, and Gerald had a generous uncle who helped out financially too. I had rented an office in a city attic and ordered some letterhead on which I was making desperate pleas to the Arts Council, Dublin Corporation, the National Lottery, and any organizations I could think of with money. I was working hard, and then up at night with the baby a lot of the time, and maybe I was more irritable than I should have been, but when I came home in the evenings after a long slog in the office, the last thing I wanted to see was my rock star little brother, sprawled across my sofa, while my wife, still sore from breastfeeding, perched uncomfortably on the dining chair, baby-sick stains on each shoulder, unkempt and exhausted.

In the beginning, I joked with him and pretended to be pleased to see him, because if I couldn't get finance from anywhere else, I was going to have to ask him, though that would be my last resort.

"Luke! Shouldn't you be out somewhere snorting cocaine off a supermodel's ass?"

Luke was twenty-three. His second album was a massive success. He had toured constantly for three years but was now on a hiatus of sorts. He lived in a big Georgian terrace house on Waterloo Road, bought for cash two years after he dropped out of college to sing in a band. We, on the other hand, were renting a one-bedroom studio apartment nearby with no central heating and unreliable plumbing.

We were mystified by Luke's stardom. Luke looked waifish with his big eyes and long hair and a thin reedy voice that would have traveled nowhere without amplification. Brian and I were jealous. We were older, and we had worked to pay our way through college, earning respectable enough arts degrees. Luke had surprised us all by getting the results to study engineering but then spent his two years smoking hash by the pond, reading poetry, and rehearsing with the Wombstones. At one point, he attached a collar to a hen and walked it through the campus. All for effect. We never knew where he got the hen or where it ended up afterward.

For some unquantifiable reason, he could attract women. I don't understand how. Women are weird. He could take or leave them and never seemed to be particularly attached to any of them. It got to the stage where I didn't bother trying to remember their names anymore because there'd be a new one along any minute.

When he got famous as a solo act, Luko, he was generous, bringing us all out to join him on tour in London and Lisbon, splashing cash around like it was nothing to him. His name had opened doors for me in the arts scene, but that spring, there had been no tour invites, no lavish awards ceremonies, no rock 'n' roll parties. He'd just turn up at our house in time for dinner, at least twice a week.

That was always the thing about Luke. He couldn't take a hint. He'd sit on our sofa staring at the television, though not appearing to take in whatever program was on. He'd eat the dinner that Susan or I prepared, ignore our baby, and as soon as he was fed, leave without much of a thank-you. Eventually, I brought up the subject of finance and my funding difficulties, but he only nodded and grunted. No offer was forthcoming. I was forced to ask.

It wouldn't be a loan as such, I said, it would be an investment, and we'd be asking him to compose the music for our film (even though Luke still couldn't read music, and we didn't actually have a film yet, *because* we had no funding). "It's not really my thing," he said. "Did you ask Brian?"

Brian at this stage was living in Paris. Mum would get an occasional letter from him written on a page torn out of a copybook. If Brian couldn't afford writing paper, he certainly couldn't afford to lend me money.

"Brian? What are you talking about? You know what he's like with money, and I don't think he's even earning that much." I tried to contain my frustration. It was so typical of Luke to be completely unaware and unconcerned. He shrugged and picked up the remote control and changed the TV channel without making eye contact. Susan got up and left the table in disgust.

It took a few weeks after that for me to tell him he was no longer welcome. If I'd done it straightaway, he'd have thought it was about the money, and it *was* about the money, but it was everything else too. He didn't appear to be showering too often. He brought, literally, nothing to our table, and he sucked the energy out of our home as soon as he entered it.

I didn't see him for most of the rest of that year, though I read in the papers that he was back in the studio recording another album and was then going on tour. I saw this in the Sunday gossip column. I wasn't about to pick up the phone.

Susan wanted that Christmas to be special, but she felt guiltier about Luke than I did. She suggested I invite everyone over for Christmas dinner, and then it would look like he was naturally included. Besides, we wanted to avoid going to Mum's house in Glenageary because she was always much louder and overbearing in her own home than in ours. Brian was home from Paris for a few days and was going to stay with Mum. It was Daisy's first Christmas. We had finally won a small Filmbase grant, and things were looking good for us. We were going into production in January for our first short film, *Fear of Life*, and I was planning to announce it over our festive lunch. I rang Luke and left a message on his answering machine. When he hadn't rung back after a few days, Susan dropped a note in his letter box.

He never showed up. We didn't think much of it. It had happened before, that he would drop off the radar for a month or two. We knew from Brian that the tour was on hiatus and that Luke was home in Dublin. Mum was put out that he hadn't called her. She sulked about it, but it was obvious that she hadn't tried to contact him either.

The family was impressed by my news, at first. Mum raised her glass and toasted me. "My son, the next Steven Spielberg!" But then when Brian heard it was a short film, and that it wasn't going to get a cinema release, he was dismissive. "What's the point in making a film that nobody is going to see?" he asked me. He ridiculed the whole project because the actors were friends from my college drama society. Mum argued in my defense that everyone had to start somewhere, and pointedly asked Brian what his career plan was. He responded defensively that he was working in an exclusive school, but Mum dismissed his boasting. "Yes, as a teacher, Brian. It's a little different from being a film producer. Show business is in our blood. You must take after your father."

Brian bristled. "Being a teacher is a very important job."

Still, I felt the need to explain myself, that I had to start small and work my way up, that nobody was going to give a bunch of unknowns ten million pounds to make a feature film. Mum said, "Well, not yet, darling. I'm so proud of you."

Brian said, "Why don't you put Luke in the film?"

Mum laughed. "Sure, if you want to make a film for teenage girls."

She was sneery about Luke's success and his teenage fan base. We all were. Mum had always belittled our youngest brother, and we usually joined in. It was a joke to us, that little Luke could be a teenage idol. I was all about making my own name, and I wasn't going to use my sap of a brother to do so, particularly when he wouldn't put up any money for it.

Brian helped Susan with the washing-up and played with Daisy. Mum got drunk early, singing aloud to *The Sound of Music* on television. The giant teddy bear that Mum had bought for Daisy sat out on the stairs, as there was no room for it in the living room. But Daisy was fascinated by it and sat at the bottom of the stairs gazing up at it. After my brother and mother left, Susan and I drained the end of the wine and went to bed.

We were awakened at three in the morning by thunderous knocking on the door. Susan sat bolt upright in bed, but Daisy, thankfully, didn't stir. I threw on my robe, initially worried that it might be bad news but prepared to be furious and to berate whoever had knocked on the door so aggressively.

Luke was standing at the door almost hidden behind a huge doll's house. "Sorry, I only just finished it, the paint is dry, but it's still a little sticky. It's for . . . your little girl." He placed it in the hallway behind me and then left. It was obvious that he couldn't remember Daisy's name. I let him wander off into the dark, because at that hour of the morning I was not prepared to entertain his drunkenness.

Daisy's eyes shone when she saw it the next day. Susan opened the hinged front of the house, but it came loose in her hand. The roof listed badly on one side, and the windows had rough edges. Daisy picked up a tiny bed and put it in her mouth. There were splinters in the wood, and it reeked of paint fumes. That night, with little effort, we broke it up into kindling and fed it into the fireplace.

A week later, Luke turned up at dinnertime as if the previous six months had never happened. He never inquired about the doll's house, and we chose not to mention it. I asked him how the new album was coming along, but he shrugged and changed the TV channel. We were too old then for me to punch him, but my fists itched.

Chapter 2

1985

Mum was the star of the family, a showband singer and actress, and Dad was always happy to let her shine. He was no pushover—he stood up to her when he needed to—but he was the quietest member of our family. Dad had established his private quarters at the end of the garden. He referred to the shed as his palace. He had a Persian carpet on the floor; an old car seat rescued from his first car, an ancient Hillman Hunter; a shelf of war history books from ancient Rome to Vietnam; a battery-operated radio; a toolbox; and most importantly for him, isolation. Dad was Dad. Not exciting or important or famous, and far from being the life and soul of the party, but just someone who was always there. Because Mum's concerts mostly took place in the evenings, it was Dad who had always cooked our dinners and made our packed lunches for the morning. I was embarrassed by this. As far as I knew, nobody else's dad cooked dinners. It was even worse that he seemed to enjoy it. He would often say fondly to my mother, "What would you do without me at all, at all?" and she might respond sarcastically that she'd get a husband her own age. I only ever invited friends over when I knew Mum was there because the humiliation of them seeing my dad in an apron was too much to bear.

I knew she had cheated on him, but I kept that to myself. Maybe he knew and didn't mind or decided to ignore it. Maybe he had cheated on her. Their marriage always seemed solid, regardless. Dad often referred to Mum as his "orphan girl," though she was no longer a girl. I think my dad liked to think of himself as her knight in shining armor, and he was disappointed that she wasn't more grateful. Nevertheless, they cared for one another, even though they could be mean and spiteful to each other sometimes. He did not trust her around other men.

Dad died when I was seventeen. He was diagnosed with prostate cancer and was dead fourteen months later, a week after my birthday. He spent the last month of his life in a hospice. He never mentioned death or dying to us in those end days, and when we went to visit him, he seemed embarrassed, as if this disease was a source of shame. Luke told Brian and me that Dad's diagnosis was terminal, and I resented that Mum had told him first and not me. I was the oldest. Luke was the kid, but she insisted on telling him every detail about where the tumors were, how they had spread, and how virulent they were. Luke secretly relayed the information to us. I confronted her about this. "But, darling," she said, "I didn't want to upset you." And I could see her point. I had my final school exams coming up.

She was increasingly tearful and seemed afraid. Luke went to the hospice every day after school and spent the last weekends there. Brian went once, reluctantly. "I hate sick people," he said.

When Dad's death was imminent—"hours," the nurse said—Mum and I were with him. "Should I ring Brian and Luke?" I asked as his breaths became more and more infrequent. "No, they'd only get in the way," she said. When his ragged breathing eventually stopped, I held Mum awkwardly as she wept.

We got home from the hospice late that night. Luke was waiting up. "He's dead, isn't he?"

Mum started to cry, and I confirmed it for Luke. Brian was already in bed. Luke went to get Mum a drink, and I climbed the stairs to wake Brian and give him the bad news.

I pushed open his bedroom door. He was reading some action thriller with a lurid cover.

"Brian? Look, I'm sorry, but Dad has died."

"Oh."

"I know. It's awful, isn't it?"

He picked up his book and started to read again. "Do you want to come downstairs?"

"No thanks, I have rugby training in the morning."

"What? Brian, did you not hear what I said? Dad is . . . dead."

"Yeah?"

"Yes."

"So what do you want me to do about it?"

The long days in the hospital had taken their toll. I'd barely seen my girlfriend in weeks. Maybe Brian *was* too young to handle such news. He was odd in a different way to Luke, but his belligerence was hard to take. Luke was younger and was already downstairs pouring gin into Mum.

"You could start by not acting like a prick."

"Piss off."

I picked up a gym shoe, threw it at his head, and left, slamming the door.

Later, I rationalized that Brian's way of dealing with grief was to ignore it, because he had never, to my knowledge, fallen out with Dad. None of us had.

Over the next few days, as funeral arrangements were made and the house filled up with relatives, visitors, and sandwich trays, Brian stayed in his room. Luke was upset, though afraid, I think, to be tearful in front of me. His eyes were red rimmed, and he started wearing one of Dad's old sweaters. Mum's family came, her sister Peggy and the others we barely ever saw. Mum put them all together in the kitchen. Her own northside family embarrassed her, and she wanted to keep them separate from Dad's friends and relations. Apart from Peggy, we didn't know any of them. They always called Mum Moll, even though her name was Melissa. She hated that. Moll was a working-class Dublin abbreviation of Margaret. When Dad was alive, he could rile her by calling her Moll. I had always thought that Mum was ashamed of her family because of Dad, because he was from this middle-class southside suburb, but now he was dead, and she was still hiding them in the kitchen.

The day before the funeral, Luke asked me if I believed that God *really* existed. It's the kind of question he would have asked Dad. I tried to think what Dad would have said. I gave the standard answer expected of an older brother. "Luke, don't be daft. Of course he exists. How did we all get here otherwise?" But Luke looked doubtful.

I played the dutiful son and was part of the decision making when it came to choosing a coffin. "The second cheapest, Mum—it's not like anyone is going to judge us, and who will know the difference?"

All three of us were tall, and it was expected that we would be pallbearers. I went up to Brian and Luke's room to tell them.

Luke nodded. "It's the least we can do."

Brian looked up from his wretched book. "I'm not doing it."

"Why not?"

"I don't want to. The undertakers will do it, won't they? It's their job."

"Mum wants us to do it."

"No."

Luke said quietly, "Dad would want us to do it, together."

"He's dead, so what he wants doesn't matter," said Brian.

"Brian! Why are you being like this?"

"People die *all the time*. I don't see why there has to be such a fuss. Do you know how many children are dying of starvation right now in Ethiopia?"

I jumped on him and yelled at Luke to help me. Luke reluctantly got Brian onto the floor, and I roughly pulled his hands behind his back.

"Get off me! You animals! Get off!"

"You're carrying Dad's coffin, and that's final."

Still he struggled and argued. "I am not, I'm not doing it. You can't make me."

Mum chose that moment to walk into the room. "What in the name of God is going on, have you no respect?" she hissed. There were relatives downstairs, who had no doubt heard the commotion.

Luke was the tattletale, as usual. "Brian doesn't want to carry Dad's coffin tomorrow."

"He doesn't have to if he doesn't want to, now get off him!" She was cried out and weary.

At the funeral Mass the next day, Luke and I stood at the front end of the coffin, two uncles and two undertakers behind us. As we passed Brian at the front pew standing beside my mother, he flipped his middle finger upward at me, a look of triumph on his face. Tears of anger came to my eyes.

In the melee outside the church, I stood by Mum's side, fielding the mourners. As Jack Gogan, one of Dad's friends, approached, I saw Luke physically push him aside, quite roughly. The man looked startled. It sounded like Luke was berating him. Afterward, I asked him what that was about. He tapped his nose. "None of your business," he said. I assumed Gogan must have been one of Mum's lovers.

In the weeks and months after, Luke and I helped Mum and each other come to terms with the loss of our father. I don't remember Brian ever mentioning him again. We were all conscious of the fact that Brian refused to discuss his death. This refusal was somehow contagious. One year later, we rarely mentioned him, not even to mark his anniversary. At that stage, we could all fend for ourselves, and I admit that, after a few weeks, I did not miss him. I'm not sure Mum did either.

Chapter 3

1992

Even though we had all moved out, Sunday lunch at Mum's had become a tradition. She took some cooking course with Peggy and was surprised to find that she enjoyed it. She proved to be better at it than Dad, though I suppose when Dad had cooked for us, it was always after a full day's work.

If Mum was in a theater show, Sundays were her only day off, and she liked to make a big effort. She always cooked for at least ten people because you never knew who might turn up. It wasn't unusual for any of us to bring along three hungry flatmates. And Mum loved to perform for them. She kept herself up-to-date with who was who in popular culture and could discuss the merits of that book or this film or that TV series. She was the "cool" mum. My friends said I was lucky. She didn't mind them smoking or cursing or drinking. And, thankfully, she did not flirt with any of them.

We were all in our early twenties by then, and Luke and I had brought several girls home at this stage, but Brian never had. We teased him about being gay, though he showed no sign of it. But he was probably still a virgin at twenty-two.

Mum noted his lack of girlfriends but approached it in her usual unsubtle manner. "Is it because of your nose?" she'd say. Brian had a deviated septum, meaning one of his nostrils was wider than the other and his nose was slightly crooked. You would never notice it unless it was pointed out. "He gets that from your side," Mum used to say back in the day, and Dad would nod and agree that his father "had an enormous conk." We never noticed it because it was part of him, but Mum would refer to it under her breath as his "disfigure-ment." At one point in his teens, Brian had asked if there was an op-eration that might correct his nose, but Mum laughed at him. While it might have been acceptable for a girl to get her teeth straightened, the appearance of boys and men was far less important. Brian later said that it didn't bother him, but in new company I noticed he al-ways faced them full on until he felt confident enough to let them see him in profile.

By 1992, Brian had completed his arts degree and teaching qualifi-cation and was teaching part-time and working odd days in a bookshop in the city center. Luke had finally recorded his second album. I was doing a film-production training course at Filmbase.

On this particular Sunday, Brian arrived with a girl. Mum nudged and winked at me. The girl was beautiful in a punky kind of way. Dad would definitely not have approved. Spiked bleached hair, scarlet lip-stick, lots of eye makeup, and most exotically, this girl had an Ameri-can accent. We only heard American accents on the TV, so to me, she already had a certain sheen to her. Luke had brought along his pothead drummer, and the two of them were so obviously stoned that after a few minutes of listening to their incoherent giggling at every inquiry, we ignored them. Mum was irritable with Luke and told him to behave himself or leave the table. My girlfriend, Irene, sat beside me. We had been dating for a few months, not serious at all on my part, but Irene had a different impression of our relationship. In fact, I hadn't even invited her to this lunch, but she knew our family Sunday routine and had just brazenly shown up.

Mum could not help herself. "Well, now," she said to Brian's guest, "has our Brian finally got himself a girlfriend?" She handed the girl a bowl of salad to take to the table, while I carved the shoulder of lamb.

"Mum!" said Brian, annoyed.

Susan smiled easily. "No, we're just friends. We work together in the bookshop." But she smiled at Brian in a way that seemed flirtatious to me.

"And where are you from, dear?"

"Detroit," said Susan. "Michigan."

"Really? Home of Henry Ford, right?"

"Well, yep, home of the motor industry. My pop worked on the production line at Ford until the day he died."

"Oh, really? I'm so sorry. But he worked in a factory?"

Mum didn't exactly boast of her working-class roots but was proud that she had worked hard to escape them. She made sure she had elocution lessons in the College of Music, where she won a scholarship. And she must have adapted quickly and easily into our leafy Glenageary avenue. She liked people to believe she wasn't a snob, but the only member of her family she stayed in touch with was Peggy, who, against the odds, had made a name for herself as a fashion designer, having started out as a seamstress in a shirt factory. Mum had relayed her elocution lessons to her older sister.

"Yes, he was in charge of the electrocoat paint process," said Susan with pride, as if her father had been the ambassador to Paris. I liked her confidence.

Mum laughed. "My late husband's family would say that I'd married out of my class. His mother once referred to me as a northside show-girl. Me! I was a trained singer and a medal winner at the College of Music. I'm a showband star."

Susan was confused by this apparent non sequitur.

Brian was embarrassed. "You *were*. Past tense. Mum, you don't have to—"

Susan interrupted. "Are you really?"

Mum was shocked. "Brian, didn't you tell Susan who I am?"

Brian sat down calmly. "Not everyone cares who you are, Mum. Most of my friends couldn't name the Three Tenors, they're hardly going to have heard of a semiretired panto dame."

Mum's jaw tightened. I was furious with Brian for being so dismissive. I kicked him under the table. Mum still saw herself as a celebrity. She measured her success by the size and placing of her photograph in the *Sunday Independent*. It had been a year since she was in any paper at this stage, and her concerts and appearances were fewer and farther between, but she expected people to recognize her. Still, she couldn't blame Susan for her fame not having reached the suburbs of Detroit.

Luke and the drummer choked, laughing on their beer. And then Irene, defending Mum and trying to curry favor, piped up, pointing at her. "This is *the* Melissa Craig! She had her own TV show when I was a kid." I could see by Mum's face that although she was grateful to Irene, this description of her put her success firmly in the past.

Susan, without guile, said, "Oh, my mom didn't have much faith in television. We didn't have one. She thought we should all read books, so I guess that's what we did when everyone else was watching *Starsky and Hutch*. So should I call you Mrs. Drumm or Ms. Craig?"

"Melissa, call me Melissa."

Melissa was a name Mum had adopted even before she met Dad. I think she must have been the only Melissa of her generation. I didn't call any of my friends' parents by their first names. Mum thought it made her modern and "with it."

"Okay, Melissa, will I open the wine?"

"Oh, no, leave that to one of the boys. They'll be strong enough." Mum was never as modern as she thought.

Brian manfully opened the wine as if he were taming a lion. He didn't say much during lunch, but Susan was funny and interesting.

A few weeks later, when I called into the bookshop, I asked Brian where Susan was. "Why do you ask?" he said, immediately suspicious.

"You said she wasn't your girlfriend," I countered.

"She's not. We're just . . ."

"Do you fancy her?"

"No!"

I knew he'd say that. He was never going to try and compete with me.

Within a week, Susan and I were dating. She had no plans to stay long term in Ireland; it was just the starting point for her round-the-world trip. She intended to stay awhile in each place and move on to Paris and Madrid before Turkey and then India. She had some qualification in American literature from a Detroit community college, but not one that would be recognized by any Irish universities. She had signed up for several night classes in sociology and languages in Dublin. She was always busy. I liked that about her. She was never going to be clingy.

A year and a half later, we had to get married. Well, we didn't *have* to, but her visa was due to expire, and she was pregnant. She didn't find out until it was too late to get an abortion. I stepped up and did the decent thing: I offered to marry her. Fortunately, it turned out that she wanted to marry me too. I was really happy. The circumstances weren't ideal, but Susan was a prize. It was a lot to take on at such a young age. I was twenty-five when our child was born and, despite Mum helping out financially, times were tough.

Luke missed his flight home from Amsterdam the night before our small wedding. He arrived eventually in the church with some almost-dressed groupie just before we exchanged rings, looking exhausted, hungover, and upstaging our precious moment.

Unsurprisingly, Brian couldn't find a date to bring to the wedding. I could tell that he wasn't entirely happy about our relationship. Not long after we got back from our midwinter honeymoon in Kerry, he went to live in France.

Susan and I were going to live happily ever after.

Chapter 4

1978

Luke was preparing to make his first Holy Communion. We weren't a particularly religious household, though Dad dragged most of us reluctantly to 9:00 a.m. Mass most Sundays. Mum often made the excuse of having performed a concert the night before. Brian and I would fidget through the readings, the offerings, and the prayers, though I liked it when the holy smoke was wafted around the church as if a genie might appear out of a bottle, or a parrot might swoop down onto the altar, but nothing ever happened. The tinkling of the bell would signal the end of Mass, but it was church etiquette to wait until all the priests had left the altar. The priests in our parish were particularly old, and it seemed like it took them years to shuffle away into the sacristy. At that point, we would race out of the church like our asses were on fire, dying for the fresh air and to escape from the atmosphere of sacrifice and suffering that haunted small boys like us.

Except for Luke. Luke was deeply interested in the concept of hell and staying out of it. Every week, he put his entire pocket money into the Mass collection box. He couldn't wait for his first confession. I heard Mum and Dad laughing about it. "What could a seven-year-old possibly have to confess?" But Luke refused to discuss his sins with us. He said it was between him and God.

Of course, Brian and I teased him mercilessly, accusing him of breaking all Ten Commandments, even the ones we didn't understand. We didn't know what coveting your neighbor's wife was, but we guessed it was rude and dirty, so we made up a filthy song about Luke and Mrs. Turner next door and tormented him with it until he cried. Brian stole a pair of Mrs. Turner's tights off her washing line and put them under Luke's pillow.

Luke never retaliated. We started to call him Saint Luke, but that backfired because he seemed to like it.

On the morning of the Communion ceremony, Luke said he was sick and he couldn't go, but Mum had bought herself a new outfit for the occasion, and Dad had gone to the trouble of polishing all our shoes the night before. A cake had been ordered. When the thermometer proved that Luke had a normal temperature, Mum wasn't taking no for an answer. She stood over him while he cried and wailed, and she forced him into the white shorts and white V-neck sweater over a shirt and tie. Even when she pinned the rosette to his chest, he did not stop resisting. We all piled into Dad's car, and Luke grew more hysterical as we approached the church. Eventually, Dad, in a rare fit of temper, pulled over to the side of the road and yanked Luke out of the car. Brian and I pressed our faces up against the back window to see what would happen next. Mum applied another layer of lipstick in the rearview mirror.

Dad had Luke up against a wall and was gesticulating furiously, while Luke cowered, covering his head with his hands as if Dad was about to strike him, even though Dad never hit any of us. Five minutes later, they returned to the car. Luke was ashen faced. Mum told Dad to speed up, as we were now running late.

We hustled into the church, muttering apologies to the other families and the teachers while Mum smiled benevolently at the people who nudged each other at the sight of her peacock-feathered hat. We sat in the pew assigned to us, Luke right at the aisle, white-knuckled, clutch-ing the missal and the pearlescent rosary beads. He was obviously ter-rified but couldn't or wouldn't say what was wrong. I felt sorry for him at this stage, so I leaned over. "Don't worry, it'll be fine. Just think of the money and the sweets you'll get afterward." He didn't even look at me but just stared down at his bare knees, blinking back tears. When it was time for him to join the line of boys going up to the altar, Dad physically pushed him into the aisle. His form teacher put her hand on his shoulder and whispered some soothing words into his ear as she guided him toward the altar.

From our spot halfway down the church, we couldn't see exactly what happened, but we heard him suddenly screaming out, "I'm not good enough! I'm not good enough!" and then there were gasps from the front rows, and Dad stepped out of his seat and was beckoned to the top of the church.

Luke had thrown up at the altar, splashing vomit on the boys around him and on the vestments of the priest in front of him. Boys started crying. The priest hurriedly left the altar, and another one stepped in to replace him. Nuns scuttled out of the vestry with basins of soapy water and tried to clean up the worst of the mess. The ceremony continued. Despite everything, Luke received the sacrament and calmed down in-stantly. He returned to the pew, a stinking mess, and as soon as possible, we all left the church. Mum pulled off his sweater and put it in a plastic bag in the trunk, gagging as she did it. Dad apologized to Luke. "We should have let you stay in bed, but you didn't have a temperature."

"It's okay, Dad, I forgive you."

Luke smiled at Mum. She ignored him.

At home, Luke was back to normal. The small gathering organized for relatives went ahead. Now dressed in clean clothes, he wore the ro-sary beads around his neck like a necklace. He partook in the chocolate Rice Krispie cakes and the decrusted ham sandwiches and read aloud from his new white Bible. We all said a prayer for our cousin Paul, who was in hospital for tests.

That night, in bed, I could hear Brian and Luke talking in the room next door.

"What was wrong with you?"

"I guess I was sick."

"You were scared, I could see it. What were you scared of?"

"I . . . I . . . the devil. He could have taken my soul."

"What are you talking about?"

"The devil told me he'd be waiting for me in the church, but I guess he was inside me. I threw him up, and now I'm clean."

"You're such a freak."

There was silence after that.

Usually, incidents like this became stories to be trotted out on regular occasions to shame or embarrass us, especially as we grew into our teens, but Luke remained deadly serious about religion. Even when we were no longer forced to, he went to Mass weekly, sometimes more often, and to confession almost every day. He never discussed any of this with us. Dad's mum was delighted. Dad said maybe Luke had a vocation. Mum said he ought to socialize more but that she wouldn't be disappointed if Luke became a priest because she didn't want to be surrounded by grandchildren when she was older. She'd had enough of babies, she said. Dad gave her one of his disapproving looks.

Our next-door neighbor insisted on having a fancy-dress party every Halloween night. All of us hated being forced to dress up in stupid costumes, except for Luke. Luke invariably dressed up as a priest or a monk until one occasion, age thirteen, when he made a crucifix out of planks of wood and stabbed himself with a bread knife in the hands and feet and went as Jesus Christ, displaying his stigmata for all to see. The wounds were not deep but bled profusely. That was the day it stopped being funny.

Dad and Mum argued that night. I could hear Dad saying, "There's something wrong with him! The boy needs help." Mum was inclined to play it down. "He'll grow out of it, it's just a phase."

Luke did grow out of his religious zealotry, after Dad's death. Whereas Brian's reaction to Dad's death was bizarre, Luke just accepted it. He said he'd been having doubts for some time, but now he was perfectly sure that God didn't exist. He never went to Mass again after that, though I often caught him whispering to himself, as if he were praying. It seemed like he was almost normal, whatever normal was, for a while, anyway.

Chapter 5

1999

I invited this actress for a drink, Amy Shine. She was just twenty-one, a decade younger than me, a fresh graduate from the new drama school in Dublin. I'd seen her in some play in the City Arts Center. I was going to see a lot of shows in those days because I was about to produce our second feature film, and I didn't entirely trust the casting director, so I accompanied him to every show. We were looking for a young male in his twenties who had to be handsome but quirky and who could convey both menace and charm. The guy we had heard about in this production had none of these things. Amy Shine, though, shone. If only she'd been able to act, she had the perfect name for a movie star. She had a small role. Nothing about the play was memorable except for this girl's incredible body. She was corseted for the part, so I guess it was a period drama. God, I wish corsets were fashionable again.

She had a small but perfect bottom and milky-white breasts. She was tall and slender, and her hair was long and golden. Her voice was terrible, but it didn't matter.

Afterward, we got talking to the cast. They knew who I was and why I was there, and they insisted on buying us drinks. We gladly accepted. Being a film producer in Dublin in the late nineties was hardly lucrative, but people thought you were important and powerful, and it was easy to let them. Amy was one of those. She pretended *not* to know who I was. A lot of them did that and then feigned surprise on hearing my name: "William *Drumm*? *The* William Drumm?" "Aren't you Luke Drumm's brother? I have all his albums." "I saw *The Inpatient*! I loved it!" Blah blah blah.

Even good actors are useless without a script. But I can't say I didn't enjoy the attention, the free entry to members' bars in nightclubs and invites to insider parties. I was climbing out from under Luke's shadow. I was something of a celebrity in my own right.

I admit that I'd had two or three one-night stands, but it was never cheating. There were no affairs, no infatuation. I was not unfaithful to Susan. It was only sex. I always woke up in my own bed, with her. No matter how late the night had been, I got up and went home and made her coffee in the morning. In the office in Merrion Square, I had a sofa where I often took a catch-up nap. She was suspicious sometimes and quizzed me about where I'd been and who I'd been with. Once, I watched her from the hallway going through my jacket pockets, examining every receipt, sniffing my shirt collars for perfume.

Women would throw themselves at me. All I needed to do was drop a hint about a part they might be ideal for or offer an introduction to Steven Spielberg. I only met him once, at an American Embassy party, but I made sure to put my arm around him when the camera pointed our way, to make it look like we were old friends. The photograph appeared on the back page of the *Sunday Independent*. It was all good for business and had other . . . benefits. Like Amy Shine, for example.

I arranged to meet her in a pub near her studio the night after her show. It was an old man's pub, spit and sawdust on the floor. A place where I was unlikely to be recognized or noticed. I told her I had a script she might be interested in, but it was a hush-hush project, she mustn't tell anyone.

In the pub, I got her talking about herself, her favorite subject, as it happened. I flattered her, told her she could have a bright future if she played her cards right. This time, I bought the drinks. Gin and tonics, doubles for her, though she didn't know it. She became giddy after a while, and when I put my hand on her lap under the table, she giggled nervously and moved her legs away, but she didn't leave, so I knew I wasn't wasting my time. She finally got around to asking about the script. I said there was no way I could show it to her in a pub. Eventually, she reluctantly suggested we could go to her studio around the corner.

When we got there, I could see the reason for her reluctance. It was tiny, and messy. Underwear was strewn across a radiator. Her half-eaten lunch was still on the kitchen table. A rather uninviting single bed was unmade in the corner. She raced around drunkenly, shoving things into drawers, throwing cutlery and dishes into the sink.

"God, I'm so sorry, I didn't expect . . . I think I'm a little drunk."

She was very drunk.

I patted the seat on the sofa next to me.

"Can I see the script?" she said, looking down at my empty briefcase.

"Let's not worry about the script. Come over here."

I stood up and pulled her by the waistband of her jeans toward me. I could feel the heat of her body.

"What are you doing?"

"I think we both know, don't we?"

"But the script . . ."

I wasn't entirely sure if she was incredibly naive or just being coy.

"You're an attractive girl, you know."

She pulled away from me at once, and her voice turned cold.

"Look, I think you've misunderstood." Her words were slurred.

I glanced around. "Do you have any wine?"

"I think you should go."

"Go? You invited me here. What is a man supposed to think?"

Her voice grew shrill. "Just leave, please, will you?"

I had never had this type of response before. I was furious. She had spent the evening making eyes at me, leaning forward in her low-cut top, biting her lip. The signals had been clear.

"I'm going. By the way, you can forget about your acting career. I know everyone in this business, and you'll never get another part." I slammed the door on my way out.

A year later, Susan and I were going out for dinner with Brian and his latest girlfriend, Gillian. Brian had moved back to Dublin after some time teaching in Paris and then a few years working with Luke on tour. We saw each other every couple of months. Luke was in and out of contact with us both, but his star was on the wane by then. The teenagers who had idolized him had grown up and moved on. He was playing smaller venues in tours that no longer sold out. On this occasion, Luke had been invited to dinner too, but didn't return our call. It wasn't unusual. Brian was talking about taking over as Luke's manager, as it looked like Sean was about to drop him. I laughed at the idea. Brian didn't have a clue how to manage himself let alone anyone else.

The restaurant we'd chosen, Hedon, was an upmarket place with a Michelin star, but it was Susan's birthday, and I could afford to be generous. We had a bottle of champagne at the bar before the maître d' showed us to our table and introduced us to our waitress, Amy Shine. After the initial jolt of recognition, I decided to brazen it out.

"Amy, what are you doing here? I thought you'd be on Broadway by now."

She blushed to the roots of her hair. "Hello, William."

Susan knew instantly. I could sense the tension in the air. "Well, Amy, how do you know my husband?" she asked.

And yet, what did Susan know? This was a girl who hadn't let me sleep with her. I was entirely innocent. I answered the question. "Amy was in a play I went to see with Carl last year. Have you done much acting since, Amy?"

I knew she'd play along. I have discovered that women will nearly always protect men from the wrath of their wives. Now, why is that?

"I gave up acting, just after that play, actually." Her tone was barbed. "I'm doing a degree in arts administration now."

"Good for you, Amy, good for you! Right, well, can you send over the sommelier before we take a look at the menu, there's a good girl."

Amy toddled off. I tried not to watch that perfect rear end and opened the menu with a flourish.

Susan said, "Don't be such a patronizing ass, William."

I felt a sharp kick under the table. Painful. At first, I thought it was Susan's heel, but I glanced up to see Brian glaring murderously at me. Susan and Gillian were buried in the menus. "Prick." Brian mouthed the word at me. I returned the gesture with a *what the hell?* look. I rubbed my shin under the table, and we all tried to continue as if nothing had happened. There was tension in the air, though Gillian seemed oblivious. She was very ordinary, but none of Brian's girlfriends was ever going to set the world on fire.

Amy never returned to serve our table but was replaced without explanation by Orla, a heifer whose efficiency made up for her lack of visual appeal. Susan and Brian talked enthusiastically to each other and to Gillian. They both ignored me for the rest of the evening. This was all the more infuriating because I was picking up the tab for all of us.

Later, as we exited the restaurant, Brian pulled me aside. "You fucking cheated on her, didn't you? Prick." Before I could answer, he took Gillian by the arm, and they went off in search of a taxi. Susan didn't speak to me on the way home. When we got there, I went to pay the pimply babysitter and Susan went upstairs. I poured another glass of wine and turned on the television. Susan appeared and threw the spare duvet onto the sofa and went back up, slamming the bedroom door behind her.

I never even fucked the girl.

Chapter 6

1983

I was fourteen in the summer of 1983, and my friends Jim and Steve and I wanted to go and see *Trading Places* in the Forum cinema because everyone in school was talking about Jamie Lee Curtis's tits, and we just had to see them for ourselves. The cinema was walking distance from our house, and for a full week leading up to the event we talked of nothing else.

It would be my first time at an over-15's film. I felt grown-up. Mum had given me permission to go without asking anything about the film. She was liberal about things like that, and she trusted me. Dad was stricter, but he was away at a conference that weekend. Only Steve was actually fifteen. He'd been held back a year in school because he wasn't too bright, but he was useful. Jim and I rehearsed our date of birth just in case we were questioned. I reckoned that if we said we were sixteen rather than fifteen, we'd be more likely to get away with it. I repeated "1967" over and over because that's how they always tried to catch you out, apparently, by asking the year of your birth. I was the tallest of us. I figured I'd have no problem getting in.

I hit the roof when Mum said she was having visitors that night and I'd have to bring Brian and Luke with me. Apart from the fact that I didn't want to be anywhere near my little brothers, especially when Jim and Steve were around, there was no way we would all get into the film. Luke had a Cliff Richard T-shirt that he was obsessed with and wore all summer long. He was a total embarrassment. Brian's acne was out of control, and it had earned him the nickname "Rice Krispie Face." I was proud of that. Even Mum laughed, though Dad said it was cruel.

Mum said we should just go to another film. I argued that it had been *arranged ages ago*, that I was going with my *friends*, that my brothers would *embarrass* me. Mum gave me five pounds and told me she didn't care where we went as long as I took the boys with me. I was livid. Brian was excited because he badly wanted to see Jamie Lee Curtis's tits too. Luke was less interested in the tits, but as he didn't get to go to the cinema too often, he was enthusiastic too. Mum often made us go to opening nights of dreadful plays that her friends were in, so the cinema was still the apex of our entertainment experience. I loved the cinema more than anything else. I saved up my pocket money and often went to films on my own. I loved the darkness and the way the characters loomed above us on that giant screen.

I couldn't dissuade my mother. I offered my brothers three pounds just to piss off, but they were adamant they wanted to see the film. In the end, I snuck out of the house early to get away from them, but sure enough they turned up and joined us in the queue.

I tried to get Luke to change his T-shirt or wear a jacket over it, but he said it would be disloyal to Cliff to cover him up. God, he was such a spaz. Brian at least agreed to wear a baseball cap, but then the idiot turned it backward. It didn't hide any of his lumpy face. Steve and Jim were not impressed.

"Ah janey, we're not all going to get in, no way. We had some chance when it was just us three."

I pretended not to know them, but Luke started to cry, and I wanted to just die on the spot. We were stuck with them. "Fine! If by any chance we all get in, neither of you are sitting anywhere near me, right? Brian, you have to say your date of birth is 1967. Luke, you can say 1968, do you hear me? If the ticket seller asks your age, you're fifteen and sixteen."

"But I'm twelve," said Luke, and Steve and Jim immediately separated themselves from us. "Sorry, Will, but we're not missing this because of *them*."

I took my brothers aside.

"Luke, for God's sake, cross your arms over your chest, try to look older." Brian ruffled Luke's hair, because Luke always kept it neatly combed. Luke looked like a choirboy. Jamie Lee Curtis's tits were disappearing over the horizon for me. I saw Steve and Jim buy their tickets, and they hovered by the popcorn booth to see if we got in. The bored woman at the ticket office took no notice of us, but my almost-broken voice wavered a little as I requested three tickets. She peered over the counter at Brian and Luke. "What age is that fella?" she said, pointing to Luke. Brian heaved a sigh of relief.

"I was born in 1967," said Luke.

The ticket seller looked at me and put her head to one side. "Do ya think I came down in the last shower? That child is nine, if he's a day. He's not coming in, and that's final. It's a dirty film anyway, you should be ashamed bringing a child into that. What would your mother say?"

"I'll have just two tickets then, please," I said as politely as I could while Luke tried not to cry behind me.

I felt bad for him, but what could I do? "Sorry, Luke, you have to go home."

Brian dithered; he obviously felt more guilt about the situation than me. But his love for Jamie Lee Curtis outweighed his love for Luke. "Just tell Mum you didn't get in. She'll understand."

The film was very funny, and we sat in anticipation of the big reveal. About fifteen minutes into it, the sour-faced ticket office woman came in, scouring the audience with her flashlight. Brian was somewhere over the other side of the cinema. Steve, Jim, and I scrunched down in our seats in case she'd start asking questions, but she methodically went through the cinema row by row until she found me. She didn't even whisper.

"You!" she said. "Your brother's outside, and he's hysterical. Come out now!" Everyone in the audience protested and shushed her, but I had to leave. I tried to look for Brian, but I couldn't see exactly where he was sitting.

Outside, I grabbed Luke roughly by the arm and dragged him away from the cinema. "What is it? You're ruining everything!"

"It's Mum! I went home and there's a man having sexual intercourse with her!"

"What?"

"In her bedroom!"

"Wait, what? Was he attacking her? Was she screaming?"

"Yes!" His lip quivered.

"Did he see you?"

"No, I was so scared that I came to find you."

I ran. As fast as I could. I didn't even look to see if Luke was behind me. The house was only five minutes away, four if I sprinted.

When I got home, Mum was in the sitting room drinking gin and tonic with Nicholas Sheedy, a musical director she had worked with from time to time. She looked perfectly demure, apart from her hair, which was like a rough-cut hedge at the back.

"What are you doing home already? I didn't expect you for at least another hour."

I bet she didn't. Luke arrived then, breathless.

"God, not you as well. Where's Brian?" said Mum.

I gave Luke a fierce look, and I could see the color and confusion rising in his face.

"Yeah, well, the film wasn't appropriate for Luke, so I brought him home."

"What a considerate young man!" said Nicholas.

"Really?" said Mum. "What wasn't appropriate?"

"There was nudity," I said.

Mum and Nicholas hooted with laughter, and I wanted to kill them both.

"I rather thought that's why you wanted to go and see it," said Mum.

That was why Mum wanted us all out of the way. I'd suspected before. She'd always been flirty, but now I had proof, or Luke had. Why didn't Dad ever do anything about this? He knew what she was like. I'd seen her touching other men in front of him. He'd be still and silent for days afterward. Why was my dad such a doormat? I'd never let a woman treat me like that when I grew up.

Later, I tried to convince Luke that he had only imagined what he saw. I swore him to secrecy. I told him that if he ever told anyone what he'd seen, Mum would go to hell. He was still obsessed by hell and heaven at that time, and which one we'd go to. Brian had come home crowing about the size and shape of JLC's breasts. Apparently, the whole cinema had cheered and thrown popcorn in the air.

So that day, Brian saw tits and Luke saw tits, even though they were Mum's, and I saw none.

Chapter 7

1998

Daisy was the best thing to ever happen to me. I couldn't believe that Susan and I had made this perfect, beautiful child. I know every parent says this, but there was something special about our child. Daisy was clever and funny and much smarter than other kids her age. Susan had done the hard work, the messy stuff like feeding and changing and laundry, and I know I got off lightly, but I happily did those tasks whenever I was around.

By the time Daisy was four years old, I was traveling a lot, to film festivals around Europe, trying to get cofinancing deals with producing partners for our second feature film, to get meetings with bigger distributors who might take a risk on a small Irish company who'd had a one-hit wonder with *The Inpatient*.

But coming home to Susan and Daisy from those trips abroad was the best thing a man could ask for. Susan was back at work in the bookshop, part-time, and Daisy was in her first year of school for a few hours every day. She had adapted to all these changes like a little trouper. And when she heard me come in the front door saying "Where's my little Daisy?" she would run full tilt toward me, arms in the air, grinning widely. I'd sweep her up, and she'd cover my face in wet, sloppy kisses, and then Susan would appear behind her in the hallway with a "Howdy, stranger!" and we three would embrace. My perfect little family.

We thought Mum would love the opportunity to babysit in the early days, but she quickly made herself clear: "I've already done babies—three of you—thanks very much. I'm not doing it again." I thought she meant the nappy changes and the feeding, but even when we visited her house with a beautifully dressed sleeping baby, Mum showed no interest. When we got Daisy to sing "Twinkle, Twinkle, Little Star" for Mum, my mother declared, "The child hasn't got a note in her head. She certainly doesn't take after me."

Susan's mum was different. She very rarely visited from Detroit, but when she did, I thought we might have to stop her from kidnapping Daisy and taking her back home. She saw what I saw, a wonderful, beautiful, and talented child full of love and promise.

So why did my mother pay no attention to her? Aren't grandparents supposed to adore their grandchildren unconditionally?

It was only after Daisy was born that I missed my dad. I wondered if he had read stories to me in my cot every night while Mum was on-stage. I wondered if he had cut the crusts off my toast or taken me out on my tricycle. I searched through the family photos but could find none of Dad and me without Brian or Luke being in the photos too. I know that developing rolls of film back then was expensive and that the camera was rarely used. Still, there were lots of photographs of Mum accepting awards in the company of dignitaries. Probably photos taken by other people and sent to her.

The earliest family photos were of all of us on the beach. Dad, Brian, pregnant Mum, and me sitting around a sandcastle that Dad must have built. I can't have been more than two years old in the photograph.

I wondered if he ever felt truly proud of me, beyond a "Well done, fella" when I got a good school report card. I wondered if he ever looked at me the way I looked at Daisy. The truth is that I always felt Dad was weak, that Mum was more important. I felt sorry for him. Did he sense that? My wife was so much easier on me than Mum had been on Dad. I never gave him credit for the way he managed her moods.

When I read Daisy a story at night before bed, she would sit in my lap and trace the words with her finger. She was an early reader—she knew the alphabet when she was three. She was chatty, and her vocabulary was definitely advanced for her age. Sometimes when I went into her room in the morning, she pretended to be asleep, and then bounced vertically into a standing position and screeched, "Daddy!" with a voice full of joy. I'm not supposed to say this, or think this, but I loved her more than I loved Susan—not that I didn't love Susan, at the time.

When Daisy fell in our neighbor's yard and was knocked unconscious on a sunny afternoon, I fell apart. Susan was out at the supermarket, and I was in the house on my own, watching the golf on TV.

The woman next door banged on our back door, distraught. She'd already called an ambulance. It couldn't have taken me more than thirty seconds to hop over the low wall and pick up my motionless child, but the horror of those moments will never leave me. I cradled her in my arms, pinching her lightly, kissing her, trying to get some reaction. The neighbor, Eve, assured me that she was still breathing, but I was too frantic to be sure. Eve's daughter, Tracey, older by two years, was hysterically screaming, "Daisy is dead!" and I reached out and smacked her across the head while gripping my child to myself. Eve said nothing but sent her child indoors. I did not speak to her in those endless minutes while we waited for the ambulance to arrive. She gabbled that Daisy must have climbed onto the wall and toppled off it. It was possible, I suppose. I had seen her do it before. Susan had scolded her and warned her not to do it again, but I had been proud that my girl was so brave and agile.

In the ambulance, Daisy regained consciousness, and I exhaled and wept. The ambulance men, who had seen it all before, speculated that it was probably just a concussion, that she'd be "right as rain in no time." She couldn't speak, though, and she didn't seem to be able to focus on my face. She was whisked away for a CAT scan as soon as we arrived at the hospital, and I tried to fight my fears as I checked in with the nurse.

Susan arrived shortly after, white-faced and thin-lipped. "Why weren't you watching her?" she snarled, and that was the first time I saw her anger and frustration directed toward me, though not the last.

I felt my face crumple again, and I was embarrassed. I turned away, and Susan put her hand on my shoulder. The gesture seemed to make things so much more serious. When I was growing up, we were not a particularly affectionate family. I had made sure I was different with Susan and Daisy. On Sunday mornings, we all had breakfast in bed together, snuggled against one another in a cocoon of warmth and love. Susan's physical act of comfort convinced me that my little girl must be dying.

Susan and I sat by Daisy's bed when she was wheeled back from the X-ray department. She was whimpering but brighter, and relieved, I think, to see us. She clung to her mother, and when I tried to take her, she screamed until Susan held her again. I was jealous. She had always been Daddy's girl.

We were informed that there was no bleed on the brain. The ambulance men were right, it was concussion, but they were going to keep her overnight for observation. The ward was busy with all kinds of kids with physical and mental disabilities. Nurses were running from one place to the next. I couldn't trust they would be able to observe Daisy properly. We had been told there was a risk of seizures. Neither of us wanted to leave her, and they allowed us two chairs beside the bed. Other parents, mostly mothers, slept on rolled-out mattresses at their children's bedsides.

Daisy improved and we were allowed to give her a little juice, which stayed down: a good sign, apparently. By ten o'clock that night, well past her bedtime, she was chatting to her bear, and apart from the grape-size lump at the front of her head, she was almost back to normal. When she eventually dozed off, I took Susan's hand across the bed, but she pulled it away fiercely. "You were supposed to be minding her."

We took Daisy home the next day. She had been checked out and deemed fit and healthy, but we both watched her like hawks for the following week. We were careful around each other too. I knew that

Susan didn't really blame me for what happened. It could just as easily have been her at home when Tracey called for Daisy. They had played together often since Eve had moved in.

Eve dropped in a note and a cake to apologize, but I didn't blame her either. Kids fall over. It's part of growing up. I accept that now. But when it's your kid, it's different, and you feel like you've let them down and failed in the most fundamental way.

We got back to normal after a few weeks. Then we noticed a For Sale sign on Eve's house. I got talking to her one Saturday afternoon. She was uncomfortable around me. "I thought you liked the area?" I said.

"I do."

"So, did you get a new job somewhere else?"

"No."

I felt like there was resentment in her voice.

"Is everything okay?"

"Ask your mother."

"What? What do you mean?"

She turned her back and walked up the path and slammed the door behind her.

Later, on the phone, Mum said she had only given Eve "a friendly warning."

"It can't have been that friendly. She's moving house!"

"Good."

"What did you say to her?"

"William, stop being so dramatic. I just told her that if my grandchild ever suffered any aftereffects from that fall, I would sue her."

"You . . . what? Sue her for what?"

"Well, I don't know, do I? It's just a thing people say. I think she should be more careful with other people's children."

"Mum, it happened five weeks ago. You haven't even called to see Daisy, and yet you found the time to visit my neighbor and threaten her."

"It's the principle. You're my son."

Susan and I both tried to persuade Eve not to sell up, but the incident had rattled us all, and the brief chats at the gate were always awkward and stilted after that. Before she moved, we invited her to dinner, and Tracey came, too, and had a sleepover. We apologized for my mother, and I think Eve accepted it. It was another two weeks before we saw Mum. When we told her that Eve had moved, she just sighed in relief. "Safer for the child, then," she said, pointing at Daisy.

I'm not sure what that said about Mum. Brian, as Daisy's godfather, had shown a lot more concern for Daisy than she did. He had phoned regularly since hearing of the accident to see how she was, and yet Mum had acted like a lioness about the grandchild she took little interest in. I knew it was because she was *my* child.

Luke phoned from Manchester about a month later and had to be reminded about the accident. "Oh yeah, Brian told me," he said. "That child is an angel, you gotta keep her safe, man," and I was proud and irritated at the same time.

Chapter 8

1981

Dad always made a fuss at Christmas. He took two full weeks off work to coincide with our Christmas holidays from school. Mum always worked a lot around the festive season, doing concerts and recitals. The showband era was over, but Mum had been classically trained and could sing an aria if she rehearsed hard enough. "I'm no one-trick pony," she would declare, and in the same breath bemoan, "The bloody Messiah, again!" but she loved it. We were forced to sit through it so often that we grew to hate it passionately.

In 1981, Dad lost his biggest client. He had an insurance company, but 60 percent of his business had come from a chain of supermarkets that had just been bought out by a bigger chain who used their own insurance company, a global brand. There was no way Dad could compete.

That year, Mum had been forced to take a job in pantomime, a theatrical form she had always said was beneath her, slapstick comedy for children, always loosely based on a fairy tale. It was grueling work. Nine shows a week for the six weeks surrounding Christmas, with only Christmas Day and Boxing Day off. Worse for her, she was deemed too old to play Cinderella and was in the role of the wicked stepmother. The costume designer had made her a fat suit, and she had to apply prosthetic warts to her face. Mum was not happy about this, and she constantly and insistently reminded Dad of the sacrifices she was making for the sake of the family. Dad groveled and made her breakfast in bed every day, and we kept the house spotless because we knew it wouldn't take much to push Mum over the edge into one of her moods.

Brian and I, at twelve and thirteen, no longer believed in Santa Claus, but we liked the fact that Luke did, even though we mocked him behind his back. Dad made us go through the whole charade of writing letters to Santa for Luke's sake. We both wanted Raleigh Chopper bikes. Luke, the martyr, wanted a new pair of school shoes because the ones he had were pinching him. Dad tried to persuade Brian and me that we should follow Luke's example and ask for something we needed rather than wanted. My brothers always got my cast-off clothes and shoes, but the zip in the jacket that was now Brian's had bust, and the shoulder had ripped. All my trousers were rising up my ankles as I grew taller, but still Brian and I wanted new bikes "like everyone else" had. Christmas and birthdays were the only times in the year when we were entitled to actual gifts of our choosing, and we weren't going to be palmed off with what should have been provided as routine by most normal parents. Dad sighed and got Mum to talk to us. She lost her temper with Brian completely. "We can't afford bloody bicycles! We can barely afford the heating oil, you selfish little pig. Even Luke understands that!"

"Luke's a spazmo," said Brian. Mum didn't disagree but raged on.

"Well, I'd rather have a spazmo for a son than an ungrateful brat who doesn't mind his mother working her ass off night and day to keep food in his mouth." Brian tried not to cry in front of us and went to bed.

"Mum," I said when I got her on my own, "I'll get a bike, won't I?" She smoothed my hair and grimaced. "We'll see, William." I wasn't very hopeful.

Usually, on Christmas Eve, we went to the panto matinee and got fish and chips on the way home, but this time, because Mum was in it, she was going for a drink with her fellow cast members after the show. That morning she had said to Dad, "It's just one drink, for God's sake. I'm entitled to one damn night off. I'll be with you for two whole days before I have to get back into the fat suit."

Seeing Mum in the panto had been as mortifying for us as it was for her. She looked garish and ugly, and the fat suit included an enormous fake low-cut bosom that I really didn't want to see. Luke had freaked out a bit when she first appeared, and I had to swap seats with him so he could sit beside Dad. Afterward, we went backstage, but she was busy signing autographs for other kids. Dad said not to worry, we'd see her later.

We stopped for fish and chips and watched *The Wizard of Oz* on TV while we waited for Mum to come home. Dad was fretful and kept looking at his watch. At 9:00 p.m., he sent Brian and Luke to bed, but I offered to stay up with him to gift wrap our bicycles. He snapped at me then.

"You're getting one bicycle between you to share. Do you ever think about anyone but yourself?" It was uncharacteristic of Dad to be so irritable or direct, and I went to bed then, upset. Not about the bike, particularly, but because Mum hadn't come home, the realization that maybe we really didn't have any money, and also because Christmas Eve, which had always been a harmonious night in our home, had been ruined.

My bedroom was over the hallway, so I heard Mum arriving home sometime after midnight according to my Timex watch (Santa's last gift before I knew he was my parents). I heard her fiddle with the keys in the door for ages before she eventually let herself in, and then Dad was talking to her and I couldn't tell exactly what he was saying, but his whispering was furious, almost hissing. Mum didn't bother to whisper. "So what if I stayed out, I earned the money, didn't I? You're supposed to be the provider. If it wasn't for me, we wouldn't even have a turkey."

Dad's voice again, and then Mum: "You're just jealous! At least Kevin can buy his wife the occasional diamond. I only wanted a bloody sandwich toaster!"

Her voice was slurred, and then doors were slammed, and I lay in bed, hoping that peace would break out in the morning like in the First World War when the English side and the German side stopped killing each other and played football instead. Why couldn't Dad be like other dads? Why couldn't Mum be like other mums?

I woke to the sound of Luke's squeals of excitement. "Santa's been! Santa's been!"

I went downstairs to find Dad disheveled in last night's clothes, pushing a blanket off the sofa.

"Did you sleep down here, Dad?"

"Where's Mum?" said Brian.

"Your mum got in late, and I fell asleep watching a film. Sorry, boys." He plastered a smile on his face.

"Santa must have been very quiet if he didn't wake *you*," said Luke, clutching his new shoes to his chest—and, in fairness, they were nice shoes, brown leather. His eyes were shining with happiness. We unwrapped other small presents, too, chocolate Santas, tangerines, a David Bowie tape for me, a Nolan Sisters tape for Luke, and a Boomtown Rats tape for Brian.

"Where are the bikes?" asked Brian.

Jovially Dad tried to explain, using Luke's presence as an excuse to play everything down. "Now, Brian, sometimes Santa sees that there are poor children in the world and he has to share the presents out equally, and you know how generous he's been in other years, so this year, he's got you and William a bike to share." Dad went outside for a minute and then lifted the gift-wrapped bike through the patio doors. I tore the paper off, while Brian sat behind me in silence. It wasn't a Raleigh Chopper. It wasn't even a new bicycle. Marks and scrapes on its frame and mudguards told us that this bicycle had already lived another life under another boy's bottom.

"Now, boys, don't be disappointed. Santa was—"

Brian interrupted. "Every single thing I get all year round is second-hand. I get William's clothes, his rugby boots, his books. I got all his old toys when he was finished with them. It's Christmas Day, and the only thing I asked for was a new bike *of my own*. It's bad enough that I have to share it with *him*"—at this point, he punched me in the shoulder—"but it's not even *new*, it's Paul's old bike that's been rotting in Uncle Dan's shed since Paul died."

Our cousin Paul had died two years earlier from leukemia at the age of nine.

"How did Santa get Paul's bike?" said Luke, his lip beginning to tremble.

"Never mind," I said. "Luke, will you go and wake Mum?" It was only seven o'clock.

"Yes, that's a good idea," Dad said, and Luke clomped up the stairs in his pajamas and his new brown shoes.

"It's only a bike," I said, displaying the mature attitude that Dad would approve of.

"It was the only thing I wanted," whined Brian.

"Oh, grow up!" I said with all the swagger of a thirteen-year-old.

This enraged Brian. He picked up the bicycle and threw it at me with all his strength. If I hadn't dodged it, I would certainly have ended up in hospital, but the weight and the force of it shattered through the glass patio door.

Rather than being stunned into silence, Brian then stamped his feet on all the other small gifts, including the unopened ones for our parents.

"Brian! Stop it!" Dad, shocked, roared at him, but Brian pulled the Christmas tree out of its pot and threw it across the sofa, then ran up the stairs to his and Luke's room, almost knocking down Luke and Mum in the process.

"What in the name of God is going on? Mother of Jesus!" Mum said when she saw the shattered glass and the absolute destruction of the sitting room.

Luke wailed, "Santa is never coming to our house again," and then Brian shouted down from upstairs, "There is no Santa, you mental gobshite. There's just Mum and Dad, who won't even buy us proper presents. Why do you think Santa uses the same wrapping paper as us, you moron? Why do other kids always get cool toys?" Then the bedroom door slammed.

Luke's lip trembled. "It's not true, is it? Santa is real, isn't he?" There was a note of desperation in his voice.

Mum looked at Dad and put her hand to her forehead. "Can you get me some aspirin, please?"

"Get it yourself," he snarled.

"But, Mum, there is a Santa, isn't there?"

"No, Luke, there isn't. Now will you please go and get Mummy some aspirin from the medicine cupboard?"

Luke was silent for the rest of the day. Dad spent the morning clattering aggressively in the kitchen, preparing the turkey and the brussels sprouts that nobody even liked. I cleaned up the sitting room, re-erected the Christmas tree, salvaged as much as I could from the broken presents. The bicycle's front wheel had buckled in the incident. Nobody was going to ride it now. Mum lay on the sofa, groaning occasionally and issuing orders for coffee and water. The television, thankfully, had been undamaged, and Luke sat in front of it, consumed by *Willy Wonka*.

Dad boarded up the patio door with some hardboard from the shed, and, in fact, it was March before we could afford to replace the glass.

When Christmas dinner was served at three o'clock, I was sent up to fetch Brian. I was sure he'd be feeling humiliated and ashamed of his own behavior, but he had wrecked Christmas for everyone, and I wanted to rub it in.

"The bike is screwed, you know."

"So what?"

"So neither of us have a bike now, idiot."

"Yeah, well, we didn't have bikes yesterday, either, so what's the difference?"

"I guess the difference is that yesterday you weren't such a complete cretin."

He came at me like a ball of fury. He punched me so hard, I went flying out of the door and was lucky not to fall backward down the stairs.

Dad came running as I went for Brian, trying to dig at him with my fists.

"*Stop!* What has got into this family?" He pried us apart, and we were left swinging at each other on either side of him, cartoonlike.

"Get downstairs for your dinner, and not another word out of either of you."

I protested. "But my nose is bleeding, he punched me—"

"I don't care. Downstairs, now."

Christmas dinner was eaten in total silence. I was trying to balance a bag of frozen peas on my nose while eating. Luke was attempting not to cry, but his eyes were glassy. Mum and Dad were not speaking to each other at all. Brian looked down at his plate and, when he'd finished pushing around the plum pudding that nobody liked, declared, "I hate this poxy family. I hate all of you!" and returned to his bedroom, slamming the door.

Mum looked at Dad and her mouth twitched, and then she and Dad started to laugh helplessly. Luke joined in, out of sheer relief. And eventually I cracked a smile too. Because, you see, in our family somebody always had to be the butt of the joke, and that Christmas Day, it was Brian.

Chapter 9

2006

Susan and I had agreed to shared custody of Daisy, which meant that I got Daisy most weekends, but it didn't always suit me because a lot of the film festivals took place over the weekend. "Bring her with you," said Susan. And I would explain *again* that film festivals were work and that I'd be having meetings and spending time with industry colleagues, trying to raise money to keep her in the style to which she'd grown accustomed. Susan didn't buy it for a second. "You forget that in the early days, when we got babysitters, I'd go with you. Those weekends were always about boozing, schmoozing, and getting enough cocaine up your nose to keep you awake until we got on the plane to come home. Take her with you. Lay off the booze—and the *other*—and mind her. You think I don't make sacrifices every week to take care of her? For God's sake, Will."

In May 2006, I took Daisy to Cannes with me. Don't get me wrong, I love my kid, but she was at that awkward age where she was shy around strangers. She used to be such a pretty child, but now her puppy fat was quite pronounced, and I was conscious of it. So was she, it seemed. Cannes Film Festival was for the beautiful girls, even the very young ones. Daisy also refused to wear dresses or ribbons or "girlie" stuff and seemed determined to make herself as unattractive as possible. She was only twelve and not interested enough to be impressed by sightings of Leonardo DiCaprio or Cate Blanchett or any of the Hollywood stars.

Much to my disappointment, she didn't even like going to the cinema, unless Brian took her. She spent most of her time with her head in a book. I know that's a good thing, but I'm a filmmaker. I'd had her out as an extra on TV dramas and feature films I'd made, but Susan told me not to use her again. Daisy didn't enjoy it and complained to Susan that she hated sitting around in a shed, eating dried-up sandwiches all day, waiting to film one crowd scene. At that age, I would have jumped at the chance to make fifty euros while sitting around doing nothing. But Daisy put no value on anything, and I think that might be because I spoiled her quite a bit. The guilt of a divorced dad. No matter what she wanted, I bought it for her. Susan was less indulgent. I suppose we should have given her a sibling, but Susan, caught out the first time, was never ready for a second pregnancy.

What was I supposed to do with my kid in Cannes? There was a Polish actress who I was hoping to hook up with, and I couldn't do that with Daisy in tow. I know that if a woman I was interested in mentioned her kid, it would really put me off. I assumed women felt the same way. I mean, you're never going to be number one to someone with a kid because the kid always comes first.

Brian, of all people, presented the solution.

"Can I come with you?" he said. He was Daisy's godfather, and they were pretty close. He brought her book shopping, and he read the books that she read so they'd have something to chat about. Good godfatherly stuff. I think he had dinner once a month at Susan's with whatever ugly girlfriend he was dating, so Daisy was used to having him in her life.

Brian needed a break, in fairness. He had been looking after Luke after he came out of treatment, and now that Luke was stable enough, Brian was free to do what he wanted. He had just finished a teaching stint doing maternity cover in a boarding school in Wicklow. He couldn't have been a great teacher because he never got a permanent contract, but he was also "managing" Luke's career and had managed to swindle Luke out of his house, so I wasn't exactly feeling sorry for him. Because his work was erratic, Brian always had more time to do the caring stuff, like helping Mum with her car insurance and house maintenance and seeing to Luke's prescriptions and psychiatric consultations.

When Brian asked to come with me to Cannes, it was the perfect answer. I got to be the generous big brother who paid for his airfare and accommodation and who could show off in front of him, and he could mind Daisy when I needed him to. Our production company rented a five-bedroom villa in the hills behind Antibes. My colleagues, Mary and Gerald, were coming too. In previous years we had partied all night with the likes of Colin Farrell and Russell Crowe. This time, I had to tell the others to keep the partying out of the villa. Daisy did not need to witness the antics of the international film industry.

Daisy was definitely excited to be on the trip. She was always happy to spend time with me, and despite our lack of shared interests, she never had any problem talking to me about her school, her friends, or her many efforts to complain about her mother. Susan was stricter than I was with Daisy. She grounded her when she underachieved at school, and she forced her to do gymnastics, which Susan had enjoyed in her own school days. Daisy did not follow in her mother's footsteps, but Susan and I had maturely come to an agreement that we were not going to tolerate Daisy's complaints about each other ever since Daisy started the "Mum won't let me have a puppy" whine.

On the flight on the way over, Daisy sat between Brian and me, dressed head to toe in black with her hair in braids like the kid from *The Addams Family*, the one film she loved. Perhaps, I thought, I could bring her to events after all, like a little mascot. She could be the cute, quirky kid, and maybe Natalia Agnieszka would find the Daddy thing charming. Women are wired differently than men, after all. She might be attracted by my loving-Daddy persona. And I wouldn't have to fake it. I adore my daughter.

May on the Riviera can be very warm, but Daisy refused to take off her sweatshirt despite the oppressive heat. I could see the sweat trickling down her hairline while we waited for our rental car at the airport in Nice. "I can see you're too hot, Daisy. You have a T-shirt on underneath, don't you? Just take it off."

"No, leave me alone!"

Brian sidled up to me and whispered in my ear. "Leave it—first bra. She's still getting used to it."

"What? How do you know?"

"Just don't say anything, you'll make it worse."

I got in the front seat and wondered about Susan telling Brian personal details like that instead of telling me.

When we got to the villa, Daisy scrambled out of the car and ran down to the pool. "Dad! My God, this is so cool! Wow!" I had impressed my daughter.

Mary greeted us, and I left her to take the bags to the room and sort out who was sleeping where. Brian looked at me. "Isn't Mary your development executive?"

"Yeah. So?"

"So why is she taking your bags and bringing you a gin and tonic?"

"Oh Christ, Brian, don't you start with that politically correct crap. Mary is well paid and gets to read scripts all day. I don't think fixing a drink for her boss is going to kill her."

"Well, if I was Daisy's dad, I'd want to set a better example about how to treat women."

"Yeah, well, if I was you and had just blagged a free weekend to the Cannes Film Festival, I'd keep my mouth shut."

A sullen Brian drove us into Cannes that afternoon after I'd showered and changed. I made him drive up and down La Croisette a few times so Daisy could get a sense of the glamour. They dropped me off, but Daisy wanted to go back to the villa and read by the pool. I told Brian to collect me at four.

I had a meeting on the terrace of the Grand with Hobie Fiernstrom, an LA-based rep from Film Capital Equity, to talk about finance for the next film. After a couple of beers, he offered me a line, but I explained I had my daughter with me and had to be good.

"How old?" he said.

"Just turned twelve," I replied. "Into books and music."

"Oh well, that's a little too young even for me." I looked at him for a moment, but he grinned and nudged me. "I'm kidding, I'm kidding," he said. I wanted to smash his face in, and I would have if I didn't need him to swing this deal for me so badly. I smiled benignly while swearing to myself that I would never party with this asshole again. Last year, we'd gone on a binge together, and some young girls had appeared, but it only occurred to me now how young they might have been.

I finished up the meeting and went back to the villa. The Swarovski Dinner was to be that night at the Majestic, and Brian had agreed to take Daisy out for the evening.

I changed into black-tie attire and met Mary and Gerald in the hallway. Mary was out to impress, tiny dress, boobs on display, tottering heels. Gerald commented, "Mary's on the pull tonight!" Mary looked at me from under her long eyelashes, and I knew I had to put a stop to any thoughts she was having because her obvious crush on me was embarrassing. I wasn't stupid enough to sleep with an employee, but I had slapped her on the ass once in front of the guys to raise a laugh. She hadn't liked that at all, had burst into tears and run from the room. It became a big fuss and there was tension in the office, but it blew over after I promoted her. She still went shopping for birthday presents for my ex-wife and my daughter and collected my dry cleaning once a week. She was a good script doctor, and she picked out projects that were original and potentially crowd-pleasing. I couldn't have done without her. I had a personal assistant *and* a development executive for the price of one. Looking at the way she was dressed tonight, I would have to make a concerted effort to keep my distance. She was not unattractive, just not my type.

"Good luck, Mary, have you got your eye on anyone?" I asked.

She gave me *the look* and Gerald laughed awkwardly and said, "Well, as long as she doesn't go for Richie Corsovo from Universal, I don't care. He's mine." And he made the purring cat gesture that drives me up the wall.

"Right, let's go."

I called goodbye to Brian and Daisy, who were out by the pool drinking from a cooler box filled with ice-cold Orangina and bottled beer. My daughter had at least taken off the giant sweatshirt and wore a plain T-shirt with shorts. Susan said it was impossible to get her interested in fashion. She would only wear clothes in which she could hide when out in public.

"Bye, Dad!" Daisy waved. Brian ignored me.

I had intended to get home around midnight that Friday night so I could get up the next morning and have a swim with Daisy. She was going to be my date for our screening of *Green Hearts* on Saturday afternoon, and I wanted Mary to take her shopping somewhere, because in Cannes there's an unofficial dress code, and if she insisted on going in her smelly black sweatshirt, I couldn't really bring her up to the stage with me afterward like I'd planned to. Susan had warned me that shopping would be difficult with Daisy, but I'd had Mary look up all the cool designer shops for teenagers. It was going to be a surprise.

Straight after dinner that Friday, I was pleased to meet up with Natalia Agnieszka, and she seemed happy to see me again. We spent most of the evening chatting on the balcony of the Majestic, right by the Palais, overlooking the Croisette while the Mediterranean lapped the shores on the other side of the promenade. I had decided I was going to play it cool with Natalia, keep it businesslike, talk about her, her career, her childhood in Warsaw, her concert-pianist father, and then maybe I'd drop a name into the conversation and mention a script we were looking at that might suit someone with Natalia's innate ability. The trick, I think, is never to mention women's appearance. It makes them needy because, as much as modern women protest about wanting to be noticed for their brains, they definitely want to be admired too. It's just more PC bullshit. I know women.

Shortly before midnight, I had made the classic move of lighting two cigarettes in my mouth and was passing one to Natalia when Mary tottered over to us, wobbling slightly and hopped-up on some chemical.

"Will, what are you doing? You don't even smoke!" she said as she swiped the cigarette out of my mouth.

Christ. She was right, I don't smoke. But I knew that Natalia did, so I'd made sure to buy some long, thin, elegant-looking tipped cigarettes, in case they came in handy. And sure enough, they had, until Mary's intervention.

"Mary, if you don't mind, we're just having a conversation here—"

But Mary wasn't listening and instead dragged one of the ornate, heavy wrought iron chairs to our private corner of the balcony, screeching it across the paving stones. "You hate the smell of smoke. I remember you giving out about Ronald, the DP on *Backwash*. You said he smelled disgusting!" And then she fixed her eyes on Natalia, who inhaled deeply and then exhaled a long plume of smoke directly into Mary's face.

"Mary, can you go and find Gerald? I'm actually having a meeting with Natalia about the new script—"

"About *Ginger Wine*? But there's no role for Natalia in that, unless she's going to play the dog sitter . . ."

"No," said Natalia, "is not that title. Is called *Beautiful Liar*. With Martin Scorsese."

Mary laughed out loud. "Jesus, Will, is that what you told her? And you fell for it?"

I stood up, grabbed Mary by the arm, and pulled her aside. "What are you doing, Mary? Are you being a jealous little bitch, is that it? Because you know I have no room in my company for jealous little bitches, right?"

Her eyes widened, and Natalia walked past us. "Good night, William, I must leave now."

"No, wait! She's just drunk. She doesn't know what she's talking about."

Natalia continued to descend the staircase behind us without looking back.

Mary laughed. "Oh my God, you told her you were making a film with *Martin Scorsese*, and she believed you? How stupid is she, exactly?"

It wasn't a punch or a dig, and it didn't leave a mark. It was a slap, though, across the face. Not like the playful slap on the ass that had gotten her promoted before. The sound of it attracted attention, and people at the far end of the balcony turned in response to the noise. I realized quickly that I needed to limit the damage immediately. I pulled Mary into my arms and hugged her to my chest. She struggled to get away from me.

"Mary! I'm sorry."

A small Englishman, wanting to be the hero of the hour, appeared at our side.

"Are you all right, love? Is this man bothering you?"

"We're absolutely fine, thank you," I said.

"I wasn't asking you, mate, was I?" he said aggressively. "All right, darling?" he said to Mary again. She turned toward him, and I let my fingers brush her hand as she twisted her body.

"I'm fine," she said stiffly.

"That's not what it looked like from down there." He gave her his business card. "Just in case you need a witness, love."

I spent the next hour apologizing to Mary. We drank two bottles of champagne as I "explained" that I'd been trying to get Natalia for a feature I hadn't told Mary about yet because it was top secret, for a script she hadn't read (because it didn't exist). She drunkenly complained that as development executive, no scripts should be kept secret from her and that if I was doing something for Martin Scorsese, then she had every right to know about it. She raked up every single grievance about how I had treated her over the past year.

She used to be the secretary. The new title had gone to her head. Why, she demanded to know, had I never replaced her as admin manager? Because now she was doing two jobs for the price of one. I made my excuses personal. I wanted to have her around, I said. I was struggling to keep things professional between us. She fell for my bullshit straightaway. She wrapped her arms around me and told me she'd never realized how much pressure I'd been under. She wanted what I wanted. She suggested we taxi back to the villa. The night was ruined for me anyway. I just wanted to go to bed.

In our atrium, as I was trying to get my briefcase together for the next day, Mary brought out another bottle of wine and two glasses. I told her I'd had enough. Her drunken messiness was unattractive, and I was bored by her. When she tried to kiss me, I recoiled.

"Mary, what are you doing? I'm your boss!"

She pulled away and then started to cry. "You hit me! I have witnesses." She pulled the man's business card out of her pocket, and I snatched it out of her hands and ripped it to shreds. I pushed her away and she fell backward onto the sofa. Perhaps I'd been rougher with her than I'd intended.

That's when I saw my daughter standing in the doorway of her bedroom on the landing above.

"Dad? Dad! Stop!"

What had she seen? What had she heard? She burst into tears, retreated back into her bedroom, and slammed the door.

Brian's bedroom door opened. "What the hell is going on?"

Mary and I said nothing, and the house was silent except for the sound of Daisy's sobs. "For Christ's sake, Will!" He went into Daisy's room and closed the door behind him.

"I'm going to bed," I told Mary. "Get your act together, you stupid tramp."

The next morning, I woke late. The horror of what had happened—and how it might have looked to Daisy—hit me.

Mary was eating croissants and drinking black coffee on the terrace.

"Why didn't you wake me?" I was still furious with her.

"I'm not your fucking alarm clock on top of everything else." She went back inside.

Brian was looking out of the window. "Daisy's down by the pool, crying her eyes out. What did you do last night?" I could see that my little girl was curled up in a ball on one of the sun loungers, and her shoulders were heaving and shuddering.

Susan and I had been separated for two years at this point. There was a lot wrong with our marriage, and we had grown apart. My infidelity was the nail in the coffin, but Susan had changed a lot too. She had become more demanding and dissatisfied. When she went back to college to get her master's degree, she started mixing with a gang of strident feminists, and they made her even worse. She started going on about the fact that I was sexist and that my mother was sexist, which was ridiculous—how could a woman be sexist? Everything suddenly became about gender and my inadequate contribution to our raising Daisy. She did all the necessary stuff, the parent-teacher meetings, buying schoolbooks, taking Daisy to the doctor and treating her eczema, doing her homework with her, blah blah blah, and I apparently got the "fun" stuff, like attending her school concerts, bringing her to film premieres, to the library and the playground at weekends.

I did not leave my family. My wife rejected and evicted me, so she wasn't the victim or the martyr she pretended to be. She was still a very attractive woman. We had, in fact, ended up in the sack six months earlier, a mistake, we both agreed, though I don't think either of us regretted it.

Over the two years of our separation, Susan and I had negotiated a kind of peace. The only rule, however, was that we would not upset Daisy. Our marriage breakup had badly affected her. In three years, she had gone from a happy-go-lucky kid to a sulky and demanding one. Now she had seen me fighting with a woman. I just hoped she saw me reject Mary's advances first.

Brian had gone to find Daisy to comfort her while I showered and changed and poured myself a fresh mug of coffee. Mary came downstairs then, with her face clean and pinched.

"About last night . . . ," I began. "Daisy's very upset. I have to concentrate on her. She's my daughter."

Mary put her hand on mine. "I understand," she said.

I flung her hand away angrily. "I don't think you do." I told her she should find another place to stay for the next two nights until we went home.

Daisy wouldn't talk to me. Brian did his best to broker a truce, in fairness to him, but she point-blank refused to engage with me and stayed down by the pool. He offered to take her away for the day. Monaco was a train ride away. He would take her to the aquarium there, and they could see a real palace and have lunch and swim in the harbor pool, if he could persuade her into a swimsuit. I was glad. At least Daisy would have a nice time, and she'd be safe with Brian. I gave him five hundred euros and told him to get her anything she wanted.

I went to our screening with Gerald and Mary. Gerald made several snide comments about all the drama and the tension off-screen. Mary was terse and polite, but we all did our jobs professionally, welcoming the clients and buyers. The auditorium held four hundred, and I guess it was about two-thirds full, which for an indie feature from Ireland at the Market was pretty good going. Natalia didn't show up and didn't respond to my texts. I had a couple of meetings that evening. I rang Brian, and he told me he was on his way back from Monaco with Daisy. I asked him if they'd join us for dinner at Le Maschou in the old town, but he said he and Daisy planned to grab McDonald's on the way home. He was keeping it casual and breezy on the phone. I wanted to speak to Daisy, but he said she was tired and would probably talk to me tomorrow.

Jesus, I was dreading the conversation with my own daughter like I dreaded a conversation with my headmaster when I was a kid. "Thanks, Brian," I said.

"Yeah, whatever." He was angry with me, too, but he wasn't going to let it out in front of Daisy.

We went to dinner. Mary, as usual, had too much wine and tried to talk to me, but I was busy schmoozing the marketing guys and a French financier who I knew had a yacht. At the back of my mind, I was thinking that if I could get Daisy and me invited to a yacht party, she might just forget all about last night. Wouldn't it be a cool thing to tell her friends in school next week? No invite was forthcoming, however, despite my heavy hints. At the end of the evening, Monsieur let me know that he was "not in a position" to offer further finance but thanked me for my hospitality and left. Mary moved into his seat smoothly, and I turned to the guys on my left with the twitching noses and went to the restroom to do a couple of lines with them. I didn't enjoy the lift it gave me, but I lingered until I became more aware of just how tired I was. I made my excuses and went back to the villa.

Brian and Daisy were already in bed. I grabbed a beer and tried to watch TV for a while, my mind wired and wandering. Mary came home within half an hour. Gerald had hooked up with the guy from Frankfurt and would see us tomorrow. Mary told me she would be handing in her notice when we got back to Dublin.

"Why wait?" I said.

I got up, went to my room, and closed the door. From the other side of the door, I heard her say, "I won't forget that you slapped me last night, and there were witnesses." I took a couple of Valium to contain my rising rage and went to sleep.

We were to go home on Sunday evening. Daisy stayed down by the pool. Brian had managed to buy her a new T-shirt with a picture of Princess Grace on it. She'd told him that she'd seen me fighting with Mary.

"I wasn't fighting with her. I pushed her away when she tried to kiss me. I'm the good guy in this story."

I knew he didn't believe me. He had explained to Daisy that grown-ups were complicated, and it would be best if she just forgot what she'd seen. He told me Daisy wanted to know if I had ever fought with Susan. She wondered if I'd been violent toward her mother. My heart broke for the kid.

I did my meetings and got back to the villa to pack. Mary had left for the airport earlier with Gerald and had sent me a snotty text. Daisy was in the kitchen on her own.

"Daisy, honey, I'm sorry—"

"I don't want to talk about it, Dad."

"You know, sometimes, adults do the stupidest things, and we don't mean them. Mary was trying to kiss—"

"Dad, please—"

"It was a really awkward situation—you know that I never laid a finger on your mum—"

"Fuck *off*, Dad!"

"Daisy!" I was shocked at her language and her tone.

"I *said* I don't want to talk about it. Ever. And you needn't worry about me telling Mum, because I know she'd be upset."

"Daisy, I'm . . . sorry."

She wandered out to join Brian at the gate with her tiny suitcase.

On the flight home, she took the window seat beside Brian, and I sat across the aisle. In the taxi back to Susan's on the way from the airport, she eventually piped up and looked me in the eye. "Dad, you need to get a puppy that I can play with when I come visit." It was an instruction rather than a request.

Chapter 10

1984

We got tickets to the Bob Dylan concert in Slane Castle through the promoter, and I was officially the coolest boy in my class, though I didn't tell the other boys I was going to the concert with my mum and dad. The sixth-year boys in school had Bob Dylan posters on their common-room wall, and while I didn't know much about his music, the guys who were into Bob Dylan were way edgier than the boys in my class who liked trendy bands like Depeche Mode and Duran Duran. My classmates wore big, flouncy shirts and ridiculous angular haircuts. The hippie older lads had long hair and wore grandad shirts. My friend Steve's brother had some Bob Dylan albums, and Steve "borrowed" them from him to give to me.

"What in God's name is that?" said Dad the first time I played *Desire*.

I heaved a heavy sigh. "It's Bob Dylan, Dad, the guy we're going to see next month?"

"God almighty, does he have sinus issues?"

Mum chimed in. "Martin, don't be such a philistine. I'm really starting to feel our age difference." Mum would jump on whatever was popular. I'd never heard her mention Bob Dylan before we got invited to the concert.

Dad was fifteen years older than Mum. Mum was twenty-two when she had me, but I hated the way she brought up the age difference so often, particularly among their friends, and how she would jokingly threaten to run off with a younger man. I feared that one day she probably would. When I grew up, I was going to marry a woman my own age so that my kids wouldn't think I was an old man, so that my wife wouldn't think I was an old man.

I was not yet sixteen, and the idea of going to an actual rock concert filled me with excitement. Mum was reluctant to bring us, but Dad insisted. He'd been to the library to read up on Bob Dylan and learned that he was a born-again Christian, and he thought it would be good for us to hear him perform.

Luke was deemed too young and too *sensitive* to cope with the crowds. We still weren't over the trauma of his freak-out when Mum sang at the Pope's Mass five years earlier.

There were going to be an estimated sixty thousand people in Slane to see Dylan in a field right beside an actual castle. Mum knew the guy who owned the castle. He was a lord. There was a photo of them together on the mantelpiece.

Dad was trying to treat this event like the Pope's Mass, talking about picnics and car parking. Mum told him not to be ridiculous. We had backstage access and would be fed and watered in the castle with the other famous people. I'd probably meet Bob.

"Will they all be hippies?" asked Dad nervously.

The look she gave him could have cut through diamonds.

I was tall for my age and could definitely now pass for eighteen. Apart from boasting rights, there would be lots of drunk girls at the concert, and that was my primary interest in attending. I knew I was good-looking. Mum often said she wished my brothers were as handsome as me.

The night before, I filled a small lemonade bottle with gin from my parents' drinks cabinet and topped up the gin bottle with water. I didn't particularly want to hang out in the VIP area with my parents' boring-old-fart friends. Mum had warned us we were not to bring autograph books, so even though UB40 and Santana were also playing, I was not allowed to bother them.

We had to stop twice on the way to the gig to let Brian out of the car to pee. The first time, he couldn't go "because there was a cow watching."

After an hour of queuing for the car park and another hour of walking through roped-off pathways, we arrived at the castle. It was magnificent. We could see a massive stage to the left of it, and in front of the stage the field was a natural amphitheater, already beginning to fill with people. The fast-moving river Boyne ran behind the castle. We displayed our VIP passes to the hostile security men at the castle entrance and gained Access All Areas.

The first embarrassing thing that happened was Mum shouting across the vast hallway at Bono. So much for *us* bothering the stars. Mum had never met Bono, but because she was famous, she expected him to know her. Mum was nearly old enough to be Bono's mother. He was closer in age to me than to her. He nodded politely in our direction, and Mum pushed me forward.

"Oh, Bono, hi! William here is a huge fan. He even has a U2 mug at home, don't you, darling?"

Oh God, this is not how I wanted to meet my hero. I wanted to be having a beer with him and some good-looking girls. Brian's hand flew up to cover his crooked nose, and he said, "Can I have your autograph?" in contravention of our rules. Bono tousled his hair and said, "Sure, buddy! Do you want to come and hang out with the other cool kids in the billiards room?" Brian produced his forbidden autograph book from his pocket. Mum had floated away to talk to some government minister who was trying to be trendy by wearing a suit without a tie. Bono signed his name with a flourish, and Brian ran off in the direction of the billiards room.

I hadn't yet spoken, and Dad nudged me forward. "William here is the biggest fan in the family, aren't you, son?" I couldn't think of anything to say to the guy whose poster hung on my bedroom wall, and following Mum's stupid rules, I hadn't brought my autograph book. "What's your favorite song?" asked Bono, and he was *actually* talking to me. My mind went blank. I could only think of him calling Brian "buddy" when Brian didn't even own a single U2 album. Brian had two records, Bananarama and the Boomtown Rats. Dad poked me in the shoulder. "Go on, Willy, tell Mr. Bono about the records you have." *Willy. Mr. Bono.*

I made a gurgling sound, and my voice, which had broken two months earlier, now for no apparent reason went full Michael Jackson. "I have all your records," I squawked.

"Cool!" said Bono.

"Can I have your autograph too?"

"Sure."

He looked at me expectantly. I didn't have any paper or a pencil. Dad saw my discomfort and took a letter and a Biro out of his inside pocket. Bono signed the back of the letter, and I looked gratefully at Dad.

"I think he's a bit starstruck," said Dad. A beautiful woman called to Bono from a stairwell. I think she was his wife, a gorgeous rock chick. I was going to marry someone like her one day. "Gotta go, enjoy the gig, man!" said Bono, thrusting the bit of paper into my hands. At least he called me a man.

Dad shoved me in the direction of the billiards room and went off to find Mum. It immediately became apparent that this was the designated crèche for the day. It was full of children. All younger than me. Brian was playing Connect 4 with a small girl who looked about five. There was no way I was staying there. I told Brian I was going out into the crowd and to tell Mum and Dad I'd be back after Bob Dylan's set.

"I'll come with you!" said Brian, jumping up.

"No fucking way," I said.

The little girl looked up. "You said a bad word."

I walked away fast while Brian was still looking for his jacket, and the little girl clung on to his arm, not wanting to lose her new friend. Brian shook his head at me and sat down with her again. I went out through the vast hallway. Mum was laughing with the politician, and Dad was looking at the paintings, pretending to be engrossed. Or maybe he was—history was his thing. Dad was definitely the oldest person at this concert. I slipped past them and out through the giant doors.

In front of the castle, I took the autograph out of my pocket. I turned over the page. Dad had given Bono a letter from his doctor with an appointment for the results of his prostate test. How disgusting. How could I show this to anyone? Worse, Bono had written *Have a beautiful day, Willy! Bono*, and drawn a flower. It was a bit gay. I had told my dad a million times not to call me Willy, but he insisted it was a term of endearment. The boys at school who didn't like me called me Willy. So I had an autograph signed to "Willy," with a flower, on the back of a letter about my father's asshole. I crumpled it up and threw it on the ground. A security guard shouted at me: "Pick that up, you little scumbag!" He came lumbering toward me, and I ran and lost myself in the thronging masses.

One of the support bands, In Tua Nua, was already playing, fronted by a pretty blond girl, but nobody who was cool liked girls fronting bands, so I picked my way through the crowd, who were mostly sitting on the grass, smoking, drinking, kissing. The litter was already widespread, and I was glad Dad wasn't out here, because he and the security guy would have been annoying everyone to pick up their rubbish.

I was on the lookout for Steve's brother, Mark, but there were tens of thousands of people in this field. I had the small lemonade bottle in the pocket of my denim jacket. I took a few swigs and tried not to wince at the taste. I had four pounds in my pocket and eventually joined the queue for the beer tent. I could see there were some people younger than me getting served, but some were being asked for ID. Dad had confiscated my fake ID a few weeks earlier, and I hadn't had time to replace it because Steve's dad's laminating machine had broken down from overuse. Steve had made a small fortune charging half the school a pound each to laminate a photocopied college ID.

The queue was half an hour long, and most people were in groups. The lads behind me were about five years older than me and ignored me completely, while the women in front of me were about fifteen years older. They were funny, even though they were ancient. They were real Dylan fans and took the piss out of me for being so young. When it came time to get served, one of them bought me a beer and saved me from the embarrassment of potential refusal. She wouldn't even take the money from me. "Drink sensibly," she said, "you don't want to get in trouble with your mammy." The three of them cackled and moved away.

The first band had finished by then, and there was a lull onstage while the crew set up for UB40. I waved and said "Hi" to two older girls who lived on our road, but they pretended not to see me, and I felt like a dick.

I settled down on a patch of grass, between two groups of drunk teenagers, hoping that one or the other might invite me to join them. But when UB40 came out, I stood up with the rest of the crowd, cheering. When they sang "Red Red Wine," everyone sang along and this, I knew, was the best part of the concert so far, but I wished I was with some friends, instead of on the edge of these groups who had no interest in talking to me. When UB40's set was finished, I set off in search of some food.

I could see that groups of men were moving down toward the stage, but I hung back, trying to spot anyone I might know. The crowd roared as Santana took to the stage, and I felt a rush of adrenaline. There was a surge forward, and I did well not to be trampled. I watched them for a while until they went into an endless guitar solo. I queued at a van for chips. Another half an hour. Nobody in this queue talked to me. The chips were the worst I'd ever tasted and cost two pounds for a measly portion. I had only stuffed one handful into my mouth when a drunk girl knocked into me, spilling the rest of the chips on the ground. "Sorry!" she yelped. Her eyes were unfocused, and I reckoned she couldn't be much older than me. She was averagely pretty. Nothing to write home about, but she was drunk, and therefore she probably had beer—or access to it—and I might even get a grope. I grinned at her, and she smiled back.

"What's your name?"

"Stella." She stumbled a little, and I reached out and held her around the waist, letting my hand slide down a little to her hip.

"Ooops." She laughed. "I'm a bit pissed. Danny raided his mother's secret vodka stash." I wondered who Danny was and felt bad that his mother was an alcoholic, but I didn't have much time to feel sorry for him because the next thing I felt was a punch in the side of my head, and then I was on the ground being kicked viciously in the stomach and ribs.

"Take your fucking hands off my girlfriend, you dickhead!" someone roared in my face.

Stella screamed, "Danny! Stop it! Danny!" and a gap opened up in the crowd around us as they scattered to get clear of Danny's fists and kicks. I raised my arms and knees instinctively to protect my head and groin, exposing my back and ass to Danny's viciousness. The jabs stopped abruptly. I looked up through a veil of blood as Danny strode away through the crowd, followed by Stella clinging to his shirttail, wailing like a banshee. Several people came over and huddled around me. I struggled to breathe and wanted to vomit at the same time. An older woman tried to hug me into her bosom, and somebody else threw a blanket over me, while another person shouted, "Give him space!" I felt dizzy and must have passed out.

I came to in the St. John Ambulance First Aid tent. "Are you all right, sonny?" said a man with a handlebar mustache, wearing a uniform and a peaked cap. He was shining a small flashlight into my eyes. He would not have looked out of place in the First World War trenches, and for a moment I thought I might be hallucinating. "You took a heavy beating, so you did. I'm not sure we'll be able to patch you up here. You'll have to go up to Navan Hospital for X-rays."

Everything hurt. I realized where I was, could hear the crowd outside, tried to ignore the vomiting patient on the trolley beside me.

"What's your name?" said Handlebar.

I told him my name and showed him my Access All Areas pass, explaining that my parents and brother were in the VIP area in the castle. He quickly established that I was under sixteen, a minor. I could see through the flaps of the tent that I was to the left of the stage. I could see the entire crowd, sixty thousand people, swaying and moving and grooving to Santana, and I almost felt like crying because I knew I wasn't going to be part of it, that the day was over for me before I'd even seen Bob Dylan, that the blood on my face and the cutting pain when I breathed meant I was going to hospital. But Mum would be here soon.

Santana left the stage as night fell and there was another lull, but the sound of excitement from the crowd was intense. They were waiting for the main man to appear. Through the gap in the tent door, I could feel the crackle of electric anticipation in the air.

A hefty cop came and took a statement. I described Danny as best I could, but I didn't think they would have much success finding a young man with long hair dressed in denim, since it was a fairly accurate description of at least thirty thousand people, including me.

I heard the crowd roar and knew that Dylan had arrived onstage. I tried to sit up, but a stab of pain flattened me, and I passed out again, briefly this time.

It must have been an hour before Dad arrived with Brian in tow. I was still in a lot of pain, though Handlebar had given me some pills that had at least taken the edge off.

When he saw me, Brian looked away. Dad was white-faced. "My God, what happened to you? We couldn't find your mother. I think she's backstage somewhere. Did you get into a fight? The medic says we have to go to hospital. Are you in pain?" His face was full of concern, and I loved my dad in that moment and hated my mother, who was no doubt flirting somewhere with someone younger than he was.

I was stretchered onto an ambulance, and Dad and Brian piled in with the paramedics. "What about Mum?" I groaned. Dad looked grim. "I left messages with everyone there. She'll find out where we are, eventually."

When we got to the small hospital, I was x-rayed and found to have three cracked ribs, a bruised coccyx, extensive soft tissue damage to my stomach, and a laceration over my left eye that needed four stitches. My chest was strapped, and I was kept in overnight for observation. The hospital was busy. We discovered that two boys had drowned trying to swim across the river Boyne to get into the concert for free. I didn't want to think about them, but I could hear the sobs of their relatives from the corridor.

There were other concert attendees there, some off their heads on drugs or alcohol, some who had gotten into fights. When I was back on a ward at eleven o'clock that night, Dad said that Mum had finally got in touch, and he had spoken to her on the phone at the nurses' station. She was going to stay the night at the castle and collect us all in the morning, as she couldn't drink and drive. She sent her love and was relieved there was no major damage done.

Dad tried to be upbeat when he delivered Mum's message, but I was annoyed she hadn't found a way to get to the hospital to see me. Dad had called up a client who lived locally who offered him and Brian beds, but Brian insisted he wanted to stay with me. He found an arm-chair and pushed it between my bed and the bed of the acid-dropping hallucinator beside me. Dad, worn-out and freaked-out by the events of the day, didn't argue and left Brian with me after seeking the agreement of the nurses.

As soon as Dad left, Brian started on me. "You really are a selfish pig, you know? Why couldn't you just have stayed in the castle? Dad was worried sick. All the rock stars were coming and going through there. I got to meet them all."

"Where? In the crèche with the other kiddies?"

"Yeah, and what's wrong with that? They were nice, and we got hot dogs and burgers served to us, and Ali Campbell came in and someone took photos of us all and I got his autograph, and Bob Dylan's too."

"You got Bob Dylan's autograph?"

"Yeah. I saw him going into the bathroom and waited till he came out." Brian pulled the autograph book out of his pocket and showed me an illegible scrawl.

"You wrote that yourself."

"I didn't!"

I knew he didn't.

"What was he like?"

"Really old and a bit grumpy. He didn't want to sign the autograph. I could tell."

I flicked through the autograph book. He had the signature of all the stars who were there that day, including ones I didn't even know were going to be there. All signed to him.

During the night, I had to go to the toilet. I climbed painfully out of bed and swiped his autograph book off the bedside table. In the toilet, I ripped out all the autographed pages, peed on them and flushed them down the pan. Then I threw the book into the special bin for incineration.

Brian was inconsolable the next day. He suspected that some other patient must have stolen his precious book. He was grumpy and uncomfortable after spending the night in the chair, and we were both relieved to see Mum and Dad approach us on the ward, though Mum took her time getting to my bedside because she was signing autographs for some of the older nurses. She did not look her best and, after inquiring about my health, asked very few questions about what had happened. Dad was angry with her but tried to cover it up.

On the journey back in the car, Dad said we were never going to a concert or a big event together again, and I think that was a relief to everyone. Mum said nothing.

When we got home, Mum and I went to our beds, and Brian went to fetch Luke from Auntie Peggy's house. I recovered slowly and told my friends about the guy I'd beaten up, about how I'd been hanging out with UB40 and Bob Dylan. They easily got the truth out of Brian when, the following week, a photo of him appeared in a national newspaper alongside members of UB40, In Tua Nua, and Santana. His face was turned to one side, and the photographer had caught the crookedness of his nose. That was some consolation, at least. He'd made a liar of me, and so I entertained my friends with stories of how Brian nearly wet his pants because he was scared to piss in front of a cow.

Unusually, Mum stayed in bed for nearly a week. She said she was under the weather but wouldn't let Dad call a doctor and insisted he sleep on the sofa. Normally, when she was sick, she was a drama queen about it. She never had a sore throat, it was always *strep throat*, never a tummy bug but *gastroenteritis*, never a cold but a *bad flu*. Dad went to work every day, and Luke and Brian rode their bikes around the neighborhood. Mum and I ate tinned soup and toast and went back to bed. Six days after the concert, though, I heard her on the phone. I padded out of my room and listened to her whispering at the bottom of the stairs. I hovered on the landing and put my ear to the banisters, filling in the blanks of the one-sided conversation.

"No, I wasn't sober, but I didn't want . . . I'd been chatting to him earlier, but I didn't fancy him, Peggy . . . He forced me . . ."

Mum began to cry.

"He pulled my skirt up. I have bruises everywhere . . ."

I was frozen to the spot. Between sobs, Mum was telling her sister what had happened.

"You know me, I flirt with everyone. I don't mean anything by it. . . . That wasn't the same thing at all, Peggy, that was a fling, and a short one, but I was involved that time. It was my choice. . . . This was different. I thought he was our friend. We've been out to dinner parties in his

house with his *wife*. I never wanted to . . . In a linen room, I think, he
backed me in there and I couldn't get past him . . . No, I didn't. I should
have, but if I *had* screamed, there would have been such a scene . . . I
just froze. I didn't know where Martin was. I was looking for William
when he grabbed me."

She had been looking for me.

"Martin had disappeared. I didn't know what had happened to William until an hour later . . . He didn't say anything . . . I tried to get away,
but he was holding my wrists above my head, he was too strong . . ."

I could tell by her voice that she was weeping.

"After he was finished . . . you know, he just said 'thanks for that,'
like I'd given him a betting tip, and he left. I didn't know what to do.
I hid down in the kitchen with all the catering staff. A girl gave me a
cup of tea, and then someone came and told me that William was in
hospital, that Martin and Brian had gone with him in an ambulance,
but I couldn't move. I just sat there. And after a while I went out, and
the concert was all over. I went and sat in the car, but I didn't want to
go anywhere. I couldn't even think about poor William. I just lay on
the back seat and cried."

I moved silently back to my room and put my head under the covers
and tried to forget what I'd heard. It wasn't my fault Mum had been
raped. I wanted to kill the man who did that to her, but I was afraid to
admit that I knew anything about it. If I told anyone, I'd have to think
about it. Dad would blame Mum for flirting.

Poor Mum.

Chapter 11

2001

Luke was in New York that fateful and dreadful September. We hadn't heard from him in a few weeks, but he was hopeless on email anyway and hadn't quite got the hang of texting. We weren't sure exactly what he was doing there. The last time I'd spoken to him on the phone in Mum's house, he was really excited about an up-and-coming project. He said he was working with a hip-hop producer I'd never heard of who had apparently done some work with the Beastie Boys. Brian was supposed to be managing him, but I shouldn't blame Brian for the fact that there was nothing to manage. Brian was also trying to hold down a job as a teacher in a school renowned for the violence of its students.

Luke's street cred as a musician was in the toilet at this stage. His teenage fan base had outgrown him and nobody wanted his synth-heavy cheesy pop songs anymore. He'd been doing private parties and a bit of daytime television but no tours and no big gigs. The stadium-filling days were behind him. He still made good money on royalties and airplay, and I reckoned he'd made at least a million at the height of his fame, so I didn't feel too sorry for him. He had a mortgage-free house. Mentally, he'd been doing okay, he appeared to be taking his meds and was generally in control of his life. He could play a guitar well by now, and his voice had improved over the years, so this new collaboration with Sharky D was supposed to be a great career move and would hopefully launch him in the US. Luke had been huge in Europe but had never broken through in the American market.

I was in the office when Mum rang to tell me to turn on the radio. And then we put the TV on in the boardroom in time to see the second tower fall. Mum had been anxious on the phone. She had been trying Luke's mobile number, but there was no answer. I guessed he was going to be fine. I told her to wait twenty-four hours for him to call back before panicking. I dropped him an email telling him to get in touch with Mum. The office had come to a standstill as we all stopped working, staring at the television as the news unfolded. Mary Cullen, the new office junior, started to cry. The phones rang constantly: "Are you okay?" "Have you seen the news?" "Isn't your brother over there?" Everyone knew someone in New York.

Gerald and I had planned to take Mary for a welcome drink—it was the end of her second day in the office—but Susan rang me and begged me to come home.

Brian was there when I got home, playing in the garden with Daisy.

"I told him to distract her," said Susan. "I don't want her seeing this stuff."

She was staring at the television, a large glass of wine in hand, but I could see tears had dried on her face where her mascara had run. I held her tightly.

"What about Luke?" she asked me. "Your mum has called three times."

"Christ, you know what he's like. He's probably holed up in some studio in Brooklyn, completely unaware of what's going on."

"Will, there can't be anyone in America who doesn't know about this! They're saying this is orchestrated terrorism. Aren't you worried about him?"

Daisy came barreling into the sitting room and torpedoed me in the stomach with her head, winding me.

"Daisy, you're too old to be doing that!" I shouted at her.

Brian stood behind her. "William," he said, "she's only a kid," and before I could point out that she was *my* kid and what the hell was he doing here anyway, he asked, "Did Luke get in touch yet? Mum's on her way over here."

Our house was always Grand Central when there was a family situation. Brian lived in a grotty one-bed studio, and nobody ever wanted to go to Mum's house, except when we were forced to for Sunday lunch.

I poured a glass of wine for myself, and then a conciliatory one for Brian, but I continued to ignore him just the same. I crouched down beside a trembling-lipped Daisy. "I'm sorry, baby, you just gave Daddy a bit of a fright, that's all. Can you go and get into your pajamas? Granny is coming over, and the grown-ups need to chat about boring things." She whined a little and tried to sit on Susan's lap. Brian agreed to take her up and read her a story, and once again I prided myself on choosing the best possible person to be Daisy's godfather.

I wasn't alarmed by the fact that Luke hadn't rung back or that we couldn't get through to his phone. Half the planet was calling New York to check on their relatives, as I explained to Mum when she arrived, grim-faced. "If he's okay and he hasn't bothered to get in touch, I don't even *want* to see him again. He's always been so selfish." This was the only time in my life I remembered Mum being genuinely concerned about Luke, but even then, she was mean about it.

"The phone networks are probably down," said Susan. She went out to buy more wine. It was going to be a long night.

When he came downstairs, Brian had to admit that Luke hadn't told him he was going to New York two months earlier. And he didn't know anything about the contacts Luke had there.

"You're a pretty shit manager, aren't you, Brian?" I said.

Two days later, we had called every single person we knew who had any connection to Luke, musical or otherwise. Nobody had ever heard of Sharky D. Pulling every string he could, Brian had tracked down someone who worked for the Beastie Boys management company. She had never heard of Sharky D either. We had called every hospital in New York and been in daily contact with the Irish consulate there.

By Thursday afternoon, I knew something was wrong but suspected that whatever it might be was unconnected to the terrorist attacks.

My old school pal Steve was relatively high up in the Bank of Ireland credit card department and was able to pull Luke's card details for me. Steve had studied economics in college, and he'd become a supercilious twat since our school days, but he was grovelingly glad to hear from me. I was already a name in the fledgling film business in Dublin at that time.

"Sorry, Will, but this is kind of embarrassing. His credit card is at its limit—"

"I don't care about that, Steve, can you tell me where his card was last used?"

"Yeah, it was in Walgreens. It's a pharmacy on Fifty-Eighth Street. He spent—"

"I don't give a shit how much he spent, what day did he spend it?"

"Yesterday."

"So he's alive? I'm going to kill him. My mother is climbing the walls."

"He seems to be paying a property leasing company on the credit card too."

"Can you tell which one?"

"RE/MAX. Only the biggest one in New York. Hold on, and I'll see if I can get the particular branch."

Steve was pretty useful.

I rang the RE/MAX branch in New York and got an automated call system. I couldn't get through to an operator until after midnight, and when I did, he refused to give out my brother's address but told me the place he'd rented was a small studio apartment. There was no phone number registered to that studio, he said. I tried to keep my temper and explained the situation.

"Sorry, sir, but rules is rules and we got to stick by 'em."

I lied then and said my mother was dying. I asked if he would leave a message at the apartment to ask my brother to call home.

"I only answer the phones here, sir, I don't make no house calls."

"But don't you see this is an emergency situation?"

"Sir, with all due respect, you don't need to be calling New York about no emergency situation. We *is* an emergency situation."

I begged, offered him money, but he said he could only do that for me if I was right there in front of him with cash. I hung up.

Brian had picked up the pieces of Luke the last time he had crashed and burned, and I assumed that Brian would do it again. He was good at that stuff. And it was now his actual job. I could usually pay my way out of a situation or call in a favor, but Brian was good at the hands-on, touchy-feely vibe. Mum was insisting that one of us had to go and bring Luke home.

"People will think I don't care about my own son if I can't even tell them where he is!"

I told Brian I'd pay for his airfare and hotel in New York.

"I think this is your turn, Will."

"What? I can't take the time off work. I'm busy. You're just a—"

"Just a what? Just a teacher? I'm fed up with you slagging off my job. I have school, Will. *I'm* busy."

"Come on, Brian, you know how to talk to him, how to deal with him—"

"Well, isn't it time you learned?"

"Look, Daisy has just started in a new school, I don't want to be away—"

He called me on my bullshit straightaway. "You were away on some junket when Daisy was born, you missed her last birthday party because you were invited to lunch by some Goldman Sachs lawyer. Do *not* use Daisy as your excuse."

I turned to a different tack. Appealed to his better nature.

"Brian, come on, he listens to you. I've barely had a conversation with him in a year. I wouldn't know what to do."

"Come with me, then."

Mum interrupted. "That's it, the two of you should go together." Brian looked to Susan. She nodded. There was no point in arguing with Susan *and* Mum.

"Fine," I said. We agreed that we would go on the first available flight.

We flew to New York five days after the terrorist attacks, on the first New York flight out of Dublin.

The previous day, Brian got in touch with Luke's psychiatrist, and she suggested that we waste no time in getting to Luke. We were pretty sure Luke wouldn't have health insurance there, so she kindly gave Brian a prescription in his name for sedatives. Totally unethical, but she had treated Luke before, she knew how manic his episodes could be, and she knew we might have to "subdue" him to get him on a plane home.

Everyone on the flight over was very quiet. There were people in tears, and some, I suspected, were going to claim what remained of their loved ones or to bring injured relatives home. I wasn't sure what we would bring home or if Luke would come home at all.

The taxi driver from JFK told us he was Syrian, a Muslim. "The people who did that, they do not represent me or my family or anyone I know. My neighbor's nephew was in the second tower. He didn't make it out." When we got to Fitzpatrick's Hotel, I tipped the driver generously and shook his hand. I wanted to go for a nap and get some food before we went looking for Luke, but Brian was in charge of this expedition. He allowed twenty minutes for a shower.

We walked to the nearest RE/MAX location, presented our ID, and explained our story to a stunning-looking girl behind a desk. She was extremely sympathetic and, unlike the guy I'd talked to on the phone, had no problem offering up Luke's address. I tried to tip her, but she wouldn't take the money. I took a chance and asked for her phone number. She was embarrassed and pointed to her wedding ring. I wrote down my mobile number on a Post-it and passed it to her. She just stared at me. Brian stepped in and pulled me out of the office.

On the street, he started shouting at me. "We are not here for a fucking holiday so that you can pick up women. We are here to find Luke, assess his situation, and bring him home if that's what he needs. You are such a wanker! A *married* wanker!"

I was enraged. Luke had been shopping in Walgreens. He was *fine*. This was no longer an emergency. But Brian had to be the good guy. Boring, broke, and single.

"Yeah, I'm the married wanker who's paying for us to be here, who paid for your rent for the last two months, and who introduced you to the headmaster who's given you a job, as a favor to *me*, so until you can pay your own way in the world, don't act the martyr."

We hailed a cab and gave the driver an address in East Harlem. Brian stared out of the window. I studied the street map in silence. Brian could harbor grudges for weeks. I tended to blow up and down quickly. After a few minutes, I started to point out landmarks on our way uptown. Brian was clenching and unclenching his hands, trying to calm down. "Harlem is a fairly rough area. Why isn't he staying somewhere better?" I said.

The taxi pulled up outside a brownstone building. The Latino driver, who had clearly sensed the tension between us, turned down his radio, turned round, and spoke softly: "You boys should get out of here afore dark, you hear me? You're screaming for a mugging up here."

The street was strewn with litter and some broken glass. Feral children roamed in small gangs and looked at us with suspicion.

"Is you cops?" said one kid, clearly the bravest of the bunch.

"No, we're Irish," I said.

"Yeah, all cops is Irish," said another urchin, and I felt something buzz straight past my ear and hit the wall behind me.

"We're not cops, we're just here to see our brother," Brian said in a friendly tone.

We trudged up the front steps of the building.

The brave kid spoke again. "Is your brother Jesus?" We ignored him this time.

The buzzers had names attached to them, but no Luke Drumm, or anything like it. There was, however, a childish drawing of a whale, or perhaps a shark, beside the bottom bell.

"Sharky D?" I wondered.

"Why is Luke paying Sharky D's rent?"

"Because Luke *is* Sharky D?"

I leaned on the buzzer. We waited. Nothing. Pressed the buzzer again. It was midafternoon. The children lost interest in us and wheeled away on skateboards. Two old ladies sat on a stoop a few doors down. We heard familiar footsteps behind the door, and then there was the sound of at least four locks and bolts being opened.

Luke pulled back the door. The first thing I noticed was how thin he was. When he was on medication after the first breakdown, he'd ballooned in weight, then after he'd stabilized he'd gone back to being just slightly hefty around the face and belly. Now, though, his cheeks were hollow. His hair was long and he had a full beard. No wonder the kids called him Jesus. He wore a filthy Grateful Dead T-shirt, a pair of stonewashed jeans, and the Adidas sneakers I'd bought him for Christmas. No laces.

It took him a few seconds of squinting before he adjusted to the daylight and recognized us. His face lit up.

"Brian! Will! I knew you'd come. I knew it. What are you doing here?" He slurred his words but did not seem manic. He smiled beatifically. I wanted to punch him.

Brian hugged him tight. I quelled my annoyance.

"So here you are! Did you not think of ringing—"

Brian interrupted. "Well, can we come in? See where you're living?"

Luke stood back, and we entered a dim hallway that smelled of piss, cat or human, I couldn't quite tell.

"Christ, what are you doing living in this dump?"

He pushed through a door in the hallway. His living quarters were essentially one room. That much I could tell before I pushed back the tattered curtains to let the light in. There was a stained sink in the corner, an electric stove, a mattress on the floor, a heap of musty-smelling laundry, one chair, a hi-fi system, a shelf full of mostly comics and Dostoevsky, a lava lamp, an acoustic guitar, overflowing ashtrays, dirty takeout containers, and empty beer cans. Brian pulled his T-shirt up over his nose and Luke spoke nervously: "Well, if I'd known you guys were coming, I'd have tidied up, you know. Like, this is a surprise."

"Let's go out and get some food or a drink?" I suggested as if everything was normal. I wanted to get out of this fleapit. Brian and Luke agreed enthusiastically.

A taxi ride took us to Rosie O'Grady's in midtown. On the journey, Luke admitted with a degree of excitement that he was, in fact, Sharky D and that he was working on some new material.

"In a recording studio? What's the Beastie Boys connection?"

"Oh, well, I'm working on my own, really. I just said that about the Beastie Boys to the papers at home so they might take me seriously, you know?"

"But, Luke, you don't have any recording equipment in that hovel you call a home."

I wasn't going to let this bullshit go unchallenged. Brian was more concerned about Luke's mental state. "Luke, are you taking your meds?"

Luke looked hurt, as if we'd accused him of theft. "Yes, I am. I know it looks strange to you, but I've made some changes in my life, like, real positive changes, and I've just stripped away all the irrelevant stuff, you know? The house in Dublin, I handed it over to a few friends."

"You what?"

The taxi stopped, and we bailed out onto the sidewalk. Luke ran to a convenience store to get cigarettes. Brian muttered to me, "Wait until we're inside, we've got to get some food into him. This house business is probably fantasy. He wouldn't even know how to give away a house."

"He sounds fairly normal to me, I mean, not what he's saying, but the way he's saying it."

"Yeah, but his voice is slurred and there could be other factors. Just stay calm, okay?"

I threw my eyes to heaven.

"Okay?" Brian asked again. I nodded.

In the restaurant, I ordered beers for the three of us while we looked at the menu.

"Should you be drinking with the medication?" asked Brian.

Luke deflected the question. "Hey, where is everyone?" he said as he looked around the near-empty restaurant. "There were very few people on the streets the last while."

"Luke, you did hear about the Twin Towers, right?"

"Oh yeah, I forgot! Wow, that was amazing, wasn't it?"

Brian and I looked at each other.

"Amazing? It was an atrocity. We don't even know how many people are dead yet, it could be five thousand. Why do you think we came? We thought you might have been . . . affected." Brian chose his words carefully.

"I saw it on the TV, though, it was beautiful! The fall of capitalism."

"Jesus Christ, Luke, have you even read a newspaper? It was a terrorist attack. The city is in shock. Haven't you noticed?"

"Yeah, what a bummer about all those dead people. Like, I'm really sorry for their families, but just the way those towers fell . . ."

"They didn't *fall*. Suicide bombers flew passenger planes into them. There has never been anything this horrific in history since the Holocaust, and you're talking about aesthetics?"

Brian kicked me under the table.

Luke looked ashamed. "Yeah, sorry, I guess I've just made a decision to see the beauty in everything. It's a life choice, you know?"

I couldn't keep silent. "There's nothing beautiful about murder." Luke started twitching as if he were being bothered by a fly. I took out my phone and passed it to him. "Ring Mum, tell her you're safe."

"Oh yeah, I guess I should have called someone, but I threw my phone in the Hudson a month ago."

"Why?"

"I guess I didn't need it."

"Call her now," I ordered him.

He went outside with the phone.

"You're right. He's not normal," I said to Brian.

"Yeah, but he doesn't seem unhappy either. And he's not manic."

"He's out of his tiny mind, and that's not his first beer today. And what's this about him handing over the house? Do you know anything about that?"

"No, but I'm sure he hasn't just given it to them. Maybe they're paying rent. Fuck it, I'd love to live there. I could really use a bit more space."

"He's living like a tramp. Aren't you supposed to be looking after his finances?"

"How am I supposed to get money to him when I don't know where he is?"

When Luke first started making money, Mum insisted that Luke ask Tony King, her accountant, to look after his finances. I don't know how well Tony looked after Luke, but the one good thing he had done was to persuade Luke to buy a house. Luke was ridiculous with money, buying extravagant, outrageous, and inappropriate gifts for us just because he could. On Daisy's third birthday, he turned up with a pony in a horsebox for her on our suburban street. He had not thought about stabling or fees or the fact that she was too small to get up on a pony. It caused chaos for a couple of weeks. The sellers had seen him coming, the animal was worth bugger all and was too old even to be trained for anything. We couldn't get an animal sanctuary to take it and had to arrange for it to be put down. Even when we tried to explain the consequences of his "gift" to Luke, he just shrugged and said he thought girls loved ponies. I always worried about how easy it was to take advantage of him. Now Brian had taken over the management of Luke's career, and it seemed like Luke had given his house away. I don't know which of my brothers was more useless.

Luke came back inside and returned my phone. "Wow, she's really freaking out, you know? Screaming at me, that I should have called. She says I have to go home."

"Maybe you should?" said Brian, and inside I was thinking no, please don't come home because then you'll be our problem. We'll have to look out for you and clear up your messes and suffer the embarrassment of your public outbursts. At least when Luke was in New York, he was out of sight, out of mind.

"She doesn't really want me home," said Luke simply, "she just wants a story she can tell on the radio. She's going on the national airwaves tomorrow."

He pushed his Caesar salad around his plate and shaded his eyes from our steaks.

"Luke, who are your friends here? Who do you hang out with?" asked Brian gently.

"You see, that's the thing I discovered. I don't need friends. I don't need much food. I only need about half the amount I was eating. My mind is crystal clear now. I only saw about the Twin Towers on a TV in a shopwindow and some newspaper headlines, but I don't buy into what the media are telling us. I haven't read newspapers in I don't know how long. Hey, what day is it?"

I was losing patience.

"It's Sunday, but, Luke, if you don't need people, maybe we should just drop you back to Harlem and go to the airport. You're happy here, right?"

His eyes filled with tears and he cried, big explosive shuddering tears.

"Bastard," mouthed Brian at me.

Brian put his arm around Luke, and Luke leaned into him the way he used to with Dad when he was a small boy. It was a pitiful sight.

"Luke, I really don't believe you're thinking too clearly. Now tell me the truth, have you been taking your meds?" Brian was good with kids. No wonder Daisy loved him. But Luke was a thirty-year-old man with the sensibilities of a seven-year-old. Tears still falling, he shook his head.

"I'm lonely," he sobbed.

I was embarrassed. The restaurant was nearly empty, but the few other diners all looked sympathetically in our direction, no doubt assuming this was some 9/11-related trauma.

"It's okay, we're going to bring you home to Ireland, and we're going to look after you. You can leave Sharky D right here. You can look up some of your old musician friends. I think you sing best when you're with other people, right?"

Brian kicked me again. I was holding back tears myself. I'd never seen Luke broken like this. I'd seen him in the psych ward when he was catatonic on antipsychotic meds, and I'd seen him jump off a forty-foot-high truss into a crowd at a gig and dislocate his collarbone when he was manically high, but this pathetic sobbing mess was new to me.

"Yeah, Luke, come home, we miss you," I said, and it wasn't altogether a lie. I missed the kid on the red scooter with the smart answers who'd always share every treat he got. I missed the shy singer who, at the beginning of his career, performed with his back to the audience, thinking he was Van Morrison or whatever. I missed the brother he could have been.

"Mum doesn't miss me. She doesn't love me." This was a recurring theme with Luke when he was having an episode. He had stored up every single way that our mother had apparently slighted him since he was a toddler and went over and over these things in his head. It was true that Mum didn't love us equally. I knew that because I was obviously the most successful and least screwed-up, and she would express it by exclaiming, "Why can't your brothers be more like you?" but she must have loved us all, in her way.

Two days later, the three of us flew back to Dublin. As Brian predicted, Luke changed his mind three times about whether he would come with us, and Brian dispensed the sedatives we'd been given that allowed us to make the decision for him. We relinquished the lease on the fleapit in Harlem and left everything behind except Luke's guitar.

In Dublin, Brian evicted Luke's "friends," who had been staying in the house he owned but not paying any rent. Brian moved in with Luke, ostensibly to supervise him, but it suited Brian, too, as he got free rent. At least, that's what I thought he got. It was months later before I discovered the truth.

Brian's act of altruism was a shocking sham. It later turned out that Luke had run up tens of thousands in debt. Managed by Brian, Luke sold him the house for a fraction of what it was worth to get himself debt-free and then became Brian's tenant. Brian had secretly shafted his own brother.

I was furious when I found out from Mum what had been going on with the finances. Mum was troubled by it but thought it was better that Brian was "in charge" of Luke. She didn't want to be his custodian either. I challenged Brian, but he pointed out sharply that I had never offered to help Luke, that Brian was his caretaker now, and that it was a full-time job. He'd had to give up teaching. He reckoned he'd earned it.

When Luke got better, he wanted to be independent. He moved into a rented apartment and made music again. Luke genuinely didn't care about money or houses or belongings. But within a year of the events of 9/11, he had slipped backward again and was living in a similarly broken-down house arrangement in Dublin. He'd stopped taking his meds and became a figure of either pity or ridicule in the media when he was photographed, shoeless, busking on Grafton Street, being heckled by teenagers.

I let Brian take care of all that. Mum and I didn't need to be linked to Luke in the gossip pages. We made no comment to the media. Besides, I was busy and my marriage was beginning to fall apart. I didn't have time for Luke. If Brian was going to live off him, he could do the babysitting.

Chapter 12

2004

Susan caught me. I had been careful, always, but women's intuition is not to be underestimated. Sometimes they just know. She was always suspicious about Mary in the office, and indeed, it was obvious that Mary had been throwing herself at me ever since she started working with us. And while I was not immune to Mary's cleavage, I was not going to jeopardize the smooth running of the office. Gerald and I were business partners. Gerald had come out of college at the same time as me and immediately afterward went to film school in London. When we met, he had been assistant director on some shorts and commercials. He knew film, actors, cinematographers, and screenwriters. He was great to work with. Our first feature, *The Inpatient*, had been an artistic success, though not a commercial one. Our second film, *Naked Bakers*, had caught the teenage market and had made us a force to be reckoned with on the European circuit, though America still seemed impossible to crack. I had studied contracts, entertainment law, Section 42 funding, and I was an astute negotiator. Gerald liked Susan and Susan liked him. We worked well together, even though the dynamic changed slightly when I hired Mary.

"Please don't fuck her," Gerald said minutes after Mary had left the interview for the job. She was clearly overqualified, but she really wanted the low-paid administration role we were offering, even though she was capable of a lot more. We were already stretched thin, and she would certainly be useful. Gerald knew I was having a few flings here and there, but he was never judgmental about these things. What happened between two consenting adults was their own business, he felt. A mature attitude. Perhaps because Gerald's homosexual activities had only been legalized seven years earlier.

But it wasn't Mary who Susan caught me with. It was Kate. I was in my midthirties and Kate was twenty, but the way Susan went on about it, you'd think I was a pedophile. Kate had nothing to do with the film business. She was my dental hygienist. Any girl who can fall for a man after wedging his jaw open and removing the calculus and caffeine stains from his teeth must be sincere. As she was taking off her surgical gloves, she advised me to cut back on my coffee drinking. "That's a shame," I said. "Would you like to join me for a cup of tea instead?"

"Sorry?" She blushed, and it was cute.

"No, I'm sorry," I said, "I shouldn't have said it." Playing bashful works with certain women, plus I was only testing the waters. She laughed then and said she was about to take her lunch break, and she wouldn't mind if I joined her. But she pointed at my wedding ring. "You're married. I'm not interested. Let's just eat." I was only mildly disappointed. She was refreshingly honest.

Lunch was relaxed and pleasant. She had started working in this practice recently after completing her two-year diploma. "Everyone thinks that hygienists are stupid, that we're just not clever enough to be dentists," she said, voicing my exact opinion. After school, she couldn't face another five years of study, so she'd opted for the hygienist course. She liked the job well enough but couldn't see herself doing it in the long term. "I guess I haven't decided what I want to do yet." She asked what I did, and when I explained, she perked up—"Oh, you're *that* guy"—and I was inwardly preening when she added, "You're Luke

Drumm's brother, right?" Her brow furrowed. "How is he doing? It must be stressful for your family."

Luke had been in the papers. His public breakdowns and bizarre behavior kept the gossip columnists busy, but I had never made any public statement or comment to the media, though my phone rang incessantly after every incident. This young girl got it. It *was* stressful for all of us, embarrassing in a way that I couldn't describe to another person without sounding like an utterly selfish pig. No matter what level of success I attained for myself, Luke always hung around my neck like an albatross. There were many days when I wished he'd never been born, for Mum's sake, for Brian's sake, for my sake, and even for his own sake because it must have been hard to live with that level of mania and distress all the time.

I wiped my forehead with a pressed handkerchief.

"I'm sorry," said Kate, "I shouldn't have mentioned it."

She was the first and only person I spoke to about Luke—the difficulty of being his brother, the humiliation he caused me, the distraction from my work and my family, the distance I tried to keep from him.

"Not everyone is built to deal with mental illness," she said sympathetically. "I mean, my granny has dementia, and I'm the only one in the family who still goes to see her in the home. And I think there's still a connection there. It's hard to tell. I know that's not as bad as your brother because you can't exactly lock him up in a home for the rest of his life—"

"Sometimes, I wish I could."

Kate put her hand on mine, but it wasn't flirtatious. I could tell it was a simple gesture of comfort. I could have used that to make my move, but I didn't.

I glanced at my watch, realizing I had to collect Daisy. I could be honest with this girl.

"I have to go and collect my daughter," I told her.

"Oh, cool! What age is she?"

"Nine."

"Well, make sure she brushes her teeth, yeah?"

"Oh, I do. Every night. Like clockwork."

"And every morning, too, I hope?"

"My wife does mornings."

At the mention of Susan, she gave me a look, and I knew, I just knew that Kate and I were going to have an affair, and that it would be something meaningful, and I desperately wanted that.

I did not pursue Kate. She called me. One week later, she rang my office and told me she'd been thinking about me and wondered if we could meet again. There was no equivocation in her voice. Kate knew what she wanted.

I'd never had a girlfriend who was sexually demanding before. Younger women were not as shy as the women of my own generation. She insisted on condoms. I didn't like using them, but with Kate, I didn't argue. It was nice not to be the dominant partner for a while. She lived in a high-end apartment near the canal in Ballsbridge. Not a place she could have afforded on a hygienist's salary alone. She casually mentioned one time that it was "one of Daddy's apartments." Daddy, I soon learned, was a barrister who specialized in criminal law cases. I'd met him once or twice at dinner parties. She was shocked when I told her that. "Jesus! I didn't think you were that old." I reassured her that he was at least fifteen years older than me. She understood the need for secrecy and wanted it for herself. "I don't think my friends would approve," she said. It seemed like the perfect arrangement.

When I wasn't traveling, we would meet after work, usually at her place, or occasionally I'd drive us out to a restaurant on the outer edges of Dublin where we would not be recognized. I never stayed overnight, and she never asked me to. She would occasionally ask about Daisy but never about Susan. Our meetings were infrequent and irregular; there were no promises of commitment. We could go a month without seeing each other and then spend three nights together in the following week. She was not needy, and neither was I. These assignations were usually arranged by text, but I was always careful about deleting the messages immediately after I received them. I listed her name in my phone as Roger. The texts were clean and coded. It added to the excitement. I gave Susan no reason to be suspicious. Kate did not wear perfume or lipstick. There were no traces to be found on my collar.

What did we talk about? The usual things: music, books, TV series, property prices, politics, religion. She was up front about the fact that she didn't go to the cinema often. She'd only seen my second film and none of the shorts or documentaries. She thought it was good, but not great. I was hurt by that. I wanted her to lie, to flatter me, but that was not her way. Even though we made no promises to each other, even though there were no declarations of love on either side, this felt like cheating. When I wasn't with Kate, I found myself thinking about her and wondering what she was doing. Sometimes when she wasn't available, I jealously wondered if she was with another man. But I never asked. There were unspoken boundaries that we both stuck to.

About a year after that first encounter at the dental clinic, she vanished. She did not answer my texts. When I called her number, she didn't pick up the phone, and she didn't respond to my messages. I called the dental surgery to make my annual checkup appointment with her, but when I turned up, a young man called Luka examined me. I casually asked where Kate was. He didn't know anything about her. He had replaced her several weeks ago. In the beginning, I assumed she was away. She had mentioned traveling to Southeast Asia, but I thought it was odd that she'd go without telling me. I emailed her, a brief, businesslike message, but got nothing back.

I missed her. Three months went by. I texted her again, left longer messages on her phone. Some nights after work, I drove to her apartment and sat outside, watching to see if she came or went. I tried to gain access one time by slipping through a buzzed door after another resident, but when I got to Kate's floor, I knocked on the door, and again there was no answer. I googled her name a hundred times, but Kate Harris was not an unusual name, and apart from an old school hockey team photo, I found nothing.

In desperation, I checked the death columns, to no avail. I called the dental surgery again, asked if anyone knew where Kate Harris had moved on to. They couldn't or wouldn't help me. I did not know any of her friends to ask. My ego was badly bruised. I couldn't believe that she would do this to me.

And then, a few weeks after I had seriously started to look for her, Susan threw the Sunday newspaper over to me on the sofa and said, "It looks like Luke has a girlfriend."

Luke never had girlfriends. He had groupies. I lifted the paper to read the headline "Is Luke Drumm Getting Serious?" There was a photo of Luke in a pavement café with "a mysterious blonde." It was Kate.

The article quoted unnamed sources who claimed that Luke had been dating this girl for six months, that she was a stabilizing influence on his life, and that he had been attending regular therapy sessions since meeting her. "When contacted for comment, Luke declined to name his mystery woman but said she made his life worth living. We wish Luke and his new love good luck for the future."

Susan was pleased when I suggested that Daisy and I have a daddy-daughter day. I volunteered to take her to the zoo, and even though Daisy felt she was too old to go to the zoo again, she knew that a day out with me meant chocolate and sweets and all the things her mother forbade. While she was in the reptile house, I fired off my first angry text to Kate.

You're fucking my brother now? Seriously? Is that who you were after all along?

Then I rang Brian. I went along with the small talk for a few minutes, until he guessed that I didn't care much about his latest tale of woe and the difficulties of trying to manage Luke's dwindling career.

"What do you want, William? It's not like you to call for a chat. Is Daisy okay?"

I tried to pretend it was all casual. "I'm just wondering how Luke is. Susan tells me he has a girlfriend."

There was a pause. "Well, why don't you ring him and find out?"

I laughed. "I'm just curious, Brian, I mean, is it true about this girl? Are they serious?"

There was another pause. "You know her, don't you?"

I said nothing.

"Oh Christ, don't tell me you're having an affair with her? For God's sake, Will!"

"It wasn't an affair. We just saw each other from time to time. It wasn't serious."

"Yeah? So why do you care if she's seeing Luke?"

"I don't—"

"I don't want to hear it. Kate is the best thing to happen to him. He listens to her. He worships her. She's not one of the yes people he's always surrounded by. She's certainly not after his money, because she seems to have plenty of her own. She cares about him."

"How do you know all this?"

"I've met her. She's sound, Will. Don't wreck this for him. When were you with her?"

"It doesn't matter."

"Recently? Please tell me there was no overlap between you and him."

"Of course not."

I had my pride.

"And Susan suspected nothing?"

Why did he always have to bring up Susan, like he was my moral guardian?

"No, Brian, I was discreet."

"You are going to get caught."

"No, I'm not. Susan and I are fine. She doesn't know anything."

"You treat her like shit."

"You must be joking! You should see her shoe closet."

"For fuck's sake, Will, that's just stuff—"

"Look, I just rang to say hello, I don't need a bloody lecture."

I felt someone tugging my coat. It was Daisy. "Who are you talking to?" she said petulantly.

"It's your uncle Brian."

Her little face lit up. "May I talk to him?"

I handed her my phone, and she talked excitedly to Brian about lizards and crocodiles and giggled at some joke he made. She wandered off with the phone in her hand, while I stood, fuming, looking at the penguins in their smug monogamy. I decided not to think about it. It's not as if I saw that much of Luke, and his groupies came and went. Kate would disappear from all of our lives soon enough.

Some months later, Susan mentioned that Brian had invited us all to dinner with Luke and his new girlfriend. "Brian says she's lovely and that Luke is doing really well. Your mom is going too."

Susan insisted that we go. She always said that Mum was really cruel and mean to Luke and that we should go to support him. I defended Mum, pointing out that Luke had screwed up so often, it was no wonder she found him an embarrassment. Susan balked at my disloyalty. It was a recurring row. She always said if her sister lived in Dublin, they'd see each other every day. She couldn't understand why I kept my brothers at arm's length.

I was furious with Brian. Did he want to embarrass me, and Kate? Had Kate told Luke about me? Was Brian doing this deliberately? But the fact was, I really wanted to see Kate. I agreed to go. Susan organized a babysitter for Daisy.

Brian was still living in Luke's former grand home on Waterloo Road. It annoyed me. Luke had a bedroom there and stayed regularly, but he'd also rented his own small apartment in Rathmines. We collected

Mum on the way to Brian's house. I listened as Susan and Mum gossiped about the new girlfriend.

"He told me he really likes her. You know who her father is? Clive Harris, the barrister who's always on the news. Luke went to stay with her family for the weekend. They treated him very kindly."

"Don't they mind about the age gap?" said Susan. "There must be thirteen years between them."

"Age gap? There was a much bigger age gap between William's father and me, you know. I don't think people worry about that kind of thing nowadays, and besides"—Mum grew catty, as she always did about Luke—"he's not the most mature of men, is he? He's not exactly grown up. They might just be evenly matched. She was pretty in the newspaper photo, wasn't she?"

"Oh yeah, totally gorgeous," said Susan.

"Luke has talked about her to Brian, quite a lot. I knew he was smitten. Let's hope he doesn't screw this up." Mum displayed her usual lack of faith in Luke. But then Luke did screw up all the time.

"What is it she does for a living?" she said. "I can't remember, something fairly menial, I think."

"She's a dental hygienist," I said, without thinking.

"How do you know? Did Luke tell you that? When were you talking to him?" asked Susan.

"Eh, no, Brian told me."

They chattered on, oblivious to my reddening face as I concentrated on the road ahead.

Brian greeted us with the usual inquiries about Daisy. Luke and Kate hadn't arrived yet. I got him on his own in the kitchen. "What's this all about, Brian? Are you trying to shit-stir?"

He sighed. "Of course not. Luke wants to introduce her to the family. Not everything is about you. You'll just have to pretend you've never met her before. It shouldn't be that hard for you, Will. It wouldn't be the first time."

I returned to the living room with a bottle of red and filled the glasses. Thank God Susan said she'd drive home, because I was going to need a lot of alcohol to get through this.

Luke and Kate arrived five minutes later. I positioned myself by the fireplace so that if my face flushed, I could blame the heat. Luke entered the room first, leading Kate by the hand. She beamed at me. "Will, how nice to see you!" Luke was taken aback. Susan and Mum looked at me. "Yes, Will was my patient in the dental surgery I worked in last year."

I feigned ignorance. "Really? Sorry, I don't remember—"

I was interrupted as Luke made the introductions, conscious of the fact that Susan was staring at me. Christ, if we were going to acknowledge we knew each other, Kate might at least have warned me.

Dinner went smoothly. I avoided Kate's eye. I was angry with her. She could have called me, texted me, emailed me. What was I supposed to think? Brian glanced between the two of us, looking for signals. Mum looked at me with concern.

"William, you're quiet today. Is everything all right? I can't believe you don't remember Kate. You've always had an eye for pretty girls. I don't mind telling you, Susan, before he met you, my William certainly played the field." Mum pretended to disapprove.

"I'm well aware of that," said Susan coldly.

"I'm fine, Mum, just a bit tired. You know, work."

"Kate, did you know that Will is a film producer?"

"Oh yes," she said, flashing her brilliant, whitened smile. "I know all about him."

She was brazen, and yet, I realized, she was telling the truth. Nothing she said was a lie.

Brian never made an effort with food, so dinner was two large shop-bought shepherd's pies and cheap Viennetta for dessert. He served supermarket wine from a box. Just as I noticed that Kate was barely sipping her wine, hadn't even gotten halfway down her first glass, Luke said he had an announcement to make, and Kate said, "No, Luke, it's too soon!" and I knew before he said it that she was pregnant. Only eight weeks, but Luke was so excited that he couldn't wait to tell people. Mum jumped up to hug her, feigning delight at the thought of another grandchild. Susan coughed, looked at me, and offered a cool congratulations. Brian shook Luke's hand and slapped him on the back as if he'd won a presidential election. Brian, it turned out, already knew.

I gulped down the full glass of wine in my hand to avoid saying anything.

"A cousin for Daisy!" said Kate, and I wanted to kill her. When she excused herself to go to the bathroom, I started to clear away the plates.

"Oh, look," said Brian, "Will is being unusually helpful," and everyone laughed except Susan. I waited in the hall until Kate emerged from the bathroom. I had decided to play it her way, light and breezy.

"So, a different condom rule for my brother, then?" My smile did not reach my eyes.

"We planned this baby. It's what Luke wanted. Oh, Will, don't be like this. *We* were never serious. We always said no strings."

"He's my brother." I couldn't keep the steel out of my voice.

A deliberate cough.

I wheeled around in the hall to see my wife standing there. Kate saw, stepped past Susan, and went back to the dining room, whispering, "I'm really sorry," in a sing-song voice as if she'd accidentally spilled wine on the furniture.

Susan grabbed her bag from the hall and glared at me. "I'm going home" was all she said, her eyes glistening with tears. Brian came out into the hall. He understood immediately. He put a consoling hand on Susan's shoulder, but she violently shrugged him off and turned on him. "You knew? *You?*" She almost ran to the door.

"What a fucking mess," said Brian. "Well done, Will!"

Brian went back into the dining room, and I heard him tell Mum that Susan had had to go home because of a sudden migraine. I had to go back and take my place at the table with the happy expectant couple while Luke told us about his house-hunting plans. This time, I tried to catch Kate's eye, but she stayed beside Luke for the remainder of the evening, gazing adoringly at him. It was sickening. She and Luke drove Mum home. Luke hugged me as he left. "I'll be looking for parenting tips from you."

Brian started to load the dishwasher as I opened another bottle of wine. "I think you should go home," he said, "tell her the truth."

Brian, the saint, who had never put a foot wrong.

When I got home later in a taxi, Daisy and Susan were in bed. I tried to talk to Susan, but she yelled at me to get out of our room. I went to the spare room and slept barely at all. I did not want to blow this marriage. It was nice to have an organized house to come home to, and Susan was a great mum. She was smart and funny, and she loved me. Obviously, the spark that had ignited us twelve years ago had faded, but she was still attractive and I'd never wanted to hurt her. Sure, she had been suspicious before, but even if she had guessed right about previous flings, that's all they were. The problem now was that this insult to her was going to be a permanent part of my family. Kate would be in our lives with Luke's child.

As I stared up at the peeling paint of the spare-room ceiling, my phone beeped. *Forgive me*, read the text, *I fell in love with him.*

Susan told me to find somewhere else to live. I couldn't believe she was taking this so seriously, but every word that came out of my mouth sounded like a cliché and made things worse: "It meant nothing," "It was just one time," "She led me on," "You weren't paying any attention to me."

Susan found me disgusting. "She's practically a child, and *she* led you on?"

I moved into Brian's temporarily. "You can stay for a week," he said.

"Luke has stayed here for months on end," I protested.

"Luke is mentally ill. You don't have that excuse."

I collected Daisy from school the next day and brought her home. Susan had told her I was filming at night, but Daisy was unsettled. She knew something wasn't right. Brian came to the rescue. Her midterm break was coming up, and he offered to take her away to Fota Wildlife Park for the weekend. Susan and I both agreed it was a good idea.

I sat in my car outside Kate's apartment for almost a full day until, finally, I caught her on her own. I jumped out of the car and followed her to the door. She startled a little when she saw me but relaxed into a smile. "Will! What are you doing here?" It was only then that I realized how young she was. She gave no thought to the consequences of our actions. In her apartment, I explained the cold, hard facts to her. My marriage was all but over. I had nothing to lose by trying to save it. Unless she had an abortion and broke up with Luke, I would go public with our affair. I could easily send some private photos to her father, to Luke, to the tabloids. I would ruin her. And that would ruin Luke. She clamped her hand protectively over her belly, and her eyes grew wide.

"You can't ask me to do that," she gasped.

"I'm not asking. I'm telling you. Go to London. Have an abortion. I'll even pay for it. Tell Luke you miscarried, and then break up with him but do it as gently as you can. The alternative is my way, and if you care about him, you won't want that to happen."

Kate chose wisely. It did not lead to the repair of my marriage, and I deeply regret that. It was a terrible thing I asked her to do. But I did it for Susan, for Daisy, and even for Luke. Susan was right about Kate being a child. She was totally wrong for Luke. He needed a mature woman, and if he really wanted a baby, he had all the time in the world. Their relationship would never have lasted. Kate was way too young to cope with his breakdowns. The one he had after she "miscarried" and left him was pretty bad, but Brian was there to pick up the pieces.

Good old Brian.

Chapter 13

2016

My lifestyle wasn't helping matters. I was never an addict, but the film business is full of opportunities for indulgences of all kinds. Champagne and fancy dining were expected at certain festivals, and cocaine was certainly readily available, but women were my weakness.

In the year after my mother's death in 2014, I struggled a bit. It seems shameful now to say it, because it's not so unusual to be an orphan at the age of forty-seven, but once Mum had died, I felt unmoored, like my anchor had slipped. She had always supported me, no matter what I did, but now that she was dead, I was lost.

Work was going well; we were climbing back from the recession. We had rehired four of the eight full-time positions we'd had to make redundant and were still getting commissions. We were making award-winning TV dramas and feature films, mostly coproductions with European partners and some American investors, but I had to keep a lot of plates spinning. My air miles could have kept me traveling for years, but I'd grown to hate airports with a passion. I was tired and irritable all the time. I got myself into unnecessary arguments about small things that would never have bothered me before.

Daisy had turned into an entitled little madam who expected everything to be handed to her on a plate. She didn't stick at any college course she started and drifted from one gang of loser friends to another. She had moved back and forth from her mother's home to rented flats, which she wouldn't keep clean—and where the rent money we gave her seemed to vanish on a regular basis for one implausible reason or another. The only thing Daisy wanted to do was play guitar and sing. We discouraged any performance-related career, citing Luke as the example of all the reasons why it wasn't a good idea. We had rows about this, which usually ended with slammed doors and sulky silences.

Daisy also ate a lot, in secret. Susan told me about the food detritus she'd found in a cupboard in her bedroom. I tried talking to my daughter about her weight, but she shut down completely. I asked Brian to speak to her about it, but he refused. "Leave her alone," he said. "She's still growing up, she'll be fine." I blamed Susan for not monitoring what she was eating. Susan flared back at me and reminded me of all the times I'd canceled plans with Daisy at the last minute and what a shit father I had turned out to be. I waved my hands around at the Dalkey mansion Daisy had now moved back into. Out of guilt, I had *always* been generous to Susan. The house was solely in her name. She got everything she asked for and far more than she was legally entitled to, but somehow I was still the bad guy. I paid for Daisy to see a therapist. She pulled herself out of the doldrums eventually, but all she wanted was the limelight, and I couldn't keep her away from it.

It pleased me that I had never been replaced in Susan's life. She had not remarried, and if she had boyfriends, I never heard about them. Occasionally, we still slept together, usually after a boozy family lunch that had dragged on too long. We certainly didn't like each other, but we knew each other, and sometimes it's better the devil you know.

I never went to the doctor when I didn't have to, but by mid-2016, I was running on empty, muscles aching, general weariness, recurring sore throats, swollen neck glands, and sporadic rashes, stomachache and backache that would come and go. Stress. Work was piling up, and I just couldn't take it anymore. I spent the June bank holiday weekend on the sofa and turned off my phone. I opened my laptop and googled Daisy's name.

By then she was a social media star, a singer-songwriter who gave TED Talks about fat shaming and body positivity. She didn't ever mention Susan or me in her interviews but acknowledged that she came from privilege and that people of her background were society's biggest problem because we didn't see the need for change, some bullshit like that. I knew she was being manipulated to a large degree by Brian, who was "managing" her media career, against our wishes. I was no longer on speaking terms with Brian, and I didn't miss him. Susan and I were furious with him. Daisy was vulnerable. He knew it and yet he still thrust her into the glare of publicity for financial gain. I tried not to worry about her. She was an adult now, but she was still my kid, even though she barely spoke to me.

On Tuesday morning, I called in sick and made phone calls to placate all the people I had let down over the weekend, claiming a virus had left me incapacitated. I didn't lie when I said I was going to the doctor that day.

My GP was a friend whose son I had used as a documentary cameraman a few times. I called round to his house casually because I didn't want to admit I was sick as a dog. It was kind of defeatist to go to the surgery. Between chats about everything else, I told him I'd been feeling lousy. He listened to my lengthy list of symptoms and agreed I was probably overstressed, but he recommended that I go to the Blackrock Clinic and get a full checkup.

I booked an appointment for the end of the month, went back to work, and delegated as much as I could. I canceled a trip to LA the following week and managed to delay preproduction of the next feature by two weeks.

I was scared walking into the Blackrock Clinic. In the intervening weeks, I had looked after myself, taken a course of multivitamins, stopped drinking, started swimming and exercising, got plenty of rest, let my social life take a back seat, and tried to remove all the stress factors out of my life. But the weariness and headaches still remained as well as new digestion issues. I knew there was something amiss. My fear was that it was cancer: a brain tumor, I imagined, or cancer of the stomach or liver. Something was definitely wrong.

A week later, I got a call from the clinic from a Dr. Galvin. She told me the good news, that my results had all come back relatively normal, but she suggested I go and see a Dr. Shabrath at the St. James's sexual health clinic, as my symptoms might suggest something else.

Syphilis.

Christ. I hadn't even heard of syphilis in years. The word made me feel sleazy, but a quick Google search told me I could be sorted with antibiotics. I was annoyed that Dr. Galvin couldn't just prescribe them herself.

In the sexual health clinic waiting room, I looked around at the other patients. There were ordinary people there, middle-class couples my own age and older, young yummy-mummy types, but also obviously strung-out junkies and a preponderance of young men. I guessed nobody was immune to a dose of something.

After the tests, another week later, Dr. Shabrath told me as gently as he could that my tests had shown I was HIV positive. He continued to talk in a tone that was reassuring, but all I could think of was Tom Hanks in *Philadelphia*, film footage of emaciated gay men in 1980s San Francisco. We didn't know—*I* didn't know—anybody with AIDS. I wasn't gay or an intravenous drug user. How was this even possible? But it was.

I had been spending more and more time in LA, where the women, whether cosmetically enhanced or not, were both beautiful and desperate for work. And I took advantage of them. I saw it as an exchange. Sex in return for the promise of a day or two on a film. I *should* have been more careful. In 2004, I'd caught a dose of the clap in time to get it treated successfully and had promised the older judgmental doctor that I would practice safe sex thereafter. But I have never liked using condoms and had rejected several women when they insisted I use one.

All the weird, wild, and wonderful sexual encounters I'd had in the previous years crossed my mind as Dr. Shabrath talked on. Which one of those bitches had infected me? There was one girl in particular who I'd really liked. She hadn't been desperate; she was smart and educated. She was the one I'd seen the most. Was it her? I tried to tune in to what the doctor was saying.

I got in my car to drive home, but instead of stopping at my house, I drove past it and kept going. I pulled over to refuel the car and put my phone in the trunk. I drove for another two hours, listening to classical music on Lyric FM because I just wanted the noise and the talk to stop. I wondered if I was having some kind of breakdown; I wondered if this was how Luke felt when he had an episode.

I stopped at a hotel in Wexford. It was a country-house-type place. I checked into a room, took a long bath, redressed in the clothes I had worn to work that morning. I drank two whiskey miniatures from the minibar in quick succession, then went down to the hotel bar, where the barman recognized me and began quizzing me about actors and films. I didn't answer his questions but went outside and walked to a nearby beach. It was still a bright summer evening, and there were a small number of families, couples, and bathers enjoying the slowly dropping sun. I took off my shoes and socks and rolled up my trousers, then walked to the edge of the water. It was freezing, and though the day was mild, a cutting north wind was beginning to blow. The holidaymakers packed up and left, and I was glad. I didn't even want to return a nod of acknowledgment.

They say a bracing walk is good for you. I walked for a mile and then a mile back toward the hotel, and still my head was full. Deals and finance and tricky actors; prima donna directors; Gemma, the girl I had been dating on and off, and Susan and their increasing demands. Brian and his making money out of Daisy's fleeting career needled me, and Luke's new sobriety was unnerving because although he seemed normal, I was just waiting until the next time he fell apart and did something to mortify me. I thought about everything except what the doctor had told me. I put up a mental wall to that conversation.

I went back into the hotel bar and bought a full bottle of Jameson for an exorbitant price, then took it back to my sea-view room, where I ordered room service and flicked from one news channel to the next until I fell into a drunken sleep.

The next morning I threw up and paid the concierge to send someone for ibuprofen and Alka-Seltzer, a clean T-shirt, boxers, and socks. I got the impression he'd had these kinds of requests before. I didn't shower or get into my clean clothes. I sat on the balcony instead. I didn't know what I wanted to eat, so I ordered everything on the room service menu. The kitchen rang back twice to check that I meant what I'd ordered. Three trolleys laden with food were delivered to my room, and I wished I'd booked a suite because there wasn't enough space to lay out all the food. Some of it was placed on the floor and on the bed, some on the vanity unit in the bathroom. I picked at bits of everything, but it all tasted like sawdust to me. Nothing made me feel good or satisfied, nothing at all.

It rained the whole day, and I sat on the balcony and watched the clouds scudding across the wide, open sky, shedding their burden of water across the deserted beach and the boatless sea. After the painkillers had kicked in, there still remained that weary muscle pain I'd been experiencing for months now. I ordered a glass of whiskey to take the edge off, and then I ordered another one. The servers took the mostly untouched trays of food away, trying to keep the looks of disgust from their faces. Then I rang down again and ordered another bottle of whiskey. I drank solidly and steadily, trying to numb the stress and pain I was feeling.

At some stage, I went out to the car park with my car keys in hand. I was wearing only my hotel robe and slippers. A top-hatted doorman intercepted me as I weaved toward my car.

"Sir? Sir. Perhaps not a good idea to drive right now? Please come back to the lobby and we'll call a taxi for you. Sir?"

I told him to fuck off and popped the boot of my car. I'd only gone out to retrieve my phone. I stumbled past him on my way back inside. He was embarrassed.

"I'm sorry, I do apologize, it just looked like . . ."

"Looked like what?" I slurred.

"Nothing, sir."

For the laugh, I stepped up to him and tipped his ridiculous top hat from his head and watched him scramble to retrieve it. I could see people staring at me. I gave them the finger and got in the elevator, but I must have punched the wrong button because when I got to my end of the corridor, my key card wouldn't work, and I realized I was outside 359 instead of 559. Furious, I kicked the door and walked away and found the stairs to the upper floors.

Back in my room, I examined my phone. There were thirteen missed calls. From Susan, Gerald, my girlfriend Gemma, and various other nonentities in my life. No call from Daisy. I wanted to call my mother. I missed her so much. There was nobody anymore who really felt proud of me. What would she have said to me under these circumstances?

I drained the end of the whiskey bottle into my glass. I felt sick and bizarrely hungry. I opened the minibar and ate all the Pringles and pretzels and then drank the wine and the miniature spirits. After the Bacardi and the vodka, I lay back on the bed as the room started to spin. I tried to close my eyes against the spiraling vortex, but that made it worse, and I sat up again. I could feel my stomach twisting and knew I was going to be sick, but I didn't make it to the bathroom this time. I passed out.

I woke up in the early hours of Sunday morning smothered in my own disgusting mess and knew that I needed help. I called the only person I thought might understand.

"Hello?" His voice was groggy; he was in bed.

"Luke, it's Will. I . . . I need your help."

"What, where are you?"

I explained that I was in a hotel in Wexford, that I'd been sick, and that I needed a change of clothes.

I started to cry. I did not cry often, though I had sobbed openly at my mother's funeral two years previously, shaming myself. I remembered Mum saying proudly, "William was never a crier, never a whiner. William always gets on with things." And yet here I was, a millionaire with a hot young girlfriend, the most successful Irish film producer of all time with every material possession one could want within my grasp, weeping like a child.

Luke arrived in a taxi a few hours later. He looked around at the mess and the empty whiskey bottle and put his hand over his mouth and nose. "Wow, man, this is some fucked-up shit."

You don't say.

He made me shower and change into a tracksuit that was too small for me, then sent me out to my car to wait while he paid the bill with my credit card. He signed autographs and posed for a selfie with the middle-aged receptionist, possessed of a face like a bag of hammers. I was furious and impatient.

Luke was in good shape. After Kate, he was a total mess for four years. Then he had a period of erratic ups and downs. But when Mum died, things changed. He had said after Mum's funeral that he was glad he no longer had to try to please her. Whatever. He was now a nondrinking, nonsmoking, healthy-living gardener and film buff. He had got into film studies in the previous years and asked me endless questions about the business whenever we met. He had grown into his looks. Now forty-five, he went to the gym three times a week and had stopped bleaching his hair. He wore respectable-looking jackets and jeans. I could have brought him anywhere knowing that he wouldn't embarrass me, and yet I didn't. I hadn't spoken to him in a month or two before this weekend. I avoided him as much as possible because I couldn't trust that he wasn't going to freak out again.

He drove me back to his suburban house, a rental in a Victorian street off Camden Street. He showed me to his spare room. He gave me a sedative from his medicine cabinet, and I slept for seven hours.

When I woke later and came downstairs, Luke was making some wholemeal pasta vegetarian dish. He served me coconut water to drink. I asked him if he had anything stronger, and he said he didn't keep alcohol in the house. He asked me about Daisy and some film projects I had on the go. He asked if I'd got my bathroom redecorated as planned after the leaking boiler incident. He talked about Brian's artist management agency and how he was glad to have left it and to be managing his own affairs, but he was desperate to get Brian and me talking to each other again. I had no interest in mending fences with Brian or talking about him or anything else. At the end of the meal, Luke took our plates away and told me I could stay as long as I wanted. He didn't ask me anything about my mental state or why I'd called him. He merely gave me a card with his psychiatrist's details on it.

"Why are you giving me this?"

"You were out of control, you might need to talk to someone. Professionally, I mean. I can listen, but to be honest, I don't understand my own mind, and I can't take on someone else's stuff, you know?"

"I'm fine. Just a bit stressed, I think. Overworked, overtired."

"Whatever, but you know, you should see someone anyway."

I assured him that my weekend had been a momentary lapse and that I was ready to go home.

As I was leaving the house, he stalled me for a few minutes on the doorstep and that's when I realized his whole act was bullshit.

"So, Will, I was thinking of getting into acting, you know, and that film you're making based on Jane Casey's book, I was thinking I could play the young detective girl's dad? I mean, physically, I know I'm right for it, and I think I could do a really good job, you know?"

It was so unexpected that it took me a couple of seconds to respond. "Luke, when we are looking for actors, we generally go to agents of actual *actors*, who have experience and training and a good track record."

"Yeah, I get that, but I was just thinking, since I helped you out this morning, that you could, like, return the favor and pull a few strings..."

I walked away while he was still talking and got into my car. He followed me, but I shut the door and turned up the radio to drown out his wheedling voice.

In St. James's Hospital after the weekend, Dr. Shabrath told me again all the things I hadn't heard the first time. He assured me that HIV was no longer a death sentence, that antiretroviral drugs were available and free for everyone at his clinic. I would be okay. I decided on the spot to get the treatment and assessments done privately. Dr. Shabrath wondered if I could have infected anyone and encouraged me to talk to my lover and ex-lovers. I assured him I was straight. He looked at me as if I'd said I was wearing a pair of trousers. He said this was entirely irrelevant. Once I was on the drugs, my viral load would reduce to an undetectable level, and I would be incapable of passing the virus on to anyone. I could go back to leading a full and normal sex life. I had no idea how long I'd had the virus. It could have been months, could have been years. It was impossible to pin down. I was clear about two things, though: I didn't want to have sex with anyone yet and nobody must know about my condition.

*I*t was suggested that we both make speeches at the service, but I suggested that instead we read from established poems. I chose a much-loved poem by W. H. Auden that had been featured in a film, popular in our youth. My brother read an irrelevant inspirational quote, unattributed, found hastily on the internet that morning. We both received a warm round of applause.

The autopsy recorded our dead brother's shattered skull, broken hands, and smashed kneecaps. I tried to get those images out of my mind. It had taken seven days to bring his body home with the help of the Irish Consulate.

We had decided against a church funeral. The crematorium was full to capacity. The curtains closed on their electric rail to obscure the coffin as it was lowered into what I suspect was a furnace. My brother released a loud hypocritical sob at that moment. I kept a dignified silence. I did not want to attract any more attention to myself than was necessary. I did not want to look like the guilty party, but neither did I want to make a show of myself.

In the face of our apparent grief, old grudges and resentments toward my brother and me dissipated. Ex-friends shook our hands and suggested drinks and dinners that we all knew would never happen.

Afterward, we hosted a finger-food buffet in a four-star hotel. It was what the undertakers had suggested, and we complied. We tried to encourage Daisy to eat a sandwich, which she declined, opting instead for a cup of mint tea. She spoke to nobody, ate nothing, and smoked outdoors, seemingly unaware of the sleeting rain that lashed her shoulders.

Luke

Chapter 14

1977

"What's a runt, Dad?"

"Where did you hear that word, Luke?" he said.

"Mum said I was the runt of the litter, and litter means rubbish—what did she mean?"

"Did she say it when she was cross with you?"

"She's always cross with me."

"No, she isn't, she's just a bit tired these days, and we should try to be a little quieter around her."

"She said she was going to leave me with the old woman who lives in the woods."

"What old woman?"

"I don't know, the one who lives in the woods."

"Don't you be worrying about that. Your mum can be a little dramatic sometimes, she doesn't mean half of what she says. There's no old woman living in the woods."

"You mean she tells lies?"

"No, she just exaggerates things. And she makes things up sometimes, to teach a lesson to little boys."

"I'm not little!"

"Well, what age are you now? Seven? You're *my* littlest boy."

Dad lifted me onto his shoulders, and we continued our stroll down the pier. I don't know where Brian and William were that day. I didn't spend too much time alone with my dad. But when I did, I really loved it. Dad always made me feel special. I think he liked me as much as he liked William and Brian. Mum definitely didn't. Mum didn't have a mum and dad after she was about two years old. I couldn't imagine not having parents. She and her older sister, Peggy, had grown up in a house with pretend parents who were poor.

At nighttime, I'd look out of my bedroom window at the woods behind our house and wonder about the old woman who lived there, even though Dad said she didn't. I'd been through the woods in day-time when we went looking for horse chestnuts, but I never saw a house there, and the only old lady I saw was Mrs. Turner from next door walk-ing her dog. I wanted Dad to be right. I was terrified of being sent to live in the woods. I could imagine the old woman really well. She was tall but crooked. She carried a large stick and wore a long black cloak. She mostly wore a hood to cover her face, but I think when the hood was down, she had long white hair and a thin mouth and a ghostly white face, and I think her voice was screechy. I think she was probably a witch. Mum never went into details about her. She didn't have to.

One day in school, Father Benedict visited our class and told us that God would protect us from evil. I loved Father Benedict. He was funny, and he could do magic tricks. I put my hand up and asked if God would protect us from witches. Father Benedict smiled and said he surely would if I studied my Bible and prepared properly for my Holy Communion.

Instead of bedtime stories, I asked Dad to read us stories from the Bible, but Brian and William complained. They said Jesus was boring and begged for *Biggles* again. I didn't think Jesus was boring. I thought he was amazing and that feeding thousands of people with five loaves and some fish was a brilliant miracle. I really wanted to do miracles when I grew up. If I tried really hard, I could be Jesus. The Second Coming. All I had to do was be good and kind to everyone.

When Mum was angry, and Dad wasn't around, she slapped me. She said that I was stupid or useless. William and Brian were able to blame me for everything they did: missing biscuits, scuffed shoes, spilled milk. All they had to say was "Luke did it" and she would believe them. At first, I tried to pray that Mum would believe me, and then later I prayed that God would forgive William and Brian so they wouldn't go to hell, but nothing changed much. This was the cross I had to bear, and it wasn't half as bad as carrying an actual cross over to Calvary.

When I went to my first confession, I didn't know what to confess, so I told the priest the sins that Brian and William had committed, kicking each other, stealing chocolate, and letting others take the blame. I was told to repent and say two Hail Marys and an Our Father, and then when it was over, I felt worse because lying to an actual priest must have been a mortal sin, but I couldn't ask Father Benedict because then he'd know.

I tried to ask Dad about it. I said that God might be cross with me for something I had lied about. Dad told me not to worry, and that I could tell the priest at confession next week. All that week, I had a sore pain in my stomach. I knew it was the devil. I knew he was growing inside me. I knew it was just a matter of time before the woman in the woods came to take me away.

Chapter 15

1989

We were invited to play a gig at midnight at the Olympia. Sean was really excited about this. It was a 1,200-seater venue and the biggest we'd played by far. I'd scraped through my first-year exams at University College Dublin and we had been touring around the country all summer in a clapped-out van, playing small pubs and clubs, but now it was November and I hadn't been to a single lecture because we were busy getting a name for ourselves. The Wombstones were on the map. We'd been busy writing and rehearsing songs, and Sean was trying to raise money to record an album. UK promoters regularly turned up at the Olympia to scout for new talent, so for the first time there was a slim chance of a record deal.

The horrific panic attack and weird visions that had overwhelmed and terrified me at our first gig were a thing of the past, and I was incredibly lucky that I had Sean on my side because after that first debacle, despite our success, Alan and Jamie had to be convinced to play with me again. I had freaked everyone out, including myself. But the second gig had gone smoothly. And Alan and Jamie were a bit friendlier to me now, though they openly called me Lucifer. Sean persuaded them that I was the person the crowds came to see, and they were mostly girls. Alan and Jamie loved the female attention. I had as much sex as I wanted, but I wasn't that interested after the first few months. They thought that was weird. I was used to people thinking I was weird.

The thing that nobody in the band could agree on was the type of music we wanted to play. Sean wanted to add a synth player to the lineup for a modern sound, but Alan wanted us to write and play old-fashioned rock 'n' roll arrangements, while Jamie's smooth bass playing was more jazz orientated, so we played a bit of everything, and I altered my voice accordingly. Sean said my range was fantastic but that I needed to work on my vocal strength.

I had developed a "look" over the last few months. I knew it was ridiculous, but it seemed like ridiculous was fashionable. My hair was halfway down my back. I washed it regularly but rarely combed it, so it was messy and curly. I shaved once a week on a Tuesday so that by Friday and Saturday my stubble was just the right length. I wore tight jeans, and because I was tall and slim, I bought the biggest-size children's T-shirts I could find and it didn't matter whether they were boys' or girls'. So they were emblazoned with Cabbage Patch dolls or toy soldiers or whatever the kids' department had. Sean thought the kiddie image really worked for me and for the band. Girls loved it. Sean had dragged me into the ladies' toilet in one club to see all the graffiti on the wall declaring how gorgeous I was. I never knew I was good-looking before that. Nobody had ever told me I was good-looking except Auntie Peggy, and she said that about all of us, even Brian with his crooked nose.

For this important gig, I had borrowed a pink-sequined jacket of Mum's to wear over my Care Bears T-shirt. She said it made me look "effeminate." I didn't care. She and Auntie Peggy were coming to this concert with Brian and William, even though they said it was an outrageously late starting time. The Olympia was popular because it had a bar license while the gigs were on. And there were few places you could drink in Dublin after pub closing time at 11:00 p.m. in winter. I'd managed to get my family seats in a box so that Mum wouldn't have to mix with the drunk and rowdy crowd.

I was feeling good during the soundcheck, and for a change, I wasn't nervous. I was about to make my family proud. Sean was hyper, saying, "This is it, lads! This is the big time. This is our chance." He kept checking with me—"Are you okay, Luko?"—afraid that I might freak out like I did the first time, and I smiled and reassured him and necked another can of Harp to prove how cool I was. We even had a warm-up act on before us, a band Sean had chosen because they were hopeless and couldn't possibly upstage us. We'd high-fived them on their way down to the stage, a bunch of Cure-heads wearing black lipstick. They grunted their warmest wishes back to us.

By the time we got to the stage, it was 12:45 a.m., and the smell of sweat, hash, and booze hit us like a wall. I let the lads go on first to tune up briefly before I strode onto the stage and bowed theatrically. I expected the usual cheers and whistles, but they didn't happen. I looked up toward the box as Jamie strummed the bassline of the intro. William was looking pointedly at his watch, as if to chastise me for being late. Mum had brought her opera glasses and was surveying the rest of the audience. Auntie Peggy was beaming at me, pride and astonishment all over her face. Brian looked mildly interested, as if he was watching a wildlife documentary on BBC2. Some girl I didn't know was sitting between Brian and William.

I sang the first lines of our opening number. There was little reaction from the audience, who all seemed to be talking and laughing among themselves. I gestured to the sound engineer to turn up the vocals on my mic. Sean glared at me. We'd already agreed the mix in the soundcheck, but we knew you had to adjust for a live audience. He nodded toward the sound engineer to turn everything up. We crashed into the second song with the more raucous chorus, and then the audience began paying attention, but it wasn't enough. It wasn't what we were used to. Sure, we'd only played small places before, but we were going to be on *Anything Goes* on TV in a few weeks' time, and this audience was showing little interest. At the end of the second song, I asked Sean off mic if I should ask the audience to be quiet and to listen. He said absolutely not. We just had to get through it.

When we announced our interval break, I glanced up into the box, and my family were all looking bored out of their minds, except for Auntie Peggy, who smiled and waved when I caught her eye.

Backstage, I was furious. "What's wrong with them? We're giving them a show. Why aren't they reacting?" We had several theories. It was a glorified bar, people weren't here for the music. They were an older crowd, in their late twenties and thirties. The front-of-house sound must be terrible because the songs that had previously worked just weren't doing it for us tonight. Sean suggested I needed to loosen up. Alan said I was singing like I had a poker up my arse. I felt like crying, but Sean told Alan to back off, that I just needed to be a bit more relaxed. Jamie threw his eyes to the ceiling.

I really didn't want to go back out there and humiliate myself further in front of my family. Will and Brian had seen one or two of our gigs before, but I knew that Mum would have something really cutting to say tomorrow at Sunday lunch. Why couldn't she have come to a gig where girls were chanting my name, where I crowd-surfed to the back of the room?

We trudged back onto the stage. My eyes flicked up to the box. It was empty. I was surprised to feel nothing but relief. The pressure was off. As we kicked into our second act, I let fly. I didn't care anymore. By midway through it, the crowd was firmly on our side. The aisles were illegally crowded with the throngs of people who had come out of the two bar areas. Every seat was taken, but nobody was sitting. We raised the roof and I felt golden again. We took three encores and still they wanted more, and when we were back up in the dressing room ten minutes later, we could hear them chanting and cheering and hammering their heels on the floor. We looked at each other and laughed, and in a moment of genuine affection, we hugged each other.

"We took that one back from the bleedin' abyss," Alan said.

We poured beer down our throats and punched the air. The venue manager came in after five minutes, offering us a residency for January and February, every Friday and Saturday night. We left Sean to sort out the details. We guessed that any A&R men or talent scouts would have left after the first ten minutes, but we hoped they'd come back when word went around about how we'd later rocked the venue.

At Sunday lunch the next day, Mum didn't mention the concert at all. Anytime the boys talked about it, she would busy herself with serving vegetables or clearing plates while clattering cutlery. Brian and William wanted to explain to me why they thought the gig was so bad. William said it was a pity I wasn't better looking and that my voice wasn't stronger. Brian said I should really start going back to lectures because the band was never going to break through. Mum eventually asked that I not ever wear her jacket onstage again, but that was the only reference she made to the night. I didn't have to say anything. Because I knew in my heart that we were going places.

I was only half-right. At the end of January, a producer from Sony got in touch with Sean. He was offering a record deal but not for our band. He only wanted me and my songs. He offered money and flights and the studio time in London that we had all dreamed of. At first, I couldn't imagine how I'd do anything without my bandmates. It would be such a betrayal. They were the ones who'd taken a chance on me and even given me second chances. And I had written only four of our songs. It was insulting that they just wanted my voice. I told Sean to tell him no, not without the band. Sean was grateful for my loyalty and went back to Sony with my conditions. He returned with a more interesting suggestion. Sony had offered me more money, as a solo artist, but Sean was offering to be my manager. I trusted Sean. I liked him. He had really been the only one to encourage me. We said yes.

Alan and Jamie never spoke to us again.

Chapter 16

1984

I wasn't allowed to go to see Bob Dylan at Slane Castle with the rest of the family because I was only thirteen. I didn't mind. I hated big crowds, even though I would have liked to see inside a real castle. I stayed the night in Auntie Peggy's house. She let me toast marshmallows in her fireplace and I played with her dog, Rusty.

Auntie Peggy was my mum's sister, but she was nothing like her. She didn't have children of her own, and she adored all of us brothers. She loved us all the same, and no matter what I did or what I said, she would never hit me. When I knocked over her favorite vase that the king of Siam gave her, she said it didn't matter because it was one less thing to dust. I loved going to her house, especially on my own. She would show me a few ancient photos of her and Mum when they were little babies in a big family with four other brothers and sisters before their mum and dad died in a tram accident. Once or twice, I met those uncles and aunts in Auntie Peggy's house, but Mum never invited them to our house. They always referred to my mother as Little Moll, even though her name was Melissa. The other brothers and sisters had never been fostered and had grown up in orphanages. Auntie Peggy said that her and Mum's foster families weren't very nice to them. She said that her real family was a bit too rough for my dad. I never knew what she meant by that. The uncles were big men who spoke with cigarettes in their mouths or behind their ears. The aunts had stalls that sold toilet paper and bleach on Thomas Street. Mum got annoyed when I asked questions about them or her parents. She said she didn't even remember them, so they didn't feel like family. I asked Dad, and he said he was sure they were good people, but it was a shame they'd never had an education. He said he was proud of Mum because she had pulled herself out of the gutter and worked at her singing and made something of herself.

They all had a terrible time at Slane Castle. Brian came home in a sulk because someone had stolen his autograph book. William was mugged and beaten up and ended up in hospital. Dad was really cross with Mum, but she was acting the strangest of all. She went to bed and didn't want any of us talking to her. Dad slept on the sofa. I guessed they'd had an argument, and then Brian told me Mum had gone missing in the castle and nobody knew where she was. I thought she might have been cheating on Dad again. Maybe he'd caught her this time. I think Mum might have been a sex maniac.

I was worried that I was a pervert too. In the previous year, I'd discovered that by rubbing myself *down there* I could get some great feelings, and sometimes it even happened in my sleep and I *leaked*. Brian shared my room, but he never noticed or mentioned anything. The priests in my senior school had hinted at it, but they said this was a great sin. Eventually, I had asked Dad about it. He said it wasn't a sin, but it was something I shouldn't talk about, and I should keep it private. So it still felt like a sin. I asked Dad if I should tell the priest about it in confession, and he said absolutely not.

That summer, my brothers would happily play with the neighbors down at the local shopping center or in the woods behind our house. Those woods were still creepy to me. I'd regularly met the old woman in my nightmares, and she always told me she had news for me. I would wake up before I found out what the news was, but I was pretty sure it was bad news that I didn't want to know. I realized these were only dreams. I wasn't a kid. I didn't believe in bogeymen anymore, but these visions came often and they still frightened me. Will and Brian laughed when I told them and made fun of me for talking about witches, so I learned to say nothing. I didn't have many friends. The boys in my class called me a weirdo and the neighbors' kids avoided me. I didn't mind. God was on my side.

One morning, about ten days after the Slane concert, Brian and Will were out somewhere pretending to be cool and probably smoking. I was lying on the sofa on my own, watching an old black-and-white film. If my brothers were home, we'd have to watch endless tapes of *MT-USA* on the dodgy video recorder Dad won in a raffle. This old film was really funny, about these two men who pretended they were lady musicians to get away from baddies, but there were two beautiful women in the film too. One of them had this funny high lispy voice, and every time she walked her bum wiggled and her hips swayed. I didn't even realize my hand had wandered down into my underpants until Mum screeched at me from the living room door. "For God's sake, you're all the same! Filthy animals!" She glared at me furiously.

I pulled my hand up instantly, but she had seen what I'd been doing. She smelled sour, and her hair was sticking up and knotted at the back. She looked like she'd been crying. She slammed the door and stalked out, and I heard the kitchen door slam too. I was nervous because Dad had said wanking was okay but private, and maybe Mum didn't know about it. I followed her out to the kitchen. "Sorry, Mum," I said.

She sat down heavily, and I offered to make her a cup of tea. She nodded but didn't look at me. "Wash your filthy hands first."

When I had my back to her at the sink, she said, "I was raped."

"What?"

"You know what that means, don't you?"

I felt all the blood rushing to my head. I didn't know what to say. Of course I knew what it meant, but I'd never talked about it before, with anyone.

"It happened when we were at Slane. Jack Gogan did it." I was afraid to turn around. "You know who he is?"

I remembered being at a Christmas party at the Gogans' house. Their two children were around the same age as us, a boy and a girl. I remembered Mr. Gogan kissing Mum on the cheek under the mistletoe, and I didn't like the way he looked at her, but that was years ago.

I continued to make the tea and placed it on the table in front of her. She gestured me to sit down.

"I might as well tell you. There's nobody else who will understand, you know, what it's like . . . to be . . . scared. I can't tell anyone else. Just sit down and listen."

I sat down and heard the words I didn't want to hear. I let them wash over me and occasionally tuned in to hear "he forced my legs apart . . . ," "I was too terrified to scream . . ."

I tried humming a tune in my head. As she continued talking, I concentrated on her mouth, old to me, with lines radiating from her thin lips. There were more lines around her eyes. I looked at her long ears, and I could see the white roots of her dyed auburn hair sprouting at her hairline. She was hunched over the table. It came to me suddenly, but with absolute certainty, that my mother was the old woman in my dream. I had already been sent to live with her. She scared me.

When she had finished speaking, she reached for the biscuit tin and gave me a chocolate biscuit.

"What do you think of that?"

For a moment, I thought she was talking about the biscuit.

"It's terrible, Mum. You should tell the police."

"If I did that, it wouldn't stay out of the papers. It's the price of fame. Don't you understand?"

"Why can't you tell Dad?"

"There are things that must not be said between a husband and wife because it changes the way we see each other."

"Like with you and Nicholas Sheedy? Did he rape you as well?"

Mum was startled. "What are you talking about?"

"I saw you . . . with him, in your bed."

"When?"

"Last year, the year before? I don't know, a while ago."

"Shut up, Luke." She cried, but her voice was filled with anger. "I thought you would understand."

I was angry too. "Yeah? Why me? Why not tell William or Brian?"

"You have nightmares all the time. I have just lived one. I thought you'd get it, but instead you fling Nicholas Sheedy in my face, as if that had anything to do with it."

"Sorry, but—"

"You think it was my fault, you think I asked for it?"

"Of course not. It's just that they were both . . . sex."

"You're too young. I should have known. Forget that we ever had this conversation. Never mention it again."

"Mum?"

"What?"

"Why do you always tell me the bad stuff?"

"What do you mean?"

"You tell me secrets all the time, but they're always about nasty things, about that young girl and her baby dying in the grotto and about us not having enough money last year."

Her mouth turned to a sneer. "I don't know, maybe I tell you because you don't deserve any good news. Did you ever think about that?"

"Why not? I didn't want to know about Paul dying. I had night-mares for months, but you sat on the end of my bed and told me all about it. He was Brian's friend, why didn't you tell Brian? You told William and Brian when you got that TV job and when you won fifty pounds in the sweepstakes. And when we're going on holidays, I always find out last. It's not fair."

She glided out of the room. Maybe that was the old woman's gift to me. Bad news.

I went to the front door. William was sitting on a wall at the end of the cul-de-sac in his denim jacket, even though it was really warm and sunny, talking to two girls. Brian was kicking a ball against the garage door. I felt a familiar knot in my stomach. I went upstairs to my room, which faced out onto the woods behind our house. In the time it had taken me to climb the stairs, a dark cloud had appeared over the woods. I shut the curtains and got into bed and prayed that Mum could be unraped and that she wasn't the witch. I was so confused, it felt like my head would burst. I had prayed and prayed for Mum to stop having sex with other men—maybe this rape was God's punishment. Maybe she would be faithful to my dad now.

That year, I got heavily involved in reading the newspapers and watching current affairs programs. Perhaps because of Mum, I got sort of addicted to bad news. I prayed to God that the IRA would stop bombing people and that Britain and Ireland could be friends, and that the Ford factory in Cork would reopen so that all those men could keep their jobs.

There was one news story that dominated the media completely. Every night, I saw reports from Ethiopia of starving children. Their hollow bellies and their sticklike limbs were shocking to look at. The flies that gathered in the corners of their enormous eyes horrified and disgusted me. I started going to Mass every day and then to confession twice a week. The guilt of not being able to help these children was more than I could take. I bought everyone in the family a copy of the Band Aid single for Christmas, and any money I had left over I sent to charities. The children still died by the thousands. God wasn't listening anymore. He didn't care what I did. I was stuck with the woman in the woods.

When Dad started to get sick and God did nothing to help, I stopped believing in him. God didn't rape Mum either. Jack Gogan did.

Chapter 17

1995

When I was a kid, I had never dreamed of being famous. Even though Dad always said I was creative and that I had an inquiring mind, I had wanted to be a postman. It seemed like such a straightforward and useful job. Other kids wanted to be footballers and astronauts, but I wanted something that had a route and a routine. Mum had laughed when I told her that and said I'd be lucky if the post office would take me.

Now, at the age of twenty-four, I was a rock star. Well, more of a pop star, I suppose. The only difference really is the age and gender of your fans. My fans were mostly teenage girls, instead of older guys. The touring and recording schedules are more or less the same. But pop stars apparently don't throw TV sets out of windows (I tried once, but the flex was welded to the wall) or do hard drugs (I had done them all).

I had everything I could possibly want: fame and fortune, TV appearances, adoring fans, more money than I could spend, world travel, sex on tap, antipsychotic medication, and an on-call psychiatrist for when things got bad. But that spring, everything was good. I felt strong and stable, and everyone said I was at the top of my game. Though, everyone always said that when I was at the bottom too. There weren't many people I could rely on to tell me the truth.

I was playing five nights in Paris at the Palais Omnisports and had three rest days there before we flew on to Zurich. It was a great opportunity to catch up with Brian. He had gone to live in Paris soon after Susan and Will got married the year before. We had been closer to each other than to Will because we shared a room when we were kids, but since my career had taken off, I had seen very little of him. After he got his arts degree, he couldn't decide what he wanted to do, so he did a Higher Diploma in education. He was now teaching English in some exclusive lycée. I envied his anonymity, though his lifestyle would bore me to tears. I think he must have picked up on that because during the eight days I was in Paris, he bizarrely quit his job in the lycée to work in a restaurant. He said it was more fun and more social. I didn't get why he'd go from a well-paid job to a badly paid one, particularly when he was always so obsessed with money, but he didn't want to discuss it.

I was staying at the Lutetia. I wanted to show off a bit. I think he was glad to see that I was healthy then. A few Fantas and a box of patisserie delicacies after a show was the most damage I was doing to myself at that time.

Brian was not especially well dressed and didn't appear to be looking after himself. When I introduced him to people as my brother, they were surprised. "You don't look alike at all!" they said. The three of us were always different, and by now I had been styled and costumed in such a way that I was no longer in control of my own image. But I was happy to let others make those decisions for me. My long hair had been cropped and highlighted, and my teeth were whitened, but they described the "look" they wanted to achieve as "scruffy chic." If anyone had known the effort and money it took to look like I'd just rolled out of bed, they would have laughed. I went to the gym for an hour every day and to weekly tanning sessions so that in the section of the show where the dancing girls ripped my shirt off, I would be both toned and tanned. I could tell that Brian thought all this was ridiculous. I thought it was ridiculous, too, but Sean, my manager, said that image was everything and it was working for me, so I didn't argue.

"You look good," Brian said. "Well, weird, you know? But healthy. How's the head?" That was Brian's way of inquiring after my mental health.

"Good," I said, and it was true. I was sleeping for full nights, and there were no longer any tiny visitors in my dreams. I hadn't told anyone about that. It was impossible to explain.

Before he quit the teaching gig, Brian brought along a gang of his students to one of my shows. Afterward, one of them tried to get into the limo with us back to the hotel. Brian was aggressive in telling her to get out of the car. But I was used to these little girls being obsessed with me and told him to be cool.

Brian didn't invite me to his flat. He said it was small and poky and there wasn't room to swing a cat. But on another evening, toward the end of my stay, he took me to the restaurant, La Saucisserie, where he had just started working. He was really excited about introducing me to the owner, Conrad. When I met him, Brian asked, "Who does he remind you of?" I looked at Conrad while he grinned at me, and there was something familiar about him, but I couldn't guess who Brian was talking about.

"Paul!" said Brian. Paul was our cousin who had died from leukemia as a child. I felt a flutter of unease in my chest, and a shadow crossed my vision. It was true. Conrad looked exactly like Paul might have looked if he had lived.

Conrad had invited the paparazzi, so we couldn't eat in peace, and it wasn't long before the place was surrounded by teenage girls. The restaurant was an eccentric, fashionable place in the sixth arrondissement. Conrad kept slapping Brian on the back and making me pose for photographs with them. He was warm and friendly and extremely camp.

Immediately after dinner, I called my driver to get us out of there. We went back to the hotel and ordered crème brûlée from room service. Brian was looking at my wardrobes of clothes and shoes. I told him to take anything he wanted, and I watched as he helped himself to silk jackets, woolen coats, shoes, waistcoats, hats, and even unopened packages of socks. Pretty much anything he could carry.

The thing about Brian is that he was never really grateful. No matter what I ever did for him, however much I bought him, it was never enough for him to say thank you. It bugged me, but it wasn't something I could ever say, except to my therapist. Dr. Shroeder wondered why I needed gratitude for things I was able to offer without any sacrifice of my own, but it was still good manners to say thank you.

Then it struck me that there was something I could do for him that might improve his life. Brian had never really had a girlfriend. There were girls who were friends and maybe they occasionally hooked up, but there had never been anyone really special, at least as far as I knew.

I fell in love every couple of weeks, but then the tour moved on and another girl would show up. In the early days, I'd had a kind of secret relationship with Sean's sister, but Sean was my manager and it seemed like a betrayal. Every time I came back to Dublin, I caught up with Sarah, but after my last breakdown she'd kept her distance, and I couldn't really blame her. Still, I could always "get" girls. I don't think Brian could. He never had much confidence. It was singing that gave me confidence, but Brian was a teacher turned waiter, and I think he felt he should be doing better.

I decided to get Brian a job on the tour. I could swing it so he could be the merchandising manager, selling posters and T-shirts and CDs. It would be easy. There were loads of women working on the tour, and I was sure some of them would be interested in nailing my brother.

The next day, I offered him the job in a discreet café he had led me to. He was horribly offended. "Seriously? You want me to sell your tacky, overpriced merch to teenagers?"

I was taken aback. "But, Brian, you'll be making proper money and you'll get to travel. We can hang out a bit."

"I'm managing fine by myself, thanks."

"Really? On a kitchen porter's salary? They must pay you well."

He looked away and fiddled with his watch. "And, what, you're going to fire the guy who currently does the merch to make room for your brother? How's he going to feel about that?"

The "guy" who was currently doing the merchandising and marketing was a tall, beautiful German twenty-three-year-old law graduate called Mila who I slept with on a regular basis, but it was clear she wanted to have a proper relationship and having her hanging around at after-show parties every night made me a little uncomfortable. I could arrange for her to be paid off. I would let Sean handle it. I wouldn't even have to see her. It seemed like an obvious solution.

"Don't worry about that. The crews on these tours move from show to show all the time. It will be fine."

"Fuck you, Luke, I'm not a bloody charity case."

"I'm offering you a job. You'll have to work. Brian, seriously, think about it! Think about the girls!" I winked.

"Jesus Christ, Luke, listen to yourself. You're offering me your leftovers. I've already been second best. This is a fucking insult." He pushed back his chair and stormed out, assuming, as always, that I'd pay the bill.

I was upset. I'd only been trying to help Brian, and he threw it back in my face without ever thanking me for all I'd already done for him. I hit the hotel bar that afternoon and drank more than I should, letting my guard down. Models, or possibly prostitutes, came out of nowhere, and I was buying them shots and champagne, and things got messy. Late in the evening, I decided to confront Brian. I got my driver to take me to his restaurant, to find out where he was living. A surly maître d', recognizing my drunkenness, reluctantly gave me an address where I could find him.

It wasn't at all what I expected. Brian's building was, like most of Paris, built in the Haussmann style, on Place de l'Estrapade, where each apartment took up one wide floor. How could he afford this? I pressed the buzzer and a voice I didn't recognize came over the intercom. I was unsure if this was the right place, so I tentatively asked for Brian

Drumm. I was wearily told to take the elevator to the second floor while the door unlocked automatically. I stepped into a high-ceilinged atrium with an old-fashioned caged lift in front of me. Nervous of such contraptions because of all the old films I'd seen, I took the adjacent stairs.

The door to the apartment was ajar, and I was surprised to see Conrad standing there in a silk robe.

"*Entrez!*" he said, and then called Brian's name. "*Brian! Ton frère est là!*"

I sat down on an opulent velvet sofa, peering at the chandelier high above me. Brian appeared, red in the face, half-dressed. He muttered something to Conrad, who disappeared down the same corridor from where he had just emerged.

"What are you doing here, Luke? It's after midnight!"

"Do you live here? I thought you said your place was tiny? This is a palace compared to what I was expecting." The cogs in my brain turned. "You live here . . . with Conrad?"

"Shut up. He's just putting me up for a few nights, that's all."

"In the same bedroom?"

"I'm not gay."

"Christ, Brian, there's nothing to be ashamed of—"

"I'm not fucking gay." He whispered it. Presumably because it would be news to Conrad.

"But you're flat-sharing a mansion apartment with your queer boss?"

He hung his head, then went to a crystal decanter on an elaborate sideboard and filled two glasses.

"You don't know anything about me. I had to leave Ireland in a hurry—"

"But why? Money? You never came to me—"

"*You* never offered. But money wasn't why I left. When I arrived here, I landed on my feet at the lycée, but last week there was trouble . . . with a student . . ."

"Jesus, Brian, did you hit him? What happened? Why didn't you tell me?"

His eyes glazed over, and he said nothing for a few moments.

"I'm the family joke, the loser, the one without a glittering career in the media. I don't want your help. I'm just staying here . . . until I can raise the rent to get a place of my own, on my own. You could lend me—"

"You're a rent boy, but you're not gay?"

"It's not like that. For fuck's sake, Luke! I swear I'm not gay. I dream of meeting a woman like . . . I don't know."

Brian broke down in sobs then, and as drunk as I was, I knew I couldn't leave him in this place with Conrad. Not that I blamed Conrad. It didn't seem like Brian had been forced to do anything.

"Where's your passport? Tell Conrad you're coming with me. Pack your bags, okay?"

"I . . . People can't find out about this, Luke."

"I'm not going to tell anyone, am I?"

"I mean, the trouble at the school . . ."

"I'm not going to say anything. You haven't even told me what the problem was."

"Maybe not when you're well, but what happens when you have the next breakdown and you say all kinds of crazy shit?"

I know that Brian didn't mean to be hurtful, but I really didn't need a reminder of my past difficulties from my "straight" brother who was fucking another man for rent and God knows what else.

"People don't believe anything I say when I have an episode. You have nothing to worry about."

When we got back to my suite in the Lutetia, Brian and I got properly drunk together.

"It's all Will's fault."

"What is?" I asked.

"Everything. Will always gets what he wants."

I could make no further sense of what Brian was talking about.

Two days later, Brian was selling my merchandise at the Hallensta-
dion in Zurich. He never said thank you. But he got laid regularly, according to the crew. All girls. I'll never understand how Brian could sell
himself like that. My therapist won't discuss Brian's issues with me, and
Brian refused to see him. "There's nothing wrong with me. It was just a
bad patch" was all he would say.

Chapter 18

1988

I was in my first year of engineering at UCD. College was not what I thought it would be like. Will was in his final year and was house-sharing with some friends while working as an usher in a cinema to pay his rent. Brian and I lived at home, though we finally had our own bed-rooms. He and Will were both doing arts degrees. Mum said the only reason I got into engineering was because I studied instead of having a social life, as I had no friends. I think she was proud, though, because she boasted about it to Auntie Peggy. Brian and Will weren't partic-ularly impressed by my high grades in the Leaving Cert. They didn't notice me much. They said I was a square and a dork.

At college, I expected more of the same. I'd keep myself to myself and be ignored and just get on with things. But college was far less re-strictive than school. There was no uniform, and I could grow my hair as long as I liked. I wore jeans every day and my combat jacket and the stripy sweater that Auntie Peggy had knitted for me. There were girls everywhere. Tall and elegant ones, cute and chubby ones, funny ones, serious ones—all types. They liked me. They thought I was funny. They said I was great, but I was way too shy to make a move on any of them. For the first time in my life, I was part of a gang. I had friends.

Some older guys wanted to hang out with us too. They were in a band, and we all went to the garage of one of their houses to listen. They played songs they'd written themselves. It was really exciting to hear them. The girls asked me if I knew any songs. I knew a few songs, but my voice was high. I knew if I sang in front of them, they'd laugh at me, so I practiced at home in the bathroom with my battery-operated tape recorder when everyone was out.

One night, I was invited to a party at one of the girls' houses. Sarah's parents were away. Her brother, Sean, was one of the older guitar players. I didn't drink much back then. I'd sip a beer to be social, but I didn't really like the taste of it. Brian and Will had been getting wasted regularly since their school days, and I could never understand why they'd want to drink so much when it repeatedly made them sick and act weird.

That night, Sarah had made a bowl of punch. It tasted like fruit juice, and I drank a lot of it until, eventually, I started to feel good and warm inside. Sean was strumming the guitar, and the room was full of hash smoke. Sarah was sitting at my feet on the floor, and Carrie was plaiting my hair. Everyone took turns singing songs, and I kept saying no, but then I realized that maybe I was better than some of the people who'd sung before me, and the booze had given me a little bit of confidence. I agreed to sing a song, but on the condition that I could pull my sweater over my head while doing it. Everyone laughed, but they weren't laughing *at* me. It was a great feeling. They really wanted me to be good.

I was so afraid of making an ass of myself. I pushed my sweater to my forehead and sang "Amazing Grace." Without the acoustics of my bathroom, my voice was thin and reedy, but I could carry the tune and hold the notes. While I was singing I could hear people moving around the room, matches being struck, wineglasses clinking, and some low chatter continued. When I finished, nothing happened for a moment, and then I tentatively lowered the neck of my sweater.

Sarah jumped up and hugged me, and Carrie kissed me on the lips. "You're really good, Luko!" she said.

Sean, the guitarist, said, "Do you want to be in our band? We won't be singing hymns and shit like that, but you've got something unusual there. Everyone I know tries to sing like everyone else, but you sound like . . . you."

Sarah beamed at me. "You really should! Their singer just moved to the States. He's living in Boston. They have gigs lined up already."

Sean looked at me. "One condition. You can't fuck my sister, right?" Sarah reddened and threw a cushion at him, and Carrie stretched her arm so that it encompassed my shoulders. I kept my promise not to sleep with his sister for at least a year, and that's how the band started.

Sean was the guitarist and the chief organizer, Alan was the drummer, and Jamie was the bass player. We rehearsed in Sean's dad's garage, which was decked out with amps, a dartboard, a few traffic cones, and a roll of offcut carpet. The walls were lined with egg boxes to dampen the echo. I felt like I finally belonged. The lads were really kind to me, though they were shocked by my musical influences and thought I was being ironic until I brought along my entire record collection to rehearsals one day.

"Right," said Sean, "we need to educate you."

They lent me their records and I listened to the musicians they liked. Led Zeppelin, Lynyrd Skynyrd, Queen, the Who, the Doors, Nick Drake, Django Reinhardt, John Coltrane, John Martyn, Pat Metheny. I wasn't completely unfamiliar with these artists because Brian and Will had some of those same albums when we were growing up. I concentrated on the lyrics, though sometimes the singers screamed them, so it was hard to make out what they were singing.

In the garage, Sean might start with a little riff, and then Jamie would join in, and I'd hum something that fitted with the music. Gradually, the humming would turn into words that popped into my head, and I realized that maybe I was a poet and not an engineer. When Dad had said I could make things, maybe he meant I could make songs. I skipped a lot of lectures over the next few weeks and worked on lyrics and my voice. Jamie taught me how to read music, and before too long, I could pick out the notes on the guitar I'd borrowed from Sean. I smoked joints with Alan, which allowed my mind to expand and tap into elements of consciousness that I hadn't known were there.

The strangest and best thing was that while I was working on these songs, the nightmares stopped. The woman in the woods who had haunted me since childhood disappeared. I had long ago learned not to mention these dreams to anyone. But, finally, I was released from them. The other side benefit to singing was sex. Girls wanted to sleep with me. I lost my virginity the night before our first gig.

This gig was in the Baggot Inn and had been booked when the original singer was still with the band. We were called the Wombstones. I don't know why or who made up the name. The others thought it made us sound edgy and dangerous. I thought it made us sound illiterate. Posters went up all over college, and swarms of girls offered to help out with promotion. I was getting nervous as the day approached. It was one thing when it was just us in Sean's garage, but it looked like this gig was going to sell out. There could be two hundred people coming.

Carrie asked if I'd get her and two friends on the guest list. I didn't know what a guest list was, but Sean said it would be no problem. Sean asked what I was going to wear onstage. I hadn't thought about any of this. He and Alan were going to wear eyeliner and spike their hair, and they thought Jamie and I should do the same. Jamie thought that was ridiculous because he hadn't signed up to "play with Duran fucking Duran." In the end we all agreed that we could wear what we wanted and that we didn't have to go for a uniform look. I wanted to wear my jeans and my usual sweater that Auntie Peggy had knitted. I felt comfortable in it. It had black and yellow stripes across the front and a red back. I'd worn it most days, since she gave it to me for my last birthday and there was a hole in one elbow. My hair was long and curly. The girls I knew loved my hair, so I didn't think I should change that. But on the morning of the gig I went out and bought Doc Marten boots because everyone said they were cool.

At the soundcheck in the venue, there were a few people milling around, bar staff, and the house sound engineer. We soundchecked and got used to playing through a PA—it was louder than anything we'd used before. We were going to sing seven of our own songs and three covers: Queen's "Bohemian Rhapsody," Zeppelin's "Stairway to Heaven," and, for fun, a rocked-up version of the theme tune to *Fame*. Sean said we'd look like pricks if it seemed like we were taking ourselves too seriously.

We stayed backstage in a tiny dressing room upstairs above the stage, with beer crates for chairs, while the venue filled up. The others drank beer, but I felt sick and could barely swallow. I tried to do some vocal warm-ups, but my thin voice sounded strangled to me. Alan sparked up a spliff and handed it to me. "You need to relax, man. It's only a gig." They had been playing together and with other bands for two years already, but none of them had been the lead singer. That morning, Mum had given me her tuppence worth of advice: "Oh, your first concert is always awful, but you have to do it, before you get a second one. I think I had three gin and tonics before I went on and was way off-key by the second song. Of course, my first concert was with a full orchestra and not in a pub." Mum came to fame as the runner-up in a national song contest before I was born. She often told us how the winner of the contest had disappeared into obscurity, while she'd had a long career, though her songs hardly got any airplay now and she didn't write any of them herself.

My new Doc Martens were tight and pinching me and I was sticky in my sweater and we weren't even onstage yet. The few pulls of the joint I was smoking made me dizzy, and I had a desperate urgency to empty my bowels. I scurried to the filthy toilet along the corridor, sweat now pumping from every pore. When I'd finished, I flushed the toilet and looked in the mottled mirror. Sean hammered on the door.

"Luko, it's showtime! Let's go."

"Give me a few seconds," I said as I repeatedly rinsed my hands under the cold tap, trying to throw cool water down the back of my neck. My face was a pale sickly blue. I closed my eyes for a few seconds, and when I opened them, the woman from the woods was standing behind me in the mirror, grinning manically. I ran out of the bathroom, terrified and shocked, shaking my head. Sean grabbed me by the shoulders. "We're going to be great. Rock the place, okay?" And I didn't want to tell him that my nightmare had just crawled into my day and that everything was going to be shit.

A huge cheer went up as Alan led the others onto the stage. They banged out a few noisy chords while I stood, shivering in the wings, rooted to the spot, afraid to open my eyes in case I saw her in the crowd. Sean came back offstage and pulled me forward into the spotlight. I peered through my fingers, and the room was thronged. I was afraid of crowds. Prolonged whistling and cheering filled my ears. The set list was taped to the floor in front of my mic, and I looked down at that because I was afraid to look at the faces.

Alan clicked his drumsticks, and Sean strummed. I missed my cue to sing, and Jamie looped back on the bass to start again. I couldn't open my mouth. I couldn't breathe. On the third round, Sean edged over to me. "Get a grip, don't fuck this up on us. Turn your back, if you need to, but sing the fucking song, man."

I turned to face Alan behind me, glowering over his drum kit. They did another round of the intro, and I raised the microphone to my mouth. The voice that came out of me was not one I recognized. Alan looked shocked, though he smiled encouragingly. I sang the whole number in this deep timbre, but the lyrics were not the ones I'd written and rehearsed. They were words spewed with hate and violence and aggression. When Sean played out the final chords, I could not stop myself and repeated the last line over and over—"I need to kill you all . . . I need to kill you all . . . I need to kill you all . . ."—and then the force that had occupied me left suddenly, and I slumped to my knees and keeled over sideways on the floor.

The crowd was rapturous and started to chant my name: "Luko! Luko! Luko!"

I felt weak and empty. Sean and Jamie pulled me to my feet. "I don't know what the fuck you're doing, but it's working. Keep doing it," said Jamie. I looked at Sean in desperation.

"Are you okay?" he said, perhaps more sensitive to my sweat-soaked body, my blue-tinged skin, and my obvious trembling.

He ambled over to Alan and Jamie, and they improvised some ambient jazz tune that had been dropped from the set list the week before.

"Sort yourself out, but don't leave the stage." He handed me a pint of lager. I drank it down in one go, eliciting another cheer, and then I leaned down and took off my boots and pulled the sweater off over my head. Bare chested and barefoot, I turned to face the crowd. I nodded at Sean. I was ready.

Chapter 19

1983

I had been praying hard for Mum's immortal soul because she had committed adultery and I didn't want her to go to hell, but a few months after I saw her in bed with Nicholas Sheedy, when William tried to tell me I hadn't seen it, I knew she was still carrying on with other men because I was looking out for it. I tried to talk about it to William, but he told me to shut up. He said Mum couldn't help it if men fancied her and that it was Dad's fault for not paying her enough attention. But the way she'd put her hand on my teacher's knee or sometimes when she was on television, and I'd see how she looked at other male guests on *The Late Late Show*, I knew she was having bad thoughts. I knew I had to make bigger sacrifices.

Kneeling in the pew after the others had raced out of church after Mass, I stared up at Jesus on the cross, begging for some sign that my mother would not be damned to eternal fires. His blue eyes were raised heavenward, his hair and beard were matted with blood, and the crown of thorns was crammed onto his head like barbed wire. It must have been agony. Each arm was stretched out, impaled at the hands, and his feet were pulled together at the bottom of the cross, staked by a giant nail that pierced both ankles. I often stood like that on my bed for an hour or more, arms akimbo, feet crossed, trying to imagine the suffering that Jesus had endured for us.

Halloween was imminent. Mrs. Turner next door always threw a tea party for the local children. She was kind and decorated her house with woolly cobwebs and made fairy cakes with scary faces. All the children on our road attended, and some of the parents came too, bringing sweets and games. We would all dress up in masks and bob for apples. Mr. Mulcahy lit fireworks in the garden. It was always good fun. This year, William and Brian said they weren't going—one of the older boys at the top of the road was having a fancy-dress disco—but I wanted to go to Mrs. Turner's.

Dad was away and Mum was at home, but she never took much interest in Mrs. Turner's parties, though at that time of year she did allow us to take certain items from her dressing room—old costumes from shows she'd been in, or elaborate hats. We had all worn her Robin Hood costume and her top-hat-and-tails outfit from when she'd been in *Cabaret*.

Instead of using Mum's stuff, I decided to work on a costume of my own. It only took a day or two, and I mostly did it in the shed after school so that nobody would bother me, and I could keep it a secret. Also, I could use Dad's gardening gloves. Out of the autumn rosebush, I'd selected several thorny branches to form a crown. I didn't actually want it to hurt, so I had a cushioned thing for the top of my head. I had a hand towel to wrap around my waist, like Jesus had on the cross, but I wore my underpants beneath it, and I was barefoot. I was really cold, but it didn't matter. I defrosted some sirloin steak from the freezer and squeezed the blood out of it to run down my face. I could have done a fake beard, but I wanted this to be taken seriously. I needed everyone to see what Jesus had gone through for us.

With a red felt-tip marker, I dug deep into the palms of my hands and pressed hard into the fronts of my feet. I had planned to stand in the pose of Jesus in Mrs. Turner's living room. I wasn't going to take part in any of the games. I was going to stare at the ceiling and say nothing. I knew somebody would call my mother, and she would understand then that I was doing this for her. I crept into the house and called out to Mum that I was going next door. "Great," she said, and I heard her turn up the volume on *Blockbusters*. She always turned up the volume on the TV when she didn't want to be interrupted.

I inspected myself in the hallway mirror. I was disappointed. The blood was real, but it wasn't mine. I tiptoed back into the kitchen, took the cushion from my head and jammed the thorny crown onto my head. It scratched and scraped but didn't hurt as much as I expected. I took the bread knife from its block on the windowsill. I clamped my mouth shut while I stabbed at first one hand and then the other. The pain was real, but I needed to go deeper. I could really only manage a superficial wound on my right hand, but on my left, I jammed my hand up against the point of the blade. Blood poured from it. I steadied myself by the sink for a moment. The shock of the pain was awful, and I hadn't even done my feet yet. I felt dizzy when I bent down, and then I realized I mightn't be able to walk next door if I stabbed my feet. I decided against it and crept out of the back door, biting my lip and trying to stop tears of pain from spilling down my cheeks.

I walked in through Mrs. Turner's front door. "Oh my word!" said Mrs. McCarthy from the corner. "Luke Drumm, you win all the prizes today. That's absolutely fantastic." She called the others to come and take a look while I moved into the front room and positioned myself beside the mantelpiece, looking heavenward. "He's bleeding," said Marian from number 42, who used to be in my class at primary school. Mrs. Turner laughed nervously. "Well, Luke, that *is* something else, but aren't you cold? I hope that fake blood is going to wash out of my rug!"

I said nothing, just threw my arms outward like I'd practiced.

"It's *real* blood!" said Marian as the drips from my left hand pooled on the dark green rug at my feet.

"Mother of God, she's right!" said Mr. Mulcahy. "He's bleeding. Get a towel, Martha, quick!"

Mrs. Turner swept all the sweets off the table, grabbed up the tablecloth, and tried to wrap it around my hand. I tried to wrestle her away. I didn't want my pose to be disrupted until Mum came to see it. But Mr. Mulcahy lifted me off the ground and forced my hand down so he could wrap it in the tablecloth. Children were screaming and running around, and the adults were all looking at me, horrified. I remained calm. I didn't speak or yell or cry. I suffered in silence as our Lord had. Somebody had gone to get Mum from next door, and she arrived, crying out, "Oh my God, what has he done now?"

I smiled at her and showed her my hand. "I'm just like Jesus," I said. "I'm atoning for your sins."

The room went quiet for a moment until Mr. Mulcahy volunteered to take me to the emergency room. Mum didn't get it. She was explaining to everyone, "Oh, he's a trial to me! Look, he can't be in that much pain if he's smiling. He takes the Bible very seriously. He's completely daft. I don't know where he gets it from. The other two are fine, you know . . ."

I think I must have passed out at that point.

Dad was by my side when I woke up in my bed later. He hugged me close. "Luke," he said sternly, "you have to get this Jesus stuff out of your head. You're a good boy. You don't need to prove yourself to your mother and me, or to anyone. From now on, you are only going to Mass once a week. And no more confession. You've become a little . . . obsessed by all this, and it's not healthy. Why would you stab yourself and hurt your beautiful hands? God wouldn't want that. He would want us to be happy."

A few days later, Dad and Mum and I had a meeting with Father Benedict. He confirmed everything Dad had said. "Jesus wants us all to be happy, and you know, Luke, half those things you tell me in confession are barely sins at all. You really don't have to atone for much."

"But what if I have to atone for other people?"

"Other people have to make their own choices, Luke, we can't be responsible for them."

I felt a weight lift off my shoulders. But only temporarily.

At home, Brian and William were half-amused and half-impressed by what I'd done.

"You'll end up in a loony bin one day," said Brian.

"I wouldn't be surprised," Mum said.

Chapter 20

1997

We don't sit around in pajamas all day, weaving wicker baskets. That's about the only stereotype that doesn't ring true. The rest is pretty accurate: the thrice-daily medicine cart that keeps us from harming ourselves and one another, the catatonia of some patients, the extreme hostility of others, the group sessions, and the twice-weekly one-to-ones with your designated psychiatrist. I wasn't in a locked ward, and I had not been committed, but that doesn't mean I wanted to stay. I was simply too scared to leave.

The record company was paying for this monthlong stint, but they had said this was my last chance. The canceled gigs and my "erratic behavior" were untenable, apparently, and my old friend and manager, Sean, had made it clear that if the next smaller UK tour did not go well, he would be finished with me. I could hardly blame him. The meltdowns, manic episodes, psychotic highs, and deepest lows had been a severe mental strain on everyone I worked with. There were several musicians who now refused to work with me. Tour managers had come and gone. I barely knew the names of half the people who shared the stage with me. And I needed a break. That's how I saw these "residencies." A rest for my body and my mind. I didn't understand how other people could get along without them.

Oh, there's another stereotypical thing that isn't true. We don't recline on sofas during a consultation. It's usually a comfortable armchair, and there are loads of boxes of tissues within reaching distance in case of crying. I've done a lot of crying.

"So, Luke, how are we feeling today?"

"I don't know how you're feeling, but I'm okay, I suppose."

"Just okay?"

"Well, if I was feeling fantastic, I wouldn't be in here, would I?"

A pause.

"Have you been having the nightmares since we talked?"

"Which ones?"

"Have you seen the baby?"

"I don't want to talk about that. I've told you that before."

"The night you were admitted here, the reports say you were terribly agitated about a baby. But in our last session, you agreed that the woman in the woods is in your imagination. You know, Luke, sometimes when we talk about things we're scared of, it helps us to quantify them and see them for what they really are."

"What do you mean?"

"Well, I'm particularly interested in the baby you talked about that night, and I'm wondering what it might symbolize in your life?"

"You're the psychiatrist, you tell me."

"Okay, I'll try. But you'll need to help me. When did you first 'see' the baby?" He did the rabbit ears thing with his fingers. I sighed deeply.

"I don't know."

"Was it when you were a child? Or later? After you became famous?"

"Yes, after."

"And how did it first appear? We haven't established if the baby is a boy or a girl, have we?"

"I don't know what it is. It's too small to tell. I was in Berlin, I think, or Dusseldorf. I know it was somewhere in Germany."

"And when was this?"

"Five years ago, 1992. Springtime."

"Yes?"

"I was in bed."

"Alone?"

"Yes. . . . No. . . . There had been a girl, but she'd left by then."

"And had you taken any . . . substances?"

"Not much. I had to be up early for a breakfast show on TV. We'd gone back to the room after the gig, got some room service, a couple of bottles of beer, and we did a few lines of coke each, that's all."

"Did you know the girl? Did you have sex with her?" He coughed. "I don't need any details."

I looked at him, weighing up whether he was some kind of pervert. I've seen a lot of shrinks, and you'd be surprised how many of them try to make everything about sex.

"Yes, I think her name was Hilda, or Gilda. She had done my makeup earlier that day at the stadium."

"Was she a friend? A girlfriend?"

"I suppose. For that night, anyway."

"And did you see her after that night?"

"No."

"Were you still high when you saw the baby? From the cocaine?"

"No, the buzz had gone, but I was still awake. That's one of the side effects, you know?"

I saw judgment in his face.

"I know, I know, it sounds careless to take a drug like that when I had an early call next day, but I was used to it by then. I'd often taken way more on a night out without bloody hallucinations."

"Luke, I'm your psychiatrist, and it would be irresponsible of me not to remind you how these substances might have a negative effect, particularly for someone with your . . . sensitivities."

"You mean, someone as mental as me."

"That's not the term I'd use. But let's get back to this hotel room. It was late, you were alone. What happened?"

I shoved my hands under my armpits, feeling suddenly cold.

"Luke?"

I shifted uncomfortably in the chair. I wished I'd been reclining on a sofa because then I wouldn't be facing him.

"I looked down at my hand, and there was a baby curled up in it. Tiny. It fitted in my palm, wriggling around, crawling up my fingers."

"A human baby? It couldn't have been a mouse, for instance?"

I stared at him. "No, it wasn't a mouse, it was a baby person. It had arms and legs, and its mouth was screaming."

"In pain? Could you hear the screaming?"

I thought about it. "No, I couldn't hear it, but I could see it. And yes, it was in pain. I was wide-awake. I wasn't asleep. I definitely wasn't asleep."

"Okay. Now you know, Luke, don't you, that it's not possible for human babies to be so small?"

"What I know is that you don't believe me. *What I know* is that what I saw was not possible. *What I know* is that I saw it. I still see it, regularly."

"I believe that *you* believe you see it, Luke. How did you feel about it, the first time?"

"Nervous. Protective."

"How do you think it got there?"

I winced, because the next part of the story made me sound even more deranged.

"The old woman put it there."

"The woman from your nightmares, yes? How do you know she put it there? Did you see her?"

"The old woman was sitting in the corner of the room. She told me to open my hand. And then she disappeared. I never saw her again. And she'd told me she was going to give me a gift, a few nights earlier."

"In your dreams?"

"Yes."

"Okay, let's concentrate on the baby. You said you felt protective of it. Did you feel like it was your baby?"

"I don't know. But I didn't want it to get hurt."

"Who would hurt it?"

"Me."

I was in my final week in the psych unit and was needed back on the road. I felt calmer by then. The meds had worked their magic, and I wondered yet again why I'd stopped taking them. When I was being good, I could perform and not embarrass myself, and I could not figure out why I had let things get so out of control. When I was myself, I knew there was no baby, there was no woman in the woods, nobody was trying to kill me. This time Sean had asked my brother Brian to act as my "minder." The previous minders, drivers and security guards, had been easily persuaded with cash or groupies to source the drugs or alcohol that I wanted, or to sneak me into Mayfair clubs. They weren't smart enough, however, to outwit the tabloids, who sent their reporters in fishnet stockings and thigh-high skirts and carrying their tiny digital cameras to catch me snorting cocaine in a brothel. My clean-cut boyish image was long gone.

At twenty-six, I was too old to be a wild child. I was fed up with singing the same songs night after night after night. I was so bored of all the pointless key changes going into the last chorus to make the song last three and a half minutes. They told me I had to replicate the radio sound. I was not allowed to experiment with my own music. I was jaded by hotel rooms and tour buses, late nights and fast food, quick fucks with strangers in dressing rooms. I was tired, really tired.

Mum came to visit with Will. Neither of them wanted to be there. I could tell. Perhaps they'd made an "I'll go if you go" pact. Will brought a cake that Susan had made for me. Coffee and walnut. I used to love that cake. I always liked Susan.

Mum asked if we could go and sit in the garden because the "nut-ters" made her nervous. Will laughed, and I led them out to the smoking courtyard. Everyone in the psych unit smoked. There wasn't a lot else to do. There were only two other nutters out there at this time, but both were self-contained, one calmly muttering to himself, the other staring at the sky in a trance. I was in way better shape than either of them, thank God.

"What's the food like?" asked Will.

"It's okay, I guess." My taste buds had disappeared two years ago, overnight. I got no pleasure from food, had to be reminded to eat all the time because otherwise I would forget. My weight loss was "a concern" for the record company. I needed to look healthy, not scrawny.

"You were always such a picky eater," said Mum, "when you were a boy."

"That was Brian, Mum. Luke always ate everything," Will interrupted.

"Oh you know, I think you're right. It was Brian. Nothing on his plate could touch anything else, and he wouldn't eat anything green except peas."

"So, I was a good eater, then?" I asked Mum.

"I can barely remember—I suppose you must have been."

Will put his hands on the wrought iron table. "So, back on tour in six weeks, Luke. Looking forward to it?"

I shrugged. "Yeah."

"Because, I mean, pop careers don't last forever. You have to be practical. If I'm honest, you're lucky you've lasted as long as you have. And I wouldn't worry about that tabloid shit. There's no such thing as bad publicity. I mean, people will buy tickets to your gigs just to see what state you're in. It's all box office at the end of the day." This was Will being kind.

"Brian's going to be my personal assistant. Sean thinks it's a good idea to have a family member with me, a stabilizing influence."

Mum laughed. "Good for Brian, that's a promotion for him rather than selling your overpriced T-shirts and CDs at the shows."

Will was annoyed. "What, so Brian is going to be paid more just to hand you a towel and show you where your dressing room is? For fuck's sake!"

Even though Will had just produced his first film, he always resented it when Brian got anything that Will didn't think he'd earned. He often referred to Brian as a loser and a waster. He'd flipped when I told him I'd put Brian on the payroll after Paris two years earlier.

"It makes sense," I said.

"Yeah, to you. Was this his idea?"

"No, Sean suggested it. It's good."

"You know," said Mum, "in the beginning, I blamed Sean for"—she waved her hand toward me—"but he's the only person who'll ever give me a straight answer these days about what's going on when you disappear for months on end without contacting me." She smiled. "It's your illness, isn't it? We can't blame anyone else for that. Your father had an aunt that got hit by a train, and everyone knew it wasn't an accident, though we all pretended it was. So there's a bit of madness on his side of the family. You wouldn't do anything like that, would you, Luke? Disgrace the family like that? I don't think I'd be able to cope with the shame. Promise me, Luke, you'd never do anything like that?"

Will looked both disgusted and horrified, as if she had placed a turd on the table between us.

"Mum! You can't say things like that!"

"Why not? Everyone's thinking it. Every time you have one of your episodes, Luke, we all wonder, is this the time he's going to finish it completely? We're worried sick, and I'm fed up not talking about it. If people were more honest, there'd be fewer suicides in this country. Everything always being brushed under the carpet. I'm sick of it."

"Mum, I'm well now, and I'm leaving here on Thursday to go back into rehearsals for the tour. I'm on my meds, and I feel stronger than I have in a long time. Something is wrong with me. I have a disease called manic depression, or neurosis, or paranoid schizophrenia, or maybe something else entirely, with a new name they'll come up with next year. I don't know how it's going to affect me. The last thing I want to do is to die, and that's part of the reason Brian is going to be by my side every step of the way. He'll make sure I stay on the meds and off the other drugs."

"Brian! He's such a good boy!" said Mum.

Will gripped my shoulder as they were leaving. "Stay in touch, then," he said.

I hugged Mum and she let me, for a moment. "Keep it up," she said, and I felt good. I couldn't remember us ever hugging before.

Chapter 21

1978

It was William's tenth birthday, and he was allowed to have a party. I had prayed that year that I might have a party for my first Holy Communion, but we just had a family lunch with Auntie Peggy, Uncle Dan, and Aunt Judy, and cake. I realized it was selfish to pray for things I wanted for myself, so I prayed that William would have one. After all, a party is for everyone, not just the birthday boy. We'd never had parties in our house before that. Mum said it was too small for "marauding hordes." We usually went to Teddy's Ice Cream on our birthdays and then out for dinner to a café. Our house wasn't small, and it certainly wasn't too small for my parents' parties where there'd be thirty grown-ups.

We were sent to bed early on those nights, but often we'd be woken by the laughing and singing and piano playing. One time, a drunk woman fell into the bedroom I shared with Brian and started to hug and kiss us. I didn't know what to do, but Brian went down and fetched my dad, who appeared and steered the woman toward the upstairs bathroom.

Boys in my class pestered me about not having birthday parties. I was invited to their parties, and they couldn't understand why I wasn't returning the invites. I told them the truth. Mum doesn't like boys my age.

Some of them suggested my mother was too ugly to be seen, or too fat to get out of bed, or that she was locked up in the attic because she was crazy.

It was easy to disprove these stories because everyone knew well that Mum was a famous singer and traveled nationwide regularly, giving concerts. Dad said the boys in my class were jealous because my mother was a celebrity. They desperately wanted to see what a famous person's house looked like. Eamon Patterson's dad was a newsreader, but everyone said his house was ordinary.

Because Mum always appeared in long and glamorous dresses on-stage and on television, with teased hair and sparkling jewelry, I think they expected a mansion. Our house wasn't exactly that, but it was bigger than the other boys' houses. We had five bedrooms. And the house wasn't attached at one side to another house like the other ones on our road. Mum and Dad shared one bedroom, Brian and I shared another, and William had a room of his own. Mum said Brian could have a room of his own if he wanted, but I didn't want to be on my own, so Brian always shared with me.

The biggest room upstairs after Mum and Dad's was always referred to as "the dressing room." It contained racks and racks of Mum's dresses, a freestanding full-length mirror, a large chest of drawers containing shoes and jewelry and belts and scarves, and a long dressing table scattered with pots of lotions, potions, lipsticks, hair rollers, and a weird-looking instrument for curling eyelashes. We used to play in there sometimes when Mum was away or tied up on the phone. But woe betide us if we were caught. The spare bedroom had a piano in it, and Mum did her vocal exercises there every day.

For William's party, Mum and Dad had pulled out all the stops. They had decided that William's friends were old enough. They greeted all seven boys, and William showed off his new tape recorder. The boys ran through the house and did one circuit of the garden with Dad and a rugby ball, but it was freezing and Mum was frantic that William would dirty the white cricket sweater she'd bought specially, even though none of us played or had any interest in cricket. A hired magician arrived to put on a show. He made a cake out of a bunch of flowers and did tricks with cards. We were all disappointed at the end when he hadn't made a rabbit appear out of a hat or cut a lady in half.

Then we had the party food in the dining room: cocktail sausages, triangular sandwiches, and chocolate Rice Krispie cakes. A boy sitting beside me, Graham, asked me if I was a neighbor. I was confused for a moment.

"No," I said, "I'm William's brother Luke, and"—pointing to Brian—"that's our other brother, Brian."

Graham nudged the boys on the other side of him. "Here, these guys are William's brothers!"

A boy on his left shouted over with certainty, "William hasn't got brothers, have you, William?"

The room went silent for a moment. Mum was standing behind William at the head of the table. "William!" she said. "Haven't you told your friends about Luke and Brian?"

William ignored the question, threw a handful of Smarties in the air, and caught one in his mouth. The others started doing the same thing while Mum asked again, "Why haven't you ever mentioned your brothers?"

William always walked to school separately from Brian and me. He never waited for us, always running to catch up with his real friends. William's friends knew us from school, but they had no idea we were related to William.

Later, after the cleanup, Dad declared we were not having any more parties until we were fifteen and no longer acted like savages. Mum laughed at him and patted William on the head. "Happy birthday, son," she said, and we listened to "Mull of Kintyre" again on the tape recorder.

That night, after we had all knelt and said our prayers, I said to Dad, "We're all brothers, aren't we, Dad?"

Dad lifted me up onto his shoulders. "You sure are, boys, you sure are." William pretended not to hear and swung the rosary beads over his head like a lasso.

Chapter 22

1994

I was lonely. When I was on tour, I was surrounded by people, security, assistants, accountants, managers, and girls, but when the merry-go-round stopped and I had to get off and go home to my big empty house, I realized there wasn't really anyone I could call. Besides the fact I don't like talking on the phone (I can never imagine the person on the other end), the many people who wanted to be in my life didn't actually want to spend time with me. I could buy drugs from them or I could share drugs with them, I could have sex with them or I could get them into the Library Bar in Lillie's or the VIP area of Renards, but they didn't want to have conversations with me. They pretended to, but nobody actually listened. And even if they did, how could I ever tell them about the baby that followed me around everywhere, the old woman who had haunted me day and night and then vanished?

My house was huge, but I was away so much that it never felt like a real home. There wasn't a lot of furniture. There was a state-of-the-art sound system and loads of giant beanbags, and the mantelpieces were strewn with souvenirs. But I couldn't always get the central heating to work. I'd chopped up some of the dining room chairs to use as firewood. I didn't open my mail often because a lot of it was technical stuff about pensions from my increasingly impatient accountant or fan mail from little girls who hadn't learned how to do joined-up writing yet. It depressed me that these children looked to me as their hero, their idol, when I knew I had nothing to offer anyone. I was a pop star with the right looks, writing predictably cheesy tunes, who could fill stadiums and arenas all over Europe, but I was scared and lonely.

I was drinking most days, enough so that I would crash out and not dream of anything. I rarely answered the door, because too often my callers were fans who didn't know what to say to me, but stood on the doorstep, openmouthed. I didn't know what to say to them either. Sometimes I just signed their autographs, and they went away. Other times, they wanted to come in and hang out, but I was too embarrassed by the state of my home. I knew the life I was living was unhealthy. I knew I needed to leave the house and interact with the world.

Will lived in a small studio a few streets away from mine. I don't know why he didn't get a bigger place, especially now that he and Susan had a child of their own. They had a real live baby, and I wasn't so crazy that I couldn't tell the difference between her and my tiny imaginary baby. But I knew that when other people were in the room, my tiny baby disappeared, so to get away from it, I used to go to Will's house regularly. I'd eat with him and Susan and watch TV. They'd ask me questions, but I was never in the mood for much conversation. Will started to hassle me about getting on board with some film project, but I had no interest in it. Then, after a few months, he told me not to visit anymore. I didn't understand what I'd done wrong, but I guess Mum was right all along, and I had an annoying personality. By the end of the summer, I had to go back into the studio to record some new songs for the highly anticipated third album. Sean came over to tell me because I'd stopped answering the phone. We'd been on a six-month break after two years of constant touring. He looked really surprised when I let him in.

"Jesus, Luke, have you been taking care of yourself? Christ, look at this house! Don't you have a cleaner? You need to take a shower, man. And shave. Hillbilly is not the look that Sony wants for you."

Sean was my only friend and my manager, but even he had insisted we take a proper break from each other during our hiatus. He would handle anything urgent, and he told me I should just rest and recuperate.

"Didn't you take a holiday? Go anywhere?"

I tried to explain that having been away for most of the previous two years, I just wanted to be home. I tried not to cry.

"Have you been eating? Luke, I think you need professional help."

Sean brought me to a psychiatrist. The first in a long line, as it turned out. I was diagnosed with depression and sent on my way with a prescription. It was a relief to know there was a reason for the nothingness I felt, the lethargy and lack of concentration. The pills definitely helped. Within a few weeks, I felt better and got busy. I cut back on the drinking and smoking hash. The baby disappeared. My nightmares became far less frequent. We recorded the new album. This time we had a full symphony orchestra behind us for the last few days of recording, so everything was on a much bigger scale. The days in the studio to prepare for this were long, but I liked the swell of music that turned bland pop songs into something magnificent. This was the album Sean said was going to break out in America. We were excited and optimistic.

In mid-December, the record company threw us a big party in the Clarence Hotel. It was one hell of a bash. Every celebrity turned up, all home for Christmas: actors, musicians, painters, poets, dancers. Glitter fell from the ceiling, and the champagne flowed. I was being sensible about the booze, though I was slightly edgy with all these people around. Sean was pretty drunk, but he noticed my discomfort. He came over and said, "It's okay, Luke, you can let your hair down tonight. You've earned it!" He poured champagne from a bottle into a pint glass and passed it to me.

I had such a good time that night that I continued partying for the next few days. I realized I'd skipped my meds, but I was feeling great and I was sure they'd fixed me by now.

There were messages on my answering machine from Brian and Will about Christmas Day. Where was I going to be? Would I like to come to Will's for my dinner? I remembered being barred from his house earlier in the year. I thought I should apologize to him. I realized I'd been a nuisance, going to his house every day like that. I decided to buy him a really extravagant, meaningful gift, but I was daunted by the Christmas shopping crowds, and then I had some inspiration. I'd make him a gift with my bare hands. I'd make a doll's house for his kid. On one of the days previously, I'd bought a couple of grams of coke, and I reckoned I'd need it to help me with the project.

I wasn't sure what wood to use. I thought it should be sturdy but thin so that it wouldn't be too heavy. I ventured out on a mission to buy all the materials I would need for the construction. I had a clear picture of it in my mind. The guy in the hardware shop recognized me. He was really helpful and said I should make it from plywood. He even gave me free sample paint pots to use to paint it with. And he gave me large wooden pegs that I could use to carve doll figures if I wanted. I felt a rush of energy as I set about the work. I'm not sure how long it took, but I don't think I went to bed for four nights. I had to start again three times because I got impatient sawing the wood and cut it wrong and ended up accidentally sawing through the dining room table.

When I was finished with the house, I decided to carve the pegs into a Mummy, a Daddy, and a little girl. I started with the little girl, but my enthusiasm turned to horror when I realized the tiny figure I had carved was the baby, and the baby was alive and silently screaming at me again.

I couldn't bear it. I tried to calm it down. I wrapped it in cotton wool and stroked it, but I could still see the tiny face twisting in pain.

I rang the psychiatrist but got a recorded message saying that his office would be reopening on the seventh of January after the Christmas break.

I didn't want to be left alone with the baby. I rang Sean, but he didn't answer. I couldn't ring Brian because he was staying at Mum's, and we weren't allowed to ring her house after 9:00 p.m.

I looked at the clock. What day was it? The early hours of December 26. I had missed Christmas Day. I remembered I'd been supposed to go to Will's for dinner. I'd been building the doll's house for his kid. I decided the only thing to do was to put the baby into the doll's house and bring it to Will's. He and Susan knew how to look after babies.

I delivered the gift in the middle of the night. I don't think Will was pleased to see me. I went home then and smoked enough blem to knock me out. When I woke up two days later, the tiny baby was next to my head on the pillow. As it crawled into the nook of my elbow, I could see the hairs on my arm rise.

Chapter 23

1979

A week before my ninth birthday, my mum sang at the Pope's Mass. Nobody was more excited about this than me. She was to sing "Ave Maria," and that was my favorite song. She couldn't get it confirmed, but it was likely she might even get to meet the Pope, that he might touch her head and pray for her. Through that blessing, I knew she would finally love me truly and forever. And better than that, if the Pope touched Mum and blessed the holy water I'd bought her for her birthday, we might be able to save Paul's soul.

Paul was my cousin, and Brian's best friend. He was always nice to me. He thought I was funny and interesting. He used to quiz me about the lives of all the saints because I knew them all by heart. He speculated that Elvis Presley was going to be a saint, but I knew Elvis was never going to be a candidate. I liked him in his films, but I don't think any saints ever went around in sports cars, kissing girls in hula skirts and wearing tight trousers. But Paul used to joke with me about all the miracles Elvis performed. For example, he could make girls scream just by waving his hand at them. I patiently explained to Paul that miracles had to be for good things, and I didn't think screaming girls qualified.

But in recent months, Paul had grown even more pale and quiet. He was in the hospital a lot these days, and even when we went to visit him, he often didn't wake up. William would eat his jelly and ice cream when nobody was looking. I told William that was a sin, but William never cared about sins. He went smoking behind the church with his friend Steve when they were supposed to be at confession, so I prayed for them too.

One day I visited with Mum on my own. It was the end of the summer holidays. And I asked Mum how Paul was going to go to school in bed. Mum looked at me, and I could tell she was cross because the two lines between her eyes deepened. "Paul won't be going back to school, Luke. Don't be so stupid."

"What do you mean?"

She heaved a deep sigh. "Paul is dying. He's not going anywhere."

I knew he'd been sick and I knew he'd been getting worse, but I thought my prayers were worth something. Father Benedict had always said that if we truly believed, God would answer our prayers. And I truly believed.

"But he can't be," I said. "I've prayed about it."

"Don't be so bloody naive. You're eight years old—"

"I'm eight and three-quarters," I said.

"You're old enough to know about death and dying. There's cancerous poison in his blood. It's called leukemia. There's no hope for him. It's very sad."

I was silent for a while. When we turned into the hospital car park, I said, "But he'll go straight to heaven, won't he, Mum? He won't have to wait in purgatory, will he?"

"I haven't a clue," she said as she hauled her bag wearily out of the car.

When we saw Paul, he was sitting up. He was having a good day. There were dark circles around his eyes. I was used to seeing him without hair, but his parents, Uncle Dan and Aunt Judy, bought him new hats every week. His favorite one was the knitted Viking helmet that Auntie Peggy had made him, even though Auntie Peggy was Mum's sister and Uncle Dan was Dad's brother. Auntie Peggy was just kind like that, to everyone.

Paul was laughing at a joke book someone had given him. He started trying out all these knock-knock jokes on me. Mum and Aunt Judy went to the hospital café and left us to chat for a while. I know he'd have preferred it if Brian was there and not me, but he didn't let it show.

"Will we say a prayer?" I offered.

"If you want."

"We should say a prayer that you go to heaven when you die."

"Die? What do you mean?"

I knew I'd said the wrong thing, and while my cheeks grew red, I tried to backtrack a little.

"In case. I mean, if you did, wouldn't you want to go to heaven?"

His eyes widened in his pale white face. "Did you hear something? Did my mum tell you I was dying?"

"No!" I could say it truthfully.

He turned back to his book and started reading knock-knock jokes out loud again. I realized he was scared. I could feel it through my skin. I was scared too. What would happen if he didn't get into heaven? I took out the rosary beads I always kept in my pocket and waved them over him. He ignored me and started laughing harder at the jokes in his book, but the laughter wasn't real. It was forced and fake.

After that day, I wasn't allowed to visit Paul again. Aunt Judy told Mum she thought I was too young. Mum asked if I'd said anything to upset Paul that day. I didn't tell her a lie exactly, just that I'd offered to pray with him.

"Prayers aren't always answered," she said. She was saying the opposite of Father Benedict, and I wasn't sure who to believe.

I asked Dad about Paul dying.

"Did your mother tell you that? She shouldn't have mentioned anything." He lifted me up onto his lap, even though I was way too old for that.

"Sometimes, Luke, people die, and there's nothing we can do about it."

"Even children?"

"Yes, son."

"Is it God's will that makes children die?"

"I suppose it must be."

"But why? And why Paul? He's really nice. Does that mean I'll die? Or Brian or William?"

"No, it's a very rare thing for a child to die. You don't need to worry about you or your brothers."

"But if I prayed really, really hard, could I pray away the poison? The poison in his blood?"

"It's not for us to choose who lives or dies," said Dad, "but let's not mention that Paul is dying to the others, okay? It's not something I want any of you to be thinking about."

That night, I heard Mum and Dad arguing. Dad said that Mum shouldn't have told me about Paul. But later, in bed, I thought maybe Mum had told me for a reason. Maybe God had chosen me to save Paul from eternal damnation.

In school that week, when we were making welcome banners for the Pope, it all fell into place. I realized I was on an actual mission from God. I constantly badgered Mum about the arrangements for when she'd sing for the Pope. Was it before the Mass or during it? Would she definitely meet him? Would she ask him to bless the holy water? Would she really believe it while he was blessing it? Because that was very important. She was vague about the details. Her schedule for the day was top secret and wouldn't be confirmed until the last minute because the Pope was a head of state, and there were big security issues about protecting him. Dad and the rest of us had good tickets because of Mum. One million of the three million people in Ireland were attending this event in the Phoenix Park, and others from all over the world were coming to see the Pope. Every window had a papal flag flying from it, and most streets were decorated in yellow-and-white bunting. People had cleaned up the fronts of their houses and swept their doorways so that the Pope wouldn't think we were dirty. Priests and nuns circled our schools, teaching us new prayers and new hymns. I was guilty of the sin of pride because I felt that finally the rest of my class and my neighborhood was catching up with me in my belief. I went to confession to tell Father Benedict, but he said it was okay and that believing was something to be proud of. Sometimes it was really hard to keep track of all the rules.

As the most religious boy in the school, I was chosen to come and have a special tea with the archbishop when he visited the school to make sure we were ready to see the Pope. I sat in a room with him and some other priests and a few nuns clucking around him, serving tea and fancy cakes. I was too intimidated and nervous to swallow any of the cakes. Eventually, when the archbishop was leaving, Father Benedict said to him, "Now, Your Grace, you haven't met Luke Drumm yet, the best boy in the school. We are pretty sure he's heading for a vocation. A devout boy, I can assure you. His mother is going to be singing for His Holiness at the Mass next week."

The tall man stooped down and shook my hand. "And who is your mother?" he said.

"Melissa Craig," I said, "she's a singer and actress."

The archbishop turned to Father Benedict and said, "That show-girl?" He sniffed. "I note she didn't take her husband's name. I voted against her personally, but she seems to be popular." And then he swept out of the room, followed by his black flock.

I didn't like the archbishop, but I had to put those feelings out of my head and find love in my heart for the task ahead.

On the day of the Mass, Dad served breakfast at 5:00 a.m. I hadn't slept at all because of the excitement. I spent most of the night on my knees, praying. Mum was collected by a state car with a papal flag insignia on the door. She was dressed demurely in a white dress topped with a yellow cardigan and white gloves. She had a white mantilla around her neck to cover her hair and face during the Mass. She carried the handbag in which I had made sure to put the bottle of holy water. I made her promise to get it blessed, and she swore she would if it was at all possible. I thought maybe just the fact that the holy water would be so close to the Pope might be enough to make it miraculous.

The whole neighborhood came out to wave her off. Everyone was in a good mood, laughing and chatting to one another over garden walls and fences about what they were bringing in their picnic baskets, and which area of the park they had been designated to sit. Some of them were jealous of us because we had seats near the front. Everyone else would be corralled into what looked like sheep pens across the vast expanse of the park in front of the brand-new papal cross. We had all watched it on the news the evening before. But there was no special treatment for us about getting to the park. We took the bus like everybody else. It was so early. The buses were leaving at 6:00 a.m. On the way to the meeting point, a rat crossed the footpath right in front of us and disappeared into a drain. A lady behind us screamed when she saw it. I tried to interpret it as a sign. I decided it was telling me that all God's creatures had a place on the earth, and I silently prayed for the rat. The bus driver was grumpy and kept shouting at all of us to sit down and move to the back to make sure everyone got on. I stood up to let an old man sit down, and Dad did the same. At the next stop, Dad slapped Brian's and William's legs to make them stand up for old people too. The mood was festive. The luggage rack was heaving with picnic baskets, and you could smell egg sandwiches or early-morning farts down the length of the bus.

When we got off, we had a mile's walk ahead of us. We passed the front of the zoo, and I wondered if the animals in there were excited, too, if they could hear the noise and singing outside. In our droves, we walked and walked, past stalls and prams selling chocolate, flags, sodas, holy statues, posters of the Pope, and lots of other memorabilia.

People in groups were singing hymns with guitars and recorders and any instrument they could carry. It was not yet 8:00 a.m. As we got closer, the crowd branched into different snakes as they queued up at their various entrances. Dad had wanted us all to bring jackets and rainwear in case of a change in the weather, but that morning I had squeezed into the white shorts I'd worn for my first Holy Communion a year earlier—they had been William's and Brian's previously, and they were uncomfortably tight—but Dad insisted I had to wear trousers: "The Pope isn't here for a fashion show, Luke." I had my communion rosette pinned to my chest and my rosary beads in my pocket.

The entrance we were guided through after our tickets were checked was an executive one, and Dad recognized ministers and judges and other VIPs. William and Brian were complaining about the long walk as we were led into a big tent. They wanted to have the picnic now, but we weren't supposed to eat until after the Mass. I was pretty sure we shouldn't have had breakfast, but a priest on the television had said people should eat breakfast that morning because the Mass wasn't happening till eleven thirty, and some people had been up since 2:00 a.m. to get there, so there was a special dispensation for people to eat breakfast before communion. I didn't like it when they changed the rules, so although I did eat, I only had dry bread and milk and ignored the smell of bacon and sausages that my brothers savaged with delight.

Dad said they could have sandwiches, but I managed just to have some tea from the flask. It would only be a few hours more. It wasn't anything like Jesus carrying a cross for miles. We stood around among the dignitaries until we were told to take our seats outside. Some people told us the Pope had landed at Dublin Airport where he'd made a speech and met our president. He was now to be helicoptered into the Phoenix Park. I was in such a grip of excitement about spotting the helicopter that I forgot about Mum singing. Soon, a million of us were standing up, cheering and clapping as the helicopter circled the park overhead, and I could tell that even Brian and William were enraptured. I sat up on Dad's shoulders, and all I could see was joy for miles around me. I was perfectly sure this was a day when miracles could happen.

Aunt Judy and Uncle Dan couldn't come to the Pope's Mass because they were with Paul in the hospital. It was my responsibility on September 29, 1979, to use all the holiness inside me and to spread love everywhere in order to make sure Paul went to heaven.

As the Mass started, we all got onto our knees. I ignored the pangs of hunger and kept my eyes on the tiny white dot in the distance that was Pope John Paul II. I tried to communicate with him through my mind. Twice, he looked over in my direction, and I was sure he was looking for me, at me. I was sure he knew. Then my mum walked to the side of the stage, genuflected in the direction of the cross, and then again at the Pope. I felt like I would explode with pride. She never sang more beautifully than she did that day, and if it's not blasphemous to say it, she looked and behaved like a goddess, beautiful and powerful, yet ladylike. I looked over at Dad and my brothers, and we were all four proud of how astonishingly dignified she was. At the end of the song, she bowed theatrically and then stood uncertainly, and I almost died of mortification, because I knew she expected applause, even though this was a *Mass* and nobody applauded at Masses. I waited breathlessly to see if the Pope was going to come over to her and bless her. He didn't. A priest had to come and lead her away from the microphone. Dad gripped my shoulder to reassure me. "Wasn't your mam just beautiful?" he whispered. And she was. I was overwhelmed by the emotions running through me. I lost concentration and somehow stopped focusing on the Pope.

I woke up to the sounds of cheering and clapping. I was slumped over my father's shoulder. I had slept through the Mass. The Pope was now driving through the crowd in his Popemobile. I was consumed by fear and shock. "Why didn't you wake me?" I screamed at my father and pummeled his head. I scrambled down to the ground and ran then, ran toward where the crowd was the noisiest, knowing that the Pope would be at the center of the cheering. I ran as though Paul's soul depended on it, and it did. I ran through crowds and barriers and climbed over deck chairs and under wire fences. I had to apologize to the Pope for falling asleep. I had to beg him not to take it out on Paul. Security men grabbed me, and I screamed and kicked and bit them, until one of them sat on my legs. I could hear the cheers dying down, and then I heard the sound of the helicopter, and I knew the Pope was leaving, and I knew Paul would die and might be stuck in purgatory forever. I sobbed uncontrollably. I was carried to a lost children's tent, and it was there that Dad found me an hour later. By that stage, I couldn't speak. I couldn't tell anyone what my deal with God had been. It was between me and Him.

On the bus home, Dad said that Mum might have met the Pope backstage, and although I knew it was unlikely, I felt a glimmer of hope that maybe the bottle of holy water in her bag had been blessed. Mum wouldn't arrive home until much later because she was invited to a reception for all the contributors at the Mass. I was frustrated that there was no way we could phone her to find out.

When we got in the front door, our phone was ringing. Dad answered it. I was about to go into the kitchen, when I heard him say, "Oh no, Dan, I'm so sorry," and Dad's voice cracked, and I knew that Paul was dead. William and Brian were stunned. Brian started to cry, and then he threw up on the living room floor. "I could have saved him!" I screamed at my dad. "Why did you let me sleep through the Mass? I could have saved his soul." William punched me in the stomach and went outside. I was winded. I watched him through the window, gripping on to the fence with white knuckles, trying not to cry. Dad was struggling to maintain order, scooping up handfuls of Brian's sick with rubber gloves and a basin, but both he and Brian were crying, Brian convulsively, heaving and shuddering. Dad later said that Brian was in shock.

It was no shock to me. I had known how sick Paul was. I had known he was going to die. Mum came home, again expecting applause, to be greeted by a house in mourning. She was quietly devastated, too, I think.

"Did you even try to get him to bless the holy water, Mum?"

"I did, Luke," she told me. "But Paul was going to die, no matter what. You couldn't have saved him."

None of them understood. I knew I couldn't save Paul's life. I was trying to save his soul.

The next day, there was a photo of Mum standing beside the Pope on the front page of the *Irish Press*. I drank the blessed bottle of holy water, but afterward I realized how selfish it was: I should have saved it for the sick and dying.

Chapter 24

2010

I was doing okay in 2010 up until that funeral. I had been taking my meds and going to my psych appointments. I still partied a bit and drank too much, but it was a bottle of wine a night instead of a bottle of vodka. My life was not settled, but it was less chaotic. I'm not sure how I spent my days. I slept a lot. I would go through phases of manic musical interest and other phases of complete apathy for any life or activity.

Brian rang me regularly enough to remind me of things like Mum's birthday, Daisy's Junior Cert exams, any gig offers, etc. A documentary maker wanted me to take part in a "where are they now?" TV special about people who had once been famous but had since disappeared into obscurity. I didn't want to do it, but Brian insisted he could get a good offer out of them. I knew they only wanted to make a fool of me and that all the tabloid stuff would be dragged up again. I argued with him a bit, but he wasn't listening and said he'd try and negotiate a higher fee. Before he rang off, he casually mentioned that he was going to a funeral the next morning, for his friend Cillian Gogan's dad.

My blood ran cold at the mention of his name. "Does Mum know he's dead?"

"I don't know yet. I was about to ring her."

"Don't worry about it, I'll call around. I'll tell her."

"Yeah? Be subtle, will you? I think her and Dad used to be really close to the Gogans back when Dad was alive. Don't get pissed."

"I won't."

"Tell her I'll pick her up at nine thirty for the funeral."

"It's okay, I'll take her."

"Sorry?"

"I'll take her to the funeral. I'm not a total imbecile, Brian, I can drive my mother to a church."

"But why do you want to go?"

"I need to be there for Mum."

I sensed the hesitation. He was going to argue but decided not to. "Okay then. See you in the morning. Sober, right?"

"Yes."

After I hung up, I had a glass of wine and got dressed in my usual hoodie, jeans, and baseball cap. My beard and hair were long, and I knew Mum didn't approve of this look, but it wouldn't matter today. Because today I was going to tell her that her rapist was dead, and she would be happy.

I rarely saw Mum on my own. I knew she was uncomfortable around me. She didn't trust my outbursts, my unpredictable mood swings. I knew I was a huge disappointment to her. She had been right about me all along. But I knew her secrets. She hadn't told anyone else about that rape, and I knew it must still affect her. I knew I had to be the one to tell her about Jack's death. I was the only one who could comfort her. We didn't like each other much, but because of the circumstances, I felt sorry for her, and maybe this could help her soften toward me. She was sixty-four years old, she had been widowed for twenty-five years, and it struck me now that losing my father just a year after her assault must have been difficult. A woman I'd been seeing the year before had worked at the Rape Crisis Center. She had told me harrowing stories of the abuse men and women had been put through; the church scandals of the previous two decades had opened the floodgates in terms of people coming forward and talking about their experiences. I had never told that girl about my mother, or why my mother had chosen to tell me, a thirteen-year-old boy at the time.

When I was dressed, I had another glass of wine, just to steady myself for what might be a difficult conversation.

"Luke, hello, what are you doing here?" said Mum, peering behind me on her doorstep.

"Oh, you know, just visiting. It's been a while."

"Of course, it's dinnertime and you're hungry."

"Is it?" I didn't wear a watch or carry a phone. Mum said it was "an affectation" of mine.

"Come in. I've just eaten, but I can make you a sandwich, if you like." The offer was begrudging.

"It's okay, I've eaten," I lied.

The television was on. I'd interrupted *EastEnders*. "Can you just shush until this is over? Put the kettle on, will you?" she said.

I saw there was an open bottle of wine on the table beside her with a half-filled glass. I looked at it, looked at her.

"Fine then, get yourself a glass from the kitchen." When I returned, the television was turned up louder. I stared at the drab and forlorn characters with their cockney vowels and garish lipstick. Inevitably, a fight broke out in the pub toward the end of the episode, and the camera focused on a young girl, a troubled look on her face, who slipped out of the door during the melee before the credits rolled. I filled Mum's glass and mine to the brim.

Mum lifted the remote control and lowered the volume.

"So. What news?"

I told her about the documentary offer Brian was keen for me to accept. I was relieved that she sided with me. "You'll do no such thing. They'll only drag me into it as if *I'm* some has-been. I'll tell Brian," she declared. Her career had recently been resurrected thanks to some stage show she'd been in, and she didn't want me ruining anything for her.

"Thanks, Mum."

"Are you ever going to get that hair cut? Or shave?"

I shrugged.

"Or get a job? Your auntie Peggy is always asking me, and frankly, it's embarrassing to have to tell her that you're doing nothing day in, day out."

"I'm okay, Mum."

"Well, it's a waste of a life—"

I interrupted her. "Jack Gogan's dead."

She sat very still.

"Mum? Did you hear me?"

"Of course I heard you. I read it in this morning's paper."

"I was just wondering how you were feeling about it, that's all."

She started to flick through a magazine on the table in front of her. "Oh well, you know, I haven't seen him in years, since before your father died. I'm sorry for Ursula and the boys. I'm sure they're sad."

"Mum. I *know*."

"Know what?"

"Don't you remember? You told me. What Jack Gogan did to you."

She stood up quickly, went to the drinks cabinet, and took out another bottle of red, much to my relief. This was harder than I had thought it was going to be. She dug the corkscrew into the top of the bottle with surprising ferocity.

"What *are* you talking about?"

"He *raped* you. You told me."

"No."

"Mum—"

"You imagine things. You always have. I don't know where you got that idea. You can't just say things like that—"

"Mum, I remember everything you told me. It happened when you all went to Slane to see Bob Dylan."

"How would you know what happened at Slane? You weren't even there!"

"Because you *told* me. I know you didn't make it up."

"Stop! Stop it." My mother stood up, agitated. "*You* made it up. I think you should leave."

"Mum! I'm not attacking you, I just thought his death would bring up some bad memories for you. I wanted to tell you that it's not too late to get counseling. I know a woman who could help. You don't have to go to the funeral tomorrow—"

"What? I'm not going to the funeral!"

"Brian expected that you would want to go, because you and Dad used to be such good friends with Jack and Ursula, and Brian is friends with Cillian."

She clutched at her neck. "I can't go to the funeral!"

"I know, Mum, I understand. Brian was going to collect you."

"I'm not going." She sat down again and put her head in her hands.

"You don't have to." I poured myself another glass of wine and topped her up. She grabbed the glass out of my hand, spilling merlot over her perfectly beige carpet.

"Shut up! You don't know anything. Get out! Get out of this house, you . . . you loser."

She pushed me away, and when I didn't move fast enough, she slapped at my head.

"Mum, please, I only wanted—"

"You only wanted to come and upset me and drink my wine. You are not welcome in my house. Do you understand? Take your dirty lies and leave right now."

I drove to a pub and got absolutely smashed. It finally dawned on me that I might be the product of a rape. Why else would Mum hate me so much? Who was my father? She would never tell me. I had no way of finding out, but it all made sense in my head. Why else would she have told a thirteen-year-old boy about what had happened? The baby was running up and down my arms now, awakened and exhilarated by the argument and the aggression. It danced across the table in front of me, sat on the lip of my glass. It told me that I was right all along. It told me that Jack Gogan had raped my mother and that maybe Slane hadn't been the first time it had happened to her. I couldn't rationalize why, but it was all my fault. I drank faster to try and shut it up.

At closing time, I bought some carryout booze. I abandoned the car and walked home. From there, I called an old acquaintance who turned up within ten minutes. He stayed for a while, saw there was nothing worth stealing from me, and left after charging me double the market value for the pills he supplied. The baby hovered in my peripheral vision, punching the air and playing a golden bugle, a malevolent cartoon character, terrifyingly real to me, although I knew, had been told, understood that this wasn't possible. After the second pill, the baby disappeared, but by then I was raving. I took my clothes off and danced, getting bored halfway through one song until I remembered another, trying to play counter melodies on the iPod and the record player at the same time, crashing into furniture, pulling down shelves.

I came to on the bathroom floor. I rubbed my eyes and looked down at my hands. There was blood on them. It seemed to be in my hair too. The clock said it was 9:15 a.m. The baby, sitting on the side of the bath, said I had to go to Jack Gogan's funeral to make sure the bastard was in the ground. I took the last pill.

I found my clothes on the floor and pulled them on, oblivious to their stink. I walked out onto the street. I couldn't find my car, presumed it was stolen again, and wished the thieves luck with a ten-year-old Fiat Panda. I walked the two miles to the church, running some of the distance, but then stopped, trying to identify the feeling in my stomach. It was hunger. Walking through St. Stephen's Green, I swiped bread out of the hands of children who were feeding ducks. Their parents came and led them away, afraid to confront me. I felt powerful and hyperalert now as I strode to the church, bent on revenge.

Mourners had gathered outside, and I shuffled among them, angling toward the church door, when I was pulled back by the shoulder. It was Brian.

"Jesus Christ, Luke, what happened to you? You have blood on your face! And where's Mum? Did you hurt her?"

The irony of his words sucker punched my funny bone, and I laughed. Was there ever anything as hilarious as the thought that I would hurt my mother, standing at the church where her rapist was about to be celebrated?

"He raped her!" I roared it at the top of my voice. "Jack Gogan raped my mother!" Brian grabbed me by the throat, but I shook him off and pushed through the crowd into the church, forcing mostly elderly people out of my way. Brian chased me, but he wasn't as ruthless with the old people as I was. The coffin was in situ at the top of the church, and the priest was tapping the microphone. I rushed to the altar and elbowed the priest aside. "You're all going to talk about how great he was, but he wasn't. He was a vile, disgusting man who needs to be exposed before he rots in hell." I could see Brian running up the aisle. He lurched toward me and headbutted me in the side, and I fell. I could hear people shouting, wails and screams, and I was dragged by several men out of the church. I think some of them were pallbearers, and this struck me as funny too. Pallbearers carrying me out of the church. Were they going to bury me now too?

I was held to the ground outside as the police were called. Brian crouched down beside me. "You are going to be locked up now, do you understand? I can't help you with this. Why do you make everything so much worse? Why did you say that shit about Cillian's dad raping Mum? You were supposed to bring her to the funeral!"

"I said it because it's true! Ask her!" I shouted before I was bundled into the back of a police car. I stayed silent then as I heard Brian discussing my "mental health issues" with the officers. The effects of the pill were beginning to wear off, and I was feeling queasy.

I don't recall most of this, and I have only other people's memories from which to reconstruct this incident. I remember when I got out of the psychiatric unit two weeks later that nobody spoke of Jack Gogan's funeral again, except I was forced to write to Jack's widow and tell her my claims at the funeral weren't true. Mum had denied the rape, even though William admitted privately to me and Brian that he'd known about it at the time. He said that was why Mum hadn't wanted to do that play about the rape victim. But now she was denying everything. My brothers declared that we should let Mum deal with it her way. My mother took out a restraining order against me. So that conversation was the last one I had with her.

Chapter 25

2003

I don't remember the address of the flat I was living in. It was either in Rathmines or Ranelagh, or perhaps I was living in both places. It's possible. I was back home in Dublin. I think the two flats must have been squats because I remember I had to get in through a back window in one place, and there was no hot running water. And in the other one, there were a few guys who stayed there, winos I suppose you'd call them, but I'd bring them cigarettes and booze, and they put up with me. But these places were temporary dwellings. Everything was chaotic. After New York, I'd been stable for a while, but I couldn't write music while I was on those meds. So when I felt well again, I cut down on them without telling my new psychiatrist, and then when I did see the psychiatrist, she kept trying to imply I was sexually abused as a child, most likely by my mother. Far from it, I told her: I'd been more or less ignored by my mother. She suggested I must have been so young that I didn't remember it. I stopped going to see her.

And then I stopped taking the meds altogether. I hung out with "friends" until they told me to leave, or to wash, or to contribute toward their bills, or not to smoke in their homes.

But I still had some income. Brian had sorted something with IMRO so that he paid income from airplay and public broadcast rights into my account every few months, but I blew through that money fairly quickly. There were some royalties from the record company, too, but they were dwindling. I wasn't selfish with the money. I took a homeless guy shopping in Brown Thomas once and spent eight hundred euros on a coat for him, but he begged me for the money instead of the coat, and we had a row about it and both got kicked out of the shop. People were pointing. "That's Luke Drumm," I heard them say. But I didn't care. I'd just been trying to help the guy. It was cold, and the coat was cashmere. I don't even remember what happened to it because I was so wasted.

Mum wouldn't let me into her house since the time I'd set fire to her dressing room a few months previously, and she bolted the door when she saw me coming. I shouted through the letter box and asked her if she had molested me when I was a baby. I could hear her screaming at me to go away, so I did, but not before throwing a brick through the front window. I knew the glass would fall onto the chair she sat on when watching TV.

Mental illness has its advantages. Not that I appreciated them at the time, but when people think you are crazy, it gives you license to do anything you want, when you want, and people put it down to your mental state. But even in moments of lucidity, I knew I could get away with outrageous behavior because it was what people had come to expect of me. I felt a certain freedom that I have never felt when well. My life had no boundaries. I could insult people to their faces instead of pretending I liked them. I miss that.

Some of the more muckraking journalists started to follow me, particularly in London, when I'd fly over for some imaginary meeting with record labels. At one stage, I'd convinced myself that EMI wanted me to record a duet with Frank Sinatra. I must have dreamed it, or maybe Brian had suggested I should have done it. I forgot that Sinatra had been dead for five years.

I turned up at EMI's plush offices in Manchester Square in London. The nervous boy in reception annoyed me by asking for my name.

"I'm Luke fucking Drumm," I said.

He wanted to know who I was scheduled to meet with. When I told him I was there to record with Frank Sinatra, he looked confused and wanted to know who had arranged the meeting, did I have any confirmation email, which producer had I been in contact with. I rattled off the names of everyone I knew in the music business, and eventually the boy asked me to take a seat while he went to investigate.

"Aren't you going to offer me a coffee?" I shouted at his retreating back.

Two burly security men showed up and asked me to leave the building. I protested and started kicking chairs, and then they got physical with me. By the time I was ejected from the building, the paparazzi were there, snapping like anoraked alligators. That was the first night I spent in a police cell.

Brian flew over to bail me out, armed with enough tranquilizers to get me on a flight home. I woke up in his house a few days later. It used to be my house. He was out, but he had hidden my shoes to stop me leaving. Either that or I had lost them. I was locked in the house, but I smashed my way out of the bathroom window and walked into the city center, my feet bare and bleeding from the broken glass. I was wearing the clothes I had slept in, and even though it was definitely winter, I was somehow immune to the cold. People looked at me and looked away quickly, not wanting to engage with the crazy man, afraid of catching my eye, and who could blame them.

On Grafton Street, I stopped and listened to some buskers. One was a pretty girl in a school uniform. She was singing one of my songs. I approached and stood next to her. She was wary but didn't stop, and so I moved closer and sang with her. She did a double take and then smiled, recognizing me for who I was. A crowd gathered, and some people with digital cameras began taking photos. After a few more songs, she stopped and thanked me. But her guitar case was full of money, and I wanted my cut. In fact, I wanted it all because I had no wallet on me. I filled my pockets with change and invited her to the pub. She protested about the money, and I called her a whiny little bitch, and then she got aggressive with me. I tried to walk away. I don't hit people. But she jumped on my back, and I violently shook her off, hearing her head thud on the concrete pavement behind me. I turned. There was blood and people shouting, and I ran. I hid around the corner, but an ambulance came and I was scared it was going to take me away.

I walked to a pub on the other side of the city, one where they didn't care whether I had shoes as long as I could pay for my drink, and I sat there, drinking cheap cider, until my face filled the television screen in the corner. I was on the news. The police were looking for me in connection with "an incident" that had occurred on Grafton Street earlier that afternoon. I pointed at the television and told the four old codgers at the bar that someone was trying to frame me for something. I bought them all pints with the last of my change to buy their silence, but at least one of them was a traitor because twenty minutes later two policemen strolled into the bar, and each placed an arm on my shoulder and took me away.

I went quietly. I saw no point in resisting. One of the officers asked me for an autograph for his sister. They were kind. They had the full story of what had happened. I guess there were plenty of witnesses. But they wanted to bring me to a hospital, they said. My brother was waiting for me there. I asked if he was sick or injured, and they humored me. I knew what was going on, but I liked that they let me act like an innocent little boy. We all knew I was being taken to the nuthouse.

In St. John of God's, Brian met me and asked me to sign myself in. I was in a good mood, and I didn't want to upset anyone. Also, I was tired, and I knew I could get tea and toast there, and I had a real yearning for the comfort of that. I felt bad about the girl. I agreed.

My tiny baby agreed too. By then I was talking to him aloud, but I knew that only I could hear or see him. I had established that he was a boy baby. He gave me instructions, and I carried them out. I was trying to get him to be a good boy, but he often got me into trouble. I could not tell whether he was friend or foe, angel or demon. He lived in the crevice of my neck below my Adam's apple, nestled into that hollow, never growing any bigger, but sometimes he took control of my voice. Occasionally, when I was in St. John of God's, he would go on holiday, and then I could get some rest.

That busking girl tried to sue me for assault. She had a fractured skull and spent a week in hospital. Even though witnesses all attested to the fact that she had assaulted me, they also said I had stolen her money. Brian said it was best to pay her off, and so for the next few years he paid my rent and bills in a small apartment and gave me pocket money, enough to live on until I could pay what I owed the girl. My tiny baby hated that girl. He wanted me to hunt her down and break her skull properly, but then I met Kate, fell in love with her, and the baby disappeared. I thought that if Kate and I had our own real baby, the ghost baby would vanish forever.

Chapter 26

2000

Sean slammed the door in my face when I turned up at his house one night. I thought he'd be my one true friend, but then, after the record label dropped me, I called his wife a bitch after she said I was too difficult to manage, and I told him I'd been fucking his sister for years. I was angry. I shouldn't have said it. Sean dropped me like a stone. He had his own thing going on by then, managing far more "serious" artists than me. It looked like my career was dead. But then Brian had stepped up and offered to be my manager, and for a while it was great, because I knew he couldn't run away from me.

In January of 2000, I was to write my autobiography. Well, that's not strictly true, but a book was being produced that would have my face and my name on the cover. Brian had somehow negotiated a deal with a publisher so that a ghostwriter would write my story. I wasn't really comfortable calling it an autobiography, but Brian said I was to keep my mouth shut about the other writer and pretend I'd written it myself. Her name was Kim, tall, blond, midfifties, businesslike. She came to my house regularly over the course of three months and would bring with her various media interviews on video or newspaper clippings about my early life, first concerts, getting signed to a record label, etc. She asked me if everything in these articles was true, if there was anything I'd like to add. She wanted to hear the stories in my own words, as I had experienced various events. She asked me about the different people who popped up in the videos, former friends, and band members. Were we still in touch? Were we still friends? The answer was nearly always no. There were some people, incidents and interviews that I couldn't remember at all. I was clearly out of my mind in some of them. It was cringe-worthy to watch myself talking utter shit on subjects I knew nothing about.

As the interviews continued, she asked more personal questions about my childhood, my relationship with my parents, how and why my career had collapsed, my stays in various mental health institutions, and so on.

I thought I was mentally stable at the time of doing this book. I was still living in my big mortgage-free home, and my royalties paid the bills, but there wasn't much money left over for the lavish lifestyle I'd been living. There was far less partying, far fewer girls, just a few glasses of wine in the evenings—well, more often a full bottle, sometimes a little more. But I felt like I was in control. Members of my family were all talking to me, which was a good sign. I even went to Mum's for Sunday lunch on a semi-regular basis. The ghosts and visions that haunted me were still around but more in my dreams than in my waking reality. And prescription sleeping tablets usually eliminated them, though I was aware now that I couldn't sleep without the tablets, and that bothered me a little.

I went to a weekly psych appointment and was normal enough to tell the shrink what I thought he wanted to hear, namely that everything was Mum's fault, but I was a grown-up now and had to stop seeking her approval. And I genuinely felt this was all true. Mum and I had called a truce of sorts. Now that I was an unemployed pop star, I fitted perfectly into her role for me as a failure, and it suited us both.

I talked to Kim, the ghostwriter, about this. I wasn't sure how much of it should end up in the book, but Kim assured me I would have final copy approval. She had ghostwritten books by sports stars and politicians. Her reputation was good, and I felt safe telling her everything. Almost everything. No need to mention the phantom baby.

She became almost like a second therapist to me, but one without the need to comment or judge or diagnose. I felt she got emotionally involved in my story and was hugely sympathetic to my trials and tribulations, even while I was relating some of the more hair-raising acts of religious zealotry of my childhood.

At the beginning of April, she handed over a rough draft of what she had written so far, the halfway point. A copy also went to Brian and to my publisher. I read it over one weekend, and I was appalled and horrified by what I had told her, what I had done, how utterly fucked-up I sounded. I felt like I was drowning in shame. Pathetic, whiny, and friendless. And I hadn't even told her the worst part.

I called her immediately and she came over, and we sat down together and deleted or toned down entire chapters, added new chapters about the positive influence of my dad, my good encounters with other celebrities, anything we could think of to make me sound more normal. I asked Kim to stall the project. I needed time and space from my own life story. That night I drank two bottles of wine and cried myself to sleep.

Susan phoned and invited me to Daisy's sixth birthday party. She and Will were throwing a kiddies' bash, complete with a bouncy castle. Will called me later and told me not to arrive pissed. I wondered if everyone saw me as a drunk. I wondered for the first time if I might be an alcoholic. I decided to quit drinking. I gave away fourteen bottles of wine to some homeless guys who used to hang out in the lane behind my house. The next day, one of them knocked on my door and asked if I had any more. I didn't have any more Châteauneuf-du-Pape, but I gave him the half bottle of gin I was saving for an emergency. I felt good and virtuous for a day or two, though edgy and nervous. I resolved to be a good uncle to Daisy.

She was a cute kid. I thought maybe I should spend more time with her. I liked her though she always favored Brian over me. Brian knew how to talk to kids. I was slightly jealous of this.

I called Susan and asked her about Daisy's favorite toys or cartoon characters. Brian had bought her DVDs of all the Disney cartoons, and Donald Duck was the one she liked best. I went to enormous lengths to hire a life-size Donald Duck costume for the party.

When I got there, I got the required response from Daisy, who ran to me and hugged me. It felt good to be hugged by a little innocent kid, to be sober and in control. Then Susan led me down the hallway to their large atrium, and I heard a lot of adult voices. Daisy ran out ahead of me into the garden and hurled herself onto the bouncy castle, colliding with some toddler who screamed, though the impact was slight. A concerned mother ran out, and then they all turned to me. I hadn't realized how big this party was. I knew there'd be other kids, but I didn't know their parents were invited too. Actors, directors, rugby players, faces I knew from TV, a guy from the Arts Council, journalists, artists, fashion designers. I felt ridiculous in my duck costume and immediately removed the large head. A few of them laughed and greeted me, not unkindly. "Luke! Well, you're certainly getting into the swing of things, aren't you?"

"Where's Will?" I asked Susan, who seemed mildly harassed.

"You tell me," she whispered. "He had a meeting this morning with some guys from New York, but he was supposed to be here two hours ago. I am so pissed with him. Most of these people are *his* friends. Can you take the salads out to the table, please, Luke? And top marks for effort, by the way. You look great."

As I moved out to the dining room next door, with platters in hand, a number of people wanted to stop and chat, asking when my next album was coming out, reminding me that we'd met at some award ceremony or backstage at some concert or that I was in the same class in school as their brother. I was now sweating and uncomfortable in the costume, and I eyed their glasses of wine jealously. A man, Tony I think his name was, noticed and fetched a glass for me and filled it. I necked it and moved on in search of another bottle, but Brian stopped me and pulled the glass out of my hand. "For God's sake, Luke, not today—or at least not until the kids have gone home. Will has gone AWOL. We need to help Susan with the lunch. He was supposed to be home by noon. And I need to talk to you later, about the book. I think it's going to be great!"

Daisy appeared at his side, pointing at me, and then she looked up and saw my face instead of Donald Duck's head and grew hysterical. Brian picked her up and tried to soothe her, whispering aside to me, "Go take the costume off! Can't you see you're upsetting her? I'll calm her down, you help Susan with the lunch." He carried Daisy out toward the patio. I went to the upstairs bathroom to remove the rest of my costume, but the jeans I had on underneath weren't too clean, and I had sweated profusely into the T-shirt and had large damp stains down my back and under each arm. In a panic, I ran to Will's bedroom in search of a clean T-shirt. Susan was in there by herself, obviously trying to get Will on his mobile phone. Will always had the latest gadgets. She saw me and hung up.

"He's not answering," she said, and began to weep.

"God, sorry," I said, excusing myself. I was unable to deal with a woman's tears, and my panic was increasing.

"Your brother's an asshole," Susan said, wiping her eyes dry and straightening her dress. I realized quickly that she meant the one she was married to, the one who wasn't here.

"Where did he go this morning?" I asked her.

"He *said* he was going to have a meeting with some lawyers from New York, promised it wouldn't take more than an hour. He was supposed to collect the cake on the way home. Not a word from him. He'd better be in the goddamn hospital because any other excuse is not going to wash with me." Her American accent became more pronounced when she was angry.

"Do you want me to get the cake?" I wanted to leave, too, and I didn't want to come back.

"No, it's okay, Brian picked it up, but can you please help me with the other things? Food, serving, clearing up? There's twenty adults and nineteen children down there. I can't do it all on my own."

I was reluctant. "Okay, but can I have a shower first and a clean T-shirt?"

She looked at me and sighed deeply. "Forget it, Luke, forget I asked anything. It's all about you, isn't it? Clean towels are on the shelf inside the door." She gestured toward their en suite over her shoulder.

"But, Susan, I dressed up as Donald Duck for Daisy," I said. "I didn't know you'd invited half—"

"Whatever." She left the room and slammed the door.

Bitch. I had been trying to do a good thing. It wasn't my fault that Will was probably screwing some trainee over his office desk.

I took my time in the shower, cut my toenails on their bed. I shaved with Will's razor and splashed on some nice-smelling aftershave. I chose a brand-new pair of Levis with the labels still attached from Will's side of the wardrobe and a plain white Dolce & Gabbana T-shirt which looked no different to the Penneys one I'd just dumped in their bin, except that it was clean.

When I got downstairs, I could hear that most of the adults were in the dining room. Children were running amok in all directions. I headed straight for the kitchen. A girl I didn't recognize was pulling a cork from a bottle.

"Here, let me help you," I offered. "I'm Will's brother, Luke." I filled her glass and found one for myself.

"Hi, yeah, I'm supposed to bring this back in to the table," she said. I studied her again for a moment. Maybe I did know her. Had I slept with her? She was wary and darted out of the room.

Brian came in bearing huge half-filled bowls of potato salad. I hid the glass on a shelf behind me. "Christ, Luke, you're supposed to be helping. Will is still missing. I'm going to kill him. Here, grab those side plates and the paper plates for the kids. I don't know where the dessert bowls are kept, they'll have to do. And call all the kids in, we're going to do the cake now. Have you got a light for the candles?" Brian was in his element. He clearly liked being the man of this house.

I drained the glass of wine as soon as his back was turned, poured myself another from a different bottle, and went outside to call the children in. Most of them looked at me uncertainly, but the two su-

pervising adults hustled them inside. I followed. Brian met me in the
kitchen. "Where are the plates I asked you for? Have you got a light?"
I assured him I did and grabbed a load of plates off the countertop.
"Luke!" he shouted at me. "Those ones are dirty. Can you not see what
you're doing? Those ones, there!" He pointed to a stack of Barbie Doll
paper plates. I picked them up and followed him into the room.

It was heaving with people and noise. A Barbie Doll cake sat in the
middle of the table, and Daisy sat on her mother's lap, ready to make
her wish and blow out the candles. "Give me the lighter, Luke," said
Brian, and I patted my pockets and realized that my lighter was in the
pocket of the jeans upstairs on the bathroom floor. Susan glared at me
while some other chivalrous smoker proffered his Zippo like it was a
golden chalice.

A loud woman excitedly said, "Why don't we have Luke sing 'Happy
Birthday'? He's the singer here, after all!" and someone clapped, and I
felt the baby dance across my eyes. My body started to pump sweat again.

"No," said Susan firmly, "let the kids do it. Luke is exhausted after
all the hard work he's done." She smiled sweetly at me, but not with
her eyes.

The kids sang "Happy Birthday" and Daisy blew out the candles. I
slipped back out to the kitchen and attacked another bottle of wine.
Then people started filtering through, looking for the cloakroom, their
children, the toilet. I smiled and endured small talk as best I could
while knocking back as much wine as possible.

Then I noticed a hush, and Will entered the kitchen, followed by
Susan, physically pushing him out into the garden. Their voices were
raised. People left quickly after that. Brian distracted Daisy with the
age-appropriate rocking horse he'd given her. I realized I hadn't bought
her a gift. Susan came storming back into the kitchen, leaving Will outside, his face red with fury. "Is everything okay?" I said redundantly.

"Go home, Luke, and take Donald Duck with you." She went
straight past me, and a door slammed upstairs. I swiped a bottle of wine
and left through the front door. Brian came out after me.

"Jesus, he treats her so badly. Tosser." He saw the bottle of wine in my hand. "Hand over your car keys, you dickhead."

They were also in the pocket of the pair of jeans on Susan's bathroom floor.

"You're both pathetic, you know?" Brian said. "Absolutely pathetic." But there was something smug and superior about Brian. He enjoyed being the one who hadn't disgraced himself.

"Daisy didn't even notice her dad was missing. That tells you everything you need to know," he went on. So self-righteous. "I'm going to drive you back to your place. You can get your car in the morning. I need to talk to you about the book anyway."

Back at my house, Brian sat me down. "I just read the first part and I love it. Obviously, we have to take the bits about Mum out, I mean, you can't do that to her, it's not fair. But the editor loves it too. You were always a mental kid, I don't know why you weren't taken to a shrink much earlier. All that stuff about religion, the first Holy Communion, the stigmata at Halloween, it's brilliant."

"But, Brian, I'm taking that out."

"What?"

"I'm taking it out of the book. Kim and I have been revising it. It's too . . . much. I don't want all those stories out there. They're too personal."

"But that's what the publishers want, that's what they're paying for."

"I don't care. They're not going in the book."

"Look, your story is brilliant—how you go from being this disturbed kid to this mega famous pop star, all the drugs and rehab. It's story gold, bro."

"I'm not doing it."

"But don't you see? It has a happy ending. You've recovered. All that shit is behind you."

I emptied the end of the wine into my glass. "Do you think so, Brian? I'm an alcoholic." It's the first time I'd ever acknowledged it out loud. "I'm hanging on to my sanity by a thread."

He didn't want to listen to me and started ranting about the 150K pounds advance I'd been given by the UK publishing house. If we didn't deliver the book, we'd have to return it.

"They'll get a book," I insisted. "They just won't get the lurid detail."

"But that's what they want, you asshole! They're hardly going to pay that kind of money for a biography of a squeaky-clean faded pop star, are they? I sold it to them on the basis of your freak-outs, your bad times. They want the dirt, that's the best bit!"

"This is my life we are talking about."

"Yeah? Well, I negotiated that deal, and I need to get my percentage out of it."

"Brian, I can't do it."

"Look, I wasn't going to say anything, but I've just gone mortgage-agreed based on my cut of that deal. Please, Luke, don't blow this on me. This is my first home. You've had this place since you were, what, twenty-one? If I don't have the money, I don't get the house."

"I'm sorry."

"Kim is going to have to be paid for the work she's already done. The publishers are probably going to insist that you pay it."

"Then I will."

He begged, pleaded, and wheedled for the next hour, alternately praising me for my bravery in telling my story and how much it could help other people, then threatening me that he'd tell Mum what I'd said about her being a witch. We were children again.

He even went out and bought me another bottle of wine, and I let him rant on while I drained it to the last drop, drinking myself sober. But I didn't change my mind. In fact, I was now adamant that the book would never go ahead in any form. He left.

The next morning, I was sick: physically sick and sick with guilt and fear. When I finally ventured out, two days later, I walked into my local parish hall and my first Alcoholics Anonymous meeting.

Chapter 27

2016

By 2016, I was in a good place. My recovery had started gradually two years previously. I had never been able to stick to AA for more than a month before that. I really noticed it one day when I went to the fridge and found I had all the components to make myself a full meal. I had gone to the supermarket earlier, and usually those trips ended with a lottery of items spread all over my kitchen. I had always been prone to bouts of food poisoning because I forgot to put food in the fridge or to check use-by dates. I'd have bought a tin of tomatoes instead of beans, but then I'd be so hungry that I'd eat them anyway. But on this particular day, I had bought fresh milk, bread, potatoes, a piece of steak, and frozen peas. Even more surprisingly, I knew what to do with these items to make a coherent dinner and have breakfast the next day.

I felt calm. I did not feel agitated or anxious or elated or depressed. I'd had some lucid days in the previous years, but this felt different. When people talk about depression, they refer to a "black dog" that follows them everywhere, but I had been plagued by an entire menagerie of reptiles and insects and ravenous lions and bears. They were gone. I could taste the food. For the first time in years, my taste buds were working again.

The only significant change in my life was that my mother had died late that summer of 2014. I hadn't seen her for four years at that stage. She was scared of me, and I suppose I had given her good reason to be. But I had also tried to make amends. I sent her flowers on her birthday, bought her expensive gifts I could barely afford, but she did not acknowledge these gestures.

Her funeral was ordinary, with just a few of her old showbiz pals in attendance, whose days in the limelight were also past. The siblings she had been so ashamed of all showed up. I couldn't understand their loyalty to her. Brian brought a suit for me to wear and stood over me while I shaved. I was warned to turn up sober, not to make a scene or a fuss, but I felt okay. Maybe I should have been tearful. All I felt was relief. Will, unexpectedly, sobbed throughout. I had not been asked to be involved with the funeral planning, so I didn't have to make a speech, though all three of us carried her coffin with the undertakers without any arguments. That was the only weight on my shoulder that day. I felt irrationally at peace, without being elated or artificially high.

Will's ex-wife, Susan, came with Daisy, their daughter, who must have been twenty by then. She appeared not to be talking to either of her parents and sat in a pew at the back, chewing gum and looking constantly at her phone. As usual, Brian was the only person she showed any warmth to. Her nose and eyebrows were pierced. Her eyes and lips were blackened with makeup. She usually avoided me at family occasions, but at the post-funeral afternoon tea, she approached me looking for cocaine. I had given up on cocaine since the overdose, and even in my chaotic episodes I knew to stay away from it. She wouldn't take no for an answer and demanded the number of my dealer. I told her to fuck off quietly, and she spat at my feet and turned away.

In the weeks after my mother's death, I felt incrementally better every day. The craziness did not vanish overnight, but that particular autumn evening when I made my own dinner and ate it, washed down with a glass of water, I knew there had been a major shift in my psyche. I cleaned the flat, took clothes to a launderette, restored books to their shelves, CDs and records to their cases and sleeves. I changed the bed linen on my salty bed. I took a long hot shower and scrubbed a week's worth of grime from my skin, washed my hair, and shaved. I went and bought a newspaper, and really, everything was news to me, because I had been living in my own bubble for so long that I was barely aware of anything that went on outside the span of my two arms.

Over the following days, I registered in my library, borrowed books that people were discussing on the radio, drank good coffee in coffee shops. I basked in this new feeling of normality, nervous, though, that it would, like all the other times, be temporary.

During the previous decade, all those stories about my "mental childhood" and psychotic episodes had been sold to British tabloids. I don't know which of my old friends or neighbors or former classmates sold those stories, but my train wreck of a life was out there in the open. I was a public joke to be ridiculed or a champion for the virtue signalers. My life had been lived mostly in fear.

By Christmas of 2014, I had not seen the tiny baby for eleven weeks. In the intervening time I had returned to my psychiatrist, the only one I had ever trusted with the truth of that constant companion. He adjusted my prescription. I was on a low-dosage antipsychotic drug, and I took it religiously. I did not touch alcohol, gave up smoking and every other drug I'd been using, even weed, which I had used so frequently, I barely thought of it as a drug at all. I went back to Alcoholics Anonymous, sat at the back and said nothing for the first four weeks, until one day an older woman invited me to introduce myself. Though it wasn't my first time at AA, this time it was different—I felt I was among family. I probably should have gone to NA as well, but even though I had taken a lot of drugs, I never needed them like I needed alcohol.

Other weeds interested me, and I wrapped up warm and dug in the rear garden of the house I was renting. I tore up weeds and planted some seasonal shrubs. I went to my local park and asked the gardeners there for some advice. One of them recognized me. He was wary of any interaction. My encounters with the police and psychiatric institutions were well documented in the press and across social media. But as embarrassing as those incidents were, I knew that I was a different and better person now. One of the older gardeners took me under his wing, and in return for advice, I would help him with raking leaves and turning soil and the more arduous tasks while the younger lads were on their lunch break.

I communicated with my brothers. I told them I was well, at least for now. I asked them if I could help with their gardens. Susan was busy at the time, so I did her garden, too, and helped her with the marriage equality campaign.

By the end of the summer of 2015, I asked Brian if I might take back control of my finances. He was extremely reluctant to hand over the reins, but Will took my side and suggested I could sue Brian if he pushed back. Brian relented then, and I quickly discovered he had all along been taking a hefty management fee out of my royalties, almost 50 percent. And, of course, he had the big house I'd bought when I was twenty-one years old and sold to him ten or so years later for some reason lost in the mists of time. Brian was unapologetic when I confronted him.

"I've been your manager, your agent, your accountant, and your caregiver. I'm the one who had to drop everything every time you got arrested, overdosed, or threatened to jump out a window, and who's to say you won't go back there. I've earned every penny of that. And the house. You did stupid things with your money. I stopped it from being wasted."

"By lining your own pockets?"

"I *saved* you. Repeatedly."

It was true, I suppose. Brian had come to my rescue many times, but now I understood that he'd done it to justify the money he took; not out of love or care for me, but as a job.

All three of us were single men now. Will and Susan's marriage had long since broken down, although he was still handsome and successful and could attract women. Brian had occasional girlfriends but nothing that ever lasted more than a few months. I tried to contact Kate again. I found her on Facebook. She was happily married with two children, living in Italy somewhere outside Rome. I wanted to know why she had left me, why we couldn't have helped each other through her miscarriage. She replied, saying she could not revisit the past, and cautiously wished me well. I felt wary of a relationship. I couldn't ever see myself with a family. And who would take a chance on an ex–pop star with a history of psychotic episodes and drug abuse, living in a rented flat with no career and no future? And no guarantee that I would not slip back down into the abyss of mental illness.

My royalty income going forward was not bad, now that it was all assigned to me and I'd cut Brian out of the picture. My erratic and well-known history meant I would never qualify for a mortgage, particularly postrecession, but I didn't have to work to keep the wolf from the door. However, I needed something to fill my days, and I wanted to be useful. I asked Will if there was anything I could do in his company. I didn't want to be the tea boy, but perhaps I could train to be a cameraman or a sound recordist.

"Christ, Luke, you don't have a clue what a producer actually does, do you? I only hire crew when I need them, on a shoot. They work for me on contract. They are not my employees, and I don't train them. They are full professionals, and when I get work-experience students in, they tend to be in their teens, not their forties. You'd only embarrass yourself."

I bought an acoustic guitar. I hadn't played in years. I strummed at it for a few days, but somehow I knew that music was not my thing. It was a career I had accidentally and catastrophically fallen into. I wondered if I could sit at a desk and sell insurance or maybe work in a library. I contemplated going back to college and finishing my engineering degree, but over twenty years had elapsed. I would have to start again with the teenagers. What does a middle-aged man do with his life when all his CV says is "former pop star"?

Word spread that I was in recovery and had regained my marbles. A few offers came in. Did I want to go into *Celebrity Big Brother* or a reality jungle show? The money they were offering was eye watering, but I wanted a job that meant something, not a springboard back into the tawdry side of the limelight. Brian thought I was mad to turn down the offers. Will dryly said I'd caused the family enough embarrassment without doing it on live television.

I met a guy I had known from the old days at an AA meeting. He had been a music journalist then, had dismissed my talent as "infantile shit" in a broadsheet, but we had both got absolutely off our faces one night at a film premiere, and I had found him on my kitchen floor the next morning in a pool of his own vomit. I had no recollection of this until he reminded me during the tea break. I laughed, told him he had no need to ever remind me. His name was Kevin, and he was now the editor of an online newspaper. When he asked me what I was doing, I was embarrassed to admit I spent most days at the cinema or watching films on DVD. He asked me if I'd like to write some film reviews. The money he was offering was barely worth talking about, and I didn't know if I could write, but I knew I had strong opinions about film.

"Sure, give it a go," he said. "Send me sample reviews of the best and worst films you've ever seen, and I'll see if you're up to it. All I'm looking for is opinion, but it might help if you did a bit of research into the history of film and filmmaking."

Now I had a project. I wasn't even sure if I wanted to write reviews, but I was definitely interested in acting and the whole film process. I watched endless documentaries on the history of film. I went to the library and got books on the subject. I went to Pulse and signed up for a course on filmmaking for beginners. One of the tutors was a woman called Mary Cullen. She seemed familiar. After that first class we got talking. She reminded me that she used to work for Will as a development executive. She now had her own production company. Even though she didn't say much about Will, I got the distinct impression she did not like him. I invited her for a coffee to pick her brains about framing a scene and the importance of lighting. She gave me a list of films to watch that were good examples.

Over the course of the next few months, Mary and I became friends. She was pretty, and she was also pretty direct. I liked that about her. She asked me about my mental health, how long I had been stable. She pointedly asked me how supportive my family had been. I explained that I'd burned my bridges and I couldn't keep asking them for help. She told me about the time Will and Brian had gone to New York to bring me back after 9/11. I had only the vaguest memories of that time and felt ashamed as she told me the secondhand details as she'd heard them. I dimly recalled watching the Twin Towers fall, on a television in a shopwindow in New York, watching it over and over again. I had no recollection of Brian and Will coming to get me or of coming home to Ireland.

I had lost years of my life. My past was a jigsaw puzzle with so many missing pieces. I didn't even want to find the pieces because I wasn't sure what horrors they held. Mary realized I was upset when I told her. She tried to make me feel better by confiding that she too had her demons. We were both AA members, though we didn't attend the same meetings. She had been sober for four years. She admitted to some hair-raising details from her own past. We started going on cinema dates. There was nothing romantic about it. Alcoholics Anonymous had no hard and fast rules about relationships or dating, but the thing most of us had in common was a past strewn with failed or destructive relationships. Sex was not something I missed particularly. I had slept with hundreds of women in my pop-star days. You can actually get bored with anything if you get too much of it. Kevin laughed when I said that, but it's true. I was happy to be celibate, happy to be studying and learning, happy to have two good and supportive friends in Mary and Kevin.

One night I ran into Will as he was walking Daisy's old dog. I mentioned that his former assistant, Mary, was a friend of mine.

"That bitch?" he said. "She's trying to compete with me for all the same funding rounds. I gave her her first job in film, and now she's trying to get ahead of me."

"Oh, come on, Will, there's at least five companies in Dublin making multiple projects, just like you. I've never heard you giving out about the others."

"Yeah, well, the others are my friends. We all worked on each other's projects at one stage or another. We came up through the ranks together."

"What? But so did Mary. After she worked for you, she went and worked for Ed and then Rebecca, and now she's out on her own. Shouldn't you be pleased that your protégée has done well for herself?"

"Mary's a liability. You'll soon find out."

"Yeah, well, she's my friend now. She's sober."

He shrugged.

"Did she do something to you? Why the animosity?"

"She should still be making coffee and ordering flowers for the boss's wife."

"Is it because she's a woman?"

"Oh, fuck off, Luke! Don't you start with this gender shit. It's all anyone is talking about these days. Feminism is fine when it suits women, but they still want you to mow the lawn, take out the bins, buy them flowers, and take them to fucking Paris."

I knew that my history with women was nothing to be proud of. I had probably used women badly in my time, but I had never thought I was better than women or that they mattered less than men do. I had been in love exactly once, with Kate, who made me a better person. Maybe we would never have worked out. The miscarriage killed our relationship. She refused to attend counseling about it, refused to even discuss it. I don't know how she could switch off love like that, because I was certain that she loved me. I definitely loved her, but then what good did it do me? As soon as I lost her, I spiraled downward again into my own personal hell. Was it worth it, loving someone, if you were going to lose them?

Will talked of women as either sex objects or inconveniences. Even though he and Susan still hosted the occasional Christmas dinner together, he never talked about her affectionately; mostly it was criticism about how she had raised Daisy, how she had failed to monitor Daisy's weight. I would point out that Will was also Daisy's parent, but I always backed off when he got angry about this. Daisy had been his pride and joy, but she'd been living an aimless life, had switched college courses several times, come out of the closet, gone back in, was drifting from job to job, and it was clear—to me anyway—that she was a habitual drug user. It takes one to know one. Then, quite suddenly, in 2015, she seemed to clean up her act and move in with Brian. He was launching her media career. Will had a huge bust-up with Brian about this. He wanted me to go and counsel Daisy that a media career was a bad idea, using myself as an example. I wanted to stay out of it. But I hated that Brian and Will wouldn't talk to each other. Now that I was experiencing normality, I wanted to find my family again. I wanted to hear from them what they'd made of our childhood. Did they see as clearly as I did that our mother had mistreated me? I had never raised the issue of my paternity with them and my suspicions that Dad might not have been my father. I wanted a family truce, but their arguments over Daisy meant I was not their priority.

I got on with my life. Despite my intention to stay away from performance, I found myself more and more attracted to the idea of acting. Out of the blue, one weekend, Will had gone on an absolute bender and ended up crying down the phone to me from a hotel in Wexford. He had never asked for my help before, but I went down and sorted him out, brought him home and put him up, thinking that now was my chance to play on his sympathy. I'd helped him out of a potentially career-damaging situation. I asked him if he would try me out in a minor role in his upcoming TV series, but he laughed at me. It pissed me off. It was a supporting role playing the main character's dad. I could easily have handled it.

I took up an adult acting course. I didn't tell anyone I was doing it. A few of my classmates knew who I was and knew my history, but most of the youngsters had never heard of me, so it felt like a proper fresh start. The fear of being the oldest in the class vanished when we started playing theater games and doing improvisations. By the end of the first week, I'd played a seven-year-old girl with a skipping rope for a prop, and a grocery store manager handling a complaint from an irate customer. We bonded pretty quickly because one of the first things we had to do was all these trust games. I had never really had trust issues. Perhaps one of my many problems was that I trusted everyone.

When we got to working with texts by Ibsen, Carr, Miller, Friel, and Chekhov, I found slipping into character as easy as putting on a comfortable old pair of shoes. These lines written by the giants of theater had been tried and tested, and performing them was a pleasure. It was so completely different to singing in an arena full of teenagers screaming my name. You could barely call both of those things performances, because they were such wildly different beasts. For me, acting involved listening intently to the other characters, picking up on cues, finding something new in the text, surprising myself, and surprising the small audience of ten or twelve fellow students and tutors.

Sometime around the end of 2016, Kevin and Mary and I went out for dinner, and I told them what I'd been doing. Kevin worried that acting might put me back into a dangerous spotlight. Mary thought it might be a form of therapy for me. I had been stable for over two years by then. A few weeks later, Mary sent me a script for *The Star Maiden* and asked me to send her a self-tape of me playing the role of a doctor. The script was really good, written by a young French Algerian woman.

It was about a middle-aged woman whose monstrous, controlling husband had kept her locked up for twenty years. The story follows her after her husband's arrest and her release, how she negotiates her way in this new world and tries to find the children she has given birth to in captivity. I was to read the role of her psychiatrist.

"Mary, seriously?"

"Well, if anyone knows how psychiatrists work, it's you," she said. She felt it would be a good start for me, if I wanted to do something professional. She would send my tape to her casting director. I emailed the footage and hoped to get the part. The next morning, Mary said the director and the casting director wanted to see me. I felt optimistic. When I went in, there was a camera set up in a bare office with lights and a lot of young people with clipboards. The English director, Ian Foster, an old man, shook my hand and asked me about films I liked, where I'd trained, etc. I only realized when we were introduced that he had directed two of my favorite films of recent years. We talked passionately about the themes and the psychology of the characters until we were interrupted by Niamh, the casting director. This was a screen test. Ian was old-school. Most directors these days relied on actors' self-tapes, but Ian wanted to meet the people he was going to work with.

I immediately felt a pressure behind my eyes, a film of sweat burst through my skin, and in my mind I was back in a student pub waiting to go on for that first performance.

They asked me to read several different roles. Ian explained a little about each character. I locked eyes with him and listened intently, terrified that the baby was back and was going to whisper something evil or poisonous in my ear. I faced the camera and gave it everything, possibly raising my voice a little too much. I left the offices feeling I'd blown it. I felt the hollow in my neck, but there was nothing there.

At my AA meeting that evening, I talked to the group about it. I didn't go into details about the baby, just being suddenly overwhelmed. They assured me that my feelings, my sweating, my nervousness were completely normal. "Everyone feels like that going for a job interview,"

Margaret said, and all the members nodded in agreement. "Just hand it over," said Margaret, "it's out of your control. Remember, accept the things you cannot change. You can't help feeling nervous. The important thing is that you weren't tempted to have a drink or anything else afterward. That's really good, Luke!"

Mary rang me that night. She wanted to call over to the flat. On arrival, she couldn't contain her excitement. "You got the part!"

"Really? I thought I'd blown it, with being so nervous."

"No, Luke, you got THE part! Not the lead, obviously, but you're playing her husband."

"What? No way!"

"Yes, it's a much bigger role. You're in all the flashbacks and the present-day prison scenes."

She pulled a bottle of sparkling elderflower out of her bag. "This calls for bubbles! Fake bubbles but bubbles all the same. You'll have to go through a medical because of your track record, but you've been so healthy for nearly three years, I don't see it being a problem. Luke, we're going to make a film together!"

"Wait, what? No, God, I don't know. I only wanted the smaller role. I've been famous. It was terrible. What if it all starts again? What if he comes back?"

"What? Who? Luke, you're a different guy now, you can handle this, and I'm producing it. We'll do it together."

She took my face in her hands and kissed it. I kissed her back. Within minutes, we were tearing each other's clothes off. I led her to my spartan bedroom and laid her carefully on the bed.

"Are you sure?" I said.

"Are you?" she replied.

We laughed like teenagers, and I pulled her to me and held her close, smelling her hair, kissing the back of her neck.

"I think we're sure," I said as she turned toward me, and for a moment we just stared at each other, as if seeing the other person for the first time.

I knew I loved her right then. I will never understand why it took me so long to see it.

"Mary," I said, "I need you to know. I have a lifetime of baggage. I could relapse at any time, and if I do, I'll be this massive burden to you. You need to be careful for your own sake."

She looked up at me. "I'm not the cure, Luke. We both know it. But I'm here, and I really think I always will be. Let's just take it a day at a time, okay?"

"Okay." I was so turned on and so frightened. I didn't want to lose her, ever.

*T*wo days after the funeral, I received a call from the crematorium to let me know that the ashes were ready for collection. We needed to go and select an urn.

I felt a moment of panic, as if having his ashes would be like having him back, accusing me of murder. Out of guilt, I chose the most expensive urn from the undertaker's website, a metallic version of a Ming vase. I did not dare to open the lid.

My brother and I argued over what to do with these ashes. The urn stood on my mantelpiece for a week, just so visitors could see and offer condolences, but I didn't want it in my line of sight. There was no Banquo's-ghost-type scene, but the urn unnerved me. I put it at the back of my drinks cabinet. Then I rang my brother and asked him to take it. He refused. "You could put it in the bin?" he said, and I wasn't sure if he was serious. But I couldn't bring myself to do that. Aren't ashes supposed to be scattered?

We met to discuss where to scatter the ashes. We tried to remember any particular place he liked and realized we didn't know him that well. And in that conversation, I realized we did not know each other well, either. We drove and then walked out to a scenic spot near Glendalough, an ancient monastic settlement, and scattered the ashes there. It was a place we had all been to before, as children and adults. It was as good a place as any.

We spent that night talking about our collective youth, our parents, our absent brother. No tears were shed.

We talked about Daisy, what was to be done for her, how we could help her. We agreed to try. We agreed.

Brian

Chapter 28

1978

Dad did the cooking in our house most of the time when Mum was working. We'd walk home from school, Will ignoring Luke and me, keeping as much distance as possible between us, and Auntie Peggy would be there with a pot of soup ready for us, or we'd all go to Aunt Judy's house if Paul was well enough, but either way, Dad would have dinner on the table at six o'clock. Some of the boys in my class thought this was funny and said that my dad must be a sissy. I didn't know what a sissy was, but I knew it wasn't cool. If Mum wasn't working, she would make dinner for us and then eat with Dad when he came home later.

I think Dad enjoyed cooking. But things were never fair at our dinner table, and no matter how much I complained about the situation, nothing changed.

First of all, Luke insisted we say grace before dinner to thank the Lord for our meals. It would have made more sense to thank Mum or Dad, but it meant we had to wait for Luke's endless prayers before we got to eat. Dad allowed this. Mum didn't.

When Mum cooked, Will always got bigger portions than me, and Luke got the smallest. I'm glad I wasn't Luke, but he didn't seem to notice or care. Mum said that Will was bigger and he needed more. He wasn't even an inch taller than me. Though Luke was two inches shorter than me. That was fine when it came to broccoli or cauliflower, but when he got more ice cream than us, I would cry and protest, and Mum would threaten to take my dish away altogether.

Dad was more slapdash about portions and who got what. How much food you got on your plate from Dad was random, though if there was an extra bit of cake going, Dad always favored Luke and told Will and me, "Your brother is only small, give him a chance." A chance at what? He was only eleven months younger than me. And Will was fourteen months older. "He has some catching up to do, don't you think?" And it's true, I suppose, that Luke was not as robust as Will and me, but the unfairness drove me mad.

One day, I counted the peas on each of our plates as Dad served them. Will had thirteen, Luke had nineteen, and I had ten.

"Dad!"

"What?"

"They got more peas than me."

"Ah, Brian, not this again!"

"And Luke's pork chop is bigger than mine."

Will piped up. "I should get the biggest chop. Mum said boys need meat to make them grow stronger."

"We're all boys, you idiot," I said.

Luke picked up the chop with his hands and put it on Will's plate. "I don't mind, you can have it."

"Ugh! Now it has your germs all over it."

I speared it with my fork and lifted it onto my plate. "Fine, I'll have it!"

Will was furious and started pulling it back toward him.

"Boys!" Dad shouted, though he rarely shouted. "Shut up and eat your dinner or I'll take it all away and there'll be no dessert either. Why can't you be more like Luke? You're supposed to be setting an example for him instead of the other way around. Behave yourselves." Luke smiled at Dad, and Dad ruffled his hair.

Will let go of the plate. I did another quick check. We had two potatoes each. Dad turned round to serve his own dinner, and as he did, Will leaned over and spat on my chop.

"What did—" The anger took me, and I could scarcely articulate my rage. I lifted his plate and threw it at the wall. Dad whirled round, lifted me out of the chair, and carried me toward the stairs.

"Will spat on my chop!" I screamed. He said nothing. He flung open my bedroom door and threw me onto the bed and closed the door behind him.

"You can stay there until I tell you to come down."

I stewed with anger, furious at the injustice of it all.

Half an hour later, Luke crept into our room with a napkin containing his smaller chop and his two potatoes.

"You must be hungry," he said. "God says we should feed the hungry."

"What about the peas?"

He looked troubled. "I ate the peas."

"Okay, thanks."

Ravenous, I demolished the food quickly and then was called downstairs by my father.

I entered the kitchen.

"Well, what have you to say for yourself?"

"Sorry."

"Right then, that's over. Your dinner is in the warming oven, but I ate your dessert."

He went into the sitting room and turned on the TV.

Will laughed at me. "Idiot. It was strawberry shortbread. Delicious." He licked his lips and went up to do his homework.

Luke watched as I ate my second dinner.

"Brian, can I have one of your potatoes?"

I gave him the smallest. He watched like a hungry dog as I ate the rest in a hurry, my arm circling my plate.

Chapter 29

1993

Will takes what he wants. He always has. He had this built-in confidence and sense of entitlement that I've never felt. Maybe it's the fact that he always knew what he wanted to be when he grew up, or because he is the oldest. He'd been obsessed with the cinema since he managed to sneak into *Jaws* at the Forum under Dad's coat when he was eight years old. I had no doubt he was going to end up being a hotshot film director, because, like I say, Will always got what he wanted.

Luke was different, and that's putting it mildly. He was odd. His childhood obsession with religion was nuts. He was always a loner, the school dork with no friends who was always pretty bright and got decent results. Then, two summers before his final school exams, I found him messing with his old Meccano set, and casually said he should try to do engineering in college. He agreed, and then studied really hard, until he got As or Bs in almost every subject. He always had an obsessive personality. But nobody—and I mean nobody—who knew him growing up would have expected that by the age of twenty-two he'd be an international pop star with his own big house.

I was envious of both of them. Luke was rich and successful and famous, and Will got Susan.

Susan and I were just colleagues in the bookshop where I worked but I had an inkling that she liked me. I hadn't had a proper girlfriend by then, just a series of one-night stands with girls I had no real interest in, though to be fair, they didn't show much interest in me either. They were mostly drunken encounters. I was sharing a house then with Cillian Gogan and Nicky Sharpe, two college friends, and bringing a girl back was always a risk. None of us were natural housekeepers, and the rent was cheap for a good reason. The house was semi-derelict. Hot water from the taps was never guaranteed. Mold crawled up the kitchen walls. The downstairs carpet had almost been eaten by moths. Consequently, we did not treat the place with much respect. We went months without buying toothpaste or using the vacuum cleaner. Nicky kept goldfish in the bathroom washbasin, but there would often be a dead one floating on the top, and he wasn't particularly conscientious about changing the water, so the reek from fish poo combined with Cillian's digestive disorder made the bathroom a particularly challenging scene for visiting girls. An old armchair in the front garden had mushrooms growing out of it.

We were a pretty chaotic trio. Nicky was an accountant during the week, but at weekends he DJ'd at raves and consumed enormous amounts of pharmaceuticals. Cillian was a bit of a drifter, like me. I was an English teacher, not a particularly good one and certainly not a committed one. Dead-eyed teenage boys in a Christian Brothers school depressed me as much as I depressed them. I was a part-timer and worked a few days a week in a bookshop in town. Cillian was a night manager of a three-star hotel on the wrong side of town. His parents had been my parents' friends when we were kids, but I think they lost touch after Dad died. They visited the flat once, recoiled in horror, and never came back. Mum never visited, thank God.

So getting a girl back to the flat was something we only did at night, and then we'd have to try to hustle her out before she got sober or dawn broke and the full horror of her surroundings became apparent.

When I met Susan at work, she always asked me to help her with the heavier boxes of books instead of the other guys, and I guess that stoked my ego a bit because I was clearly fitter and stronger than them. Then we started taking lunch breaks together. We'd conspire to get scheduled together on the staff timetable. It was all platonic. She referred to me as her friend when talking to other people, but she'd wink and put her hand on my arm in conversation in such a way that led me to think she was interested in more. And that American accent was so unusual in Dublin. She looked and sounded like someone in a TV show.

A few weeks into our "friendship," over lunch, she squinted at me and said, "You have coffee foam on your nose," and I wanted the floor to open up. I wiped my nose with my handkerchief, and trying to make light of it, I said, "Yeah, I have a weird nose."

She saw my embarrassment and peered at my face and laughed. "Oh my God, it's not bad or ugly. Come on! We've been lunching and working side by side for months, and this is the first time I've even noticed. Are you seriously self-conscious about that?"

Yes, I was seriously self-conscious. Mum and Will in particular would often mention it. I'd spent most of my teenage years with my hand in front of my face. It was hard to believe that Susan was only noticing it now, but then, I wondered, maybe she was just being kind or else she hadn't been looking at my face as much as I'd been looking at hers. Her skin was milky pale, her huge brown eyes were full of expression and mischief, and her lips—her lips were kissable. She was slight and slim, and extremely attractive. She dressed in a flamboyant punky style, spiky short hair and scarlet lipstick. She belonged on an album cover.

Susan had a friend who worked in the box office of the Abbey Theatre, and occasionally she'd invite me to see some awful show with her, and I'd sit beside her in the dark, wanting to take her hand but terrified that she might recoil. And then I decided I would invite her to Mum's for lunch. Our home was larger than most, I suppose, and way more impressive than my shared house, which I was ashamed to show her. I knew Mum would make a fuss, so I didn't tell her in advance that Susan was coming. I wasn't sure what Will and Luke would make of her. I just prayed they wouldn't say anything to embarrass me or to insult her.

Will and his girlfriend, Irene, and Luke and the drummer from his band were there when we arrived. Irene was hanging off Will, while he more or less ignored her. I guessed he was bored by her already.

Over dinner, Mum was fascinated to learn that Susan grew up in a house without a television.

"But what did you do, in the evenings, for entertainment?" she said.

"Well, mostly we'd read, play cards and board games, or discuss current affairs, argue about politics. My family would have been Republicans originally, but Detroit is beginning to get real run-down these days. No more Motor City. My mom and I voted for Bill Clinton last year. My dad would turn in his grave if he knew."

Will joined in the conversation. "But didn't you feel left out, when you heard other people discussing television programs?"

"Not then, but we went to the movies every week. We weren't completely unaware of the big-name actors and actresses. When I started sharing apartments with my friends, it took me ages to get used to the tiny TV screen . . ."

We were heading into dangerous territory then, because Will could discuss film until the end of time, and I could see he found her interesting.

"William is going to be a film director," said Irene, and Will scoffed and corrected her. "A producer, actually. Directors are just hired hands. Producing is where the power is, and the money."

There was an awkward silence then, and I was glad because Will had just made a tit out of himself. The rest of the afternoon went fine. Susan had come to one of Luke's gigs with me; she'd met him before. He and his drummer were so obviously stoned that Mum just ignored them. They left early to meet some visiting French music arranger in Windmill Lane.

I walked Susan to the bus stop, and she kissed me on the cheek when her bus came. I thought I could make my move soon. I liked her; she liked me and my family. I wasn't going to wait around.

I had full teaching hours for the following week, covering for a sick geography teacher, so it was Saturday before I got to see Susan again. She had made a cake. We were going to St. Stephen's Green on our lunch break. And then, about an hour after the bookshop opened, Will walked in. I was surprised to see him, but he wasted no time.

"Where's Susan?"

"Why?"

"I broke up with Irene, I like Susan."

"Fuck's sake, Will, you can't just pick up women and drop them like that."

"You mean, *you* can't."

"Susan's a friend of mine."

"I know, but it's not like she's your girlfriend, is it?"

I couldn't say anything. I was furious. He found her in the children's section, and afterward, when he'd left, she came to me, smiling and blushing.

"Your brother's just asked me out for dinner, like, on a date!"

I stared at her. "What did you say?"

"Well . . . I said yes. Why? Is he a monster? Should I have said no? Tell me all about him."

The most hurtful thing was that she didn't appear to notice how hurt I was. I made some excuse to cancel our lunch plans and worked in the education section for the rest of the day.

I expected that Will would date her for a few weeks and then drop her, but as the months went by they became closer, and she delayed her plans to go traveling. My dreams of mending her broken heart and putting her back together again after Will had dumped her faded. They were a couple, and they seemed to be solid. I tried to maintain our friendship, but she would talk about Will and Mum and Luke, often telling me things about my own family that I didn't know. I found it increasingly hard to be around her, but even harder to stay away. We would all three go for drinks together sometimes, but it killed me to see their hands intertwined, her head nestling into his shoulder.

Did Will know I was in love with her? I honestly don't know. And would he have cared if he did know? Ultimately, Susan chose him. If she had been interested in me, she could have said no when he asked her out that first time, but was it just lousy timing on my part? I didn't have any ownership of her. I'd read *The Female Eunuch*. I'd discussed it with Susan. She was free to do what she wanted. She said I was a good feminist. But I did not like it. Not one bit.

In the summer of 1993, Luke was headlining Ireland's largest summer music festival. It was a big deal for him, and he was nervous about it. There had been hints in gossip columns about his bizarre behavior, but he laughed it off when we questioned him. He was hugely successful abroad, but the home crowd was always tougher and readier to ridicule him. He would perform in front of fifty thousand people, and his manager, Sean, was turning up at his house every morning to take him to the gym and bring him to dance rehearsals.

Luke, to everyone's surprise, could really move. Mum said he got that from her. I think it's the only thing she ever claimed that Luke might have inherited from her. He had a way of dancing that was original. He could move elegantly across a stage in an almost balletic style with this boyish charm that he simply did not possess in real life. He was not as good as Michael Jackson but better than George Michael. They had a damn good choreographer. He had a troupe of twelve stunning-looking girls who danced with him and around him, and sometimes on top of him. Some of it seemed a bit indecent considering the age of his fan base. There had been complaints to the phone-in radio show *Liveline* about him. Mothers saying that he was perverting their children. His videos were played on heavy rotation on MTV Europe. But I think the attraction of Luke for these kids was that he looked so young. No matter how he danced, he still looked more like a child than an adult, and his appeal lay in the fact that he appeared asexual and therefore nonthreatening to prepubescent girls.

Luke had arranged for backstage passes for Will and Susan and me for this festival. Now that school summer holidays had started, I was working full-time in the bookshop. Avoiding Susan and missing her like crazy. I was determined to find a girl to come with me so that I wouldn't be Will and Susan's gooseberry, but the closer it got to the day, the more I thought about spending a whole day in Susan's company, and I didn't want to waste any of the time on someone else. And then, the best news of all—Will got finance for a short he was going to produce, and he needed to fly to London to convince some English actor to be in it. He invited Susan to go with him, but she wanted to see Luke's gig, and I took that as a sign that maybe she wasn't fully committed to Will after all. I mean, who would turn down a weekend in London to see an Irish teenybopper pop star in a field, but then she told me she was going "to support Luke and to represent Will." There were a few other more serious support acts on the bill, and I knew she liked the Sugarbombs. Maybe that was the attraction. It certainly wasn't me.

Backstage that night, in Luke's dressing-room trailer, Sean tried to calm him with some positivity mantra bullshit. We hung out with him, reassured him that he was going to be great. Sean left the room, and Luke pulled a bag of pills out of his pocket, bit one in half, and put it on his tongue.

"What's that?"

"It's new stuff. It just gives you a huge lift, makes you feel ace! Want to try one?"

"No!" I said. "You can't perform in front of that crowd when you're off your face, Luke. Are you mad?"

"I'll try one," said Susan, and I immediately felt like some old fuddy-duddy dad character, ruining everyone's fun. Luke picked a pill out of a small plastic packet and pushed it into her mouth. Susan grinned at me. "Come on, Brian, we have to let our hair down a little!" Luke laughed and gave me a pill too. I swallowed it with a bottle of warm beer.

"They're quite strong. I've only taken half because I have to go out there, but I guarantee, you two will have a great time." Luke went to get ready, and we were left alone in the dressing room.

"I take a few pills with Will now and then, it's no big deal, Brian."

"Sure," I said, not sure at all and grasping at excuses to seem cool. "We all do that from time to time, but I'm not sure Luke is the most stable of people to be taking this stuff. We don't even know what it is."

"Yeah, maybe nothing will happen, in which case we've nothing to lose."

"Or maybe we'll all end up in prison or in hospital."

"Brian, you are so cute." But she meant cute in the American way. Cute like a bunny rabbit.

Ten minutes later, at the side of the stage, waiting for Luke's big entrance, I felt a warmth spreading out from the pit of my stomach, and a feeling of contentment and satisfaction reached my fingertips. Everything was going to be fine.

Luke burst onto the stage at the center of a whirling dervish of dancing girls in scanty space suits, and the drumbeats cracked the air like fireworks. His energy was electric. Susan, beside me, clapped her hands in joy like a little girl, and I felt like doing the same thing. I caught her hand and we laughed at the sheer madness of it all. "We're not in Kansas anymore!" she yelled. "Are you feeling it?"

I was feeling grace and love and acceptance and joy and positivity and beauty and all good things. We hugged, and didn't pull away from each other, and I stood behind her with my arms around her waist, her head against my shoulder, as we watched my little brother work his magic. God, I loved that weird kid, despite everything. Even the older crowd who might have been there for the support acts were energized by him, and we watched as the crowd surged toward the stage.

Susan's hand brushed my thigh as we moved rhythmically to the music, and it was the most erotic thing I'd ever felt. I moved my mouth down and kissed the back of her neck. She didn't stop me. She moved back into me, pushing her ass against my groin. I knew she wanted it too. Without words, we slipped away from the side of the stage and walked, almost ran, back to Luke's trailer, giddy with laughter and anticipation. Once inside, I locked the door and we kissed hungrily and undressed each other in a hurry.

Afterward, we sat naked, tracing our hands over each other's bodies, talking about how much we cared about each other, how good we felt together, and then, consumed by lust, we delved again into each other, tasting and touching and caressing, together in ecstasy.

Later, we found out that was the name of the drug. Ecstasy. In the following years, it seemed like everyone took it, but I feel like we were among the first. I was never a drug taker, so perhaps it affected me more than most, but Susan's ardor matched mine that day, and when we melted away from each other late that night, it was as if a beautiful dream was crumbling. We got a lift back to Dublin on Luke's tour bus, holding hands under the table, while everyone around us celebrated with drugs and booze. Luke offered us more pills, but I think we both knew we had transgressed, that the loss of control was something we would have to deal with. I was sober enough to know I couldn't invite Susan back to my grotty flat, and when the bus stopped at the end of her road, I hoped she'd ask me to come with her, but she kissed me chastely on the cheek, thanked Luke for the brilliant concert, and said she'd see me next week at work. Luke, in his own selfish world, had noticed nothing.

The next morning, I woke with The Fear. All of the previous day was hazy. Had we really talked about running away together and opening a bookshop by the sea? Had I told her that I loved her from the moment I saw her? Had we even mentioned Will? We definitely talked about how emotionally connected we felt. And yet, in the cold light of day, I was sure the words were hollow. Even if we had meant them, they were artificial, drug induced, fantastical. Her body had been amazing, and the sex better than with anyone I'd ever been with before, but was that the drug too? Had I imagined some of it? Had I been tripping?

Susan and I avoided each other in the bookshop. The manager asked if we'd had a row. And then we did have a row. When finally we were forced into unpacking boxes together, Susan told me that I shouldn't have seduced her. I balked. We had seduced each other. She conceded it was the drug, insisted she had no romantic feelings for me, and wanted to forget it had ever happened.

Spurned, I turned nasty. "So you don't want to run away with me?"

She burned crimson. "You mustn't tell Will. It would kill him. I'm going to look for a job elsewhere. We can't continue to work together anymore, Brian. It's just too awkward."

I was miserable. I went back to teaching in September, a full-time position. I hated it. I couldn't settle into anything. At least, with my increased financial security, I was able to rent a small one-bedroom flat in Ranelagh. For months I sat around waiting for Will to dump Susan, waited for her to discover that he was cheating on her, waited for him to get bored and move on, but at Sunday lunches, they seemed closer than ever. And then, in late October, Will announced he had three pieces of good news. First, Susan and he were moving into a house together. My heart sank. Second, they were getting married. I stared at her as he popped the champagne cork, and my heart flipped in my chest. He filled a few glasses and passed them out. I couldn't drink mine.

"And in even better news, Mum, we're going to make you a granny!" Mum leapt up and hugged them both, though she declared that she would not countenance being called "Granny." Mum was not the type to disapprove of sex before marriage. I think Dad would have been horrified.

"Is it a boy or a girl?" she said. "How pregnant are you?"

Susan faced my mother as Will placed a proprietorial hand on top of her head. "Oh, we think about fourteen weeks, past the danger zone anyway. We've decided to let the baby's gender be a surprise."

"Surely, the baby is enough of a surprise?" I said. "You didn't plan it, did you?" I tried to keep the spite out of my voice.

Susan did not look at me but laughed. "Well, all the more champagne for you!" she said, and Luke swiped the bottle and filled his glass to the brim.

"A baby? Seriously?" he said.

Will glared at him. "What's your problem?"

"Nothing," said Luke and the mood grew tense.

Luke became morose and drank everything in the house before Mum told him he should leave. She commented on how quiet I was. "Loads of homework to mark when I get home," I said. I had been silently doing the maths in my head. "About fourteen weeks." *About.* If it was sixteen weeks, it could be my baby. I kept trying to catch Susan's eye, but she looked everywhere except at me.

Mum admired the modest diamond engagement ring and discussed wedding dates with them. "Of course, you'll have to tie the knot before the baby comes!"

As I was leaving, Will said, "You haven't congratulated us yet, Brian."

"Haven't I? Sorry. I'm so happy for you." I tried to get Susan to look at me. "You'll make a brilliant mum."

"Yeah? And what about me?" said Will. "I'll be a brilliant dad too." I could see he was happy, proud, and excited.

"Yes," I said, "a brilliant dad. Congratulations."

Chapter 30

1979

I wished Paul had been my brother instead of Luke or William. Our birthdays were a month apart, and we were first cousins because our dads were brothers. We even looked alike, although there was nothing wrong with his nose. Paul was blond like me. My brothers had darker hair. We were in the same class in school and sat beside each other. He lived around the corner.

Paul and I shared comics and sweets and catapults, unlike William, who shared nothing with me, or Luke, who just gave me anything of his that I wanted because of God. I heard Mum say that Paul was spoiled by Aunt Judy, but he wasn't. He got all the same stuff we did, he just didn't have to share it with anyone. Except when he shared it with me.

Uncle Dan's house was much smaller than ours. But they didn't need as much room as us. When I had a sleepover at Paul's house, it was fun to sleep on the floor beside his bed on a pull-out mattress. We could have midnight feasts and play with our soldiers and dinosaurs long after we were supposed to be in bed. We never did that at home. Luke was always scared that everything was a sin. When lights went out, Luke closed his eyes and crossed his hands over his chest. "In case the Lord takes me in my sleep," he explained.

Paul saved my life once. We had a joint eighth birthday party in his house. We never had birthday parties in ours. I was excited. His mum, Aunt Judy, had cooked two cakes, one with Dennis the Menace on it and the other with Gnasher the dog. We were both big fans of the *Beano*. We even had the badges to prove it. It was October, even though my birthday wasn't until the following month, and Paul's had been three weeks earlier. Though it was pretty wet outside, Uncle Dan had bought a swingball set, and we all took it in turns until Will whacked the ball too hard, and it detached from its string. My brothers had been invited along with our school friends. Will was throwing his weight around, reminding everyone that he was the oldest. Luke clung to his scapular medals and gifted Paul a book about Saint Paul that he'd bought with his own money.

After it got too cold for swingball, we went inside and Uncle Dan said we could play hide-and-seek. It wasn't going to take long to find anyone, but I knew Paul's house better than everyone else, and I knew exactly the right place to hide. There was a false floor inside their airing cupboard. I think Paul and I were the only people to know it was there. We found it by accident, and we never told his parents because we kept our secret treasure in there: the spud guns that we weren't allowed to have, the old-fashioned money stolen from Uncle Dan's box, the gun holster that we'd found in a dumpster—at least we *decided* it was a gun holster; it may just have been a small broken leather satchel. I reckoned if I scrunched myself up small and tight, I could just about fit under the false floor. So that's what I did, and then I moved the piece of flooring on top to cover myself completely. Only it got airless quickly, and I lost all my energy, and there wasn't enough room in the space to kick the lid open, and then I started feeling dizzy and sick. One of our school friends was doing the seeking, and I guess it was probably ten minutes before they realized I still hadn't been found. I had fainted by then, and it was Paul who realized where I must be hiding. He raised the alarm when he found me purple and motionless.

I don't remember much about being found, but I remember their next-door neighbor, Dr. Hallinan, rushing in, and I remember being hit hard on the chest and crying.

I was completely fine the next day, but Paul had saved my life. His dad nailed down that floor afterward, and we were banned from ever playing hide-and-seek again. It turned out to be a dangerous game. At another party on our road just a year later, a little girl got trapped between two panes of glass, a foot apart, and the window had to be smashed to release her. But if I worshipped Paul before that day, I was even more steadfast in my loyalty to him afterward. We spent all our time in each other's houses. We cut our thumbs with sharp knives until they bled a little and swore ourselves to be blood brothers.

After Paul died a year later in 1979, I wondered if that bloodletting might have caused the poison that killed him. He got sick so gradually that it became kind of normal. Before that party, he had complained of pains in his legs, and his mum said it must be growing pains, but I didn't have growing pains. At first, he was home with a flu or a cold for a few days, and then he had to go to hospital for tests, and then there were more tests, and then his hair fell out, but that was cool because we both loved *Kojak*, and I'd bring him lollipops. He didn't run around much anymore, but we were happy to discuss the characters in our comics, and then his mum gave him a magic set, and it wasn't even his birthday, and we learned how to do all the magic tricks.

I missed him at school, but I visited every chance I got, whether he was in hospital or at home, except for Thursdays, when I had judo. Sometimes, I'd visit and he'd be asleep and I wasn't allowed to disturb him, but I'd write him notes about funny stuff like Mr. Gallagher's mustache or Father Matthew's sandals with the purple socks underneath.

I never thought for a second that he was going to die. I'm not sure I understood what death was, though Luke was always talking about it, and crucifixion and resurrection, but the idea that I would never see

Paul again, that we'd never do our funny walks and our secret codes, I didn't know how to cope with that.

Paul died the day we went to see the Pope. I remember nothing about the Pope—except that Luke went apeshit at the Mass and we spent hours looking for him. Afterward, when we got home and learned that Paul had died, Luke got hysterical and screamed that it was his fault, and I was paralyzed by fear. How could my friend, my blood brother, be dead? I threw up, and everyone was upset. Even Will went out to the garden and stayed there for an hour by himself. Dad was trying to pacify Luke—and it turned out Luke knew all along that Paul was dying because Mum had told him. Paul saved my life, but Mum said there was nothing I could have done for him.

The days after his death were colorless and pointless. The yellow-and-white papal bunting and flags everywhere felt so wrong. There was nothing to celebrate. I felt that I'd be better off dead too. At the funeral, the boys in our class made a guard of honor for the coffin. Our teachers came and handed out tissues, and even the roughest and toughest boys used them. Luke wasn't allowed to come because everyone was afraid he'd make a scene. I never saw so many people crying. Even the choir kept breaking down in the middle of hymns and having to start again. Uncle Dan was openly sobbing. Aunt Judy could barely stand up. I realized, suddenly, they didn't have other children. They only had Paul, and now they'd lost him. Mum bawled her eyes out, and Dad tried to be strong but kept making this weird choking sound as he tried to contain his emotion. One of the guys who carried the coffin down the aisle tripped and nearly dropped it, and part of me hoped the coffin would fall and break open and that I'd get to see my friend one last time. I'd pick him up and carry him away and find a way to fix him. It was the worst day of my life. I was never going to another funeral ever again.

Chapter 31

1976

It is one of my earliest memories. We were all small, just five, six, and seven years old. I was in the middle, distinguishable from my brothers by my blond hair and crooked nose. We were in the back garden of our house, playing or fighting. In those days, we were not big or strong enough to do lasting damage. Playing and fighting were the same thing. Mum was inside, behind the open French doors in the sitting room, ironing, with the radio on. She was careful about sun damage to her skin, and we were at all times slathered in lotions. Before that day, as far as I can remember, she protected us all equally.

We had sticks in our hands, and by some stroke of luck, mine was the biggest. William, the oldest of us, was trying to grab it out of my hand while I tried to wallop Luke with it. Luke was jabbing his stick at me in the manner of a sword-wielding pirate, but I was already conditioned to carry everything with two hands, and my grip was stronger and carried more heft. I lashed William across the middle of his back with all my tiny might, releasing a wail of injustice from his shocked red face. Mum knocked on the window, shouting at me to leave William alone. I shouted back that I hadn't done anything, even though I had, but then we all turned to the sound of a low growl.

Crouched in the side passage of the house, hackles raised, was an Alsatian dog, teeth bared, snarling, ready to pounce. While Mum, oblivious, continued to shout at me that "William doesn't tell lies!" we were frozen with fear. I remember that feeling, knowing that something awful, even catastrophic, was about to happen, and nothing I could do would prevent it.

The dog leapt into the air and crashed into the middle of us, knocking us all to the ground like skittles. Mum came barreling out of the sitting room, capsizing the ironing board, with a heavy table lamp in one hand. It was the closest thing she could grab. She swung it toward the dog and pulled at William and me with her free hand and ran with us toward the house. Luke was left out there, cornered by the slavering dog, screaming, hysterical as he reached for one of the abandoned sticks, but I watched as the jaws of the dog wrenched his ankle, and the animal tossed its head from side to side as if trying to unscrew Luke's foot from his leg. I turned away then, in terror, but caught William watching the scene unfolding, his eyes narrowed as if studying the incident for something he might like to explain later.

I looked to Mum, who was watching also, blank eyed. "Get Luke!" I screamed. She lurched outside again, slamming the doors behind her to keep us safe, and this time she had the pipe of the Hoover in her hand. She landed it squarely on the dog's head, and it released its grip on Luke's leg, running away down the side passage, never to be seen again.

She ran and closed the gate behind it before returning to Luke, whose lower leg was a bloody mess. He was no longer crying but pale and shaking. "Why did you leave me out here?" he shrieked.

William and I looked at each other. We did not have the vocabulary then to articulate what we had always felt but somehow, from that day on, knew. That we were loved more.

In later months and even years, that story became family lore. Mum would laugh and say she should have had three arms that day. She lied that she had grabbed William and me in each arm. In the retelling, the dog grew in size and breed. It was a Doberman before we heard of Rottweilers. Its fangs grew in length and sharpness. Luke's foot nearly had to be amputated apparently, when in reality he had suffered only flesh wounds. We had gone to pick out a wheelchair for him, according to William. Dad said it was the first time he'd heard of a sabre-toothed tiger escaping in suburban Dublin. Mum said it would never have happened if Dad had fixed the handle on the side gate. Dad might tease William and me, and call us Mammy's Boys, but we knew it was better to be in a gang of two than to be on your own.

Luke never said anything on these occasions, even when it was decades behind us. We all knew the experience had scarred him deeply, but it was one of our family's little cruelties to revisit it, often.

Chapter 32

1989

I was in my final year of an arts degree in college, studying French and philosophy with no idea of what I wanted to do when I graduated. Three evenings a week, I waited tables at a pseudo-French restaurant where the only French thing was the word *restaurant*.

I was good at French, but most of the philosophy bored me senseless, and I couldn't wrap my mind around the concepts of Kierkegaard and Confucius and Aristotle without my head exploding. With French, I could get to grips with the language, the history, and the culture, but in philosophy I resorted to learning off the text in our books and regurgitating it in my own words to pass exams. I half wondered if the examiners even read our papers. The guys in my class were earnest about all this and would sit around discussing nihilism and obscure Dutch cinema. They bored the hell out of me. French lectures were much livelier.

Luke had stopped attending lectures in engineering to sing in a band. Mum said he was always doomed to failure, but Luke's band was the talk of the campus. Everyone was saying they were the next U2. I rode on the coattails of their success. Even though we attended the same university, I rarely saw either of my brothers. Will had graduated the year before and had got a job as a trainee on a film, *The Courier*. The way he talked about working "on set," you'd swear he was directing it, but he clearly loved it and had found his career path, even though I think his job was to fetch coffee for the crew. I was treading water. I'd decide what I wanted to do later. I assumed it would come to me, like a lightning bolt, or that I would naturally gravitate toward some job or other, but at the time, I had no idea what that was.

Luke and Will were getting laid left, right, and center. Will had been sexually active since he was sixteen. I'd had a few fumbles but was still embarrassingly a virgin until I met Sandra.

Sandra was in my French lectures. She was always late or absent, and there were times when I was sure she'd thrown clothes over her nightdress to try to make the lectures on time. She reeked of booze and cigarette smoke, and those things would have put me off except for the fact that she was hilarious. She lived her life in chaos with a family of eleven siblings and various pets with human names like Emily or Stephen, so that when she told a story about home you could never be sure whether she was talking about her dog or her brother. She was often the center of attention in the student bar, and even though we were all pretty broke, we would scramble to find money to buy her an extra pint if it meant she entertained us for another half hour. She was shameless in the way she talked about sex and lovers and masturbation (girls masturbated—who knew?), and naturally most of the guys thought they had a chance with her. She wasn't especially pretty and was quite chubby, but she was attractive in the best way. Everyone wanted to be in her circle. Since I took copious notes at lectures and photocopied them for her when she was absent, I was firmly in her circle.

Luke was playing a gig in the Olympia. It was a big venue for the Wombstones and, like everyone else, I wanted to sleep with Sandra. I thought I could seduce her with tickets to Luke's show. The only drawback was that we'd have to share the box with Mum, Auntie Peggy, Will, and whoever he was bringing to the gig. Sandra was thrilled when I suggested she come as my date, though I was dismayed when she described

Luke as "a total ride." It amazes me how girls lose their minds over average-looking guys if they can sing a bit. Everyone in college had bootleg tapes of Luke's previous gigs. She knew all the lyrics to the songs.

I invited Sandra to our house for dinner first. Luke's gig was at midnight. Mum was pissed off about this. "What kind of concert starts at midnight? It's ridiculous!" The truth was that at midnight all the pubs in town would be shut, and the Olympia had a late serving license. You could legally drink there until 2:00 a.m. I didn't want to tell her that most of the crowd would be drunk.

Will was to collect us at eleven thirty, and Auntie Peggy would meet us there. Sandra arrived for dinner half an hour later than the time I'd told her, which was exactly what I'd expected. I'd told her that dinner was at eight and asked Mum to prepare it for eight thirty. Mum said she wasn't going to go to much trouble. She said she'd prepare a hearty soup and buy a loaf of crusty bread and made a big deal of how we'd all have to drink copious amounts of coffee to keep us awake. Sandra burst into the house like a grenade, fawning over my mum. "I loved you in *The Silent Garden* in the Eblana," she told her. "Our whole family went to see it. We took up nearly half the theater!" Mum was immediately mollified and flattered that Sandra was a genuine fan and overlooked the fact that Sandra was dressed as Madonna in her "Like a Virgin" days, years behind in fashion terms, cheap and trashy—bra straps on display, a ripped miniskirt, and badly bleached hair that lay flat on one side of her head like cattle-trampled straw and wildly backcombed on the other side like a haystack.

Mum and she chattered happily and, as with all Irish meetings, soon found people in common. Sandra's aunt had been a makeup artist in RTÉ when Mum was in the soap opera. Sandra's next-door neighbor had been Mum's obstetrician when all three of us were born. Mum winced and paled. "I don't think we need to go into any stories of childbirth, do we?"

Mum changed the subject then, moaning again about the late hour of Luke's gig.

"You don't have to come," I said, not unreasonably but knowing that Luke would appreciate seeing her there.

"Of course she wants to go," said Sandra. "This is Luke's big night, you don't want to miss it, do you, Melissa?"

Mum smiled wanly. "Of course not."

When Will arrived to collect us, he looked Sandra up and down, then gave me a quizzical stare. As we were getting into the car, he muttered, "Where did you get *that*?"

"What?"

"Her, it—Jesus, the state of her. Brian, tell me you're not serious about her. She's an embarrassment."

I felt the blood rush to my face. Will didn't know her and was judging her solely on her appearance. He hadn't heard her laugh or tell stories or sing a bawdy song. "Fuck off, Will, she's brilliant craic. Don't be so shallow." He snorted.

I was fuming. We all piled into the car, and I thought he might warm to Sandra as we drove into the city center and she regaled us with some hilarious tale of their childhood bunk bed arrangement in the modest three-bedroom house they grew up in. Will remained silent while Mum hooted with laughter and I fake-laughed, too, even though I'd heard the story before, because I needed to counter Will's rudeness. As soon as we were parked up, he strode ahead of us, making it clear he didn't even want to be seen with her. Will didn't have a date for this night. His natural confidence usually ensured he had some gorgeous blonde on his arm, but he made it clear that going to this gig was an inconvenience to him, and both Mum and he joined forces then to say how selfish Luke must be to put on a concert this late. It was nonsense, obviously, Luke had no say in the timing of the performance. He was lucky to get this venue. It was a break for him. Auntie Peggy met us at the stage door, rattled by the late-night action in the laneway: semi-naked teenagers, street pissers, and glue sniffers were to be seen the length of the lane. We were admitted and shown to a box by a doorman, and Mum patronized the guy by insisting on tipping him when there was no need.

The support band came on first. They were so bad that we all stood in the corridor behind the box to get away from the noise. Will offered to go to the bar to get drinks. Mum, Auntie Peggy, Sandra, and I stood around chatting, but Will took his time, and when he eventually came back, the warm-up act had finished, thank God. We went back into the box and took our seats. It must have been after twelve thirty. Mum was yawning, and Will kept looking at his watch and muttering "for fuck's sake."

Then the Wombstones arrived onstage. Luke looked utterly ridiculous in one of Mum's pink-sequined jackets over a cartoon T-shirt. Mum took a pair of opera glasses out of her bag and peered down at the stage. Sandra stood up and cheered. Auntie Peggy and I joined her. The crowd below was sparse. They hadn't come back from the bar after the first band had left the stage. The noise of chatting, squealing, laughing, and the fog of smoke drifted upward toward us. The crowd wasn't reacting well at all. They barely acknowledged the band onstage.

I tried to catch Luke's eye, but he was concentrating on his performance, strutting around like a lonely parrot as the band behind him desperately tried to generate some energy. It was embarrassing. His college gigs had been much livelier. At those, Luke had been way more animated. Mum was at the far side of the box from me, and I could see Luke several times turning toward her, but when I looked to see her reaction, she was chipping away at her nail varnish on one hand with the other. She wasn't watching the stage at all. Auntie Peggy nudged her and whistled and cheered, but Mum made her disinterest apparent. When the interval came, she said she was too exhausted to stay a moment longer and insisted that Will take her home.

I had always been aware that Mum favored Will and me over Luke, but I think she *must* have loved him in some way. She was furious and frustrated by Luke's dark moods and the crazy things he'd done as a kid, but that's because he embarrassed her. I think maybe once or twice I remember her saying something fond about him, but never to him. Luke definitely felt unloved by her. He had been closer to Dad. But

Dad was the same with all of us. It was the way it was, though, and I didn't question it.

Will took Auntie Peggy and Mum home in his clapped-out Nissan Micra, leaving Sandra and me on our own in the box with their unfinished glasses of beer and wine. I snaked my hand around her waist, and that's all it took. She responded passionately, and I lost my virginity on the floor of that box in the Olympia Theatre. We never saw the second half of Luke's show, but we certainly heard it, and by the end he had turned it around. The audience were stamping their feet in wild adulation, but we were too busy to watch. I had nobody to compare Sandra to in terms of a lover, but she was very generous with her affection, and I like to think I satisfied her too. In fact, I know I did because she panted and squealed her head off, and the sounds of her desire were thankfully drowned out by the noise from the stage and the crowd below.

At Sunday lunch the next day, Will went on and on about how ugly Sandra was, how I could do better than her, how embarrassing it was to have her with us last night. I told him to piss off and lied that she was just a friend anyway. "I hope so, because if people see you with her, they're going to think you're a bigger loser than you already are." He then turned to Luke and told him that he couldn't sing, the band was awful, and he needed to go back to college. To take the heat off me, I agreed with that part.

"Luke, seriously, you're going nowhere. One gig in the Olympia isn't going to make you a star."

"But none of you saw the second half," he whined, "we rocked the place. We're booked in again, they want us back. Twice a week in January and February, in fact."

Mum came in then. She didn't mention Luke's concert at all, except to say she wanted her jacket back and that Luke was not allowed to help himself to her wardrobe.

I saw Sandra in college the following week. She had already moved on to Frank, but she regaled the student bar with the story of how we had shagged on the floor of the box in the Olympia Theatre. Everyone thought it was brazen and hilarious, and I knew I'd scored brownie points on the social scale. I didn't have feelings for her especially, but Will's cruel words about her washed through my head. I slowly detached myself from her circle, and within a few months, we rarely met, apart from in the lecture theater. I don't think she noticed that it was deliberate on my part, but I'll always be grateful to her for ridding me of my wretched virginity in the most exciting way, and for not being ashamed or insecure about it. One day at the end of the last term, she saw me in the corridor and pulled me aside. "Brian, no regrets, right? You didn't think I wanted a relationship, did you?"

I blushed. "No, of course not."

"Good, because I'll always remember that as one of my naughtiest nights," she laughed.

One of.

"By the way, I didn't want to mention it at the time, but your brother is a shithead. Not Luke, Will. He tried to feel me up that night while I was sitting between you and him, and he hadn't even spoken to me. What a wanker."

I couldn't have agreed more.

Chapter 33

1995

I was living in Paris, teaching English in a private school, Institut Charles Sorel, in a large town house in the sixth arrondissement, not far from the Sorbonne. The job came with rooms at the top of the building, five flights of stairs up, small and sparse, but functional.

At the age of twenty-four, I'd had to leave Dublin for the sake of my sanity, and Paris seemed like the type of place where I might be able to forget everything and start over. I did several interviews to get the job. It was a very exclusive school. I lied on my CV that I had given English classes to the children of the French ambassador in Dublin. I even forged a reference to support the lie, but my French was good, and I'd studied their curriculum and devised my own lesson plan, which impressed them. It was an open-ended contract.

I thought teaching English to French students might be a bit more meaningful than teaching it to kids who thought that because they already spoke the language, they had no need to read it. The reality was a disappointment, however. Teenagers seem to be the same the world over. To show interest in a subject was to show weakness. Apathy ruled the day. There were one or two bright students in my class, a girl called

Arabelle and a boy, Sacha, who were both engaged and attentive. I ended up redesigning my classes for them and ignored the rest as they ignored me. I knew I wasn't a good teacher: it was something I'd fallen into after college; it wasn't something I'd actively pursued. I guess I still didn't know what I wanted to be when I grew up.

A month into my teaching job, one of the senior teachers retired, and the staff were all invited to lunch at La Saucisserie. The restaurant prided itself on being quirky. It was popular and expensive, but the food was nothing extraordinary. Cheeses and charcuterie, salads and quiches, the ubiquitous French onion soup. People came for the ambience and the decor. Meals were served on mismatched plates, wine was splashed into large coffee cups. Instead of chairs, there were rescued bench seats from old churches. Shaving mirrors adorned the walls as well as semi-pornographic shots cut out of magazines and slotted into expensive ornate gilt frames.

The moment I walked in, Conrad caught my eye. I didn't know who he was, then. I thought he was just a diner like us, but I gradually realized he belonged to the restaurant, as he sat at a front table totting up receipts on a calculator.

It had been fifteen years since my cousin Paul had died. We had been children, but when I thought of him, which was often, I always imagined him as the age I currently was. Conrad, with his big eyes and sandy hair, was *exactly* how I imagined Paul would be as an adult, except maybe a little older. He looked physically strong, average height, broad shoulders, large square hands. I watched him with fascination, imagining that he must be some kind of reincarnation. I mostly ignored everyone at my table. At one point, Conrad looked over, caught me staring, and smiled in acknowledgment. It was an indulgent smile, one from a proprietor to a customer, nothing more, but I was desperate to speak to him, to hear how Paul's voice might have sounded when broken, to see if his mannerisms were the same. It is said that we all have doppelgängers somewhere in the world. Few people actually get to meet theirs. It was unnerving to think that one would carry on living if the other one died.

At the end of the meal, I approached him and apologized for staring, told him in my accented French that he looked like my cousin, that they were almost identical. He laughed and responded in English— "A handsome fellow then, yes?"—and he had the same tone in his voice and mischief in his face. It was uncanny.

"Well, yes, though my cousin is dead."

His eyes grew sad. "I am sorry to hear this."

I struggled to explain that it was a long time ago, that Paul had died as a child, that I imagined he might have grown up to be like him.

I'm not entirely sure he understood what I was saying, and it was for the best because it sounded crazy. Nevertheless, he put out his hand and introduced himself. He invited me to sit down and join him for a glass of pastis. And he raised his glass in a toast: "*À Paul. Je suis vraiment désolé.*"

I had never toasted Paul before. It hadn't crossed my mind, but this seemed noble, correct. I smiled at Conrad. "*Merci.*" We fell into casual conversation then. He told me he had owned this place for a year, after spending some time in the West Village in New York. He ran it with his hands-off partner, André, who worked in investment banking, and I understood immediately that André was not just his business partner but his romantic partner too.

"And you?" he said. "Do you have a wife? A lover?"

How to explain to a stranger that I had only ever loved my brother's new wife, and yet the intimacy I had shared with Paul seemed to be present and I told this complete stranger about my love for Susan.

"This will not do," he said, tapping a cigarette on a silver cigarette case. "Paris is exploding with beautiful women. You must find one, *et vite!*"

I laughed. "It isn't so simple when I have to measure up to Frenchmen. You have a reputation, you know."

We shook hands and I left, with promises to return. It was an all-day place. I could pop in for a coffee anytime, and it became my regular haunt. Conrad and I struck up a friendship, and although he could never be Paul, we liked each other well enough, and even when my

French colleagues commented on the fact that Conrad was gay and people might talk, it didn't bother me. Growing up in a house with a singer/actress at the center of it, I didn't find the company of gay men or women strange or unusual.

I bumbled along in the school for over a year, taught private classes in the summer months. If I had been a better teacher, I might have foreseen the problem, but in Ireland, most of the time, girls went to all-girl schools and were taught by women and nuns, and boys went to all-boy schools and were taught by men and priests—I had never taught a mixed class before coming to Paris. I must admit, I was fascinated by the sexual politics among the teenagers. The girls were much more mature than the boys. They swatted them away like flies most of the time. They were well-groomed and expensively accessorized. Over the age of fourteen, they conducted themselves like young women, while the boys were children until the day they left school, and perhaps beyond. I know I was.

Arabelle Grasse was like the rest of the girls in appearance. She was physically developed with the attitude of a thirty-year-old world-weary divorcée, but she was a child. She hung back after class often to ask questions about the texts or her homework. She loved English, she said, and she would apply to study in Cambridge before doing *le bac*. She was a pretty fifteen-year-old with flawless skin and perfect teeth and long honey-brown hair, which hung down to her waist. I wasn't too familiar with girls' fashion, but although their uniforms were ordinary enough—blue blazer, white shirt, blue skirt—the girls all rolled their skirts up above their knees, they knotted their shirts at the navel, and opened enough buttons to reveal cleavage if they had it. I could see how the boys were easily distracted, but they were all children to me.

Unfortunately, from Arabelle's point of view, I was not a teacher but an object of misplaced affection. It was a teenage crush. Completely irrational, as crushes are. I was not handsome or successful or rich. I did not possess a car or a fine linen jacket. I did not even smoke. When she presented a letter from her mother asking for private tuition that September, I was frankly glad of the opportunity to earn a bit more cash and ignored the fact that Arabelle didn't need the extra classes. She was well ahead of her peers.

It was agreed that two evenings per week I was to go to her elegant apartment on Boulevard Saint-Germain and coach her through Shakespeare, the Brontës, and Thomas Hardy. I sensed it was not the happiest home. Arabelle's father worked in Lyon, and I assumed her parents were estranged. Her mother suffered from persistent migraines, and on the few occasions I saw her, she would appear disheveled in her robe, standing at the kitchen sink, swallowing painkillers with a glass of water. There was a brother who was at university in New York. Clearly, these children did not want to live at home, and university was their opportunity to escape.

The first time I came to the apartment, I met Madame Grasse, who admitted me, showed me to the study and then announced she had to go and lie down. The apartment was shuttered from daylight, and I could see outlines of old dark furniture through the gloom with the occasional glint of silver from large candelabra sitting on sideboards. Arabelle's study was bigger than my room in the school. She had baked a cake, and before we began our class she was anxious that I taste it. She had to be reassured several times that I liked it and insisted I take the entire thing home after the class. I had come with a lesson plan, but she requested that we start each lesson with conversation in English because, that way, she was in the right mindset when we came to the text. I conceded to fifteen minutes of chat and kept the conversation banal. Where did she go on holidays? What did she like to watch on television? Who was her favorite pop star? I asked this question with a sense of mischief. I had not told anybody that Luke Drumm was my brother, but he was pretty big in France too. She named some other French group that I'd never heard of. But then she asked me questions. What was Ireland like? Did I prefer it to France? What was my favorite food? She pointed to my hand and asked if I was married and if Irishmen wore wedding rings. That should have been the first alarm bell, but I didn't hear it.

The next time I came, she had prepared my favorite meal, even though it wasn't dinnertime. She was wearing a skintight dress with a slit up the side that revealed her bare shiny legs. That day, I felt a little uncomfortable. I sat on the other side of the table to her, whereas previously I'd sat beside her. She looked at me a lot more than at her book, and this time I limited the conversation to five minutes, and I asked the questions, keeping them mundane and generic.

Within a few weeks, at school, she had started acting familiar with me. She called me by my first name in front of the other students, even though I had never told her what it was, and it had always been "Monsieur" before. The others mimicked her and called me Brian, too, but in a simpering girlie voice. Some of the boys made smooching noises when my back was turned, and I realized that, whatever she had told them, I had lost any respect I had from this class.

I posted her mother a note, requesting that our next lesson take place in the school library, which stayed open until seven. Arabelle came to me in school, tearfully asking why I didn't want to come to her home anymore. I lied and said I had a part-time job in a restaurant closer to the school, and her home was too far away. Of course, she wanted to know which restaurant, and on the spur of the moment I told her it was La Saucisserie.

She must have staked out the restaurant for days because the next time I was there, perhaps a week later, after school, she passed the window and waved at me. She came in and sat beside me, uninvited, in her school uniform. "Hello, Brian! How are you? I'm going to order a coffee. Do you want another? Perhaps we could continue our lessons here? The library is so airless, and this is comfortable, isn't it? Are you waiting to start your shift?" All these questions, delivered in perfect English, while I blushed with embarrassment, knowing that I was caught in a lie and a potentially dangerous position.

"Arabelle, even though we are not at school, you must call me 'Monsieur,' and this is not an appropriate place for classes."

"It's my favorite restaurant. Do you work here weekends or just evenings?"

I guessed she had never been here before.

Conrad appeared at my side, surprised. "Brian, who is your young friend?" he asked.

"This is Arabelle, my student." I emphasized the last word. I tried to make some eye contact with Conrad, but he was looking at her with disapproval. "Conrad, shall I start my shift now? Arabelle, you must leave. Conrad doesn't like to see me chatting with customers when I'm working." Conrad raised an eyebrow at me but nodded, saying nothing. He was not going to actively lie for me.

She left, not before blowing me a kiss and saying she would see me tomorrow.

In French, Conrad expressed his discomfort. "Brian, I told you there were beautiful women in Paris, but what age is she? Sixteen? It is wrong to encourage her. Why did you tell her that you worked here?"

"I know. Honestly, I haven't encouraged her. I told her I worked here in order to get out of teaching her private classes at her home because I felt so uncomfortable. She just showed up today. I think she has a crush on me. I don't know what to do about it."

"It is not right!" said Conrad, and I could see he believed me. "You must tell her. Tell the school. Put a stop to it."

Easier said than done. Most of the students were not impressed by me, and I knew the faculty members thought me strange, a loner. I didn't socialize much with them. If there was to be a suggestion that a schoolgirl had a crush on me, would they even believe it? It's not like there weren't better-looking and way cooler male teachers on staff. Perhaps that's why Arabelle singled me out. She thought there would be less competition for my attention. She needn't have worried. The other girls treated me the same way they treated their male teenage counterparts.

I should have acted straightaway. I should have done something. But then I got a call from Luke saying he was coming to Paris for a series of concerts in May and had a few days off directly afterward. I put Arabelle to the back of my mind until I walked into the classroom one day to be surrounded by girls asking me about Luke. In advance of his concert, he had done an interview with a teen magazine, *Jeune Jolie*, and mentioned that he was hoping to catch up with his brother Brian, who worked as a teacher in Paris, while he was here. "Is it you, Monsieur? Is it you?" Instead of denying it, I realized that maybe I could gain back a little kudos by admitting the truth. There was uproar and cheering, they all wanted tickets and to meet my famous brother, and I said I would see what I could do. Suddenly my status among the students shot up.

It was no problem to get twenty free tickets. The Omnisport venue where he was playing was vast. I decided to raffle the tickets but make the students pay half price because I could do with the extra cash. They thought I was doing them a favor. There were far more than twenty children from the three classes I taught, mostly girls, who were interested in going. I deliberately did not choose Arabelle's name out of the hat. She came to me afterward, upset. "But we are friends! Why can't you bring me as your guest?" I gave her my best Gallic shrug and lied that it was the luck of the draw. I should have made it clear that we were not friends, but I was afraid of tears and recriminations. I didn't want to hurt her feelings.

Ever resourceful, Arabelle found a way to come. On the night of the concert, she turned up, having bought a ticket at great expense. Afterward she wanted to be introduced to Luke with the other selected teenagers. I had arranged a fifteen-minute meet and greet with autograph signing, and Luke obligingly posed for photographs with them and some of their parents who had come to collect them. The happy children then dispersed, but Arabelle stayed behind, and when I got into Luke's limo to be whisked off to the Lutetia Hotel, she climbed in behind me.

I was annoyed by her presumption and arrogance. "Arabelle, you must go home. I need private time with my brother." Luke was kind to her. He gave her a poster and some CDs. I insisted angrily that she had to go. She sulked but got out of the car.

Luke assumed she was a fan of *his*, and I didn't bother telling him the truth. I went back to Luke's hotel and got drunk while I watched him eat French pastries and drink Fanta. Every time he mentioned Will's name, I changed the subject. Luke was easy to distract.

The next day when I went to school, I was summoned to the headmaster's office in the afternoon. I knew instantly that this meant trouble. My hangover added to the paranoia.

"What is going on between you and Arabelle Grasse?" He was livid. He stood behind his desk, his hands gripping the chair. I squirmed in mine.

"Absolutely nothing, Monsieur le Proviseur, except I think she may have a crush on me. I have done nothing to encourage it."

"I believe you have a brother who is a 'pop star'"—he loaded the words with disgust—"and that you took her and twenty other students to see him last night, on a school night?"

"Well, yes, I arranged tickets, the students were most enthusiastic. But I raffled the tickets, and Arabelle didn't win one. I made sure of that. Their parents were aware, Monsieur, I got written permission from them."

"Oh yes, the parents are certainly aware, Brian. One of them rang me this morning to tell me that Arabelle Grasse was seen getting into a limousine with you and your brother."

"She tried, but I told her to get out."

"And am I to believe you have been giving her private tuition, even though she is one of the brightest students in the school?"

I looked down.

"All of these things organized without consulting me or the *proviseur adjoint*. Are you aware Arabelle has told other students that you are her boyfriend?"

"What? No! That is ridiculous—"

"Have you given the girl any reason to believe you have romantic feelings for her?"

"No! She's a child. Of course not."

He sat then. Did he believe me?

"This shows poor judgment on your part. I am sorry to say this, but there will have to be an immediate inquiry. We will be talking to Arabelle and her mother, and"—he peered at me—"we will be checking your references. We should have done so before. While the inquiry is conducted, it would be better if you stayed away from the school. And for God's sake, stay away from Arabelle."

"What? But I've done nothing wrong. And I *live* here." I felt my temper rising. I have always had a temper, but most of the time I've been able to contain it.

"*Au contraire*, you have behaved entirely inappropriately. I suggest you seek alternative accommodation, at least temporarily."

I stood up, shaking with anger. "Fuck you! Are you going to take the word of some manipulative little bitch over mine? You're implying that I'm a fucking pedophile! Do you know what that could do to a teacher's reputation?" I leaned forward across the table and grabbed him by the collar. "Are you trying to destroy me?"

He yelled for help, and that made me angrier because I hadn't even intended to hit him, but the secretary burst into the room, misread the situation, and started screaming.

I was wrestled to the ground by the caretaker and the geography teacher and escorted from the office. The consequences were devastating. I received a note under my door later that evening from the head of the school board informing me of my immediate dismissal and ordering me to vacate my apartment within twenty-four hours unless I wanted *la police* to be involved.

I had blown everything by losing my temper. But it made me even angrier, if anything. I knew my emotions were high. I packed my suitcase with my few belongings, walked to the Jardin du Luxembourg, and sat, contemplating how I had screwed up my life so badly.

Luke was still in the Lutetia for another few days. I couldn't tell him. He was stable now, but God knows what he might say or who he might say it to when having one of his episodes.

I turned to my only friend, Conrad. By the time I talked to him, I had calmed down and was feeling foolish, humiliated, and guilty. It was all my own fault. Conrad had warned me. Arabelle was just a child. I couldn't blame her for any of it.

When I turned up at the restaurant, I was close to tears. Conrad did not say "I told you." He gave me a glass of pastis, offered me a small room in his apartment "just for a week or two" and a job in the restaurant. I would chop vegetables and stack and empty the dishwasher in the kitchen. I would take orders from the chef only. I told him I had waited tables in restaurants in Dublin through college, thinking that washing dishes seemed appallingly menial.

"Brian," he explained, "in France, being a waiter is a career. It is not something we do to pass the time while waiting for something better to come along. All of my staff have at least three years' experience. I would not insult them by giving you a job. You do not belong in a restaurant, but you can stay here until you decide what else to do."

Despite my dive from grace, it was generous of Conrad. His apartment was large and ornate, filled with light, gilt, and crystal, and well located on Place de l'Estrapade. I met his investment banker boyfriend, who eyed me first with suspicion and then curiosity.

André was much older than Conrad; he was clearly financing the restaurant and the apartment. They had met in New York. They were an established couple, though I could tell André was relieved I was not gay. Through the walls, I heard him say, "Okay, one week, but no more. We don't know anything about him. Maybe he did do something with that child?" I sat on my hands in the bedroom, wondering if that rumor might follow me for the rest of my life, wondering if there was any way I might counter it. Conrad later counseled me: "Anything you do will make it worse."

He reported that Arabelle had hung around the restaurant for a few days, loitering on the corner, perhaps hoping to bump into me, but I was in the basement kitchen, unseen by customers and staff. Conrad had approached and told her I had gone back to Ireland and that there was no point in hanging around. Apparently, she burst into tears and ran off. That was a relief. By then, though, I was able to feel sorry for her. What a troubled child she must have been.

To thank Conrad, I made Luke and his entire entourage come to the restaurant for a meal toward the end of his eight-day visit to Paris. Conrad released me from the kitchen for the evening, but he contacted the press in advance. I didn't stop him. Free publicity for the restaurant was the least I could do to express my gratitude while I wondered what the hell I was going to do with my life.

Luke and I went back to his hotel that night. He invited me to take anything I wanted from his wardrobe, but he was patronizing about it. He had wardrobes full of brand-new expensive clothes, some of them with labels still attached. I took as much as I could carry.

The next morning, we met in an expensive café I could not afford. His shades and baseball cap covered him sufficiently so that we weren't bothered by any fans. He asked why I didn't have a proper job and offered to fire someone on his staff to give me a job selling his merchandise. I needed the job, but I couldn't humiliate myself by working for my little brother. I could only imagine what Will might say. I swore I was fine on my own. "Really?" he said in the most pitying tone of voice. I felt my temper flaring and left before I lost it completely. I went to La Saucisserie and put in an eight-hour shift, being roared at by a stereotypically obnoxious chef because the batons of carrots I had cut for a bloody garnish were an eighth of an inch too thick. I headed home with Conrad, in low spirits. André was away on business. Conrad poured us a brandy and asked me if I had thought about my plans for the future. It was an unsubtle way of saying that I needed to find somewhere else to live. I was going to have to reconsider Luke's offer.

I was startled to be awakened in the middle of the night by the buzzer. Nobody knew I was there. I assumed it was a friend of Conrad's, but it was Luke, drunk and messy. Conrad, trying not to be furious because of the publicity Luke had given the restaurant, went back to bed. Luke had discovered where I was living from someone in the restaurant. He looked around at my opulent surroundings and immediately concluded I was in a relationship with Conrad. I was so tired, I could barely argue with him. I didn't take much persuading this time to pack up my stuff and leave Conrad's to go on tour with Luke.

I had avoided my family for the best part of two years. I hadn't wanted to think about them or hear about them, because every time I did, I thought of Susan—and the baby I was convinced was mine.

Chapter 34

2005

I was the loser brother. Despite Luke's madness, he had already achieved a significant level of fame, and infamy, in his life. Will was enjoying huge success as a film producer. What was I? My brother's manager, whose career was in free fall, and a part-time teacher who nobody ever recognized, who only got invited to events because Will or Luke put me on the guest list. When photos were taken for the papers, I was asked to step aside to make way for my brothers and their notable friends. I envied them both.

I always loved Susan, even when she lied to me about her happy marriage, even when she swore that Will was the perfect husband. We both knew he'd been cheating on her for years, but she desperately wanted to keep the charade going. I tried to believe in the "if you love them, let them go" theory. I let them be.

When Will asked me to be Daisy's godfather after her birth in 1994, I was in emotional turmoil. Daisy had been born two weeks before her due date, exactly as I expected. But Will had told me that the baby was an accident. He didn't use condoms, and Susan was not on the pill. He was convinced they must have been careless one night. I knew there was a strong chance she was my child, but when I confronted Susan about this the night before her shotgun wedding when her belly was swollen at five months, she denied it to my face. I begged her not to go through with the wedding, told her I loved her and that I would go back to Detroit with her and make a new life for the two of us there. I knew she missed her mom and her sister, Lynn. She told me I was crazy and that she wished *I* would leave the country and let her and Will get on with their lives and their baby. A month after the wedding I flew to Paris. I didn't come home for the christening and was named as Daisy's godfather in absentia.

But now, nearly ten years later, I was back home, trying to get Luke's career out of the gutter. God knows I needed my percentage, but he continued to lurch from crisis to crisis. I ignored Will's philandering and tried to stay in Susan's life in whatever capacity she would have me. I used Daisy—I got to see Susan a lot because of Daisy.

Daisy and I were close. She was a great kid, full of beans and mischief. She told me things she wouldn't tell her parents. Silly, innocent things, but I kept her confidence because she was possibly my daughter, and I enjoyed having a piece of her that neither of them did. She was the image of Susan. I could see nothing of Will in her. Nor of me. There were no clues. I thought long and hard about getting a DNA test—it would be easy to take a strand of her hair from a comb—but then I thought, what if she's not my daughter? Would that change the way I felt about her, or about Susan? As long as I didn't know for sure, we three were bonded in my head.

In 2004, Luke met a girl, a middle-class rich girl who was pretty and funny and smart. She was way too young for him, but I thought it was all good publicity. I leaked the story to the tabloids myself, as I had leaked lots of stories since Luke had stopped me from making money out of his autobiography. The British tabloids paid good money for those stories. And if journalists suddenly had the contact names of the people who had attended a Halloween party in 1983 when Luke pulled his Jesus stigmata stunt, and if those people "spoke" to the press as "sources," nobody could link those stories back to me.

I know it made Luke paranoid every time those stories came out, and he wondered if he could trust anyone from his past. I felt guilty about it because I had already gotten him to sign over his house to me when he wasn't right in the head, but I had to take out a small mortgage on it for living expenses, and the mortgage needed to be paid. Luke's music was getting less airplay these days, and his public appearance fees were paltry. My "official" 25 percent as his agent/manager and accountant didn't amount to much, and I had to make money somewhere. The tabloids were the obvious route.

But this girl, Kate, was a good influence on him. Luke cleaned up his act, stayed away from the usual narcotics, cut back on his drinking, which was clearly his biggest problem, and behaved normally, taking his meds. He told me he was doing it for her.

"Luke," I said, because I'm not a complete bastard, "why don't you do it for you?"

"She's worth it, I'm not," he said, and it was the saddest thing I ever heard. He adored her. He declared himself to be in love. I'd never heard him talk about a girl like that before, and I was glad for him, though I knew he was investing his emotional well-being in their relationship, and that wasn't altogether healthy.

When I learned from Will himself that he had already had an affair with Kate, I couldn't contain my anger. First, I was furious on Kate's behalf. She was just a kid being taken advantage of by an older married man. Then on Susan's behalf. He was cheating on her again. But mostly I was incandescent with rage that he could do to Luke what he'd done to me, and steal the love of his life. When Luke told me Kate was pregnant, I knew it was the right time to act. It was me who engineered the dinner party that broke up Will's marriage. He had never deserved Susan in the first place, and she needed to finally see it. Kate meant little to me, and I was sorry for the way things turned out because I think maybe she did love Luke, but Susan was more important. When

Kate and Will excused themselves from the table at the same time, it was me who sent Susan after Will on some pretext, knowing she would overhear something that would crush her.

I had some idea that Susan might turn to me for comfort. There was no way she could accept Kate as a member of the family knowing that Will had slept with her. I hoped it would be the nail in the coffin of their marriage, and I was right. I felt completely vindicated.

But then Susan turned on me because I had known about it and hadn't told her. It was completely unreasonable of her, and I hoped in time she would accept my story that I didn't want to hurt her. I did, however, want to hurt Will. Ironically, when she threw Will out, he came to live in my spare room until he got a place to rent.

I never thought of the fallout for Daisy. I regret that. I took her to Euro Disney for the weekend on Will's guilt dollar and distracted her with Paris, but she was smart enough to know that something was up at home. I was present when Will and Susan told her they were separating but that they still loved her. They asked me to be there, and I watched her little face crumple in confusion and hugged her while sobs racked her small body. I wish I'd thought it through.

A week later, Kate miscarried her baby and maybe the trauma of that made her think about what she was doing with Luke and the implications for Will's marriage. Luke knew Will and Susan had split up, but he didn't know why. I'm sure Kate knew. After the miscarriage, she ended her relationship with Luke, leaving him brokenhearted and vulnerable to another breakdown, which was exactly what happened. When Will moved out, Luke moved back in so that I could keep a suicide watch on him. I needed to get him functioning and available for work. I couldn't be there 24-7, but if I had to go out, I rang home constantly to check he was okay. He went to a dark place in his head. I had to force him to take his meds, but he stayed in his room, hardly ate, hardly spoke, rarely showered.

Mum, who knew nothing of the story behind Will and Susan's breakup, declared that she had never liked Susan, that she had always thought of her as white trash, and that it was cruel to deprive poor Daisy of her father. God knows what tale Will told her. When I told Mum that Luke was having a breakdown after Kate's miscarriage and abandonment of him, she said it was typically selfish of Luke to think only of himself and that he should be there to support Will in his time of crisis. I bit my tongue until I felt blood on my lips.

Chapter 35

2011

Money was tight. The agency was working on a shoestring. There was only one full-scale film made in Ireland that year, and two of my clients had only small parts in it. Mum hadn't been well, and even though she was in demand for stage work, chest infections kept her at home.

Luke was back in residential care, and although music royalties were coming in, he wasn't making any additional money. His income was eaten up by medical bills. I now had thirty-two clients, mostly actors. I had three in a soap opera and two others in TV dramas, but most weren't working, or working on profit-share theater shows, which never made a profit. They called me constantly asking about auditions, but I couldn't get them seen for parts that weren't there.

Will had started churning out cheaply made documentaries using archive material that he could sell internationally or as in-flight entertainment.

So, financially, things were terrible. But my love life had taken an upswing. Somewhere in the last few years, I had given up fantasizing about the life Susan and I could have had together. She had been single since she and Will split up seven years previously. I had made no secret of the fact that I was there for her, but she had never once given me any indication she was interested. I still saw her regularly when I took Daisy out. In the beginning, I grilled Daisy about Susan's love life. Children answer questions far more honestly than adults if you put them the right way. "Did Mummy tell you if she had a good time last Thursday when she went out in her pretty dress?"

"Yes, but her friend Sarah came home with her and got sick on the sofa. Mummy was really cross with her."

Now that Daisy was seventeen, she was barely speaking to her estranged parents and seemed to be permanently plugged into social media. I reckoned it was her age. At first, she brought home a black boyfriend. I don't think she liked him much but was using him to provoke a reaction from her parents, which was more racist than a thing either of them would do. They said nothing but were extra nice to the boy, which ensured that Daisy dropped him fairly quickly. Having failed to get much attention that way, she declared herself bisexual and started dating a girl in her class.

But she still allowed me into her life. Not every corner of it, obviously; she refused to discuss her girlfriend, for example, a bad influence who treated Daisy like crap, according to Will and Susan, who rarely agreed on anything. As her uncle (or possibly her father), it suited me to look at all this behavior objectively. She complained to me about her parents all the time.

But she liked being treated like an adult when I took her out to dinner to a pizza place or to a film premiere or to see a play. She was a cheap date, thank God. She had strong opinions about plays. She hated most of them, but she came along all the same. I was flattered that she still wanted to spend time with me until the day she said, "Don't you get lonely, Brian?" (She had dropped the "uncle.") "No girlfriend, no kids? It makes me feel sad." That was my wake-up call. A seventeen-year-old thought I was pathetic.

I had not lived like a monk. There had been a lot of one-night stands and a few short-term flings, but nobody lasted more than eight months. Women my own age were mostly desperate to have children, and although some of them were genuinely great, I could not take on any financial burden, no matter how much I liked the girl. Some of the women expected me to pay for dinner every time we went out. I tried to date women who were good earners or ones who had rich ex-husbands and good maintenance payments, but most of them weren't interested in me.

After Daisy's declaration that I was "sad," I realized that maybe I did need to find a life partner. Growing up, our family dynamic had been strange. Mum and Will were close, Dad and Luke were close, but I was neither close nor distant with either of my parents. I thought that was healthy, but now I wondered if maybe there was something wrong with all of us and our relationships with women. I thought about my two brothers, who weren't exactly successful at dating, either, though Will had his chance and blew it. Was I lonely? I didn't even have a cat. I went back through my lists of ex-girlfriends and looked them up on Facebook. So many had photos of children and husbands, but then there was Gillian, who advertised her status as single.

I had gone out with her for a few months over a decade previously. She had dumped me, but only because she was moving to Galway for a job. According to the posts I could see, she was certainly back in Dublin. She looked great, if anything better than she had a decade earlier, though I guess she wasn't going to post unflattering photographs of herself. I sent her a Friend Request and instantly got accepted. Now I was able to see all her info. She was a fully qualified lawyer working for a big company. Back in the day, she had worked for the Inland Revenue. From the photos, she lived in a decent-looking house in Goatstown, though it wasn't clear if she was renting or was a homeowner. She had a puppy (more likely to be a homeowner; landlords don't like pets) and watched a lot of reality TV. She went on many "girls' nights out" and had been a bridesmaid several times in previous years, but never a bride.

I sent her a direct message asking how she was doing, and we began a flirtatious conversation that went on for some time until I suggested meeting for coffee. There was a brief pause before she agreed. We swapped phone numbers. I was slightly miffed by the pause. What was her hesitation? We had always gotten on.

When we met the following week in a café near her office, we slipped back into familiar ways, joking with each other, talking in cockney accents and backing up each other's opinions by vehemently disagreeing while nodding. I'd forgotten how much fun she was. As expected, she wasn't as stunning as she was in the photos, but she looked well and seemed happy. At the end of our coffee date, which had turned into lunch (I paid), she suggested a drink later in the week. I was in.

After drinks we went back to her house, which I discovered she owned—worth quite a bit, nicely furnished—and she led me to her bedroom. She had clearly learned more than me in that area in the previous decade. I invited her for dinner to my place a few days later. She was impressed by the house. I didn't say how I'd come to own it and let her believe that I'd earned it. She was slightly less impressed by my cooking. Well, I hadn't done any cooking, but I'd been to Marks & Spencer and bought some pasta-ready meals in a three-for-two offer. I laughed and suggested she could teach me to cook. She said I hadn't changed, but I wasn't sure she meant it in a nice way.

After a further few dates and outings she told me I was cheap, when I had to remind her that it was her turn to pay. I am not cheap, but I have always been careful with money and don't see the point in squandering it. That date ended badly, and we parted company. At the weekend, I went to collect Daisy from hockey and drop her home. Susan made me coffee, and after some conversation, I asked her if she thought I was penny-pinching.

"God, yes!"

"What?"

"You make Ebenezer Scrooge look good, Brian. You are a skinflint."

"That's ridiculous! I don't splash money around like Will, but he loves flashing the cash. He thinks it makes him look like the big man."

"Yeah? Well in terms of generosity, you look like the small man. Who finally called you on it?"

"That's all very well coming from you. You haven't *had* to work in years."

"What are you talking about? I slaved in that bookstore while Will was getting his career off the ground. I went back after Daisy was born. I worked my ass off to get my degree and then my master's, and now I'm a social activist. Sure, I don't earn a lot, and Will still supports me to some degree out of guilt, but if he stopped tomorrow, I would manage perfectly well. How dare you suggest I don't *work*?"

I was forced to back down then and told her about Gillian. Susan thought my ready-meal dinners were hilarious, and my keeping account of who paid for what on each date outrageous.

"How is it outrageous?" I asked her. "Isn't equality what you want?"

"Damn it, Brian, there's a difference between equality and accountancy. When you take Daisy out, for example, you take her to the theater because you get free tickets. Or you take her to a film premiere because you're on the guest list. You don't actually spend any money on her."

"That's completely unfair. I took her to Pizza Slice a few weeks ago."

"Yes, but you said that was her birthday present, you didn't buy her an additional gift, and for Christmas you gave her some CDs of musicians you represent who she has no interest in. You might have noticed that she listens to everything on her iPod? You gave her CDs that you got for free."

"But I thought if she liked them, she could spread the word in school, make these young guys popular."

"What? You're making it worse! So, you were using her for promotion instead of spending money on something she might actually want?"

This conversation was going badly astray.

"I bought her an amazing rocking horse."

Susan was exasperated. "That was for her sixth birthday. Eleven years ago! And it wasn't even new. You got it secondhand somewhere, because there were crayon marks under the saddle." Well, she had me there. I had bought it in a junk shop for twenty pounds.

"Brian, I say this as a friend, okay? If you want to keep a girlfriend, you have to go into it with an open wallet and an open heart. You have money. We know you do. There might not be a lot coming in, but you got that amazing house for half nothing, and you don't spend a cent. What are you saving it for? I don't understand."

"But I think she earns more than me."

"So what? You must have thousands stashed away. Try spending some of it. You'll enjoy it. Seriously, take the girl to Madrid for the weekend. Surprise her. And don't bring any more women to your mother's Sunday lunches pretending it's a date. I cringe for them every time."

"I've only done that a few times."

"Yeah, well, that's not a date."

"Christ."

"Honestly? I've been hoping to have this conversation with you since I met you. Back in the bookshop days, you used to tell me how much you'd spent on coffee compared to me, and when it was your turn to buy lunch, you'd bring in sandwiches."

"I thought it was nice to spend some time in St. Stephen's Green."

"Not in fucking February."

"Those weren't dates."

"Weren't they?"

I faltered. "Did you think they were dates?"

"I . . . I don't know. I was never sure. You never made a move."

"Are you saying that if I'd paid for lunch, you might have chosen me over Will? That's a bit mercenary, isn't it?"

Her hackles raised, along with her voice. "You know what, maybe it is, but it would have made you far more attractive. Will was earning no money then either. He still made me feel special. He might order a pizza to his flat, but he'd have bought an expensive bottle of wine. Something to show he valued me."

"And look how that turned out."

"Fuck you."

We were shouting at each other now. I couldn't believe what she was telling me. I stormed out of the house and slammed the door.

A few days later, I texted Susan.

I'm sorry I got it so wrong. Would you like to come to Madrid next weekend?

Five minutes later she replied.

Yes, I would. Tell nobody.

That weekend cost me two thousand euros. Best money I ever spent.

Chapter 36

2008

I got a call from the Abbey Theatre, asking if Mum would audition for a new play. I had taken over the management of her career, too, in tandem with Luke's. I had convinced her to fire her agent. Why should she make money out of Mum when I could get it? I had the contacts, and I had a private relationship with some journalists who gave my clients publicity in exchange for insider stories. Some of Mum's friends had dumped their agents for me too. I was now officially an artist's agent, representing just twelve singers and actors, but I was making a living, and I had finally been able to give up teaching.

Through Luke, I had built up enough contacts in TV and radio and with music producers. I couldn't say which of my family members was more difficult to handle. We were offered great money at one stage to take part in a documentary about the two of them, but they were both horrified at the thought of it. They barely tolerated each other.

I was able to get Mum lots of voice-over work and quite a few radio dramas, and that was a good income for her, but by 2007 she had barely worked in a year. Luckily, Dad's pension plan was watertight, so she didn't need to rely on any of her own income to put food on the table.

Her showband singing was now wildly out of fashion, and no matter how much dieting, self-tanning, or makeup she did, she couldn't disguise the fact that she was now in her seventh decade, and her once-strong voice was beginning to crack. When the work dried up, her voice had, too, but mostly because she gave up doing her daily vocal exercises at the piano, which had been the soundtrack to our childhood. She and her actor friends would get together and bitch about their employed friends, but if one of *them* got a job, that person would then become the subject of the bitching. Mum knew she wasn't fully accepted as an actor by her gang, since she had made her name as a singer first. There weren't many acting roles for older women, and the competition and jealousy between them was savage.

When the call came about the tryout, Mum was at first outraged that someone with her extensive experience and ability was being asked to audition. "Everyone knows me!" she declared. I persuaded her that the English director wouldn't necessarily know her work and that she should go along and give it her best shot. She told none of her pals, because the humiliation of not getting the part would be too much, but when she turned up, they were there, all going for the same job.

Mum said the role specified a character in her "early seventies." Mum was sixty-one. She was the youngest auditionee and felt it a mixed blessing. She might have the advantage because her energy levels would be greater than those of her competition, but on the other hand she was afraid if she played "a crone" she would be typecast for the rest of her life. Sixty-one was by no means old, and I assumed they'd never give her the part exactly because she was so fit and healthy-looking. But I hadn't reckoned on Mum's desperation to get back on the stage and to hear the applause.

She rang me afterward and said the audition had gone well, and she was optimistic. Mum was always optimistic about work because she thought she was more deserving than everyone else and would then be bitterly disappointed when she didn't get the part.

On this occasion, however, she got the part. It had been a long time since I'd seen her happy and excited about something. It turned out it was the lead role in a new play by an established playwright. She had only seen part of the script because it was still in development, but she insisted on taking us all out to dinner in the Trocadero to celebrate; even Luke, who she more or less ignored these days. Robert, the maître d', greeted us all by name, as usual remembering my dad's name and recalling us all being there together when we were teenagers. Mum was delighted by the attention. She felt she was back on the scene at last.

Will arrived with his twentysomething girlfriend, Hilary, herself an aspiring but so far unemployed actress. Luke arrived late and drunk and morose, and spent the evening folding his napkin into smaller and smaller pieces, while skulling wine into his maw as fast as it could be poured.

Will had put Mum into two of his films, and although they were minor roles, she was always treated like royalty on set with a big trailer and the crew fawning over her because she was the producer's mother. She used the fact of this new play to tell Will that he needed to commission a screenwriter to come up with a story about a middle-aged woman, since clearly it was fashionable now that the Abbey were doing it and Helen Mirren had just won an Oscar for *The Queen*. Will promised to think about it, and then Hilary ruined things by saying she could play Mum's granddaughter. I think Will kicked her under the table because she gave a gasp. Luke laughed. "Or . . . ," he said, slurring, "you could play my loving mother, but you'd probably need years of rehearsal for that, wouldn't you, Mum?" There was a moment's silence.

"You're drunk," she snapped at him. "I don't know why you bothered coming."

"Oh, I thought this was a family dinner, was I wrong? Maybe I'm not really a part of this family. It would suit everyone, wouldn't it?"

I put my hand on his arm. "Luke, relax, it's fine, nobody's attacking you. We're just here to celebrate Mum's good news, okay?"

I was still managing Luke. Some American rapper had done a remix of one of his earlier hits, one that he had written himself, and it had been a huge success over there. Royalties were coming in again, and Luke was back on the talk show circuit in Britain and Ireland, with tentative offers to record from studios in America. He performed well in front of cameras, recalling his glory days, if I could keep him sober until the interview was over. Luke and Mum were more alike than either of them would ever admit. Two has-beens clawing at the dregs of their earlier successes.

Hilary was crimson with embarrassment. Will did nothing to reassure her. He moved the bottle of wine away from Luke's glass. Luke was about to react when two women approached our table and asked if they could take a photo with him. Luke immediately morphed into his pop-star persona and stepped out of the booth to oblige the ladies. Mum contained her jealousy. Altogether, it was a failure of an evening. Luke never came back to the table.

Two months later, I was sent the theater script for Mum. The cover note said there had been significant rewrites and a redefining of roles. It was a three-hander play with the other two actors doubling up and playing multiple roles while Mum would be onstage for the entire performance. Thankfully, it was one act with an expected duration of ninety minutes, but it was still a pretty demanding role. I understood why they'd given the lead to the youngest auditionee. I skimmed the first few pages. The character was light, funny, and charming. Mum could play to her strengths. Rehearsals were to begin the next day.

That night, Mum rang me. "I don't want to do the play. You have to get me out of it." I was shocked. A lead role on the stage of our national theater would be the pinnacle of most actors' careers.

"What? Why?"

"I . . . I don't like the director."

"But you only met him on the day of the audition. You said he was kind. Did you meet him again? Did he say something to you?"

"No. It's . . . I don't know, I just don't want to work with him."

"Mum, you've only met him once, you can't judge him on that."

"Look, it's not just him, I don't like the other actors. They're younger than me, they're going to be patronizing, making sure I have a chair and running to get me coffee as if I'm not able to myself."

"I'm perfectly sure they'll be happy to let you get your own coffee."

"It's the Abbey, I don't like the atmosphere. I feel like the place is haunted by dead actors, judging me."

"What?" This was unusual. Mum had been excited about the part, and she had just come up with three nonsensical excuses not to do it.

"So, you seriously want me to ring the Abbey and tell them you no longer want the part that is due to start rehearsal tomorrow, to break a contract that's already been signed? You realize this is career suicide? You know we won't be able to keep this quiet?"

"You can make up something. Cancer?"

"Mum!"

"You'll think of something."

"Are you nervous about it?"

"Of course not, I've been performing since I was sixteen."

"Look, if you pull out of this role, people will assume you are seriously ill. Are you prepared to go into hiding for the next three months? What is going on? You were desperate to get this part."

"I know." Her voice was small, childlike. "Did you read the script?"

"I read the beginning, it seemed like a fun part."

"It's not a fun part, it's a horrible part. She has all these awful things happen to her."

"Okay, but you're an actor, right? Isn't that what the job is?"

"Oh God, I have to do it, don't I?"

I needed my 18 percent of her fee. I had negotiated to get her more money, had promised she could generate media interest, that she could get bums on seats. Whatever her problem was with the show, she had to get over it.

"Yes, Mum, you have to do it."

I worried that she would deliberately act badly or misbehave with cast and crew to get herself fired, but her lifelong professionalism wouldn't allow her to do that. I rang my contact in the Abbey a week later to casually ask how things were going, to be told that everyone loved Mum, that she was playing a blinder, that she was brilliant in rehearsals. It put my mind at ease. Whatever was up with her had passed. Maybe it was nerves after all, or the fear of aging.

She canceled Sunday lunches for the rehearsal period. Will called me: "Is Mum all right?"

I didn't want to tell him she'd had a crisis of confidence and I'd pushed her into doing the show. Will resented the fact I was Mum's agent as well as Luke's and made constant digs about how I'd exploited my family to make a living, always referring to my house as Luke's house. I'd owned it for nearly six years now, *and* I'd let Will stay there when Susan kicked him out.

"Yeah, she's fine. Why?"

"She told me not to come and see her show."

"What?"

"She said she's terrible in it and she doesn't want any of us to see it."

"She is being a bit weird about it, but the Abbey are happy with her. I spoke to them last week."

"Well, she's not happy, and you're her agent. Sort it out." He hung up. Will was always Mummy's boy. They were close. Will could do no wrong in her eyes. She idolized him. And he thought she was the perfect mother. To him, she was.

I pulled the script out of my desk and read it through properly. Yes, the play took a dark turn after the first third when Mum's character was raped by her daughter's charming boyfriend, but the rape scene wasn't dramatized, it emerged from the dialogue after a storm scene outside a country farmhouse. It wasn't as if she'd have to simulate being raped. And there was a resolution, in that she murdered the rapist, and mother and daughter buried the body, so justice, although savage, prevailed at the end. It was a terrrific role and a strikingly well-written play. It skewered society's attitude to sex, motherhood, and aging in a way I'd never seen before. And it would be great for Mum's career to be seen in this kind of part. I wondered if Will might consider a film version of it. I sent him the script with a note suggesting this could be a great film with a starring role for Mum.

He emailed me a few days later and said the script wasn't something he was interested in and sarcastically congratulated me on trying to squeeze another few quid out of Mum.

Despite not being invited by her, Will and I went to Mum's opening night. As a film producer, Will automatically got an invite. Perhaps the playwright had the same thoughts as I did regarding its suitability for a screen adaptation. Luke said he had something else on, although that was unlikely. He never saw it.

Mum was electrifyingly good. I had been vaguely embarrassed by her showband singing and her stint on a bad soap opera, I had cringed at her panto performances, but in this play I saw a side to my mother I had never seen before. I fully believed she was the character and forgot she was my mum. The post-rape scenes were devastating. Tears filled my eyes as I saw her transform from a jovial widow into a destroyed and broken creature, and then resurrect herself into a vengeful, angry warrior. The other two actors were great, too, but it was Mum's show. Everything revolved around her character. As the lights went down on the final scene, the audience stood as one and clapped for a full five minutes. It was touching to see Mum's tears of gratitude. And, I thought to myself, this is a game changer for her career. Surely Will would see her capability now? He said nothing until we made our way out to the theater bar.

"She was something else, wasn't she?" I said, my voice still quaking with emotion.

"Yeah, brilliant. Look, I've got a headache, not feeling the best, I think I have to head straight home—"

"Hang on, you're not going to wait to congratulate her? For fuck's sake, Will, she just gave the performance of her life, you need to tell her."

He was already heading for the exit. "She told me not to come. She doesn't know I was here. I'll call her tomorrow," he said as he almost ran down the stairs.

The other two actors emerged from the backstage area, and there were cheers and claps on the back for them, but no sign of Mum. Usually she was first out of the traps on an opening night, looking for adulation and champagne, but on this night, when she deserved it, she didn't come out at all. The stage doorman told me she'd gone home on her own in a taxi.

I reasoned that she was overwhelmed, and probably exhausted, but I couldn't let the night go without letting her know how incredible she was. I jumped into a taxi and went to her house.

I gave the standard family knock before I let myself in with my key. I found her sitting in her armchair, sipping a large glass of brandy.

"Mum! Are you okay? You were amazing. Why didn't you stay around afterward? Everyone is going nuts over you. You were incredible." I almost hugged her, but she didn't smile or laugh or accept the congratulations.

"All my life, I've been performing, posturing, entertaining, and now I know that none of it was authentic. None of it mattered a damn. It's quite a thing to discover you've been faking it for forty years." Tears rolled down her cheeks.

"It's never too late," I said. I held her hand but found it was trembling.

"I just don't know if I can do that every night." She was booked for a six-week run.

"Of course you can. You're a trouper. Dad always said it." I don't know why I mentioned him. We never talked about him.

"I miss him so much," she said.

"Then do the show for him. He'd be proud."

I stayed the night that night in my old bedroom. Mum did the play for the full six-week run. She got rave reviews in all the media. The play subsequently toured Ireland, returned to the Abbey for a second run the following year, and then went to the West End in London for six months. She put her foot down then and refused to play the part any longer, even though there was an offer from Broadway. I begged her to think about it, but she had had enough. The role was recast and opened in New York to mediocre reviews and small houses before being pulled altogether in the second month.

It was all good for me, though. Actors defected from their agents and asked me to represent them, crediting me with turning around my mother's career, when the truth is that some casting intern at the Abbey had spotted Mum's potential.

Of course, when Will heard that other TV and film production companies were courting Mum for big roles, he capitulated and had her cast in a new drama series and in two films. I wasn't surprised when he tried to get the production accountant to cut me out of the deal and negotiate directly with Mum. She told me, and I hit the roof. She ordered Will to cut me in for my percentage.

Then the recession hit. Two of the productions were canceled. Will said nobody would take a risk on investing in an Irish production. Even though it meant lean times for me, and less work for Mum, I was delighted to see Will struggle. By now, I had an almost mortgage-free home and no family to support. Will had put stupid money into property deals and shares. He had to let a number of staff go and pay support to Susan for Daisy. There was another reason for never getting that DNA test. I loved Daisy, but I didn't need the financial burden of her upbringing.

Chapter 37

2015

At Susan's insistence, I told nobody about my relationship with her, if you could call it that. I was forced to accept her terms if I was to have any part in her life. She kept me at arm's length. I tried to persuade her we should go public, but she said it would hit the tabloids, horrify her dying mom, and disturb Daisy.

Daisy was already disturbed. She complained bitterly about her parents and how they disapproved of all her lifestyle choices. She would move out of Susan's house for short periods of time but boomerang back when life got too much. Luke told me she was a drug user, and I had tried to talk to her about it, but she denied everything. Daisy was cutting herself too. I noticed scars on her arms, and Susan confirmed my suspicions. Her weight ballooned.

Daisy mostly sat in her room playing her guitar, writing songs about people who had committed suicide or died of drug overdoses. She had a sweet voice, but her subject matter was grim and depressing. She had been to a number of therapists. Susan, in an echo of my mother, said, "She obviously gets it from your side of the family," which brought up the whole issue of Daisy's paternity. Susan finally admitted that she didn't know: Daisy's father could be Will or me. We agreed it would do no good for Daisy to find out even if Will wasn't her father. I agreed not to get a DNA test and didn't tell Susan I had already ruled it out many years earlier.

Susan and I negotiated our relationship carefully. We went away for weekends together, on separate flights on separate days. I only ever stayed in her house when Daisy was elsewhere, and if she stayed in mine, she parked in a lane two streets away and came in the back gate. Our assignations were always planned in advance. I wanted Susan for herself, not to spite Will or to stave off loneliness. I had always managed on my own, but I loved her. It was as simple as that. When I was with her, I became a better person. She had taught me to be financially generous, and though it felt uncomfortable and didn't come naturally, I saw the benefits of it. I accepted my role in her life. I realized it didn't matter if nobody else knew about our relationship, as long as we did.

By this stage, Susan had done a master's in equality studies and was at the forefront of the Marriage Equality campaign. In May 2015, Ireland was to vote on the right for gay people to be fully married in the eyes of the law. I had helped her with this by asking Luke and the better-known actors on my books to publicly endorse the campaign, and sometimes we spent evenings knocking on doors or boxing YES badges, bulk ordering T-shirts and making banners.

Daisy sometimes joined these activities. She now identified as bisexual. She could have identified as a chimpanzee for all we cared. We just wanted to see her happy. Susan's house became a hub of activity for the YES campaign at weekends, and it was great to see Daisy take an interest in something. She had written a song for the campaign but only performed it once at a rally. I wasn't there that day, but Susan recorded it on her phone, and it was a good song. Daisy wanted to post it to the campaign Facebook page, but Susan refused to allow it. She said it would end up on the internet and be stolen by some other singer. Susan told me privately that Will was worried people would post comments saying Daisy was fat or ugly or worse; and having read the below-the-line comments on social media concerning even the most beautiful girls, I was inclined to agree with her.

Luke came to help on these weekends too. He hadn't had a psychotic episode in quite a while. He had become a bit of a film buff. He was on his meds and had joined AA but, annoyingly, had begun to ask questions of my management of his career, asking to see a statement of accounts for the previous decade, suggesting that the record companies must have ripped him off. I assured him that wasn't the case. And it was easy to explain that all music revenue was down because of music streaming. It was mostly true. Airplay still paid, but CD and iTunes purchases had tanked. Everything was on YouTube or Spotify.

I had planned a surprise for Susan, and when it came through, I wanted to be there when she saw it. I didn't represent Saoirse Ronan, or any A-lister Oscar-nominated actors, though I had some promising graduates from acting school who were getting noticed, so business was looking up. But I knew people who knew Saoirse, and she had agreed to do a piece on camera advocating equal marriage. I knew this would go viral and that Susan would be delighted. It was the kind of thing Will should have been involved in. He'd actually met Saoirse loads of times. It would have cost him nothing to ask her, but Will showed no interest in the campaign. The way he mimicked his director partner Gerald was extremely irritating, but he'd be the kind of guy to say "How could I be homophobic when my business partner is gay?" This infuriated Susan, and that pleased me.

I knew that Daisy had moved out again, to a flat in the city, so I thought nothing of driving over to Susan's early on a Wednesday morning. I picked up some bagels and the ridiculously expensive coffee she liked. I thought we might spend the morning together before I had to head back for work.

My reaction when Will opened the door in a T-shirt, a pair of boxers, and Susan's dressing gown was one of stunned silence.

"What are you doing here?" he said as if it was the most natural thing in the world.

"Who is it?" I heard Susan calling out from upstairs.

"It's Brian. And he's brought coffee." He took the two containers from my hands. "Come in," he said.

"Are you . . . are you and Susan . . . ?"

"Ah, you know yourself, the occasional roll in the hay for old times' sake. Don't let on to Daisy. It will only confuse her. Poor thing has been having a dreadful time."

He led me into the large open-plan kitchen, and I sat on the sofa on which I'd made love to Susan the weekend before.

Susan appeared, stricken, as well she might be. "Brian, what are you doing here?" Her voice went up an octave.

"He bought coffee. Oh, I guess this one is for you. Here." He handed it back to me and went to the Nespresso machine to source his own coffee. He had never lived in this house, yet he clearly felt comfortable moving around it and acted like lord of the manor.

I couldn't speak. I simply stared at her. She glared defiantly back at me.

"Brian? Brian? Are you okay?" Will was talking to me, snapping his fingers in front of my eyes.

"What? Yes."

"Oh, cool, you brought bagels too. We can share them, can't we, between the three of us." It wasn't a question. Will always took what he wanted.

"Are you here about your little gay rights campaign?"

Normally, Susan would have taken him to task for that slight. But Will rambled on, oblivious to my shock and Susan's embarrassment. "Daisy being bisexual? It's just a phase, you know, she'll grow out of it. It's like a craze among young people. It's because of the internet. They're seeing all this stuff that turns them on. It'll be something else next month. Daisy is as straight as a die." I nodded and grunted a few times. Susan made herself busy wiping the spotless countertop over and over again. Normally, she would have attacked him like a bull for a statement like that. So would I. Not today.

"Right," said Will, "I'm going to have a shower, and then I have to shoot off to the office. Let you two have your 'campaign' meeting."

Neither of us responded. We heard her bedroom door shut.

"I can't believe this, after everything . . . after all the years . . . you despise him. You told me. What the fuck, Susan?"

"I'm sorry . . . It doesn't mean anything, it was a one-off . . ."

"Don't make it worse by lying! He just told me about 'the occasional roll in the hay.'"

"Brian, please, look, we'll talk about this later when he's gone, okay? It's hard to explain."

I didn't want an explanation. I needed to leave, because if I didn't, I was afraid I would punch her, or murder him, or both of them. I ran to my car and drove as fast as I could back to the city. At home, I bypassed the office, went upstairs, lay on my bed, and stared at the ceiling.

The next morning, the answer came to me. Revenge. Daisy. They both cared about Daisy. I cared about Daisy. But I needed to hurt them both, and I knew I could take Daisy from them. I had the video clip of her "Say Yes to Love" song. I posted it to YouTube under an anonymous name, linked to it on all the anti-gay rights pages, and waited. It didn't take long.

Within a few hours, the stream of vitriol was savage and relentless. I worried that I'd gone too far. She would find out quickly that she'd become a target. I called her.

"Daisy?"

Her voice was tearful. "Brian, someone put my video—"

"I know, love, I'm coming to collect you. Stay where you are. I'm on my way."

I drove straight to her flat and whisked her back to my house. I let her smoke a joint, with shaking hands, while she sat on my sofa, crying and freaking out.

"Daisy, I'll fix this. Don't worry. I'll fix it."

I posted the YouTube video to all the pro-equality Facebook pages and realized it had already popped up on loads of them. Thousands of messages of support were rolling in.

Daisy Drumm has a beautiful voice and a beautiful soul.

We heart you Daisy!

Ignore the haters, Daisy Drumm, we're going to get you to number 1!

Where can I download this amazing song?

"Daisy, did you upload this to Spotify yet?"

"No, I wouldn't know how."

The golden egg had tumbled into my lap. I could actually monetize this. I could make Daisy happy. I could make her famous and take her from Will and Susan in one fell swoop.

I had a Spotify account. I told Daisy to watch the pro-equality sites to see all the positive messages coming in. I told her I would negotiate with the person who had stolen the song and put it on YouTube (me) and get them to take it down. Meanwhile, I created a YouTube channel in Daisy's name and uploaded the song to iTunes at 99p per download, with the promise of a donation going to the Equal Marriage campaign.

"Daisy, would you like me to be your manager?"

"Manager?"

"Yes, I think you're about to become a media star, and I want to handle things in the way you are most comfortable with, because we are not going to let the haters win this one, okay?"

She jumped up and hugged me, a thing she hadn't done in several years.

I drew up contracts and had her sign them within the hour. I would courier them to my lawyer first thing in the morning.

"Will I have to go on TV?"

"Probably not until the referendum's over, but the vote is next Friday, we have to move fast."

"But I'm not—"

"Daisy, come on! This is the break you need. You've been so aimless for the last few years. You've written great songs—"

"But Dad says I'm fat . . ."

"You're beautiful, Daisy. And look at how brave you are, standing up for your rights and your friends' rights? How about standing up for your body shape too? Stop hiding yourself. I can get you a stylist and a makeup artist."

"Can you get me a personal trainer?"

I almost cried for the kid. My motivations may have been warped, but I was going to help her see how great she was. She didn't need a personal trainer. She just needed affirmation and goals and a reason to get out of bed in the morning. That evening, I collected all her stuff from her flat. She agreed to live with me for a few months while we sorted out her career path. I let her ring her parents and tell them the news. She and I had ignored their calls all day.

Will was livid when he spoke to me. "You had her sign a contract without talking to me or Susan? You're 'managing' her now? Are you taking the piss here, Brian, because I do not consent to this."

"Didn't you talk to her? She's happy. And she doesn't need your consent. She's twenty-one."

"I'm going round to her flat to get her. This is ridiculous. I don't want my daughter to be a poster child for gay rights."

"Will. Seriously? You're so homophobic."

"Don't be so ridiculous, I just don't want her used and abused on the internet. She's fragile. You know it."

"I know you think I'm on the make here, but I love that kid like she's my own." I let the words sit for a second. He didn't notice. "I'm not going to let any harm come to her."

"You'd better not, Brian. She's my child and I don't want her hurt."

I think that's when I made the decision.

Susan was more difficult to pacify. "What are you doing, Brian? Is this because of yesterday?"

"We're finished, Susan. I was just convenient for you, but you know our relationship meant everything to me. I can't make you love me. I couldn't back in the day, and I can't now. It's over."

She didn't even care about that. "So why are you dragging Daisy into it?"

"That's got nothing to do with you, Susan. Some idiot got hold of Daisy's video and posted it on YouTube and linked it to all the right-wing homophobic sites. So far today, I have turned Daisy's worst nightmare into a dream. Tell me why you have a problem with that?"

"Why has she moved in with you? Why can't she stay in her own flat or come home to me?"

"Because I need to watch her, to make sure everyone treats her right. She's safe here."

"It's all very coincidental, isn't it, Brian? You find Will in my house, and the next minute you've moved my daughter into your house."

"Let's not forget, she could be my daughter too."

"You asshole!"

"I don't care what you think anymore, Susan. I waited twenty-two years for you, and even then I was your dirty little secret. There are lots of dirty little secrets in this family, aren't there? I loved you."

"I never loved you, Brian. If you hurt her—"

I hung up.

Daisy burst into the room. "I'm number three in the Spotify charts!"

Great. I'd be able to sell ads on the YouTube channel.

In the few days before the referendum vote, I put Daisy into intensive media training with a friend in that end of the business. Thankfully, she enjoyed it. It was a risk to invest in her because if the equality side didn't win, she wouldn't be in much demand, but I was watching the polls, which suggested the referendum would pass by a narrow margin.

And on Friday, May 22, it did even better than we hoped. We won with a 62 percent vote. The celebrations that night and the next day were as wild and colorful as you'd expect. I brought Daisy to Dublin

Castle, where the official announcement was made. Loads of people in the crowd recognized her. They started chanting her name and begged her to sing. I pressed her forward through the crowd toward the front where a makeshift stage had been erected. When the organizers saw Daisy, they beckoned her to come forward. She was lifted over the barriers with her guitar and led to a microphone. She said nothing, stared at the ground for a minute, and then strummed her guitar. I saw Susan in the distance. Her eyes were on Daisy, a look of pure worry.

Daisy only had to sing the opening bars to the song in a slightly wobbly voice before the crowd sang with her. The entire upper courtyard was singing Daisy's song, and all had phones in the air recording this historical moment. The Taoiseach came over and hugged her. She was then carried shoulder high through the crowd. She had become their mascot and their emblem, and the joy on her face was something to behold. I saw Susan approaching through the mayhem. She simply said, "Thank you," but I didn't even respond. My plan was only starting. I put a press release together announcing Daisy's availability to talk on the subjects of equality and fat shaming and to sing onstage or on-screen.

Daisy was elated and exhausted after the first week of interviews and appearances. The impromptu performance had given her the confidence boost she so badly needed. I did not take Susan's or Will's calls. Daisy told me they thought she was doing way too much, too soon. Luke called to the house under instruction from Will and told me Daisy was too young for this attention and that I should learn from his own mistakes. I tried to disarm him by asking him to join me in managing her. He knew better than anyone the pitfalls of early stardom. "I don't know, Brian, it's different now, everyone's filming everything and putting it on the internet. It's much crueler than my day. You can't protect her from the shit anymore."

I tried. I got her into regular twice-weekly therapy sessions. I allowed her to smoke cannabis in the house on condition she did it with her pals and not on her own. Her girlfriend wasn't a bad kid, but she was jealous of Daisy's success. Daisy was now strong enough to dump her. I monitored her drinking. I treated her like a daughter, and she responded like one. She said she liked living with me. I said I liked having her there. We fell back into the tactile ways we'd had when she was a kid. She hugged me at night when she was going to bed. I lavished her with attention.

I agreed when she said her parents were nagging her. I implied that Will had said cruel things about her weight (he had), but that he'd just said them out of concern. I suggested that Susan might not like Daisy being an independent woman with money and a career of her own because Susan was bored now that the referendum was over and had a need to be nurturing. In all kinds of small ways, I broke down the trust Daisy had in Susan and Will. It was like pushing an open door.

And then, two weeks later, Will and Susan turned up on my doorstep demanding that Daisy pack her bags and go home to Susan's right then. I sat back and let Daisy stand up to them. Susan said she should check how much money I was making out of her. Daisy countered that she'd never made any money before and that she was living rent-free thanks to my generosity. Will made the fatal mistake of suggesting out loud that Daisy had put on weight. Daisy accused her father of fat shaming her, admitting that she'd spent years hating herself for not being able to live up to her father's impossible standards.

"What are you doing, Brian? Why are you doing this? She doesn't want to be a media star. She's too young. You saw what it did to Luke. How can you do this?" Susan demanded.

Daisy screamed at her mother. "Stop making decisions for me. I'm an adult. Brian is the only person who ever cared about me. Leave me alone! I can make a difference to people's lives now. You are just jealous, both of you. I don't even know if I want to be a media star, but it's worth trying to be something, to be an advocate for people like me." She dissolved into tears and rushed from the room.

Susan couldn't look at me. I suspect she knew what this was all about. Will gave me hell. "There's a difference between a father and a

godfather, Brian! You have completely crossed the line. Mum is probably rolling in her grave right now."

"Poor William, such a mummy's boy." I couldn't help saying it.

He grabbed me by the shoulder, but somewhere among the clumsy
wrestling and struggling, I landed a punch squarely on his nose. Susan
clamped her hand over her mouth, afraid to scream in case it alerted
Daisy upstairs. Will staunched the blood with a linen handkerchief.

"You prick," he said through the muffled handkerchief as he stormed
out of the door. Susan followed him.

That night, from a comb left in the main bathroom, I took a strand
of Daisy's hair with the follicle attached, a swab from the inside of my
mouth, and a strand of my own hair and sent them off to a DNA lab
in the UK.

II

STRANGERS

Chapter 38

2017

WILLIAM

I bumped into a journalist at the Galway Film Fleadh. Grace Kennedy was a woman I knew who wrote a column for one of the weekend supplements. She had always given me favorable coverage, and in return I bought her drinks and secured one-on-one interviews with our film's stars, but she was more beholden to me than I was to her. We had slept together once or twice over the years, but not since my diagnosis. My doctor had reassured me that I could have a full sex life again without the need for a condom, as my viral load was negligible. I'd had some dalliances with women in the intervening year, but the shock was still raw, and sometimes I needed Viagra to help me along. I was reassured over and over that I would live a full and healthy life as long as I stuck to the tablets. My daily pills were kept in a vitamin bottle beside my bed so that even the cleaning lady would never suspect.

Grace sidled up to me at the bar of the Radisson on Friday night, elbowed me. "Would you get me a margarita, Will? I need to talk to you."

"Sure, any particular tequila?"

She grinned and pointed to a table outside on the patio smoking deck. I dutifully ordered the drinks and followed her, curious as to what she had to say. She'd already given my new film, *Brazen Souls*, a great write-up and interviewed the three leads.

"It's about your brother." I assumed she meant Luke.

Mary Cullen, who I had employed and trained, had made a feature film, *The Star Maiden*, with Luke in a major role. I laughed when I heard it first. Luke had no experience, and the chances of his actually showing up for the job were so bad, I was sure they'd never get the necessary insurance to cast him. But I'd heard from people in the know that not only was the film good, but that he was great in it. He was playing a psychopathic husband opposite an A-list actress. The film had gone down well at international film festivals and was gaining traction. It was getting its Irish premiere here in Galway.

My film, *Brazen Souls*, was about marathon running, and I was sure it was going to capture the zeitgeist of modern-day fitness fanatics. Gyms were opening up at the same rate that pubs were closing down, and college students seemed to be spending more time working out than drinking. The millennial Instagram generation. *Brazen Souls* was released on the festival circuit around the same time as *The Star Maiden* and was getting the same kind of attention.

There was an Oscar buzz about both films. I'd been around the block long enough to know this meant nothing, except perhaps a bigger release on more screens. Mary and Luke were less experienced than I was, and overexcited at the prospect. I sat back and waited for their bubble to burst. The Irish media made much of the fact that the two Drumm brothers were in fierce competition with each other while the third, Brian, was managing the careers of most of Ireland's young talent. My daughter, Daisy, was at the forefront of Brian's stable of performers, musicians, and activists.

Luke and I were not in competition. We still spoke to each other and met up from time to time, mostly at film industry functions. He had sent me a screener of his film and invited me to various showings, but I made excuses not to watch it. I know he was desperate for me to see it and to say something positive about it, or at least his performance in it, but I guess sibling rivalry never goes away. Luke had been a star when Susan and I were struggling to get the money together to feed Daisy. He had not helped me then. Why should I congratulate him now? I suppose it was a positive development that his mental health was stable at the moment. The stories about him in the papers now were usually optimistic. I tried to be glad for him. I tried to ignore that he and Mary seemed to be a committed couple.

"What has he done now?" I said to Grace wearily, worried that he might have slipped back into a bad emotional state.

"Do you trust him with your daughter?"

"What? He barely has anything to do with her."

"Isn't he managing her?"

"Oh, you mean Brian?"

"Yes."

Brian had more or less taken control of Daisy. I knew she was vulnerable, but I had to accept she was now a twenty-three-year-old adult making her own choices. Luke said she'd come back around to me again, but I hadn't seen her in seven months, and Susan only saw her occasionally. Susan seemed to want to let things lie. I couldn't understand why she wasn't as furious with Brian as I was. Brian and I had not spoken in months either.

"What do you mean?"

"Okay, now I know this is delicate, because it's family, but I was in Paris a few weeks ago doing a story about how the Irish music scene has failed to penetrate the European market apart from the obvious people like U2, and your brother Luke back in the day, and one of the people I interviewed was in a class that Brian taught, oh, it must be . . . twenty years ago. And you know—"

"Sorry, but what has this got to do with anything? How did Brian's name even come up? It's not like he's famous."

"This woman was a fan of Luke's when she was in school. I said I knew you and Luke. She told me that Brian brought all the students to Luke's gig in some arena . . ."

"Right?"

Grace exhaled smoke that floated innocently out over Lough Atalia, and as she spoke, I watched the hairs on the back of my arm stand up.

"And . . . well, look, it might be nothing, but . . . she said Brian was fired from the school for having an improper relationship with a student in her class. The girl was fifteen and he would have been twenty-five, so not a huge age gap in adult terms, but still illegal, and she was a *child*, and I just wondered if this was something you were aware of, or something you should be aware of? Especially now your daughter is . . . you know . . . living with him. Don't worry, I won't be writing this up, but if someone from the *Mail* were to get hold of this story, well, there's nothing I could do . . ." Grace was a freelancer. She wrote for nearly all the dailies, but that wasn't what concerned me.

"You see, normally, Brian came to us with all the dirt on Luke—"

"He what?"

"Oh, Will, where do you think we got all the stories on Luke? For years, Brian sold stories about him. His childhood, his freak-outs, psychiatric committals . . . and he'd give us a name of some friend or neighbor who would verify the story with a little prompting. But I just wanted to give you a heads-up, you know, because I can't guarantee this will stay out of the papers, you understand, Will?"

I don't remember the rest of what she said. In my mind's eye, I saw all the times Brian had hugged Daisy, from when she was small until quite recently when she no longer hugged me or Susan. He was always physically affectionate with her. When they watched TV, her legs would be up on his lap. She'd never done that with me. I thought of all the times I had come home to find Brian "playing" with Daisy when she was a child. He told me about her first bra. Could he possibly . . . ?

Was it normal for a man in his late forties never to have had a long-term relationship with an adult woman? Had he been grooming Daisy?

Was he in a relationship with her? And hadn't Daisy broken up with her girlfriend shortly after moving into Brian's house? Had something been going on since her teens?

I sat through the screening of our film, made a speech on autopilot. I tried in vain to get a taxi driver to take me back to Dublin after the film, but it would be a five-hour round trip, and they all refused. I'd had quite a bit to drink. I had a sleepless night in my hotel, and early next morning, I threw my suitcase into the back of the car and broke all the speed limits getting back to Dublin. I parked outside Brian's house—*Luke's* house— and watched and waited. After an hour, Daisy approached the gate on foot along with two other androgynous-looking types her own age.

"Daisy?" I called out to her.

"Dad!" She seemed surprised but not annoyed to see me there. "What are you doing here? Aren't you supposed to be in Galway?"

I needed to stay calm. I was glad to hear that she was keeping up with my movements, though.

"I'm going out to your mum's for lunch. I thought you might like to join us. It's been a while."

She gave her pals the key to let themselves in and hung her head in the car window.

"I'm glad to see you but, y'know"—she pointed at her friends, who were going in through the basement door—"I have plans with these guys."

"We never see you, Daisy."

She sighed. "I miss you, I really do, but you have to accept my life choices and that I'm happy here with Brian. He takes care of me. He doesn't judge me."

"We'd take care of you too, Daisy. Please, come with me now. We miss you as well."

She bristled.

"So I should just cancel my plans right now because you say so? That's the problem, Dad. Brian would never expect me to do that."

I had to grip the steering wheel and keep smiling at her.

"What about lunch tomorrow?"

"Okay. Is Brian invited too?"

"Let's take it one step at a time, okay, sweetie?"

"Dad! For God's sake! I am not your *sweetie*. I'm a grown woman."

"Right. Sorry, sorry. But please come to lunch tomorrow?"

"In your place or in Mum's?"

I knew this was a gender challenge. I always let Susan do the cooking for family meals. Daisy said I was a typical example of the patriarchy.

"Come to mine. I'll cook. I'll even wash up."

She eyed me suspiciously. "What are you going to cook?"

"A roast chicken dinner." It was Daisy's favorite.

"Okay. What time?"

"Twelve thirty. Just you. No Brian."

"Fine." She rolled her eyes but agreed as if she was doing me a reluctant favor. She walked away toward the door.

Maybe I was wrong. Daisy was "woke," as they say; there was no way she would allow herself to be taken advantage of by her uncle. She seemed to be comfortable in her skin, and though she was clearly overweight, the strained and pained look had gone from her face. Brian had sent us emails telling us about all the counseling he had arranged for her. We were so angry that we hadn't replied. Daisy's friends were obviously free to come and go; it all *looked* innocent. But what had happened at the school in Paris? What had Grace said about Luke doing a concert in Paris at the time Brian was teaching? I needed to talk to him.

Luke was thrilled with the advance reviews of his film, particularly the ones that singled out his performance as Oscar-worthy. But he had shied away from doing any press junkets, didn't attend any of the film festivals if he didn't have to. He was determined to stay out of the limelight, and Mary was protecting him from that end of things as best she could.

I called him.

"Luke."

"Hey, Will, are you in Galway? Did you see my film? Mary said she saw you . . ."

"I'm not ringing about that. Can I come over and see you?"

"Well, sure, but what's wrong?"

"I don't want to talk about it over the phone."

"Sounds serious. Are you in trouble?" And then his voice rose. "Am I?"

I was so tired of Luke always thinking the world revolved around him.

"No, it's—look, I'll be there in twenty minutes, okay?"

"Okay, but I've moved."

"What?"

"I moved into Mary's house two weeks ago. I meant to tell you."

I sighed. "Fine. What's the address?"

An apartment overlooking Dun Laoghaire Harbour as it turned out. Well furnished, nicely decorated. But definitely a woman's apartment. There was no trace of Luke there, except for Luke himself.

He looked smart, his salt-and-pepper hair only slightly receding at the forehead, whereas my bald patch was creeping toward my ears. His manner and movements were calm. Three years of mental stability was a record for him. It couldn't last. I almost felt sorry for Mary, though I had never forgiven her for wrecking my relationship with Daisy. Daisy always saw me differently after that weekend at the Cannes Film Festival all those years ago, and I'd been stupid enough to let Brian take my place as her father figure. I should have tried harder.

"Luke, when you were touring in Paris years ago, I mean, like twenty years ago, when Brian was living there—"

"Yeah?"

"Were you stable then? Do you remember that time?"

He looked offended. "Yes, I was, William."

"Sorry, I didn't mean that the way it sounded, it's just that . . . look, a journalist has told me some weird stuff about Brian, and I wondered if you'd remember anything?"

"Oh, *that*? Yeah, I remember. It was weird all right, but he denied everything."

"You knew?" I was incredulous.

"Yes, but who am I to judge? Maybe he was just experimenting. We were really young, Will. Is some tabloid trying to expose that? It's pathetic!"

I was alarmed by Luke's casual attitude. "He wasn't as young as the girl."

"What girl?"

"The schoolgirl!"

"What?"

Our conversation was at cross-purposes. It took another ten minutes to ascertain that Luke thought my brother Brian had been in a gay relationship with a restaurant owner.

"Look, I'm not a hundred percent certain, but it looked that way to me. Brian was living with him in his swanky apartment in a pretty salubrious part of town, and he couldn't have afforded that on a dishwasher's salary."

"A dishwasher? I thought he was a teacher."

"Yeah, I don't remember the details, but he switched jobs the week I was there. The guy he was living with owned the restaurant. I had dinner there. I think Brian was actually fired from the teaching job."

"Why?"

"I can't remem—"

"Luke, think! This is important. Why did he get fired from the teaching job?"

"I don't know. Honestly. It was something to do with a student."

"Had he interfered with her? This student?"

"What? God, no! At least, I don't know. He never told me. I thought he'd hit a kid. You know how he used to have such a temper. But he refused to tell me what it was about. He came on the road with me after that. Remember? He was doing my merch."

"Right. With plenty of access to teenage girls."

"What are you saying? That's not cool, Will."

"What's not cool, Luke, is that Brian has been selling your stories to the tabloids for years. Remember all the times you said you couldn't trust anyone? It's Brian you shouldn't have trusted. He made money out of you, not just by being your agent but by selling your history."

Luke stood up. "No! He wouldn't, he couldn't. We know he's always been tight with money, but he wouldn't do that."

"To be honest, I don't give a shit about that right now—I need to know if he is or was in a relationship with my daughter. The whole gay thing sounds like a smoke screen to me. He's into young girls, and I'm fucking terrified that Daisy is one of them."

Luke started pacing the room, his hands on his head. "Oh my God. That prick!"

"Calm the fuck down!" I barked at him. "Try to remember all the details of what Brian was doing in Paris, the name of the school, the name of the restaurant and its owner. There's a chance this could all be wrong."

"But he sold the stories on me? Definitely?"

"Yes, Luke, this is all about you."

I drove out to Susan's then. It was after five when I arrived, and she answered the door in her bathrobe, looking shattered. I was momentarily taken aback.

"Are you sick?" I asked as I followed her into the kitchen. She paused before answering.

"Menopause. I feel like I've been run over by a train. Everything hurts."

"Sounds more like flu to me."

She stopped and glared at me.

"Yes, Will, because you'd be an expert on the menopause." She hadn't lost her sarcasm.

"I'm here to talk about Daisy."

"Can't it wait?"

"No, it can't. She's coming to my apartment for lunch tomorrow, and I'd like you to be there. We have to confront her."

"About what?"

"God, I don't even know where to begin. I'm worried she might be in some kind of weird relationship with Brian."

Susan sat up from her reclined position on the sofa and pushed a greasy strand of hair behind one ear.

"What are you talking about?"

"They're too close. They always have been. The way he is with her. You've seen it yourself. They hug each other. Why would he have encouraged her to live with him? It's weird, isn't it? Like Michael Jackson weird?"

"God almighty, what goes on in your head? Do you just dream up fantasy scenarios to satisfy your jealousy? I'm as pissed off as you are that he has Daisy under his thumb, but throwing accusations like that is just disgusting and dangerous."

I was surprised she was so dismissive. But she hadn't heard the full story.

"He got fired from that school in Paris for inappropriate behavior with a fifteen-year-old girl. It's all about to come out. A journalist told me."

"Nothing happened there, that girl got obsessed with him. He never touched her. But he punched the headmaster in the face when he was questioned about it. That's why he was fired."

"What? How do you know?"

"I went to Paris with Brian a few years ago. We met up with an old friend of his, Conrad, the gay guy who owned the restaurant. They talked about the whole thing."

I thought I was misunderstanding something.

"You . . . what? Why did you go to Paris with Brian?"

She pulled at her hair again. Something she always did when she was uncomfortable.

"I was at a loose end. So was he. We just decided to go."

"And why didn't I hear about this?"

"Because it was none of your business."

"Oh my God, he's been grooming you to get to Daisy!"

"No, he wasn't! Why are you so determined that your brother is some kind of pedophile?"

"Because he's always been way too friendly with her. At the time, I thought he was a great godfather but, oh Jesus, he took her swimming every week, don't you remember? When we weren't getting on, she'd have sleepovers at his house. Doesn't that strike you as weird? Why would an adult man want to spend time with a little kid, or a teenager?"

Sweat broke out on her forehead.

"Because he's her father."

At first, I thought the menopause was making her delusional, but she burst into tears, and the truth came flooding out. She and Brian, creeping around behind my back.

"It was just one night," she said, "at Luke's gig, before we were married."

"Well, obviously *before* we were married," I snapped. "I wouldn't have married you if you hadn't been pregnant." This was a lie.

"Oh, because you're so *honorable*?"

She said that she and Brian had some kind of druggy one-night fling.

"Brian doesn't even do drugs!"

"He did that night. I swear, you can ask him."

Susan said she never knew who Daisy's father was until recently, but she chose me.

"Brian and I . . . we started to have a proper relationship a few years ago—"

"What?"

"He was always mad about me. He always felt that if he'd asked me out first, I would have married him. I know, it's deluded, but it all went sour after the time when he called here that morning and found you making breakfast in my dressing gown. He was so furious we were still sleeping together—"

"But that was, what, two years ago—?"

"I know, but I think that's when he decided to get the DNA test."

Susan took down a copy of a DIY manual from the kitchen dresser. From between two pages she revealed a copy of the DNA test that proved Brian was Daisy's father. Susan had made him swear never to tell Daisy.

"And me?" I said. "Did you form some pact not to tell me?"

"Yes," she said, tears rolling down her cheeks.

I had to get out of there. I tried to be rational about it. I had not always been faithful to my wife. I accept that. But she had cheated on me with my own brother before we married. And yet it was *my* infidelity that broke up our marriage? She had made me believe that Daisy was my own child, and Brian had played along. How was I going to face Daisy? How did I feel about her now? I knew how I felt about Brian. I wanted to kill him. The deceit, the betrayal. My daughter, who was not my daughter.

I left Susan's house in a state of total distraction. Part of me wanted to confront Brian, but I was afraid of what I might do to him. I went home and sat up all night. Susan had given me photo albums after our separation. I don't think I'd ever looked at them, but they weren't the type of things to throw away. I looked at the photos now. Daisy on my knee, sitting up on my shoulders, celebrating her birthday parties. Susan, Daisy, and I, a self-contained unit.

But there was the evidence in too many of the photos. Brian, pushing Daisy on a swing. Brian, teaching Daisy how to tie her shoelaces. Brian and Daisy lying on the sofa together reading or tickling each other. My mother appeared in some of the photos, always beside me, beaming with pride. What would she make of this turn of events? Poor Mum would be horrified. Luke only appeared in a handful of photographs. I don't know who had the photos of our childhood, but Luke was rarely at our adult family events, and when he was, he was in the background, guzzling wine.

Coffee after coffee kept me wired. I went back through the photos of Susan and me. It had never occurred to me to remarry. I hadn't really wanted to go through with the divorce, but it was cleaner for tax reasons. Even at the times when I couldn't stand her, there was a part of me that loved her.

There it was—our wedding day. She was five months pregnant. We'd had to get special permission from the parish to avoid the three-month waiting time to get our church wedding. And yes, didn't Brian leave for Paris the month after the wedding? I remembered the argument Susan and I had about appointing him as godfather. She didn't want him in that role, and I thought she was being ridiculous. Her sister was godmother, after all. But then, Brian never came home for the christening, even though I offered to pay for his flight. He must have suspected he was Daisy's father her whole life. But why had he waited until so recently to get a DNA test? The date on the form proved it was shortly after Daisy moved in with him. Just two years ago. After our fight. After he discovered that Susan had cheated on *him* with *me*.

The buzzer in my apartment rang. I woke with a start, confused and exhausted.

"Yes?"

"Dad? It's me, Daisy."

"Come on up."

Susan wasn't coming; there was no roast chicken dinner. I was not her father. If anyone deserved to know the truth, it was Daisy.

Chapter 39

2017

———————————— **BRIAN**

Susan had phoned me to warn me on that Sunday morning. Will knew. He had picked up some ridiculous rumor from Grace Kennedy that I was a pedophile, and Susan thought it was the lesser of two evils to let him know that I was Daisy's father. I panicked. I didn't know what to do about either situation. I wanted to go out and see Susan, but she claimed to be sick. She knew that Daisy was going to Will's for lunch. Would he tell her? Surely not.

I decided to call Conrad in Paris. I had been in and out of touch with him for years. He and André had come to Dublin for rugby weekends and to Wexford for the opera. And when Susan and I went to Paris together, shortly before I discovered Will was back in her bed, we had dined in La Saucisserie. Conrad knew the truth about Susan and me. He knew that she was the reason I had turned up in Paris in the first place. He was the first person I told about the DNA test results. He insisted I tell Susan and let her decide whether or not to tell Daisy.

I could hear Daisy and her pals laughing and messing in the basement as I lifted the phone to call him. Two of her pals had stayed over.

They were such weird kids, but I had learned quickly not to ask Daisy if they were boys or girls. They were just "they," apparently. I let Daisy have her private life. The basement was hers. It had its own front door, large bedroom, small shower room, and kitchen. I still played the benign, indulgent uncle, but since I'd discovered I was her father, I'd grown more protective of her career and her mental health. I think I'd done a better job than her parents. Daisy was happier with me than she had been for a very long time. I did not want anything to spoil that.

But first, I had my own reputation to protect. I represented a lot of young people in my agency. Any suggestion of impropriety could sink me.

Conrad and I spoke in French and English, switching back and forth, both of us fluent in each other's language. He told me he still saw Arabelle occasionally in the neighborhood of the restaurant. She was usually in the company of a handsome young man and two little girls. He suggested that I trace her on social media, warn her that muckraking journalists might try to track her down. I should try to get some admission that she had a teenage crush on me.

I told him Will had discovered I was Daisy's dad. He drew in his breath, and I could almost hear the Gallic shrug at the other end of the phone. "It is a crisis for your family, yes?"

When I hung up, I searched for Arabelle Grasse on Facebook, Instagram, and Twitter. I used these platforms for my agency work. I didn't know how to use the others. There were a number of women with that name on social media, but none of them matched up to the girl I remembered. They were the wrong age, the wrong nationality, a different color. I realized if she had an account, it might be under her married name, assuming she had married the handsome man with whom Conrad had seen her. I racked my brains to think of the boys in her class. There was Sacha Kippenberg, the bright boy who sat beside her. I prayed that would not be a common name. I put his name into Facebook, but nothing came up, and then into Twitter. Bingo, there he was. He was now the editor of a literary journal. I spent hours going through his twelve

thousand Twitter followers one by one until I found her. Arabelle Beau-
champs, "*femme et mère de deux anges*," living in Paris. She didn't appear
to have a career. The photo was unmistakable. Her high cheekbones and
pert nose. Her hair was blonder, but it still had that lift at the front of
her head. I trawled through her posts. Mostly photos of her home, her
family, her dogs, her nights out, her afternoon walks, her sunny skiing
holidays. She had done okay for herself. I "followed" her and asked her if
she would accept a private message from me. Then I waited.

And realized that Daisy had already left to go to Will's for lunch. I
wondered how his attitude to her would change. He loved her, sure, I
knew he did. I was certain he wouldn't do anything to hurt her. He was
her uncle, after all.

I spent the afternoon refreshing Arabelle's Twitter page, waiting
for a response. I had been able to send a message to Sacha Kippenberg
asking him to warn Arabelle that journalists might want to talk to her.
His instant response was reassuring. He was in regular contact with
her. She had become obsessed with another teacher the following year
and had been removed from the school. Most of her classmates knew
she was a liar and a fantasist. He would be happy to speak to the press
on my behalf and he would let Arabelle know what was happening. He
said her childhood had been unstable, but she was now happily married and settled and totally embarrassed by her teenage crushes. He
guessed she would refuse to speak to the media.

And then I got a call from Susan, distraught. Daisy was at her place
and refusing to speak to her mother. She had locked herself into her
bedroom. I grabbed my car keys and drove straight out to Dalkey. I
couldn't believe Will had told her.

When I got to the house, I saw Will's car was there too. He swung
open the front door and came charging at me like a bull. I put my hands
up in submission.

"Will, let's think about Daisy, okay? She needs to know that nothing has changed."

"You fucked my wife!" He was simmering with rage.

"Well, technically, I didn't. The first time, when Daisy was conceived, was before you were married, and the other times were long after your marriage was over, so no, I didn't *really* fuck your wife. I fucked your girlfriend, and then your ex-wife—"

He swung his fist, which didn't land, but as I avoided it, I fell backward onto the gravel.

Susan came to the door. I'd never seen her look so awful. She had lost weight and there were dark circles under her eyes. Her hair was lank and her skin looked gray.

"Stop it!" she yelled, but her voice was weak and the effort it took made her stagger and sway.

Will and I both stopped in our tracks. I picked myself up off the ground while Will led her into the house. Susan limped over to the sofa and lay down, shivering.

"I can't deal with this right now, okay? Can you both just leave? And I'd really appreciate it if one of you could take Daisy with you. I'm just not up to it."

These words came out breathlessly. It was alarming.

"What's wrong with you?"

Will answered. "She says it's menopause."

Susan began to weep.

"I thought it was, at first," she said. "I haven't been sleeping properly over the last month, you know, night sweats. I googled it and asked my sister and they all pointed to menopause, but the last few weeks, my throat is sore and my neck is swollen, and I just feel like shit all the time. My doctor sent me for a biopsy on Thursday."

The word *biopsy* scared me. "Biopsy for what?"

"What do you think? Cancer."

My phone buzzed annoyingly in my pocket. I ignored it.

"Doctors overreact," said Will dismissively. "It could be glandular fever *and* menopause, or any number of other things. They're just covering their asses and racking up the bill to charge the insurance company."

Susan brightened a little. "Do you think so?"

Will was right. How many times had I heard of people getting dire diagnoses that turned out to be minor ailments. The weight loss, though, was worrying. I decided to be the practical one. "Do you have everything you need, Susan? Can I pick you up some painkillers? I can open a tin of soup if you like?"

A door slammed upstairs. Daisy appeared on the mezzanine over-looking the kitchen. She was calm and spoke in a singsong voice, the way she used to when she was a child.

"Playing happy families, are we? You liars and hypocrites. And now the whole world knows what you're like."

"What do you mean?" said Susan. "Darling, please calm down, we can all talk about this rationally. Nobody ever meant to hurt you. We all love you, sweetheart, but right now, I'm just too sick. Please under-stand." Susan's voice was so weak that she barely sounded convincing.

"I understand everything," Daisy said, "and I've written it all down in my blog and published it. If you start to get some press attention, don't be surprised. I'm only here to collect my clothes, and now I'm going back to your house, Brian—*Dad*—to collect the rest of them. By the way, I'm firing you as my agent. I'm moving in with a friend. I don't want to see any of you again until I'm ready. That might be next week, or it might be never. You disgust me, all of you." None of us said a word as she charged down the stairs carrying a backpack over her shoulder, a suitcase in each hand.

She checked her phone. "The taxi's outside. Have a nice life, you parasites. To think, I always thought Luke was the weird member of this family. You're all freaks, and you've even made a freak out of me."

Susan protested weakly. Will tried to apologize. I followed her out and tried to help put her bags in the cab, but she pushed me roughly away. The car door slammed, and the wheels scrunched on the pristine white gravel, leaving grooves in their wake.

When I went back into the house, Will was holding a sobbing Susan in his arms. It should have been me holding her, but it struck me then. I had always thought Will took what he wanted, but now I realized—Susan always chose Will. I was never her first choice. For her, it was always Will. I loved her still. She loved him.

I left, hoping to catch Daisy before she cleared her things out of my house. How could she see me as the bad guy? I had always tried to do right by her. I didn't know exactly what Will had told her. I'd forgotten to ask, I was so rattled by Susan's appearance. I hadn't asked when the biopsy results were due either.

I pulled in at a petrol station. My phone continued to buzz with messages from journalists, friends, clients, all outwardly sympathizing but wanting the scoop. Daisy's blog had gone viral.

When I took Daisy in, I had warned her to stay away from social media, and she had obeyed me as far as I knew. She hadn't seen the cruel and vicious comments from unidentified strangers calling her a fat attention-seeking whore, the doctored photos of her surrounded by mounds of food, the ones where they superimposed her face onto the image of an elephant. The casual cruelty of it all shocked me. But her counselor had agreed with me and warned her off social media. She had a separate lifestyle blog called *FitandFat* unconnected to any social media accounts and hundreds of thousands of followers from all over the world who were mostly kind and supportive. She wrote about body positivity, mental health, plus-size fashion and where to get it, travel, books, and food. I had accompanied her on whirlwind tours of America and Canada, and we were on the verge of sealing a TV deal whereby she would host her own talk show on Netflix. It would be filmed in Ireland but networked around the world. The stakes were extremely high. There were book offers on the table, too, but I didn't want to rush Daisy or bombard her with too many decisions. I didn't want her to be overexposed. One thing at a time. I was taking care of my daughter. In the garage forecourt, I clicked through to her blog.

She had written up the whole shitstorm while I had been trying to track down Arabelle. How her father had pretended to be her uncle, how she had once caught the man she thought was her father physically attacking her other uncle (Luke's) current girlfriend (Mary). She told how Will had always referred to me as a loser and a money-grabber. How her uncle had married her mother believing he was the father of her baby. How her other uncle, who had been a psych patient so many times, was the most normal member of our family. The Drumms sounded like characters from a Greek tragedy or the shoddiest soap opera there ever was.

On one level, I was relieved. Although I didn't come well out of the story, the pedophilia rumors were totally overshadowed, and when I checked Twitter to see if Arabelle had responded, I discovered she had blocked me. Good. This was the best outcome. Grace Kennedy now had a bigger story, but so did TMZ. We were trending on Twitter.

When I got home, I went down the back stairs to the basement. Daisy was flinging things into black plastic bags, tears streaming silently down her face. I saw an extremely distressed young woman. All I wanted was to be able to comfort her and make her pain go away. Whose fault was this really? Susan's for not telling the truth when she was pregnant, Will's for telling Daisy the truth yesterday, or mine for doing the DNA test? We were all to blame.

"Daisy, please—"

She wouldn't look at me.

"I only knew for sure two years ago."

"I don't want to hear it. Please go away. I'll be out of here in an hour. I'm going to get a new agent tomorrow. I've been approached by loads, and I always turned them down out of loyalty to you."

"I don't care about that. I care about you."

"No, you don't! Dad—I mean, Will—told me everything yesterday. You manipulated me to spite him and Mum. It was never about me."

"That's not true. Look, we've always been close, haven't we? I certainly suspected the truth. I desperately wanted you to be my daughter for all those years, but then when I did the DNA test, I was worried what your reaction might be."

"So when were you going to tell me?"

"I don't know. Honestly? Never. Because look how upset you are. We could all have just carried on as normal."

"Jesus, Brian, this isn't *normal*. None of this is normal. Just leave me alone. I can't bear to see you."

"Can I call you? Tomorrow?"

She screamed at me. "No, you can't call me. Leave me alone!"

Will had a lot to answer for.

By the time Daisy left, there were already press photographers at the door. I tried to hold them back, repeating "No comment" over and over, but Daisy ignored me and told them: "My comment is on my blog. My family are trash. That's all you need to know." There were five smartphones in my face, recording everything.

She departed again in another taxi, and I quickly turned away from the press and ran back indoors. They shouted through my letter box: "Do you have any comment to make on why you were fired from your job at a Parisian school twenty-two years ago, Brian?"

Fuck.

I swung the door open again.

"In 1995, I was teaching English in the Institut Charles Sorel. A young student, Arabelle Grasse, became obsessed with me. I did absolutely nothing to encourage her, but she told some of her friends I was her boyfriend. When the headmaster implied I was having some kind of improper liaison with her, I punched him and was fired on the spot. That is all that happened, and you won't find a shred of evidence of anything else. If any of you even hint at me being a pedophile, I will sue you and your newspapers."

I turned on my heel and closed the door behind me. And that's when I realized the scale of the mistake I had just made. I knew exactly how they'd run this: "Brian Drumm denies pedophilia rumors." I should have said nothing at all. I was about to be ruined.

Why had I opened my mouth to the press? It could all have been sorted calmly and quietly, but I had given them my denial. And Will had spoken to the bloody journalist in the first place.

I sat up late watching Twitter. Already my name and the word *pedo* were linked in tweets. #DrummFamilyFreakShow was a hashtag already, lifted from Daisy's blog. I got hostile emails from clients requesting to be taken off my books with immediate effect. I didn't respond to anything. About midnight, there was an unmerciful pounding on the front door that I couldn't ignore. I found Luke on my doorstep, eyes rolling back in his head, swaying like a blade of weak grass in the wind. He was drunk.

I let him in. He shouted abuse at me for selling his stories to the media. I denied it.

"What are you talking about? Who told you that?"

"Will!"

"Luke, why are you drunk? This is really bad. You can't believe anything Will tells you anymore. He hates me because I'm Daisy's dad."

"What?"

Clearly, Luke was the only person who hadn't been watching the social media storm that had exposed our whole family. He'd been drinking for twenty-four hours after three years of sobriety.

"Shall I call Mary for you?"

He slumped onto the sofa and quickly passed out. Christ, this was the last thing I needed.

I was hoping my days of looking after Luke were over. I removed his shoes and threw a blanket over him. I locked all the booze in the house into the pantry, left two pints of water and a bottle of Tylenol on the coffee table, and a large plastic bowl on the floor beside the sofa. I rang Mary.

"Brian! What the hell is going on? Where is Luke? I just got back from Galway to all these messages, and my apartment is trashed, and I can't get hold of Luke. His phone is here. Are you really Daisy's dad? What is going on with your family?"

I didn't go into much detail about the family end of things but warned her not to believe anything she read about me being some kind of child molester. I reassured her that Luke was with me but told her he was upset. I didn't want to tell her he'd fallen off the wagon. I knew it would jeopardize their relationship.

"Can I talk to him? Please?"

"He'll call you in the morning, Mary, okay? It's been a really long day."

"Has he had a drink?"

I paused for too long before I denied it.

"Tell him not to come back until he's been sober for forty-eight hours, and get him to a meeting as soon as you can. There's one in Blackrock at one p.m. tomorrow. Make sure he goes."

I resented how it was just assumed I'd be the one to take care of Luke. I was no longer his agent. I owed him nothing.

Fuck Will. In one day, he had destroyed my career, my relationship with *my* daughter, and my reputation, as well as Luke's sobriety and, possibly, his relationship with Mary.

I turned off my phone, took the battery out of my doorbell, and went to bed.

In the morning, I made strong coffee and toast and got Luke to shower before I agreed to tell him anything. He was shaking and tearful. He looked terrified.

"Brian, did you really sell my stories? How could you do that to me?"

"Look, I never said anything that wasn't true, and most of the time they were things that had happened in the distant past. I badly needed the money. And I was keeping you in the public eye. There's no such thing as bad publicity, right?"

"You did all that *for me*?" His sarcasm was evident.

"I hated teaching, and you refused to write the book, remember? It wasn't malicious, I swear. I'm sorry, I just . . . needed the money."

"Christ, it's always money with you. I don't know how I let you take this house from me. You really took advantage of me. I wasn't well in the head."

"Yeah, well, look where you ended up last night when you weren't 'well in the head.' I hope that was a temporary slip, Luke, you have to stay away from alcohol and whatever drugs you were on last night."

"Are you going to tell the papers about this?"

"No, the papers are more interested in Daisy and Will and me than they are in you, Luke. It should make a nice change for you. But there are a few things I need to tell you."

Luke was shocked to discover I was Daisy's dad. He didn't remember that I'd told him last night.

"Brian! How could you do that to your own brother?"

"He did it to me first, and"—I remembered—"he did it to you too. Remember Kate?"

"What about Kate?"

"Will had an affair with her before you met her. Don't you think it was strange that she dumped you after you were engaged?"

"But she never told me that! She had a miscarriage."

"I know. Susan and Will split up because she found out about him and Kate. He was desperate to save his marriage. I wouldn't put it past him to have blackmailed Kate in some way. Susan was never going to take him back while Kate was a member of the family."

"What? Who knew about this? My God, is there nobody I can trust? We're supposed to be family."

I wasn't finished burying the knife in Will.

"You know that Will hit Mary when she worked for him back in the day?"

His face paled.

"My Mary? My girlfriend?"

"Yes."

"But she never mentioned it."

"He treats women like shit. Yes, I made a few quid out of you when it was financially necessary, but Will is the one who really betrayed you. What did he ever do to help your career? When you were looking for acting work, he did nothing. Direct your anger in the right direction, Luke."

He said nothing but shook his head violently as if there was a bumblebee inside it.

"I can't take this. I can't take it."

"Luke, come on, nothing changes for you. You're a film star with a cool girlfriend, leading a sober life, right? This was a *slip*. I'm driving you to an AA meeting in Blackrock. Stay here tonight and then go home to Mary tomorrow, and ask her, just ask her what happened between her and Will. From what I remember, he used and abused her, like he did everyone else. She was probably too embarrassed to tell you. Don't ruin what you have with her. Look where she has brought your life and career. Don't fuck this up. She's crazy about you."

After I dropped Luke to the meeting, I called Susan. I had barely thought of her all weekend, but I couldn't bear to think that Will might be the person consoling her after all the trauma.

"Susan?"

"Yes." Her voice was faint, weak.

"Are you okay?"

"I have lymphoma. Burkitt lymphoma. I'm in St. Vincent's. They're doing blood tests and scans. Brian, I'm scared. I'm really scared."

A lightning strike of pain crossed my forehead.

"What is that? Cancer?"

"Yes."

"Who's with you? Is Will there?"

"No, I was trying to get hold of him."

Why him? Why *always* him?

"Stay put. I'm five minutes away. I'm coming right now."

I was with Susan when a doctor asked to speak to her in private. She insisted the doctor could speak freely in front of me. Dr. Shaw asked what my relationship to Susan was. I thought it was a strange question, and when Susan said I was her brother-in-law, Dr Shaw asked again if Susan was sure she didn't want to speak to her in private.

I knew there was something serious going on. Susan had already been admitted to a private unit from the emergency room because treatment needed to start straightaway. She had nothing with her, no overnight bag, not even a toothbrush.

Susan was perched on the bed, looking pale and sick. I took her hand, but she shrugged it away.

"Whatever it is, please just tell me!" she begged Dr. Shaw.

"Your blood-test results came back and—well, there's no other way to put this, but you are HIV positive."

Susan looked at me, and we both looked at Dr. Shaw like she had lost her mind.

"That's not possible. It's a mistake."

"We did the test twice, to be sure."

"It's a mistake."

"I'm afraid not. Now, this won't necessarily affect your treatment, and an HIV diagnosis is very treatable and really, in the ordinary scheme of things, nothing to be worried about, but as Burkitt's is a particularly aggressive form of cancer, we have to start you on chemotherapy straightaway, and we have to be very careful of infection. Of course, we will start you on antiretroviral drugs too . . ."

Afterward, the doctor asked Susan if she had any questions.

"How long have I had this virus?"

"It's really not possible to tell. If you have indulged in any needle-sharing activity—"

"Don't be ridiculous."

"I'm sorry, I understand you're upset, but if you didn't contract it through blood transfusions, and there are none in your medical history, then we must assume it was through sexual contact. Your partner may not know he has the virus—"

Susan glared at me.

I had an HIV test the next day. It came back negative. I almost cried with relief. Susan insisted that if it wasn't me who had infected her, it must have been Will. She hadn't slept with anyone else in two years, not since that morning I'd found her with Will. She had sworn off men after that. There had been some men in her past, but nobody except Will or me in the last six years.

Two months later, Susan died from pneumonia, an infection she was unable to fight because of her compromised immune system from chemotherapy. The medics said it was not HIV or AIDS that had killed her, but that did not stop me from blaming Will for her death.

Chapter 40

January 2018

I had been cast in two other films with big-name American and UK directors. I had moved to LA temporarily in October 2017, where my new agent was, where the work was, to live the dream. It was supposed to be the pinnacle of my career, but it didn't feel like it. Mary tried to be understanding about my depression. She wondered if taking on a big role so soon was too much, but I enjoyed the character I was playing. The sets were dark and gloomy, almost candlelit. A welcome contrast to the blinding sunlight of the boulevards of LA. The rest of my life had fallen apart, as had my family. I felt like my brothers were aliens. They had both betrayed me in all kinds of ways and I felt like the child my mother had rejected all over again. Mary stood by me, but I knew I was pulling her down.

Susan died. Her cancer was advanced and virulent, but it was pneumonia that killed her, just two months after diagnosis. Brian and Will were both distraught.

Her sister, Lynn, had flown in and banned all of us brothers from visiting. Lynn reported she was very weak but incredibly angry. She knew her death was imminent. My brothers were devastated to be excluded from her life at the end.

Daisy blogged about it all, unable to stem the flow of the anguish she had been dealt, spewing it all out onto the page for four hundred thousand strangers to see. Her followers were her tribe, her *real family*, she said. We couldn't stop her. Daisy slept in her mother's hospital room, feeling overwhelmed by guilt for the way she had refused to speak to her mother until she learned that Susan's condition was terminal. Susan couldn't let go of her anger, even at the end, ruing the day she had met the Drumm family, furious with Daisy for abandoning her.

Lynn, obeying Susan's final wishes, made it clear that none of the Drumm brothers were welcome at the funeral. But I saw the photos in the newspaper. Daisy, openmouthed and wailing, surrounded by her friends and fans, but too young to recognize the difference between them.

I had managed to track down Kate, who admitted that Will had forced her to have an abortion and to break up with me by threatening to expose their affair. She had left me for my sake. She cried over the phone. I hung up.

Mary told me the truth about Will too. She had been infatuated with him when she was his young assistant. He used and abused her. Daisy had caught them drunkenly fighting when she was just a child. Will had hit Mary in public at the Cannes Film Festival. I was outraged. The #MeToo campaign was in full swing, and Will's behavior had hit the headlines, initially because of Daisy's blog and what she had witnessed at Cannes, but then the floodgates had opened, and soon there were fifteen different stories from women who had been bullied or sexually harassed by Will.

Brian released his HIV test results to the media. Daisy had blogged about that too. Will remained silent. How many women had he infected? Had he told them? Brian had proven his innocence in the French schoolgirl scenario, but people said there was no smoke without fire. Twitter mobs piled on to take down each one of us brothers, to investigate every detail of our past, and when they weren't sure of the facts, they made them up. On Twitter, everything was black or white and devoid of facts, nuance, or understanding. I got a certain degree of sympathy because my indiscretions were the result of mental illness and were in the past.

Except that my mental illness wasn't really in the past. The baby was back now, dancing in front of my eyes whether I was awake or asleep. It screamed in pain and told me I was bad and useless and that my life wasn't worth living. Vodka helped me sleep, but now I was a secret drinker. Mary had come with me to LA. She was doing movie deals, and I could no longer avoid the publicity trail. It was in the contract of the distribution deal. I made sure the interviewers could not ask me anything about my brothers, though my previous career as an erratic pop star with mental health problems was always dragged up. I put a little vodka in my water bottle and sipped it through these interviews. I sipped it while filming my new movie. I sipped it through AA meetings, sitting beside Mary, holding hands, and reciting the Serenity Prayer.

Mary knew the revelations about my brothers had shocked me. Will, Kate, and the abortion; Brian selling my stories to the tabloids. She made sure I was back in therapy, but this LA shrink was different from anyone I'd seen before. Dr. Mukherjee was a small Indian woman who insisted on going back to the beginning. She wanted to know why I felt that my mother hated me. When I explained that I thought I was the product of a rape or an affair and told her how my mother had treated me, deprived me, ignored me, burdened me with shit I was way too young to handle, Dr. Mukherjee asked me to dig into my past. It was homework. I wasn't going to bother, but Mary insisted I try. I couldn't talk to Will or Brian. I finally flew back to Ireland to see Auntie Peggy, well into her seventies now. I had lost touch with her years ago. But she still lived independently and welcomed me with warmth and kindness. She told me she was horrified by what she had heard on the radio about us all, and shocked by Susan's death.

Peggy was the person who finally told me the simple truth.

"You have to understand, Luke, your mother gave birth twice in fourteen months, and two months after Brian was born she was pregnant again. She really didn't want another baby so soon. Your father, well, he worshipped your mum, particularly in those early days, he really wanted to look after her. We were orphans, and all he wanted was to protect her. Our fostering situations had not been good, and we hardly knew the rest of our siblings because we'd been torn apart as children. You know contraception was completely illegal in those days. Your birth almost killed her. She was in the hospital for weeks. She had to have blood transfusions. She was terrified, and I think it traumatized her for life. I tried, Luke, I really tried to make her see that it wasn't your fault. I know she was hard on you. I tried to talk to her about it, but you know what your mother was like."

"Why didn't you ever tell me this before?" I asked her.

"It wasn't my story to tell, love. And you need to know something else. Your mother was raped, many years later, and I think that brought all the trauma back."

"She told me about that rape. I was only twelve or thirteen at the time."

"Did she?" Peggy was shocked. "But I think that explains why she told you. Those two incidents, your birth and the rape, they were linked in her mind. Pain and fear. I think she might have been a little unhinged. Your . . . illness, it's not unique in our family. We told everyone our parents had died in a tram accident, but your grandmother committed suicide when we were tots. Our father disappeared. Moll and I were fostered, but the rest of our siblings grew up in orphanages."

I couldn't believe what I was hearing.

"How did your mother die?" I asked her.

"She threw herself under a train. Moll was the youngest, she was barely two years old. I was only four."

"But she told me my father's aunt had done that?"

Peggy shook her head. "No, it was *our* mother. It was so shameful in those days. A suicide and then our father vanishing, to Scotland we think. He never came looking for us, and we never went looking for him. I thought about it years ago, tracking him down, but your mother was horrified by the idea. And as the years went on, it became pointless because he couldn't still be alive."

"I wish I'd known this."

"But when Moll met your dad, she thought he was the answer to her dreams, you know. He was almost old enough to be her father, and posh compared to us. She adored him in the beginning, but Moll got bored easily, and even though your dad was only fifteen years older, in those days it was like a generation gap. Moll came of age during the sixties. He was a clerk in an insurance company when she was a school girl."

I was overwhelmed with sadness. If Mum had told us any of this, we might have been able to understand each other and to help each other.

I made no attempt to see my brothers on that visit home. On the business class flight back to LA, I drank straight vodka and checked into a hotel for a night before returning to the condo I was sharing with Mary.

Dr. Mukherjee thought my mother's attitude to me, although cruel, was understandable. I had caused her the greatest fear she had ever known. I must try to see things from my mother's point of view. I must try to forgive her. The baby that haunted me was *me*, asking me to love him, she said. She prescribed more antipsychotic drugs and encouraged me to confront my phantom visitor, to welcome him, nourish him, and cherish him. Easier said than done. He terrified me. I terrified me. I didn't know what I or he was capable of. And I didn't tell her I was drinking again.

On Christmas Day 2017, three months after the death of her mother, Daisy took an overdose. Mary and I were back in Dublin for a few days to see her family. I had a week's hiatus from filming. Daisy had been living in a flat with some friends who had all gone home to their parents for Christmas, leaving her alone. She was still refusing to see Brian or Will. She had stockpiled Tylenol and took enough to fell a horse. But before she passed out, she had written a blog to her followers to say goodbye. Some of them who knew her called an ambulance and Brian, and they broke the door down and got to her in time.

That kid is going to grow up to be me. I feel sorry for her. But her near-death caused an uneasy truce between Brian and Will. They came together for her sake. And they got in touch with me. On her release from hospital, Daisy moved back into Brian's house. Will and I visited her there regularly, and I pretended to like my brothers in front of her. Daisy was heavily medicated and often stared into space. I wanted to ask her if she was seeing a tiny baby, but I was afraid that by saying it out loud I might accidentally infect her with my illness. My madness is hereditary, after all.

In January, I was back in LA, filming *Innocence*, a biopic of the painter Caravaggio, based on the play by Irish playwright Frank McGuinness, when the Oscar nominations were announced. *The Star Maiden* was nominated in three categories. I was up for Best Supporting Actor and we had nods for Best Score and Best Screenplay. Will's *Brazen Souls* had one nomination, for Best Cinematography. The Irish media were ecstatic, though some speculated that *Brazen Souls* might have gotten a Best Film nod if it wasn't for Will's involvement. Will had given an in-depth interview to Grace Kennedy about living with HIV and the grief he felt after Susan's death. He publicly told all the women he had slept with to get tested. He agreed to be a spokesperson for an AIDS charity and fronted a public awareness campaign about how HIV almost never led to death because of the free availability of antiretroviral drugs, but the accusations of harassment toward women damaged him badly. He won back a little sympathy from the public, but not much. Will had had to put his next project on hold because the financiers had pulled out.

Brian emailed us both and asked if he could bring Daisy to the Oscars with us in March. It would be just the lift she needed, he said. He begged and wheedled, said he didn't have the money for accommodation or airfare but that it would mean so much to Daisy. Will and I both said yes. We could hardly say no.

Chapter 41

March 2018

I met Will, Brian, and Daisy in the Cabana Cafe on Sunset Boulevard for breakfast early on the morning of the Oscars ceremony. We greeted each other at the outdoor table with suspicion but faked warmth for the sake of Daisy, who stared vacantly at her hands. She had lost an alarming amount of weight in the six months since Susan had died. Her once moon-shaped face was gaunt. I couldn't help staring. Where her cheeks had been, there was slackness of skin, and her collarbones jutted through the silver top she wore with jeans, which hung loosely from her hips. She didn't speak much, pushed her scrambled egg around her plate, and drank exactly two sips of her freshly squeezed orange juice, despite Brian and Will's desperate urgings for her to have some toast or a bagel. I warned them to leave her alone. She looked up and smiled at me gratefully. Brian tried to encourage his daughter to talk and asked her about her blog. Daisy said she'd lost interest in blogging. Brian persisted with the conversation and asked her about her future plans. Daisy said her plans were between her and her new agent. That shut Brian up.

My tiny baby was squirming around, scratching at my skin.

BRIAN

The breakfast reunion was full of awkward silences. We hadn't all been together in months. Will proposed a toast to Susan, and we raised our coffee cups, but I glared at him. Luke had dark circles under his eyes. He was anxious and fidgety, and kept raising his hand to his neck and rubbing the hollow beneath his Adam's apple. This was a bad sign. It's a thing he always did before he had an episode.

I ate heartily, knowing that Will or Luke would be paying the bill. I told them how difficult it was for me to get clients since the scandals had broken. Will suggested I sell "Luke's house" and get a small apartment in the city center. But I didn't answer him.

I changed the subject and speculated as to who would win which Oscar tonight. Then, magnanimously, for Daisy's sake, I congratulated Will on *Brazen Souls* and said it was a fine film.

Will said he hadn't got around to seeing Luke's film, *The Star Maiden*, yet but hoped Luke would get the Oscar, though he couldn't resist the urge to say that it was unlikely because Luke hadn't even been nominated for a Golden Globe or a Screen Actors Guild Award.

I was really surprised that Will hadn't seen Luke's film yet, since *everyone* was talking about it. And Luke announced he had written an acceptance speech, just in case.

"That might be tempting fate," said Will.

"You should really hope I don't win, you know, because you'll all get a mention in the speech if I do, even Mum."

"You won't mention me, will you, Luke?" asked Daisy nervously.

Luke pulled a folded sheet of paper out of his pocket and drew a line through his script on the page. Will and I leaned in to see what was written, but he refolded it and replaced it in his pocket before we got a chance.

Daisy excused herself to go to the bathroom.

"Is she going to throw up?" Luke said to Will.

"Ask her father. How should I know?" he replied.

I wiped my forehead with a napkin and said quietly, "She's in therapy, but it's expensive. I couldn't get medical insurance for her after the overdose. I can only afford for her to see someone once a month. The public waiting lists are really long."

Will glowered. "I raised your child financially for twenty-two years, Brian. Such a coincidence that you only did that DNA test well after her eighteenth birthday. No prizes for guessing why you took so long."

"That's bullshit," I said. "Susan always denied she was my kid."

"Don't bring Susan into this," Will erupted.

"I'm not the one who cheated on her. I'm not the one who gave—"

Luke slammed his glass down on the table. "I'll cover the cost of Daisy's therapy, okay?"

He took out the page and scribbled something onto the bottom of it. Will and I strained to get a glimpse again, but Luke was quick and discreet.

Daisy returned to the table then, looking pale and red eyed.

"What are you wearing tonight, Daisy? Or should I say *who* are you wearing?" I said, increasingly desperate to make things normal for her.

"My mother," said Daisy. "I mean, I'm wearing Mum's wedding dress. She was five months pregnant when she wore it, so I've had to do a lot of alterations, but I think it's going to look good."

Her eyes brightened with hope, and the tension eased. Daisy was the glue holding us together. A smile from her lifted us all.

WILLIAM

Once Daisy had lightened up a bit, we joked about our designer tuxedos, and Luke said that Mary had been given a dress to wear by an Irish designer. "She's not doing the red carpet with me, though."

"Why not? She's your partner," said Brian.

"Not anymore." It wasn't news to me. "Anyway, she doesn't want the attention."

"Oh, Luke," said Brian, "what did you do this time? Did you fall off the wagon again? Just go to a few AA meetings. You'll patch things up." Luke put his hands up. He wasn't prepared to discuss it.

Brian paused. "I know! Why don't you take Daisy on the red carpet? Would you like that, Daisy?"

Her face lit up, and a genuine smile appeared. "Really? Really? Thanks a million, Luke."

What a terrible idea.

We were staying in the Regency Oriental Hotel, a mile from the Dolby Theater, where the ceremony would take place, but we brothers took separate Ubers and said we'd see one another at the ceremony. Luke and I, and now Daisy, were the only ones due to walk the official red carpet. I was prepared to decline any interviews. I was sure *Brazen Souls* would have been up for Best Picture if it hadn't been for the #MeToo brigade. Mary and Brian would meet us inside. Brian and Daisy had seats in the upper balcony. Luke, Mary, and I were all to be seated in the front tiers.

Los Angeles had been buzzing for a week. Luke, Mary, and I had been at all the right parties: the Screen Ireland Fundraiser and the Oscar Wilde party at Bad Robot in Santa Monica. Luke didn't take the hint to leave these parties with everyone else at 9:00 p.m., despite Mary begging him not to make a show of himself. He would disappear with random strangers and return to the hotel late. His room was next door to mine, and his lunatic raving kept me awake until the small hours. We had all conducted interviews with the media, but it was already being noted by some journalists that Luke's behavior was "unpredictable" or "morose." They did not use the words *drunk* or *stoned*, but I was pretty sure he was drinking again. He certainly wasn't sleeping.

Mary and I, as independent producers, used the week to make deals, and to hustle for funding and distributors. Our schedules were full. We were relieved the parties ended so early. LA parties were not like wild Irish parties that ended in the small hours. We nodded politely at each other. The Irish media were watching us like hawks.

Daisy had confided in me that her new LA agent was disappointed with her. He had suggested she live-tweet the Oscars, but she had refused to do it. She told me she might have to sleep with him to smooth things over.

"Daisy!" I said, horrified.

"It wouldn't be the first time," she said. "MeToo is a fashionable hashtag, but next year it will be forgotten. I'm not going to be a victim. I'm the one who can manipulate my agent, I know he prefers me thin. 'Much better for business,' he says." I looked at this girl who used to be my daughter, who I had loved more than anyone in the world. She was a stranger. I missed Susan. I missed Mum.

LUKE

Mary had summoned me to her hotel room. She begged me to come to an AA meeting with her. My drinking was no longer a secret between us. She had already told me our relationship was over. We were only together for the sake of appearances and so she could keep me straight through all the media focus since the nominations were announced. Hollywood was less concerned with my antics than the British and Irish media. #MeToo was the topic this year, and the media was buzzing with which studio heads were next to roll as women came forward with their accusations. Will was the one they were after.

I had wanted Mary to go public with the abuse she had suffered at Will's hands, but Mary point-blank refused. Although she did not contradict what Daisy had written, she refused to confirm it either. She feared a backlash against the #MeToo movement, and as one of few female producers, she did not want to get caught in its wake. She was also worried that she might herself be implicated, because when she worked for Will all those years ago, she had arranged private meetings between him and a lot of young actresses. She did not know what had happened in those meetings, but she had always suspected that when girls left "auditions" with tears in their eyes, it wasn't always because they didn't get the part.

"You knew what he was up to and you did nothing to stop it?" I said.

"So did you! Everyone knew. Look, he's no Harvey Weinstein, but everyone is throwing rape and bullying and harassment into the same pool of shit, and I do not want to be identified as an enabler or a victim."

We had argued about this for weeks until, out of anger and frustration, I stopped hiding my drinking, and Mary asked me to move out. The ground beneath me moved to one side, and I fell.

I refused to go to the AA meeting. I was going back to my hotel room to work on my speech. Mary looked at me. "Luke, you may not win, you know?"

"Oh, I know that," I said, "but I think I need to make this speech anyway. Maybe not onstage, but somewhere, tonight."

"Just please, no matter what happens, be kind. Remember Daisy. I don't think she can take any more scandal. Don't drink today. Please. For her sake." I saw the tiny infant sitting in the crook of my arm. He was laughing at her.

"Daisy is screwed. It's too late for her. Nobody can save her now."

"Oh, for God's sake, pull yourself together. Why can't you see that this might be the best night of your life? Why can't you ever appreciate the good stuff?"

"I don't deserve it," I said. Or maybe the baby said it. I wasn't sure who spoke.

"Fuck you, Luke, you have an opportunity that people would kill for, and you are throwing it away. Look beyond yourself for five minutes. I don't know if you were always selfish or if it was your mental health that made you so self-obsessed. I've never been able to figure it out. For a while I thought you loved me, but now, I don't think you ever did. You needed me. It's not your most attractive quality."

I said nothing, afraid of what might come out of my mouth. She gathered her briefcase. She had one meeting to attend before she went to some salon with Daisy. "Will you please leave?" she said. I walked toward her bedroom door but stopped at her minibar and removed the miniature vodka bottles. She tried to grab them out of my hands, but I held tight and laughed in her face. The baby was running across my shoulders, cackling in glee.

BRIAN

I knocked lightly on Daisy's door. "Daisy? It's Brian. May I come in?" She answered the door in a hotel robe that swamped her tiny frame. The change in her was so drastic. In eight months, she had gone from chubby to skeletal, and I was terrified for her.

"Look, Daisy, I bought Twinkies and Junior Mints and Reese's Kisses. You can't get these in Ireland. Want to try some?" I enthusiastically bit the end off a Twinkie to demonstrate how enjoyable eating was.

"I'm not hungry, Brian," she said.

"You must be, honey, you ate nothing at breakfast. Please, just take a bite of something. I mean, how embarrassing will it be if you faint on the red carpet? You don't want that to happen, do you?"

"I won't faint."

"Daisy, love, what can I do to help you? Just tell me."

"Go back to the way things were."

"When?"

"When? When Mum was alive and I thought she and Will were my parents, when I thought you were my uncle. When Will and Mum were together. To when I was ten years old."

"I wish I could. I really do."

"Go back to when people weren't so hateful on the internet."

"I begged you to stay away from social media. It's poison, but none of those people know you. None of them know the real Daisy." I changed tack. "You're going to be on the red carpet tonight! Isn't that just amazing? Wait until all the keyboard warriors see that."

"I know exactly what's going to happen. They're going to say I'm too thin. That I sold out by losing the weight, that I betrayed all my followers and let them down. They're going to speculate if Luke is my father now, or if I'm sleeping with my uncle. They're going to say I'm pathetic for wearing a cheap old wedding dress."

"Well, why do you want to do it, then? You don't have to."

"I want to look pretty for once. Haven't you noticed? I fit in here. Almost every woman here has some kind of eating disorder. I blogged about it two years ago. I could actually live here. My LA agent thinks I should stay. He thinks I could be the poster girl for weight loss. All I have to do is smile and pretend I'm happy. It's not that hard, *acting*."

"Listen to yourself. Think of all the positive things you wrote about being overweight, how much your body was capable of, how comfortable you felt. You were happier and healthier then, you didn't have to fake it."

"I wasn't faking it. I was much happier then, but everything is different now. I miss Mum so much. I wish I hadn't written all that family stuff on the blog. It's my fault everything turned out this way."

I told her I loved her, that none of this was her fault. We could try again, she could be herself with me. I begged her not to move to LA, not to live in such an unhealthy environment where the pressure on women to look impossibly perfect was greater than anywhere else in the world.

She allowed me to hold her bony hands. "Maybe. I don't know what I want. I just want to be normal."

We both cried and hugged. She ate half a Twinkie.

WILLIAM

I told them all I had a meeting with WME about a future project, but instead I went to look up an old friend. Talaya Fuentes was a woman I had spent a lot of time with in the early part of the decade. She was in her early thirties, and like most of the women in LA, she was an aspiring actress and screenwriter. I had cast her in some minor roles, but I had genuinely liked her. I felt our friendship was mutual. If we had met under different circumstances at a different time, I might have dated her properly and acknowledged her as my girlfriend. Her scripts weren't bad but not quite good enough to get over the line when I brought them to my development team. Still, I had made special efforts for her and talked her up. I had avoided LA since my diagnosis, but now that I was here, I felt like I should pay Talaya a visit. I had followed her career online. She had done a few pilots, been a hostess on two seasons of a game show. She had written an animation series but had no screen credits for the last year. Now, according to her website links, she was making personalized cakes from her home in Santa Barbara.

I borrowed Gerald's rental car and drove out to see her, knocking on her door shortly before 11:00 a.m. She answered the door, looking flustered. Surprised to see me, but smoothing her hair and removing her apron, revealing long tanned legs in denim shorts as she came to the porch.

"William Drumm! Why didn't you call? Are you in town for the Oscars?"

She was glowing, full of health, and her whitened teeth beamed at me. "I don't suppose you need a date for the big night?"

I passed through her kitchen and into her lounge, ignoring the mess of baking trays and kitchen scales.

"Talaya, I need to ask you . . . to tell you . . . A couple of months after we last hooked up, I started to feel . . . bad and . . . well, I had to get tested—"

"Oh, honey, HIV? Me too. Did you give it to me? I should have forced you to use condoms. I got hit in 2016. Swear to God, I thought I was gonna die. But these drugs are great, right?"

"Wait, I don't think *I* gave it to *you*."

She threw up her hands. "Well, we weren't exactly dating exclusively, so who knows? How are you doing, though? Your cell count okay? You got the antiretrovirals in Ireland, right? You look good!"

"Yes." I sat down and began to shake. "I infected my wife, before I knew I had the virus . . ."

"I thought you weren't married?"

"I wasn't . . . we'd been separated for a long time, but occasionally, we fell back into . . . bad habits."

"You never mentioned her. Is she doing okay?"

"No, she . . . well, she got cancer, a really fast-growing lymphoma, and that's when we found out she was HIV positive, too, but it was too late for her. I swear I never went near her after the diagnosis, but I must have infected her before I knew. I mean, it wasn't HIV that killed her, but—"

"Oh no! Will, I'm so sorry. You can't blame yourself for that. Sounds like you really cared for her, yeah?"

"Yes, I did. I don't blame myself for her death, but she was so angry with me."

"Who all knows about this?"

I realized that Talaya had not been keeping tabs on me the way I had on her.

"Everyone. And now those MeToo bitches are on my tail. Jesus, all I did was grab a few asses. I'm not a monster."

Talaya turned to face me slowly.

"MeToo *bitches*? Will Drumm, you are lying to yourself. You played nice with me because you knew I wouldn't accept it, but I have seen the way you treat other women. More vulnerable women, younger, those poor little pretty ones hoping for a break. You're a predator."

Her tone changed. Was Talaya going to turn on me too? After everything I'd done for her?

"What are you on about? I didn't notice you standing up for your 'sisters.'"

"Fuck you, it's not my responsibility to manage your grabby hands and your filthy mouth."

"But you came out to dinner with me. You played 'the game' very well." I could be sarcastic too.

"I'm calling you on it, Will, I'm a witness. I have seen you grope women. I have heard your nasty comments. I have seen you nudging the other male execs, like little-ass teenage boys. You think because I let you in my bed that I'm just some dumb bitch. I'm trying to make a living, same as you. And you were useful, for a while."

"I'm not a rapist."

"You don't have to be a rapist to be an asshole."

"Why are you being like this? I never hurt you. I never raped anyone."

"No, but you sure as hell don't think of us as equal. MeToo? I don't give a damn what *you* do. I look after *me*. Don't worry, I'm not going to expose you. I have better things to do with my life. But I think it's very interesting that you have waited, what, two years to tell me you had the virus?"

"Yeah, well, I highly doubt I was your only lover. I bet that ass has been all over town."

She laughed in my face. "Get out of my house, Will, and never come back. And by the way," she wiggled her little finger, "you'll never be able to find a clitoris with *that*."

I left Talaya's house thinking what a bitch she was, what a whore. You can't trust any of them.

BRIAN

I had called Will and asked him to come to my room as soon as his meeting was over. He turned up in a dark mood. Obviously, the business meeting hadn't gone well. He anticipated exactly what I'd wanted to talk to him about.

"We're going to have to do something about Luke." I paced my room as I spoke. "He's not going to win that Oscar, but he's a liability. He could say anything to anyone. It's obvious that he's really edgy. He's drinking again."

"Tell me something I don't know. Is this going to turn into an episode or is he just depressed?"

"If he was just depressed, his ex-girlfriend wouldn't be here babysitting him. I'm worried. If he releases some crazy statement, we could be headline news for the next week. This is the first time since her death that I'm glad Mum's gone. Can you imagine what he might say about her in public?" Mentioning Mum always got Will's attention.

"What? Would he?"

"I'm more concerned about Daisy. If he does anything to upset her on the red carpet—"

"Exactly. And if Mary is no longer going to be responsible for him, then it's back to us," Will said.

"Maybe we could get him sectioned?"

"Here? Today?"

"I don't know. Daisy's face lit up at the thought of the red carpet. I don't want to take that away from her. But she's not able to take any more drama. She told me. I couldn't bear to lose her, and I don't think you could either."

"Lose her again, you mean?" William was still angry at me for that.

"We would all lose. Are you prepared to take the risk?" I was definitely not prepared to take the risk.

"Look, let's just go and confront him now," Will said.

"Okay, but don't lose your temper with him. We have to be really careful. Talk him down. Or find a way to shut him up. Whatever it takes."

WILLIAM

Brian and I went together to Luke's room on the ninth floor. As we were about to knock on the door, a young man in a baseball cap and leather jacket exited. Brian held the door open with his foot, and asked the teenager who he was, but the boy pulled his baseball cap down and almost ran toward the exit door at the end of the corridor. When we entered the room, Luke glanced upward but did not stop what he was doing. A rolled-up dollar bill in his hand, he snorted three fat lines of cocaine off the glass-topped coffee table and took a swig from a bottle of Stolichnaya, already half-empty.

"You know, I think they put glass-topped tables in these rooms on purpose?" he said, hopping up out of his chair to go to the minibar. "What can I get you, gentlemen?"

"For fuck's sake, Luke! What are you doing? Are you mad?" Brian shouted. And he had urged *me* to be calm.

"Yes, but I thought you already knew that."

Brian continued to berate him, while I scanned the room for the jacket that Luke had worn to breakfast. It was lying across the bed behind Luke.

"I'll have a Jack Daniel's if you have one," I said as I positioned myself at the end of the bed. Brian glared at me.

Luke offered me the rolled-up dollar bill. I shook my head. "I'm too old for that shit. So are you."

Brian looked at Luke in exasperation. "I'm not letting Daisy walk up the red carpet with you while you're coked out of your head."

"Good, because the last thing Daisy needs is a red carpet," said Luke. "Daisy needs to go home, go back to college, get away from all of us, and try to lead a normal life."

"As if you'd know, Luke, you've never been a father," I said. I was hardly going to take a lecture about Daisy from my psychotic brother.

"Nor have you," he said. "Neither of you have done a great job of being her dad, and you both got a turn, didn't you? And I might have been a good dad, and a good husband, if you hadn't bullied my girlfriend into dumping me and having an abortion."

I sighed. "Kate told you that? I did you a favor. Look at you, you could have fucked up two more lives."

Brian looked at me. "My God, you are far worse than I ever thought. You forced her to have an abortion?"

"Yep," said Luke, "he blackmailed her into it. And she went along with it, for *my* sake." He chopped out more coke on the table.

"You are such a prick," Brian said to me. "That poor girl."

"Oh, Brian, what about you?" Luke turned his attention to Brian. "We'll never really know, will we, whether you fiddled with a schoolgirl—"

"That's bullshit—you know that's not—"

"But we do know how you ripped me off, how you manipulated me into selling my home, the only asset I had, when I was clearly out of my mind. We know you sold stories about me to the tabloids. Your craven jealousy was always obvious. But so was your meanness. You took advantage of every deal you got for me, and you're a cheater, too. Sleeping with your brother's girlfriend? You have nothing to be smug about."

Luke was right, and given his state of inebriation, he was surprisingly articulate about it. He took another swig from the vodka bottle and bent toward the table, dollar bill in hand.

"Susan was mine before Will ever set eyes on her. And he knew it!"

"Yours?" said Luke. "She wasn't a piece of property, Brian. She was an adult woman who chose Will, and you never got over it."

"Fuck you, fuck you both," said Brian.

While they were arguing like the schoolboys I remembered, I had reached back and riffled through the inside pocket of Luke's expensive linen jacket.

"What is this supposed to be?" I said, and they both turned to look at me. I was holding the pages that Luke had tucked neatly away. I held up the two sheets of paper, turning them back and forth. They were full of childish squiggles and indecipherable hieroglyphics.

"That's my speech. I'm going to tell everyone about my loving family," said Luke, and his voice had turned childlike again.

He put his hand to his throat and then watched intently as if an invisible spider was walking down his arm into his hand. He turned his face away and jumped over the sofa to the balcony doors behind him, flinging them open. He stood out on the balcony overlooking the Hollywood Hills. "Please," he whimpered, "please, leave me alone."

Brian and I looked at each other and followed Luke onto the balcony into the LA sunshine. Luke was having an episode.

"Who are you talking to, Luke?" I asked. It was as if a firework had exploded in his head.

"Luke. You need to calm down. You can't go to the ceremony in this state. Where's your phone? We need to call your therapist."

Brian automatically reverted back to the nanny role he was so used to. Luke didn't answer. He was murmuring incoherently into his hand.

"I think it's better if he doesn't go to the ceremony. For all of us," I said.

Brian looked from me back to Luke.

Luke started to cry and wail, hysterical, talking to some invisible tormentor. "No! This can't happen, you can't do it to *her*. No!"

"We have to get him sectioned. Now," I said.

Luke crouched in the corner of the balcony, flinging his left hand forward as if trying to swat a fly or shake water from his hand.

"What?" said Brian. "What's happening? What's wrong? Come back inside, Luke!"

Luke looked back down into his hand. "It has Daisy's face now. It's got Daisy!"

He backed away and jumped to sit up on the edge of the balcony with cocaine-fueled energy, throwing his hand outward as if trying to get rid of the spider that neither of us could see.

"Luke! What are you doing? What are you saying about Daisy?" I said, but Luke was wild-eyed and determined.

He stood up on the balcony's ledge. It was eighteen inches wide. There was a sheer drop below to the paved area beside the pool. "Daisy," he said, "she's in trouble, I know she is."

Brian and I looked at each other. We didn't dare to acknowledge the thought that I am certain was flitting through both our minds. It would take so little effort.

"Daisy is with Mary at some beauty salon. She's fine," I replied.

"You don't understand. You'll never understand."

Brian looked back at me and shook his head. He put his hand up toward Luke and gestured to me, and reluctantly I did the same thing. "Take our hands, Luke, get down and come back inside."

We three brothers all looked, one to the other. We knew it was inevitable. In that moment, we realized we had always known, but the moment dragged, and eventually, not trusting either of us, Luke reached forward for our hands. As our hands touched, Brian looked at me and pulled his away first, unbalancing Luke, who lurched backward. And then, just as Luke tried to grasp my hand, I jammed it into my pocket. Brian and I would never speak of this moment for the rest of our lives.

Luke fell backward, and we saw him smile at us as we betrayed him. The saintly, martyred smile we remembered from childhood. And then he disappeared from view.

We stepped to the edge, but he was already smashed on the patio below. Implausibly broken. Brian and I locked eyes, reflecting in each other's dark pupils something between horror and elation. Before the hotel staff hammered on the door of the suite, we held each other, weeping. We told each other it was okay, that it was for the best, that Luke was finally at peace.

DAISY

*W*ill and Brian are taking me out for my birthday lunch today. They have put the issues surrounding my paternity and my mother's death behind them. They are friends now, apparently. Or they are trying to give that impression. They have left show business behind and are working in property development. They have told me I can think of both of them as my dad or as my uncle.

I miss my mother so much. She was the stable person in my life, the constant. I wish I could take back all the awful things I said to her. I always knew that Dad was unfaithful, but I thought Mum was the steady one. I couldn't forgive her until it was too late. I think she died hating me, hating all of us, and I can't blame her.

Luke's death put us all in the spotlight. The Oscars went ahead, but black armbands, hastily rescued from some prop store, were handed out on the red carpet, and that whole galaxy of stars who had never met my uncle gave interview after interview about him and their shock at the news. Out of respect, they suspended the announcement of his category that night. As it turned out, he hadn't won. But his film, after his death, made $700 million at the box office, one of the top-ten grossing films of all time. Luke would not have been able to enjoy that success. His death was ruled as a drug- and alcohol-related suicide. His fame is now legendary, like Marilyn Monroe or Kurt Cobain. Teenagers make pilgrimages to Glendalough, not to see the monastery founded by Saint Kevin in the sixth century, but to be at the site where his brothers scattered Luke's ashes.

Brian and Will and I went to a rented villa in the South of France for a month after Luke's suicide. We all agreed not to respond to emails or phone calls from the media. We closed our social media accounts. When we came back to Ireland, we locked ourselves away and demanded our privacy. I like it. Brian and Will have been able to move on. I am stuck in a loop of relentless grief and guilt and horror. I can see no escape.

When Brian was managing Luke, he ensured that Luke made a will. Having no children of his own, he left his entire estate to me. I don't know why. I'm guessing Brian suggested it. Luke and I were never particularly close. He found me annoying. I think perhaps he wanted me to be financially independent so I wouldn't have to rely on fame to make a living. But when Mum died, I got her house and estate, so I have plenty of money without having to work for it.

I have no agent now. I don't go on social media and I don't blog. I don't leave my house very often, except to get food, and even that I can get online, if need be. Food is always going to be an issue for me, but at least I have someone who tells me what to do. She is like a toddler's voice in my head. In my mind's eye, she is the doll I had when I was a child. Only I can hear her. Sometimes she tells me to eat. Sometimes she tells me to starve. I listen to her because I don't think there is anyone else I can trust.

I have dressed up for my lunch date with Will and Brian. I have decided to wear the dress that I had altered specially for the Oscars last year. It will unnerve them. I am still very thin, even thinner than I was then, so I had to adjust the dress again. I am angry with them. I want everyone to be punished in the end. So does my little friend.

I look out of my bedroom window. I can see the two of them getting out of Brian's car. They are both carrying gifts. Will's is twice the size of Brian's. I can see they are eyeing each other's offerings. Brian's is in a blue Tiffany bag, and Will is worried that Brian will upstage whatever he has bought.

You can't buy your way out of guilt, gentlemen. I am determined to make you suffer. When we go to this very exclusive restaurant, I intend to order the most expensive thing on the menu, and you will be so pleased with yourselves, and then I'll watch your faces fall when you realize I'm not going to eat any of it. We will enjoy that, my little friend and I.

Acknowledgments

Thank you to my mum and dad and my family, in-laws and out-laws. I promise you that none of you are reflected in this book.

Professionally, first and always, thanks to my agent, Marianne Gunn O'Connor, who has talked me down from many a cliff and up from many an abyss. A constant friend and supporter, her tenacity and loyalty are notable in what can sometimes be a fickle business, and to Pat Lynch, who ably assists Marianne in every way, and Vicki Satlow, who does the business in Europe and buys me champagne in Paris.

To my incredible New York team: editor Jackie Cantor at Scout Press/ Gallery Books for trusting me and guiding me toward the light. Her wisdom and thoughtfulness have taught me so much. Also lovely Aimée Bell, Jen Bergstrom, Lisa Litwack, Molly Gregory, Sally Marvin, Lauren Truskowski, Caroline Pallotta, and the eagle-eyed Tricia Callahan. I am blessed amongst women!

Thanks to all the excellent team at Simon & Schuster Canada, especially Nita Pronovost, who has been relentlessly positive, and to Kevin Hanson, Felicia Quon, Adria Iwasutiak, Rita Silva, Shara Alexa, and Greg Tilney.

For all kinds of expertise and background information, Sue Leonard was great for the secrets of ghostwriting; Lucy Nugent, CEO of Tallaght

University Hospital, and Helen Enright, Consultant Haematologist gave expert medical advice; Rebecca O'Flanagan knows the Irish film industry inside out; Lucas Webb knew what happens and where at the Cannes Film Festival; Tara Flynn and Sinead Crowley were my Oscar experts; Jean-René Fouquerne told me all about being a Parisian school teacher; Conor Horgan and Michael Gallen knew about Parisian neighborhoods and architecture; Cathy Belton gave me actress insight; Clare O'Dea was able to tell me where a rock star might play in Switzerland; Peter Nugent gave me legal advice; Fiona O'Doherty was great for psychological and psychiatric data. Any mistakes or factual errors are mine alone and cannot be blamed on my informants.

A debt of gratitude is owed to Nora Hickey and all at the Centre Culturel Irlandais, Paris, where I was writer in residence for the month of April 2019, and to all at the Tyrone Guthrie Centre who don't mind me turning up regularly like a bad penny to be inspired by the resident muse, the ghostly Mis Worby, the lake and the food, and to Paul Maddern at the River Mill Readers and Writer's Retreat for never knowing how much is enough food.

To all the people who visited me (or really wanted to—sorry, but sometimes I just wasn't up to it) when I was in hospital for three months from the end of 2019 into 2020.

I'll always be grateful to my immediate family and to: Maria O'Connell, Bríd Ó Gallchóir, Rachel O'Flanagan, Grainne Killeen and Mike Seibert, Lucy Nugent, Shane Nugent, Sophie Nugent, Ingse Nugent, Tania Banotti, Katherine Cahill, Ger Holland, Grainne Nugent, Martina Devlin, Sinead Moriarty, Claudia Carroll, Rick O'Shea, Bob Johnston, Michael O'Loughlin, Judith Mok, Fiona O'Sullivan, Susan McNamara, John O'Donnell, Barry McGovern, Susie Sheil, Alex Barclay, Mary Lou McCarthy, Sarah Ryder, Jane Casey, Patricia Deevy, Cliona Lewis, Aoibheann Sweeney, Níamh Ní Charra, Sinead Gleeson, Cathy Belton, Clíodhna Ní Anlúain, Elaine Butler Doolin, Beta Bajgartova, Mary Kate O'Flanagan, Eimear Murphy, Marian Keyes, Tony Baines, Anne McManus, Karen Dervan,